"BISHOP IS ONE OF THE MOST IMPORTANT NEW WRITERS TO EMERGE IN SF IN THE '70s...

CATACOMB YEARS

Berkley Books by Michael Bishop

CATACOMB YEARS
A LITTLE KNOWLEDGE

MICHAEL BISHOP

CATACOMB YEARS

A BERKLEY BOOK
published by
BERKLEY PUBLISHING CORPORATION

This Berkley book contains the complete
text of the original hardcover edition.
It has been completely reset in a type face
designed for easy reading, and was printed
from new film.

The author and publisher wish to acknowledge the following
publications where some of these chapters first appeared:
"If a Flower Could Eclipse," from *Worlds of Fantasy*, Issue 3; "Old
Folks at Home," from
Universe 8, edited by Terry Carr;
"The Windows in Dante's Hell," from
Orbit 12, edited by Damon Knight;
"The Samurai and the Willows," from
The Magazine of Fantasy and Science Fiction;
"Allegiances," from *Galaxy;*
and "At the Dixie-Apple with the Shoofly-Pie
Kid," from *Cosmos* #4.

The selection from James Dickey's Kudzu which appears on page 157
is copyright © 1963 by James Dickey,
reprinted from Poems 1957–1967
by permission of Wesleyan University Press.
Kudzu first appeared in the *New Yorker*.

CATACOMB YEARS

A Berkley Book / published by arrangement with
the author

PRINTING HISTORY
Berkley-Putnam edition published January 1979
Berkley edition / February 1980

ISBN: 0-425-04050-X

A BERKLEY BOOK® TM 757,375
PRINTED IN THE UNITED STATES OF AMERICA

ACKNOWLEDGMENTS

Catacomb Years is a labor of several years. I'm unable to let it appear without thanking several people. It would be tempting—although altogether churlish and inaccurate—to hold them accountable, too, for the book's aesthetic and philosophical shortcomings. But, fearing my solitary conscience and the prospect of their righteous joint wrath, instead I had better acknowledge their very real contributions, whether deliberate or inadvertent:

My wife, Jeri, who more than eight years ago suggested that I write a story about a little boy whose favorite color is black. Francis R. Burnham, better known as Bill, who sold me a title for two cents a word and thereby earned, in addition to my gratitude, a dime.

Ejler Jakobsson, for buying my first story, and the second (which is incorporated here), and for later asking for more. Damon Knight, who spared me the wrath of a network television executive and, for learning my lesson, introduced me to orbital flight. James Baen, for sending the mail under trying circumstances. Edward L. Ferman, for quite frequently liking the different sorts of work I seem to do. Terry Carr, whose universe it took me quite some time to enter. And Bob Frazier, who cared enough to take his shoelaces out.

Thomas M. Disch and Robert Silverberg, in whose very different visions of future urban life I have found

v

material so inspiringly theft-worthy that I have...well, clumsily helped myself.

Several anthologists—Harry Harrison and Brian Aldiss, Donald A. Wollheim, and Gardner Dozois—have provided incidental assistance and encouragement along the way. Perhaps they didn't know.

Gerald W. Page, for rehearsing and re-rehearsing with me the episode I've called "Death Rehearsals," which he may now fail to recognize. Virginia Kidd, for too many things to mention here—although I ought to cite in particular her patience, steadfastness, and good advice. And Bob Phillips, who has entitled himself to half my kingdom; I hope he never tries to collect.

And, finally, David Hartwell, my editor—who will perhaps know what I mean to convey if I simply reiterate, "And, finally, David Hartwell...."

MICHAEL BISHOP
June 25, 1978

This book is for the grandparents of my children: Nora Hobeika Bishop and Lee Otis Bishop. Minnie Ellis Whitaker and John Gregory Whitaker. Maxine Elaine Willis and Charles Edwin Willis. With much love, always. (My children are luckier than most.)

CONTENTS

CHARACTERS

```
                2000
85  90  95    |    05  10  15  20  25  30  35  40  45  50  55  60  65  70  75  80  85
```

```
-----------------Almira Longhope---------------------------
-----------------Paul Erick Ferrand-----------------------
-----------------Parthena Cawthorn---------------------------------**************************
-----------------Helen Mitchell-------------------------
-------------Martin Luther King Battle-------------------
-----------Kazuko Hadaka (Fowler)-------------------
-------------------Jeremy Zitelman---------------------
---------------Joyce (Toodles) Malins------------------
---------------Zoe Stevens (Breedlove)------------------------
-------------------Vivian Millar Escolana Tyndale Klemme-----------------
--------Gerard Nettlinger---------------
-----------Gregory Greer--------------------------------
--------Carlo Bitler---------------------
-------------Leland Tanner----------------------------------------------
---------------------Jonah Trap~---------------------------------------
-----------------Fiona Foe (Bitler)----------------------------
------Simon Hadaka Fowler-------------
----------------------Sanders Noble---------------------------------
----------------Melanie Breedlove (Noble)--------------------------
----------Saganella Ruth Lesser--------------------------
----------(Raymond) Ardrey-----------------------------------
------Alexander "Menewa" Guest--------------
-----------Asbury Holman --------------------
------------Emory (Coleman) Nettlinger --------------------
---------------Tyler Kosturko---------
------Georgia Cawthorn (-Kosturko)-----
---------------------Newlyn Yates--------------------
---Margot Eastwin (-Cawthorn) ------
------Clio Noble-----------------
-----------Julian Cawthorn-----------
```

CATACOMB YEARS: A CHRONOLOGY

Documents	Dates	Historical Data: Technical, Social, Human
	1968	Robert F. Kennedy & Martin Luther King assassinated.
	1972	Apollo 17, final American manned flight to Moon.
	1973	Maynard Jackson, first black mayor of Atlanta. Mrs. Martin Luther King, Sr., dies at hands of gunman in Ebenezer Baptist Church.
	1976	Celebration of American Bicentennial. Viking I & II put down on Mars. Saigon falls.
	1978–1994	Soviet Union & Red China at military & political loggerheads. Pan-European Ecumenical Movement provides foundation for New Free Europe (NFE). Continuing homogenization of American landscape. Adoption of "Preemptive Isolation" as guiding foreign policy.

Documents	Dates	Historical Data: Technical, Social, Human
	2029	Bitler assassinated.
If a Flower Could Eclipse *Interlude:* The Testimony of Leland Tanner	2034	Disappearance of Fiona Bitler & Emory Coleman (Nettlinger), son of her husband's assassin, from Atlanta Nucleus. Septigamoklans officially approved. "Death" of Vivian Millar in Miami.
Interlude: The City Takes Care of Its Own	2035	Retrenchment Edicts. Covenant ceremonies of original septigamoklans.
Old Folks at Home	2040	Office of First Councilor instituted.
Interlude: The City Takes Care of Its Own	2041–2045	Bondville riots & repressive aftermath. Nonviolent but antiauthoritarian hoisterjacks in hive. Combcrawling becomes popular urban pastime. Telemetric biochemical monitoring of most urban dwellings begins.
	2043	NFE, with Amity Moon Base, test-advances spacecraft four light-years; retrieves it in 93-day period.
The Windows in Dante's Hell	2045	
Interlude: Volplaning Heroes	2045–2046	Latin revolutionary armies, with advisors from reunified China, begin tentative assaults in RAU.
The Samurai and the Willows	2046	
Captives of Hieronymus Bosch	2047	Saganella Ruth Lesser becomes Atlanta's First Councilor, forces resignation of Leland Tanner as

Documents	Dates	Historical Data: Technical, Social, Human
		head of UrNu Geriatrics Hostel, disbands septiga-moklans. Continuing conflict in RAU.
	2050	Treaty of cooperation and nonaggression between RAU & Sino-Sudcom Alliance. Ships of NFE go from lunar orbit to six different computer-selected solar systems.
	2050–2068	Resource - reclamation teams sent into Open ("Fifth Evacuation Lottery"). Intensive immortalist research in Japan & NFE. Funkphalt music.
Interlude: First Councilor Lesser	2063	"Glissador Revolt"; marital law & police-state tactics.
Allegiances	2066	Fiona Bitler & Emory Nettlinger return from Scandipol to Phoenix Plantation near Toombsboro. Resource-reclamation team sent to escort them back into City.
Interlude: The Cradle Begins to Rock	2067–2071	Pair of alien visitors installed in Hyatt-Regency "ecologarium." Five more arrive via Amity Moon Base & 61 Cygni A. NFE & Japanese scientists performing sophisticated gene-splicing and limb-regeneration procedures.
At the Dixie-Apple with the Shoofly-Pie Kid *A Little Knowledge*	2071	First public appearance of alien. Several Cygnusian conversions to Ortho-Urbanism. Publication in newstapes of "ethnography" devoted to aliens'

Documents	Dates	Historical Data: Technical, Social, Human
		penthouse society. Attempted assassination of Cygnostik priest. Urban guerrilla episodes. Death of Fiona Bitler.
Interlude: The Fall of Saganella Lesser	2071–2072	Bloodless coup removes First Councilor Lesser from office. "Council of Three" expels all but two of remaining Cygnostikoi from City. Emory Nettlinger returns to Scandipol.
	2073	Vivian (Millar) Klemme meets with Nettlinger in Polity of Rhine, NFE, to discuss immortalist research. Leland Tanner returns to Atlanta from 26-year exile in Washington Nucleus.
Death Rehearsals	2073–2074	Deaths, nativities, resurrections.
	2075	
	onward	ERA OF MULTIPLE POSSIBILITIES

Prelude: The Domes

Toward the end of the twentieth century, history branched in a way that would have struck its human captives—had they only had the power to view their counterparts in the divergent branch—as curious and unforeseeable. But they had no such power. Like most of us, they believed their lives linear and single, the results of a host of successive past choices that were now indelibly beyond recall. The captives of one branch had no significant belief in the captives of the other, who mirrored them exactly in the only aspect of their divergent lives that they continued even in their alternate realities to share: the splendid crazy-quilt robes of their humanity.

This narrative, then, is a history of the divergent branch and its otherwise inaccessible human captives.

In 1994 the American Republic ceased to exist. For more than twenty years the nation had been doing a drunkard's walk toward collapse. The Jeremiahs who foresaw the end harped on different strings, usually plucking out monotones that were drowned in the full orchestral resonance to which their partisans remained unbelievably deaf.

The threat, argued these one-note prophets of doom, was *(choose one, and only one)* Communism, fiscal irresponsibility, military unpreparedness, technological disaster, or spiritual

1

decay. If the People didn't *(choose one, and only one)* reassert
the values of the Founding Fathers, restore the credibility of the
Dollar, restock the nation's nuclear and paranuclear arsenals,
reject the temptations of machine and computer, return to
Nature, or rededicate their souls to Christ, the United States of
America would fly apart like an ill-made wheel.

As it happened (at least along the divergent branch of history
that this narrative randomly chronicles), the Republic collapsed
not so much because things fell apart as because the center could
not hold. The central government, under an unremitting barrage
of regional priorities and narrow local solutions, gave way to a
number of virtually autonomous city-states, or *Urban Nuclei*,
that cut themselves adrift from the heartland. The United States
of America became the twenty-five poleis of the North American Urban Federation.

The symbols of this new social order were the immense,
computer-designed Domes capping the Cities. Linked one to
another by seldom-used transit-tunnels, these Urban Nuclei rose
like giant geodesic mushrooms from the cluttered neon and
aluminum wilderness of the nation. The country had so
homogenized its landscapes that the forests of New England and
the deserts of the Southwest were mere local variations on an
inescapable suburban theme. It took a decade for the Cities to
put up their hemispherical shells, and resources that the
plundered countryside yielded only grudgingly, and so many
admirable   human   qualities—cooperation,   ingenuity,
perseverance—that few of the people under the Domes realized
what stifling secular infernos they were creating for themselves
and their descendants.

Or why they were doing it.

The why had to do with many things, not the least of which
was the irrational popular notion that the ultimate urban
environment must exist beneath a bubble or a Dome. A
science-fiction given for decades, this notion proved—if only in
retrospect—an embarrassment to those who had taken it up
secondhand without examining the preconceptions on which it
was based. It eventually proved such an embarrassment to these
people, in fact, that in order to deny the sources of their chagrin,
they resisted resurrecting themselves to the light and invented
reasons for staying as they were. As a consequence, many of the
inhabitants of the Urban Nuclei believed that they lived in
Domes to protect themselves from the unbreathable air,

polluted vistas, and pathogenic sunlight of the World Outside. This belief was in error, but for most it sufficed.

For those demanding more stringent or at least less facile explanations, a number of other theories arose. One stipulated that the Domes had gone up because the materials and methods for building them had suddenly come to hand; that, in other words, the ability to do something not only presupposes but actually ensures the doing. Another theory posited the idea that the Domes were the Cities' means of declaring their economic and cultural independence of the rest of the nation, a divorce made possible by the wonders of climate control, intensive rooftop and hothouse cultivation, "tank farming," and the manufacture of a startling variety of chemical foodstuffs. (In truth, trade between the Cities and the countryside continued unabated, but it was conducted in secret through fortified urban "receiving points"—as if to admit even a degree of dependency were wretchedly shameful.)

A third theory embodied the bizarre but useful concept of "Preemptive Isolation," by which it was meant that America's major Cities were concertedly resisting foreign attempts to entangle them in a patently unworkable Government of the West. The perpetrators of this idea were the nations of New Free Europe. Meanwhile having engaged in a protracted conventional war along their common frontier, the Soviet Union and the People's Republic of China had effectively neutralized themselves as threats, making a confederation of domed Cities in North America a viable alternative to union. In turn, the efforts of New Free Europe to incorporate the United States as one of its western "polities" had led to the local conclusion that the Domes were not merely an option but an absolute necessity. They represented an architectural prophylaxis against the spores of foolish optimism and utopian meddlesomeness that were being wafted across the Atlantic.

Finally, a few discerning Americans believed that the impulse behind the Domes was not substantially different from that behind the Egyptian and Mayan pyramids. The Domes were monuments to privilege, and tombs for all those who found themselves trapped within. They were unparalleled feats of engineering, prodigious works of art, and unutterably loony memorials to human folly. They seemed, once they had arisen, as abiding and inannihiliable as the Earth herself. Like Everest and Annapurna, forever and always they were *there*.

* * *

Atlanta followed New York and Los Angeles in the raising of a Dome. While it was still being built, the City's leaders summoned beneath its naked honeycombing a half a million people from the surrounding countryside. This was the First Evacuation Lottery, a random computer selection of Georgia's rural inhabitants. Surprisingly, most of those selected chose to obey their summons—probably because they were either proud of themselves for having won a lottery or half-panicked by the realization that someone had deemed an evacuation from the countryside essential to their health.

Between 1998 and 2004, then, three more Evacuation Lotteries—each larger than the last—emptied the fields and old-fashioned town squares of the state and swelled the City's population to the bursting point. By the time the Dome had been completed, Atlanta was housing the greater part of its citizenry in surfaceside tenements, dilapidated hotels and motor inns, and tiny cubicles along the spooky concourses of its nine recently excavated understrata. Catacomb years, the people called them, and at the turn of the new century they looked to be endless.

Living during the Catacomb Era, you could go crazy without ever realizing the depths of your own madness. The outwardly well-adjusted and the uncompromisingly deranged were often indistinguishable. You lived from day to day in the submerged hope that your old age would deliver you to the immaculate dignity of death under a clear blue sky. In the meantime you tried to form fragile human alliances against the terms of your imprisonment. . . .

CHAPTER ONE

If a Flower Could Eclipse

1 / "My Favorite Color is Black"

It was white. That was what struck me most forcibly about the classroom when I first saw it. The walls gleamed like porcelain; the light fixtures glistened with a preternatural frostiness; the tilework on the floor was as clean and hard as ivory. The classroom was white and beautifully equipped. From the observation window (it was a two-way mirror, but they termed it otherwise) I could see the drawing tables, the easels, the glass display cases, the sliding chalk boards, and the small soundproofed projection unit in its hard white casing. In a way, the children in the room seemed meant merely as extensions of the equipment. Still observing, I spoke:

"Do you show many films?"

Mz Bitler turned toward me in the outer darkness of the observation chamber. In profile she had the tall head of an African princess; her flesh was darkly chocolate, and she wore two small white pearls in the long lobes of her pierced ears. I tried not to look at her, but as I studied the children I heard her voice like a drill in my consciousness.

"We sometimes do, Dr Greer. We occasionally show films on *hygiene*."

She spoke resentfully. She spoke the last word in particular as if she were breathing ashes. I could feel her testing the syllables on her firm heavy lips. But I could not immediately determine the sources of her resentment.

"And films on the life sciences," she said. "Current films geared to their intelligence level and suggestive of the modern predicament."

"Very good," I said. "You have that down nicely."

The children were busy at the long tables. They worked with crayons and fingerpaints. They worked with plastic T-squares and drafting pencils. A few were shaping delicate white flowers from tissue paper, constructing elongated stems from wire and florist's tape. Several appeared to be fashioning mobiles out of cardboard and tinfoil. One such mobile hung in the center of the room, a silver mock-up of the atom, slowly turning.

"Which one is Emory?" I asked curtly.

Again, her voice grated like the insidious burr of a drill: "I expect you can pick him out if you look."

Momentarily unsettled, I turned to rebuke her.

But Mz Bitler was staring fixedly through the observation window, her chin jutting forward like the cowcatcher of an old locomotive. The analogy was strange, but I felt she carried her pride like a cowcatcher, a means by which to scoop up obstacles and push them insensitively away. Her dark lips were trembling very slightly. But despite my pejorative images, she did not look ridiculous. She looked strong.

I turned back to the window and looked.

"All right, Mz Bitler," I said. "I expect it's that one."

The boy looked like a miniaturized monk. He had cloistered himself away from the others at the only single-seating table in the room, a desk with a slanted top. He was in the farthermost corner. Leaning arthritically forward, he perched atop a white enamel stool and pressed a crayon against a sheet of paper. He might have been copying a manuscript.

"Is he as creative as the others?"

"I suppose that's for you to determine." She still had not looked at me.

"Well, then, Mz Bitler, let's go in."

We emerged from the observation room's darkness into the enameled clarity of the classroom.

A few children looked up, but Mz Bitler rotated her gaunt wrist and set them working again. The classroom smelled antiseptic; and the boy we had seen through the two-way mirror seemed an immensely long way off, humpbacked and isolated. He did not look up, but continued the tedious copying movements of shoulder and arm that made him seem a monk.

Even from across the white, out-of-time room, I had the feeling he was pressing his crayon mercilessly into the paper, his face screwed in a grimace of pain and unboyish concentration. There would be tight blue veins ticking on his forehead.

I could guess that much. Mz Bitler had volunteered nothing. But if the boy had not posed a small tunneling menace to classroom stability (and to himself) I would have never been sent for. All I knew was his name.

Emory Coleman.

Now I stood in the middle of all that encompassing whiteness and stared at Emory's back. The other children were no more than blurred pockets of color to me, and I wished that Mz Bitler would also blur away to an indistinguishable hue, leaving me to deal with the boy. Even in the narrowness of her hostility, she must have sensed this desire; for she stopped between two tables and let me proceed alone. Over the quiet rustling of paper and the children's hushed voices, my footsteps on the tiles were deafening.

But Emory did not look up.

Locked tightly away in its hard white casing, the projection unit was at my back. Nevertheless, I believed that in approaching the boy I was walking through the brutal flood of the machine's projection lamps. It was as if my journey toward him somehow demanded the consecration of light. All of it could be explained, however. Mz Bitler had put me on edge, and I was therefore projecting on the boy the light of anxiety that she had instilled in me.

After what seemed a long time, I reached Emory. I pulled up a stool from an unattended easel and undiplomatically peered over his shoulder. He still had not seen me. Mz Bitler, the other children, the room itself—all were far away, drowned in an ocean of stabbing light. I put my glasses on. Things momentarily untangled themselves, but Emory had detected the movement. He swung his face toward me.

"This is my corner. Who said you could come in?"

"Do you want to see my passport? I have papers."

"They won't suffice," he said quickly. Then the corner of his mouth sagged, as if in chagrin, and he emended his original statement: "They ain't any good."

"No? I'm surprised that anyone would stake out claims in a public facility. A big wide room like this."

"It's not so big. And maybe it's *too* public."

"Look," I said. "Don't you have a buddy in this group?"

"No. I don't have any *friends* here." He was correcting my use of a patronizing colloquialism. "You see, I don't choose to have any."

"Now that's what we call a manifestation of antisocial behavior. Did you know that?"

His eyes narrowed, became two lozenges of intense brown, then went opaque. He turned back to his drawing and began pressing his crayon against the paper so fiercely that I heard it snap between his fingers. I moved my stool beside his desk. Blue veins ticked on his forehead, and flakes of crayon wax lay scattered on the desk's surface like pieces of shrapnel. His knuckles were white with the vehemence of his anger.

"Whoa," I said softly.

He threw the broken crayon on the floor.

"Come on," I said under my breath. "Mz Bitler's going to think I'm an absolute incompetent."

Emory looked at me warily for a moment, shuffled all his crayon sketches into a pile together, and abruptly deposited them in the compartment beneath the desk's lift-top surface. I put my hand on the desk.

"Can't I see them?"

"Sure," he said.

His face softened and he reached into his desk, withdrew the sketches.

I took the drawings and shuffled through them, reflecting on one or two and making no comments about either young Coleman's craftsmanship or his unorthodox subject matter. The single most obvious detail of his work was that he had executed every sketch in black. There were black octopi, black starships with black bodies spilling from ruptured bulkheads, black children standing in showers of black fire, black eels and scorpions, charred madonnas and burnt-out planets, witches with black capes, and strangely beautiful black flowers. One sketch was morbidly poignant.

I held it up. "Would you explain this one?"

"No."

"How about telling me the title?"

He paused long enough to make it evident that the idea appealed to him and that he was extemporaneously creating a title.

"Two Entities Exhumed," he said at last.

"Very apt."

It was, I suppose. But the sketch seemed to embody a compassion that the boy's awkward title did not even suggest. Two figures of uncertain age, sex, and race lay sprawled in faintly smoldering rubble, mere sockets for eyes, their mouths blackened and agape. But the hand of one figure was touching the hand of the other. In spite of the desolation of the scene, an infusion of life obviously was taking place.

"My favorite color's black," Emory said. His eyes were the color of brandy. His close-cropped hair was blond.

"You realize that may be an affectation?"

"No," he said quickly. "It's an assertion."

Puzzled, I examined his face. "About what?"

Instead of answering, he lifted the top of his desk again and withdrew a tissue-paper flower, which he extended to me with decorous reserve. The flower was black, like those in the drawings. It was an aggressive parody of all the pale tissue-paper flowers that the other children had made or were making. The delicate tissue was so imbued with black stain that it seemed evil. I took the flower, half expecting the head of a snake to strike from the ebony heart.

"Emory," I said. "If you carry this sort of thing too far, it becomes self-conscious."

He took the flower back, held it deftly in thin fingers and studied its corolla, the separate petals in the center. Was he looking for my snake?

"What is it, Emory? A black rose? A black carnation?"

With no self-consciousness whatever, he looked me square in the face. "If a flower could eclipse, it would look just like this."

"Especially a sunflower?" I ventured.

"Nobody ever sees the sun," he said.

"I've never heard of a flower eclipsing. You're not using the word with its scientific definition, are you?"

"No, I'm not." He put the flower inside the desk again and took Two Entities Exhumed away from me. My last question had thrown up a small blackness between us. The barrier was almost touchable.

"That's the assertion," he said. "Now go away."

"You believe in blackness?"

"Sometimes there ain't anything else, is there?"

"You believe in Mz Bitler?"

Emory put his head on the desk. I looked at the tiny blue

veins in his temple for a while, then stood, turned the enamel stool to its original position and faced about. The classroom came into focus again; the whiteness of its walls, ceiling, floor, equipment, was an ironic counterpointing of what I had just discovered. But even more ironically, for one slippery moment I thought I had grasped the gist of the boy's final sardonic question. Emory stayed in his corner. I returned to Mz Bitler past the well-adjusted prodigies who manifested their talents in a reasonable, socially acceptable manner.

Mz Bitler and I retreated into the dark observation chamber. We stared through the two-way glass like visitors at an aquarium, standing together, not touching.

"Well," Mz Bitler said.

I continued to look at the children. From here Emory became simply one of the group. In the world of concrete and plexiglass and reinforced steel to which we all belonged, these children still believed in flowers and madonnas and even joyously wriggling eels. Inside the tight clean cubicles to which they returned after school, they still contrived horror stories about witches and ogres, made up romances and fairy tales. With his insistence on black, even Emory was a romantic. But outside—above the huge bubble which encysted Atlanta, beyond the architectural miracle which housed us—a nightmare threatened to stifle all our dreams. We had forgotten the exact nature of that nightmare; we no longer remembered its beginnings. We knew only the clean but finite world of the Dome. Within that world I still believed in the children. They were starships who would take us into the freedom of the void.

I turned.

"Don't say 'Well' again, Mz Bitler. I heard you the first time. What will the children be doing this afternoon?"

The black woman faced me haughtily.

"Integral calculus. Then a session of kinetic relations—dramas that the children extemporize. Then a break."

"And after that?"

"A film," Mz Bitler said defiantly. "On hygiene."

"Wonderful. These children possess quantitative intelligences in the genius range, and we're showing them movies about their non-existent pubes."

"I don't formulate policy or curriculum, Dr Greer. You're a fool if you don't know that. I do my job."

She stood before me with awesome dignity, a tall

white-frocked tribeswoman aloof from her wizened children. With one dark hand she toyed with the single pearl on her necklace, the pendant at her throat. I backpedaled.

"Mz Bitler, I'm sorry."

"And maybe you should know something else. Emory Coleman, the little boy whose favorite color is black, he's our projectionist. He runs the films."

"Thank you. I appreciate that information. I'll be back this afternoon, in time for the film."

I left Mz Bitler and the Van-Ed classroom. The outer corridor was hung with a series of reproductions, all of them abstract and geometric. At last the corridor ended, and I took a lift-tube several floors up to the heart of the education complex. I spent the next two hours at my private carrel in the library. I scanned the visicom tapes and took notes. Our preoccupation with light becomes more and more intense as we discover the unfathomableness of the dark.

2 / Two Biographies

Some of the things I tell you now are beyond my power to explain. We live in shells, encapsuled in our plexiglass blisters, bound up in the peasecods of our personal isolations. I am going to tell this story as it happened. Little of this appears in the report which I filed with the Vanguard Education Program. Logic and good order prevail in the Program's manifold computer banks.

No one intruded upon my carrel.

In the quiet I took advantage of my access to Van-Ed information. The librarian, a purse-lipped little man with pale jowls, helped me find the tapes that detailed the biographies of Mz Bitler and Master Coleman. Then he wandered off into the antiseptic stacks, losing himself amid plastic cartridges and immaculately rebound old books. I heard his voice once or twice, distilled from afar, and knew that other people were actually in the library.

No one intruded. I fed the tapes to the visicom. Information unraveled itself in golden impulses. Letters appeared against the dark green background of the screen in my carrel. I read the information carefully, monitoring the speed with which each electronic sentence unraveled.

The gold filigree, developing against the deep green background, simply displayed information; it made no distinction in emphasis between the name of one's Siamese cat and the death by assassination of one's relatives. Because the visicom system merely advanced a golden chronology, it was for me to interpret and give emphasis.

Fiona Bitler.

She was black. She was tall. She was aristocratic in her bearing. Those things I knew. But the visicom system told me things that could conceivably aid me in fathoming the mystery of Emory Coleman. The boy's teacher was thirty-four years old, and she held a doctorate in applied psychology from the University's urban extension (that extension now comprising the whole of the University, although the old designations refused to die). No one addressed Fiona Bitler by the title she had earned, however; she refused to permit it. This last fact made me consider her in a different aspect.

Then the visicom system deluged me with so many visual impulses—dates and names—that I let the information burn on my retinas and fade into conscientious forgetting. I remembered the gnawing trivialities and the forehead-bludgeoning shocks that make a biography and slowly sculpt attitudes. With maddening slowness I began to learn about Fiona Bitler's heart. Although the process did not have a chance to fulfill itself, I can make a beginning.

Born in a stagnant backwater hamlet, Fiona Bitler came into the geodesic cocoon of Atlanta with her parents during the third Evacuation Lottery. She had been six months old, alive because of the random impartiality of the computers that sifted through the names of remaining rural inhabitants. Her father's name had been Amos Foe. When the family arrived in Atlanta, the authorities boarded them in a walk-up flat in an unrestored ghetto building; they gave her father minimal janitorial duties in a clearing house for organic foodstuffs, a stopgap position. The family existed.

At the age of four, Fiona was reading. Amos Foe found her one evening on her knees on the cold peeling linoleum, hunched over an open spread of newsprint, deciphering the letters by a legerdemain that neither parent could comprehend. Amos Foe and his wife had had only the barest rudiments of education, but

their four-year-old daughter was sitting in the drafty halfdark-
ness reading a newspaper.

The next day Amos took her to the educational complex. He
waited six hours in a carpeted anteroom and finally spoke with a
tall lean man in a technician's smock. The man talked with
Fiona for a few minutes, then made her father return to the
anteroom. The interview lasted half an hour. The technician let
Fiona read from a thick book with a stippled black binding; he
watched the way she touched the words and magically
deciphered them, saying them aloud tentatively. Then he took
her back to Amos.

The Foes received new accommodations.

White rooms inside a self-luminous white building that
looked monolithic from the street.

Their neighbors were black. But the Foes found themselves
in an entirely unique predicament. They did not conform to the
patrician ethos of their neighbors' blackness. Throttled by aloof
white administrators and supercilious blacks, the family grew
introspective. Fiona grew up in her books. At sixteen she
processed a six-page application and secured the nomination of
one of her private Van-Ed tutors. Consequently, the urban
extension accepted her into its psychology programs.

With her father's permission, wary as it was, she quartered
herself away from home. She took a room in the extension's
sexually and racially integrated dormitory-terraces. Eight floors
up, sealed away in an internal section of the complex, she
pursued her studies. The walls were still uniformly white, but the
people had changed. She emerged from her books.

Upon obtaining her first degree, Fiona Foe married Carlo
Bitler.

Here the visicom screen seemed to blur; the gold letters
backed up on me and I was lost elsewhere. At last the images
became clear again, and the sentences resumed parading silently
down the green face of the console.

Of course, I recognized the man's name: Carlo Bitler. But I
had never associated that name with marriage, and I had
difficulty in associating it now with the darkly proud, but
somewhat resigned woman who was Fiona Bitler. I saw her
among the children, fierce, commandingly gentle, mildly
haggard. She was working within the streamlined creakings of
the System, but not particularly liking it. She was not very much
like her husband, whom I knew by reputation.

Though this line of narrative may seem momentarily tangential, Carlo Bitler is extremely important. He has a great deal to do with the story of Emory Coleman, as well as with that of his wife. Therefore I ask you to fix the vision and voice of Fiona Bitler in your mind that you may understand the contrast which her husband provides. As quickly as I can, I will detail the most significant events in his biography.

Before his marriage, Carlo Bitler had graduated from the urban extension with degrees in both theology and political science. *A combination of the spiritual ideals and the crass realities,* he often said. He was neither a black man nor a white man, but his soul apparently gravitated to that which was dark and primordial in his makeup. He was wide-nostriled and narrow-lipped; his flesh was the color of coffee; his eyes buoyed within their irises small flecks of golden light, like shattered coins. Unlike Fiona, he had never experienced the stale self-negating existence of the ghetto. The ghettos were roach-infested anachronisms, but unofficially they received sanction and were still standing. Carlo Bitler damned the authorities for niftily pulling their caps over their eyes, for ignoring that which needed change.

He *felt* the inconsistencies. In a closed world supposedly cleansed of its inner pollutions, all the residual hates gnawed at his gut. (Perhaps I am editorializing; the visicom tapes are as matter-of-fact as a newspaper obituary.) But he fought off the hates, looked up, and realized that no help would be forthcoming from without.

So he made noises that he hoped would send groundswells through the concrete, and tremors through every Dome-supporting girder in Atlanta. He raised his voice.

He preached from the pulpits of all the back-alley churches. Over the grizzled heads of antedated laborers who still called themselves Negroes, he shouted the necessary one-and two-syllable words. The city buried these people. He wanted them to come out of their ratholes. Always, Fiona watched him from the backmost pew of the urine-stained synagogue to which his rudely formulated purpose had led him. She watched him out of an uncomprehending love that simply endured. She herself now held a teaching position; she would not question her husband's calling. Finally, the electric glow that seemed to suffuse Carlo Bitler as he reached out with tortured hands to his congregations, as he gesticulated, became a physical adjunct to his person; he generated the charisma that brought to him the young.

As Fiona watched, others in our closed world took note. Something was happening. Here was a man who should not be practicing such demagoguery, the Others said. After all, didn't he have full rights of citizenship? Full protection under the Federal Urban Charter? Unlike his own wife, unlike eighty percent of the middle-aged blacks who now found air and subsistence under the Dome, he had never been an integer in an Evacuation Lottery. He held the franchise of any urban-born individual. That he should be making these noises was inane, an affront to the City that sheltered him.

The pressures were of two kinds. Carlo Bitler had one such pressure inside him, and he released it in those innumerable harangues which returned him to Fiona drained and sallow. The other such pressure was that which grew in the proletarian whites. They remembered just enough history to envision domed Atlanta a racial battleground. Those who felt so threatened had no outlet but invective through which to release their bewilderment and anger. For a time, the City ignored both factions.

At this point I halted the unraveling of information. The words stood obediently on the console screen, unmoving. Then I shut off the tapes altogether, so that the gold vanished from the background. I knew what was going to happen.

Deliberately, I stalked out of the cluttered study cage, leaving yellow notepaper strewn carelessly about. I walked to a lift-tube. The book stacks through which I found my way all smelled of disinfectant. Somewhere the purse-lipped librarian was mumbling to himself. I rode the clean transparent lift-tube upward until an amber light glowed in the glass carapace just above my head. Then I was alone on the uppermost rampart of the Ed-complex.

No sky was overhead, only the colossal honeycombing of steel and opaque plexiglass that still challenged my belief. How had we accomplished this? and why?

We are inside a walnut, I thought. *Who in our walnut is king of infinite space?*

Let me complete for you the biography of Carlo Bitler, as incidental as it may seem to this account of his wife and the Black Period of her grim nine-year-old prodigy. On that parapet

I completed his biography in my thoughts.

I had shut off the visicom tapes precisely because I remembered too well.

Carlo Bitler demanded and received the opportunity to address a combined session of the Urban Council and the Conclave of Ward Representatives. His clamor had bought the time but it didn't buy much.

They gave him twenty minutes on a slow Monday, between two sessions of a debate on fund allocations. Money was wanted for cleaning several monuments. Bitler's remarks would provide an interlude, as if he were a jester or a magician.

From the back of the chamber he threaded his way to the platform. He stood stolidly alongside the podium and surveyed the slack-jawed legislators, black and white. He began. He attempted to define his purpose. He spoke to fulfill himself, rocked and leaned to define his own limits in space.

In spite of the air-conditioning, the assembly chamber smelled of sweat.

Carlo Bitler said that he was going to run for ward representative next time around, so that he would not have to threaten in order to be heard. He railed at the legislators, damned them for worrying about chipped and irrelevant statues while ignoring the crumbling edifices in which black people slept.

"We are entombed!" he shouted. "We are all entombed! Every mother's whelp among us. Yet this assembly aspires to dig the black man even deeper. The old buildings stink. They crawl with vermin. You want to replace them with still deeper ghettos. For several decades, the exigencies of history have spared you this confrontation. And now you are burying us..."

He stopped in midsentence.

A tiny red circle appeared on the right side of his forehead. The report of the pistol sounded through the chamber like a single amplified cough. He tried to complete his sentence.

"...burying us in light..."

The circle on Carlo Bitler's forehead sent out crimson runners; it let them drop across his eyes. Soon the wash of blood obliterated his features so that his face was no more than a horrible Greek mask. One arm still reaching toward his audience, he slumped in a heap beside the podium.

Death by assassination. End of incidental biography.

Of course, there was an untidy aftermath, but that didn't

concern me. In the five years since her husband's death Fiona Bitler had pulled her life together, shunned the role of the martyr's widow. She taught children, taught them within the cold white system that her husband had railed against. "No longer involved socio-political activity," the tapes had said.

I looked down at the City. The circulating air touched my garments slowly. Beneath the Dome I could see the old Regency complex with its tall central tower and smoky blue turret, also the blinding lofty cylinder of the Plaza Hotel. A dull and all-pervasive luminosity seemed to hang in the air, like dust. But there was no dust. Only light.

We no longer concern ourselves with the medieval terrors of the dark, I thought.

Then I rode the lift-tube down.

When I returned to my carrel, I found the librarian. He rose diffidently, with a small snorting sound. A number of yellow sheets lay before him on my desk, but it was obvious that his curiosity was merely a purposeless corollary to his job.

"You've had a telecom," he said.

"Who?"

"Oh ho," he said jovially. "A woman. A female."

"Mz Bitler?"

"She told me to tell you you're going to miss this week's instruction in hygiene. The projectionist waits for no one."

"No," I said. "I don't imagine he would."

"You want me to replace the tapes for you?"

"No. Just leave them. I only used one. I may want the other one."

He made a deferential bow, pursed his discolored lips, and rearranged the papers on my desk.

"A woman," he said playfully. "A film on hygiene."

I raised my fist in mock anger, but did not touch him. He grinned lopsidedly and left the carrel. Even as he retreated, I pictured not his back but his moist silver eyes fading, fading into the fluorescent labyrinth around us. After sorting out the mess he had made of my papers in trying to arrange them neatly, I left.

The librarian's empty whistling followed me.

3 / *The Witch of Tooth Decay*

I wrote that some of what I must tell you is beyond my power to explain. Let me reiterate. Occasionally people try to live so strenuously by the processes of logic that they become irrational. Therefore, do not expect explanations of me. I refuse to contribute to the insanities into which you will rationalize yourselves. Darknesses of all sorts exist, and sometimes it is best simply to accept them.

They exist.

Meanwhile, we carry the gnarled rudeness of our souls like shillelaghs. We either stump around or bludgeon aside those things that we don't understand.

It was nearly three when I stumped into the Van-Ed observation room. Through the two-way mirror I could see Mz Bitler standing to one side of the classroom. Tables and chairs had been shoved against the walls. Engaged in kinetic relations, the children held forth on the ivory parquetry which they had cleared. They were enacting a conflict of some kind.

There was utter polarity in that conflict. Two groups stood facing each another. Chins jutted forward bellicosely, and hands fisted and unfisted. There seemed to be an unwritten law that no one touched anyone else during these supposedly cathartic little dramas, for all the jutting chins and clenched fists. Whether any such provision in fact existed, the children unanimously obeyed it.

I turned the dial beside the window. The voices of the children came lucidly through several small circular speakers.

They were arguing about the time when the geodesic Domes of the twenty-five Urban Nuclei must eventually suffer demolition, releasing us to the sun. The two sides made no concessions, reached no compromises. At last I recognized that my own charge, Emory Coleman, belonged to neither group. He was sitting on the table that supported the projection unit, one lank white arm draped over its casing. He was looking at his feet.

The argument among the other children went on: "We should destroy the Domes as soon as we can." "We must keep the Domes even after the conditions which prompted them no longer exist." "The Domes are a monument to man's stupidity."

"No, they are a demonstration of all that mankind can do in cooperation." And on it went.

Emory Coleman looked up at the group, the two groups, which stood in forensic confrontation. His legs continued to swing back and forth, pale hairless legs that ended in a pair of dark blue moccasins.

"Why doesn't everybody shut up?" he demanded. "You've gone over the allotted time. We ought to be watching our movie."

He dropped the metal canister from which he had already removed the reel of film and let it clatter on the floor.

Every head turned toward him, and he began carefully to thread the celluloid through the sprockets of the machine. The hard white casing sat on a rack beneath the projection table. He had removed it almost without our noticing, as easily as he might doff a beanie. Now he was standing and working efficiently at his one apparently gratifying duty.

The other children stared blankly for an instant or two, but Mz Bitler nodded her stringent approval and they began to move their chairs into position for the film. Then Mz Bitler dialed the lighting down, turning the classroom into a glossy crypt.

It was into this gleaming darkness that I finally stepped. My presence in the classroom caused no stir. Mz Bitler, with no evidence of surprise, turned and indicated a chair beside the projection unit.

Emory saw but ignored me. "It's ready," he said.

One of the children drew a white panel out of the wall at the opposite end of the room; the panel was a screen. Then we sat in the darkness, Mz Bitler and I, looking over the silhouetted heads of the children and occasionally glancing at Emory's intent profile as he ran the projector.

The film flickered onto the screen in veined splotches of gray and black; it stuttered and blazed like a fire in a wind tunnel. The film was inestimably old, and the frames seemed to jump one another. Numerals burned on the celluloid, then disappeared: 9, 8, 5, 5, 4, 2, 1. My eyes ached.

"This *is* going to be a talkie, isn't it?"

Mz Bitler looked at me but spoke to the boy: "Emory!"

"What?"

"You've shown this before, haven't you." Her inflection did not suggest a question. "I can tell it's not the scheduled one."

"I've shown it before," he said, "Sort of."

"I think once is enough."

"No," he said. "It's not enough."

The projector contributed a gentle whirring to the otherwise silent room. Either chagrined or acquiescent, Fiona Bitler leaned back in her chair and watched the screen.

"What's going on?"

"Just watch." She refused to look at me. "Just let your eyes show you what later you'll reject altogether."

The meaningless lead-ins at last gave way to a series of scripted titles, all in flourishing longhand. Scratchy marching music came from the stereophonic speakers. Trumpets made scrolls of victrola cacophony in the air. I almost expected to see phalanxes of goosestepping soldiers come striding through the screen. Some of the children turned cautiously in their chairs. Was there some mistake? They looked at Emory. Undaunted, he continued to stare at the screen.

"Well," I said. "At least there's sound, isn't there?"

The main title came up. In fancy longhand. *The Dental Institute of America Presents . . . Your Teeth and the Witch of Tooth Decay.* Trumpets and drums rattled from the speakers. The film jitterbugged on the screen.

"Where did he get this thing?"

"From his father." Fiona Bitler still did not turn her head. "He got it once upon a time from his father."

I will not dwell on the preliminaries. A narrator spoke of proper dental care. A crude line drawing showed the alignment of the upper and lower dentures. Arrows appeared in miraculous animation to designate the individual teeth: molars, bicuspids, canines, incisors. There was a somewhat clinical sequence in which a child demonstrated proper and improper methods of brushing the teeth.

The film continued to pop and flicker unsteadily, and the narrator (he never appeared, but I pictured him with a slick mustache and a shiny pompadour) lectured pontifically over the fading martial cadenzas of the trumpets.

Then I heard one of the children murmur, "She's coming next," and they all shifted in their chairs, readying themselves. I, too, stared nervously at the screen.

Envision, then, that same screen.

You see a close-up of the girl who has been demonstrating brushing techniques. Then another close-up, this one of her soft cherubic mouth. Her lips part. The camera takes us inside the moist dark cavern where her teeth grow up like so many porcelain-hard toadstools, the enamel glistening. We are in another world, an enclosed universe in which moistness and darkness strangely commingle. We are no longer dry and illuminated.

The narrator is still talking, but each of us ignores the insidious drone of his voice. At last he ceases; the music also ceases. All we hear is the whirring of the projector, the odd static in the film itself.

Into this hush comes the hag.

Deep in the sacristy of the girl's throat there appears a conical hat; beneath it, a hideously sutured face. Flickering, the hag arises from the epiglottis, balances on the meat of the child's tongue, and approaches us through a sheen of spittle. She carries a gnarled staff. She proceeds up the row of baby teeth, tapping on their bonewhite crowns. At last she consumes the whole screen. A frightening close-up.

She grins maliciously at us, her audience. When she speaks, her accents are unmistakably those of a previous time's touring-company player.

> *Acid, acid, stinging poison,*
> *Mixed in cauldron, stirred in chalice,*
> *Poured atop the clean crown chosen*
> *Object of our special malice.*

> *Fester, fester, let the sickness*
> *Plague the pulpy heart within,*
> *Rot the capsule 'round the quickness,*
> *Send the crownlet crashing in.*

> *Sour, sour, Carrie's power.*
> *Burns the lustre from your smile,*
> *Chars to chalk the children's hour*
> *Grinning ashen, black and vile.*

Carrie the hag falls silent. Her expression undergoes a metamorphosis that renders her even more hideous. She hunches her shoulders, scrunches her head on her neck, cocks an oyster eye at all of us. It is as if she cannot hear the stinging poison of light from the projector, the flooding lantern light to which she owes her existence on celluloid. She grimaces horribly and draws up her cape to shield her eyes.

The camera records her agony.

Inside the child's mouth she crumples to her knees. Her conical hat totters. At last she looks painfully into the projector lamp again, and haltingly recites.

> *Lamp of logic, burning straight*
> *Through the grottos of our hate,*
> *Let thy brightness amplify*
> *The mote of love in each man's eye.*

But it is strange. It looks as if someone has lip-synched these words to the contorted movements of the witch's mouth and tongue. What has logic to do with any of this? Then Carrie the hag falls silent and collapses in her billowing robe.

The little girl's mouth closes, eclipsing her. The martial music begins again; so does the narrator's unctuous blabbering. The closing titles appear in their elaborate longhand, caught in the wavering filaments that have accompanied the entire showing. The screen goes white.

And at last you can hear the film itself going *slap slap slap* on the take-up reel.

4 / *Gerard Nettlinger's Son*

The lights were dialed up; the children shuffled their chairs back into some kind of order; and Emory carefully replaced the film in its canister. Fiona Bitler sat unmoving in the small plastic chair that had been made for nine-year-olds. Her eyes had pulled down on her thoughts.

She said nothing.

Waiting for some word from her, the children grew restless. They whispered and fumbled with their school supplies. I stood up and inanely rushed in to fill the vacuum.

"Well," I said jovially. "What did you all think of the movie?"

"We've seen it before," said one little girl, speaking over her shoulder from a table. "But it was different this time."

Emory looked at me. "I've closed the projector up. It's time for us to go. We're seven minutes late already."

Mz Bitler at last stood up. She smoothed away the folds in her rumpled smock and turned bewildered eyes on Emory. Then she spoke to the class as a group.

"All right. It's time to go. Place your materials in your desks—everything but the texts you have to read tonight. Tomorrow we'll have language, urban history, and a seminar discussion about the effects of superstition on both primitive and rational societies. You all know which parts you're supposed to take." She looked over the top of Emory's head. "You'd better take that film back to your family's cubicle."

"No," he said. "It has to be shown again. I'll leave it on top of the projection stand."

As the other children began preparing to leave, Mz Bitler took an awkward step or two toward the boy. She had no idea what she was going to do, so I interposed myself and spoke to him.

"If you could stay a few extra minutes, I'd like to talk to you a little."

"No." His face tightened. "It's very important I get home when my parents expect me."

"Your stepfather?" Mz Bitler asked.

Emory turned away. I watched the other children leave by a clean white panel next to the door to the observation room. They filed out in an anonymous blur of satchels, brightly colored paperback texts, and red and yellow moccasins. Emory went all the way across the room, opened his desk, and removed all the crayon drawings that I had looked at earlier. He also removed the delicate black flower, cupping it in one palm. Across the intervening whiteness of the classroom he spoke to us.

"You can only look at the ones I show you."

Then he too left, his soft blue moccasins padding through the door. With him he carried nothing but his drawings, and the flower. When he was gone, the room was childless.

I sat down on a table and turned toward Mz Bitler. She was standing like a tall African sculpture at one end of the room.

"That was a very odd film."

She said nothing.

"A very odd film on hygiene."

She said nothing.

"I mean, even for these youngsters that was a rather erudite presentation of a subject like tooth-brushing. And weird."

"Didn't you hear the little girl?"

"Which?"

"The one who said that it was different this time. Emory sneaked that same film into the classroom once before, and showed it. But this time it was *different.*"

"How?"

"Carrie. The old witch. She didn't speak in poetry. She didn't slump into a pathetic heap after reciting a Blakeian stanza about love. It was *different.*"

"Are you sure you remember correctly? Are you certain Emory just didn't bring along another film?"

"I remember. How often do you see a spliced and tattered movie from the middle of a previous century? Besides, everything was the same this time except for the performance of that old witch."

"A fitting prelude to a seminar on superstition."

She looked at me sharply.

"Is he trying to annoy you?" I asked. "Is he trying to make you hate him?"

"I'm afraid I don't understand him well enough to answer that." Fiona Bitler still had not moved; her face was averted from me, darkly sorrel. I tried something new.

"Why are you teaching, Mz Bitler? Some would hold that you've let the calling of your husband slip by."

She changed position and fixed me with a long critical look. "You have a long memory, Dr Greer. And a remarkable ability to make difficult associations."

"No, ma'am. I have access to the Van-Ed tapes."

"The biographies?"

I nodded.

"Well," she said. She touched the pendant at her throat. "You must be amused by the irony of my position in regard to Emory. Do you think it's funny?"

She had lost me. *"Irony?"* I said.

"Let me tell you right now," she said, approaching the table. "It's not a coincidence that I'm teaching that child. It's not a droll little quirk of our destinies."

"I hadn't presumed it was. What exactly are you talking about?"

She stopped, and we made our positions clear. When Fiona Bitler at last understood that I had reviewed only one of the biographies (and that one hers) we sat in conference for nearly an hour.

She believed Emory Coleman had suffered from understanding the mystery of his father. The boy now lived with his mother and a taciturn stepfather whom Fiona—for no good reason—distrusted.

The boy's real father had been a dentist, dead now for five years. While alive, he had made his living working for the urban medicaid programs, caring for that segment of the population confined to the sweat-stained tenements. The man's name had been Gerard Nettlinger; his background was Austrian, and he recalled, as if in the darknesses of racial memory, a prenatal time when witches and unnameable demons had controlled the destinies of men. In the Urban Nucleus, however, these things capitulated to expediency and science. He became a dentist and a good one. He gathered to himself all the supplementary aids of the meticulous practitioner.

But he was a bitter man. The medicaid professional received a fixed salary, one beyond which there was little advancement. The City provided; that was all. Gerard Nettlinger consequently felt some antipathy toward the system which sheltered him, but which denied him the opportunity to govern his own rates. He wanted to practice among an elite cross-section of the City's governing hierarchy, where, if not advancement, he might find other benefits.

The black man—and the black man's need—prohibited him.

The outlet for Gerard Nettlinger's bitterness toward the urban system was in his overweening hatred for those whom he involuntarily treated. He despised the black patients into whose mouths he probed with tongue depressors and drill bit. He considered them inferior, he despised their docility, he raged inwardly that his career should belong so utterly to their helplessness. The City was using him.

"I understand that," Fiona told me. "He was discriminated against."

But apparently he worked the more fiercely for all his bitterness. He stopped dragging himself to the boxlike office the Urban Health Bureau had assigned him. Instead, he made voluntary trips to the ghettos. He set up his projector in walk-up flats, bullied the residents into becoming an audience, and showed out-of-date movies on the cracked plaster of the walls. He showed the film that Emory had just shown. Carrie the hag permitted him to play to the primordial Austrian instincts in himself while simultaneously frightening his audience. After the movies he lectured from the tops of stairwells. Sometimes, in the middle of the street, he intimidated skinny black children into opening their mouths; there he brusquely examined their teeth. But he hated those upon whom he so impulsively showered his attention.

"His impulsiveness was not at all unlike Carlo's. In some ways the two men were much alike."

Gerard Nettlinger followed the news. Many things made him angry. Although he had a young wife and a new child, the political affairs of the Urban Nucleus concerned him more than his family. He grew angrier. Finally, one slow Monday afternoon in a legislative assembly chamber, he vented his frustrations through the muzzle of a pistol. Sweating, he stood up in the midst of an august body of politicians and fired at the gesticulating man behind the lectern; the bullet created a victim for him. He knew he had succeeded even as four or five men grabbed wildly at his arm and bore him uncomplaining to the floor. Noise abounded, but he had heard the last few prophetic words and almost sympathized with them.

"*...burying us in light ...*"

Gerard Nettlinger died in a small sterile chamber, the fumes anesthetizing him forever. His son was a prodigy, an immature genius who no longer carried his name but might conceivably carry his primordial guilts and social hatreds. Science did not think that acquired attitudes were in the genes—but which are acquired, which innate hatreds?

Fiona Bitler folded her hands, a movement of gentle finality. The story was over.

"And you tell me it's no coincidence you're teaching the son of the man who murdered your husband?"

"No," she said. "There's no coincidence. I manuevered to obtain this position, showed credentials, deluged the Van-Ed offices with references."

"Why?"

"Because I had to get close to the boy."

"Why? To carve your own initials on his psyche?"

She leaned forward, her nostrils flared.

"To teach him forgiveness, Dr Greer. To communicate through personal contact something like moral understanding."

"Fine sentiments. But whose forgiveness are you teaching him?" I silenced her with an upraised hand. "Do you believe the sins of the father are visited on the son? If so, will the boy forgive you for forgiving him?"

Fiona Bitler touched her taut throat and made a helpless gesture. I was holding my glasses by the frame, letting them dangle in my hand, waiting with blurred eyes.

"All right," she said. "We haven't communicated and

consequently I haven't been doing any real teaching."

"The fault isn't entirely yours."

"If I thought so, I'd quit. Now, Dr Greer, why don't you leave me to straighten things up a little and correlate my notes? You can always interrupt class tomorrow."

"Yes, ma'am. Tomorrow it is." I stood up and surveyed the austere porcelain luster of the room. It seemed achingly empty now that the children were gone and our conversation was over. I made an attempt to cover the emptiness: "Why won't you let anyone call you doctor?"

"Titles are barriers," she said.

"There are others, maybe more important ones."

Mz Bitler extended her hand and I took it. The flesh was warm and supple and brown in my grasp. I held her hand a second or two longer than etiquette would dictate proper, but her expression did not change. Then she let her hand drop, I nodded goodbye, and the observation room swallowed me soundlessly. Standing in the darkness, I looked out on the woman who seemed to be an African princess contemplating other worlds from a plain of ice. That was the last time I really ever saw her.

Looking through the two-way mirror, I had the inarguable feeling that someone had preceded me into the observation room. The air was warm, as if with the residual warmth of a spy who had just retreated. But no one was there. I calmed my suspicions, opened the panel sealing off the aquarium and left through the Van-Ed suite's outer chamber. I was going home. My head throbbed with the kaleidoscopic pulsing of new information, and I wanted a drink.

One moment I was walking down an empty hallway, too preoccupied to look at the canvases spaced along the walls; the next moment I was facing an individual who had seemingly materialized from the sterility of the corridor itself. I halted, my footfalls echoing away into the labyrinth.

Emory Coleman faced me, his drawings clutched tightly in one hand. With the other he thrust the purplish black flower at my chest. I took the flower and wondered where everyone had gone, where Emory Coleman had come from.

"Are you giving me this?"

"You were talking about me," he said. "About my father."

"I thought you had to be home when your parents expected."

"I went to that room where the teachers spy on us."

"And you listened?"

"Yes."

"Well, what did you think of the conversation?"

"Neither of you learned anything," he said. "You never think about things that happen when it's dark."

"Like your father?" I suggested.

Emory merely eyed me with disdain, the blue veins working in his shaven blond temples. More and more I began to feel exposed, vulnerable, that the corridor was a place of neither comfort nor privacy. As I shifted from foot to foot in that open whiteness, I could hear my very thought echoing. Insidiously, the paintings on the walls retreated to a distant vanishing point.

"Is that why you brought the film, Emory? To make us think?"

"It's a film on hygiene," he said. "Just like the Van-Ed people wanted. But there's a witch in it, ain't there?"

"Yes. There certainly is."

"Mz Bitler ought to know about blackness, like my father did. But she doesn't. That's why I brought the film with the witch."

"Look, Emory, Mz Bitler said that the movie was different this time. So did one of the girls. Was it?"

I stared deep into the heart of the black flower, still half-expecting the coral snake to emerge from the central petal cluster. Emory ignored my question. He turned to study one of the paintings and spoke without looking at me.

"She wants to understand what my father did to her husband by understanding me. But she doesn't want to understand me *first*. And that's why she can't do it, why she can't touch me."

"That's difficult reasoning," I said. "Do you dislike her?"

"Sometimes." He turned back to me from the painting. "But I wouldn't ever do anything malicious. Even if it somehow looked that way."

"I'm afraid I don't understand."

"Do you know what *paradox* means?"

"I believe so."

"Mz Bitler taught us that word, but she doesn't know what it means. Hygiene and witches is paradoxical, though, isn't it?"

"I would say so. If for no other reason than to appease you."

"Well, something else is paradoxical, too. Blackness is. Do you want to hear how?"

"If I have to stand in this hallway much longer, I want to hear something either helpful or interesting. One or the other."

Emory composed his features, and stared past me down the hall when he finally began reciting. "Black pushes things apart," he said, "by separating and making outlines. But it's the oldest color, and it pushes things together by covering them all up so that they're just alike. That's what Mz Bitler doesn't seem to understand."

"I'll try to remember that."

Then I regretted my tone, for Emory Coleman's eyes suddenly went opaque, like those of a lizard, a creature of another species. Before I could react, he stepped violently forward and knocked the tissue-paper flower out of my hand. My response to his philosophizing had violated years of training. Now I watched the results of that error. Emory Coleman fled down the corridor and all too quickly disappeared into the brightness that held us both. I picked up the fallen blossom and turned it in my hands. Footfalls echoed. I was alone again.

5 / If a Flower Could Eclipse

I spent the evening with my feet hoisted on an oversized red ottoman, a perspiringly cold glass of Scotch and water in my hand. Watching the patterns that my water-lantern threw against the white fiberboarding, I stared at the ceiling. The shapes enthralled me. In the intense quiet, my mind was empty of everything but the phantasmagoric images overhead and the slowly befogging incursion of the Scotch. I stared at the ceiling for two hours.

Then I stumbled to bed.

The telecom unit woke me. Its buzz sounded inside my skull like the amplified whirring of a dentist's drill. I imagined myself gagging as Gerard Nettlinger probed relentlessly into my jaws. Perhaps I had not come fully awake.

"Hello?"

A voice curled into my ear, not to be mistaken for any other—a shrill contralto that I had heard earlier in the day chanting about Carrie's power. Unmistakably, it was the voice of a witch.

"Who the hell is this?" I shouted.

My mouth tasted as if I had been chewing the tongue of an old canvas shoe, horribly wrong.

"Mz Bitler . . . Fiona . . . is this your own patented variety of a practical joke?"

A hesitant cackling. Then silence.

"Come on now. Who is this?"

Nothing in response but the voice of the hag: Shakespearean accents which pieced together a message. I cannot remember if she recited her message in the trochaic meters of Emory's film, but she very clearly ordered me to follow her directions.

Dr Greer, you will come to the educational complex . . . to the Van-Ed suite . . . And you must come this very moment.

I raged impotently into the telecom unit, demanding answers, begging for elaboration: the unit began to hum.

Groggy from sleep and alcohol, I pulled on my tunic and left the apartment. Fluorescent lamps burned over my head in every corridor; crystal lift-tubes carried me up and down the gleaming levels of masonry; an individual transit-car whisked me through the echoing stone vaults. Anticipating, my stomach churned.

In twenty minutes I burst into the outer office of the Van-Ed suite. The door stood open, the panel sheathed inside its frame. Silence. The quiet that one encounters in a cathedral sanctuary. A sentient hush. I activated the panel into the observation room, but I could see nothing through the window.

The classroom was an inscrutable black cave.

I rapped on the glass with my knuckles. "Mz Bitler, are you there?" Another tattoo on the glass. "Fiona!"

I looked down at my other hand and saw that I had unmercifully crushed the black flower Emory had given me that afternoon. Without realizing how or why, I had carried it with me all the way from the apartment. Turning to the panel into the classroom, I found further evidence that Emory was manipulating my comings and goings. Taped to the middle of the panel was one of Master Coleman's drawings—the sketch that he had shown me on my first visit, fourteen hours ago. I removed the tape and held the sketch uncomprehendingly in my hands, along with the crushed paper flower. There was a legend, in flourishing longhand, just beneath the two figures in the sketch. Two figures who touched in the rubble of Emory's unspecified holocaust. I read the legend.

Only you should look at this one. It explains.

It explained nothing. I held the drawing and the flower, and waited for something momentous to happen. All I could hear was my breathing.

I decided to discover the prankster, whether it was student or teacher. I entered the classroom and dialed the lights up. No one. Rows of red and yellow plastic chairs. Several mobiles turning slowly in the emptiness. The absence of any human being was a palpable thing.

I walked into the classroom, toward the corner where Emory had cloistered himself. The only desk in the room.

Facing that desk, I heard the reverberating clatter of a movie canister on hard tiles. The noise jerked me around. No one. I was looking at the projection unit in its creamy white casting. The battered movie canister lay beside it. No sound but the fading clatter and my own amplified breathing.

What I did next has neither motive nor explanation.

I picked up the canister, removed the reel of film, set aside the projector casing, and carefully threaded the film through the correct sprockets. My hands were shaking, but I made no mistakes. Never before had I operated a projector; nothing in my work had ever required the use of a machine considered by many obsolescent, if not strictly primitive. But I operated this one. The screen was still in place.

As the lead-in frames of numerals and letters flickered on the screen, I dialed the lights down and perched forward on the edge of a plastic chair. Both numb and expectant, I concentrated on driving down the alcoholic blur that had seeped into my eyes. Victrola music. Trumpets.

What in God's name had manuevered me to this idiocy?

Envision the screen.

A crude chart depicts the upper and lower dentures. Animated arrows point out the biscuspids and molars. A little girl (one who has since grown old, died, and blown into the night as dust) is brushing her teeth. The narrator's lubricated baritone slides back and forth in your ears. A close-up of the girl's cherubic mouth.

Then the screen goes totally black. You can hear the film as it bunches in the sprockets and subtly tears.

But even as the film seems to be tearing, the picture reappears. But we are not gazing into the child's enormous mouth; no hag grins at us from her Carlsbad throat. Instead, the confrontation is something other, something terrifyingly other.

You are looking at the aristocratic figure of Fiona Bitler; and

Fiona Bitler is standing in the middle of the very classroom in which you are watching her stand. The film depicts her looking pensively at her folded hands, a secret preoccupation playing in her mind. She appears irredeemably isolated and alone. But maybe she is waiting.

(I know that I started and came to my feet at some point in this initial sequence of frames, but the woman's herky-jerky image assured me that she was indeed on film. I sat back down, shaking with disbelief.)

Into this uneasy reverie, flouncing through the classroom door like a miniature Mack Sennett cop, comes Emory Coleman. The action develops at twice the normal pace. The child gesticulates, waves his hands and moves back and forth in front of her in comical sparrowlike hops. Mz Bitler frowns, places her arms akimbo, speaks, tries to touch the boy's face and watches him hop away with mincingly censorious steps. The room seems to revolve about their pirouetting bodies.

You realize there is no sound.

Merely a whirlpool of black and white ribbons.

But then Emory (on film) scurries to the projector, takes the film from its canister, winds it onto the machine, and points emphatically at the lighting dial. Mz Bitler whirls to the dial, flicks her wrist and plunges the screen you are watching into darkness. You can dimly see both figures in the darkened classroom; they stare toward the deeper screen that exists in their circumscribed celluloid world.

Now: Envision a screen within a screen.

The filmed persons of Emory Coleman and Fiona Bitler are viewing the same film the boy showed that afternoon. But their movie begins with Carrie the hag proceeding forward from deep in the little girl's throat. She fills the more removed of the two screens with her puckered eyes and stitched alligator's mouth. But no longer does the action waltz by at twice its normal pace; Carrie's slow smile forms in thirty dragging seconds of agonized stasis.

Then the camera dollies back for a long shot and Carrie steps clumsily out of the little girl's mouth. She hoists her ebony skirts over the child's moist bottom lip and carefully plants one bony bare foot . . . *into the classroom.*

She is still a two-dimensional character to you, but to the woman and the boy in that filmed classroom she is a three-dimensional reality, coexisting with them in time.

Draw back to your first screen: the *real* one.

Emory Coleman and Fiona Bitler rise. The witch is in the classroom with them. She has descended from that other screen. Her eyes grow as wide and bright as silver coins and she points a crooked finger at the two human beings who confront her. She draws a looping circle in the air.

Fiona Bitler grasps the boy protectively to her body. He does not resist. The two of them face their antagonist, locked one against the other.

At that instant the screen bursts into color. You can see the red and yellow chairs, the violet tones of Carrie's wrinkled mask, Emory's soft blue moccasins, the warm chocolate of Fiona's skin. Then Carrie sweeps the darkness of her cape over the screen and reduces everything again to black and white.

A blinding phosphorescence blots out your vision. Glow-worms swim in the water of your eyes.

You recover in time to witness a vivid tableau: On the bonewhite floor lie the charred remains of both Emory Coleman and Fiona Bitler. Each face is punctuated with the black crater of a burnt-out mouth. Their hands are extended and touching.

Things concluded swiftly.

I did nothing so melodramatic as to scream or faint away, but I did rush forward from where I had been watching and stop in the middle of the room—exactly on the spot where the two lay outstretched and incinerated; exactly on the spot where the film had shown them. But nothing was there.

Then I smelled sulphur and heard a sound like the popping of grease in a skillet. Again the room filled with light. I turned and saw flames skirling over the surface of the projector, threading between the spokes of the take-up reel, running across the curling film itself. I waited for the fire to burn itself out.

And I waited for Atlanta's Dome to collapse in ruins of plexiglass and tangled steel.

All that happened was that the burning stopped. I stood in the empty classroom. When I looked at my hands, I found that I was still clutching Emory's flower. I let it slide to the floor. So white were my hands that I believed myself stricken with some leprous disease. There were ashes in my palms.

But when I looked at that crumpled paper flower, I knew that it had done something other than merely eclipse.

Interlude: The Testimony of Leland Tanner

Transcript of a taped deposition taken during the official hearing convened four weeks after Dr Gregory Greer's hospitalization. The purpose of this hearing was to determine the cause of Dr Greer's breakdown and to fix the degree of his responsibility in the unsolved disappearance from the Urban Nucleus of Fiona Bitler and Emory Coleman.

The questions posed in this exchange are those of Assistant City Attorney D. L. Kahn. The responses are those of Dr. Leland Tanner, an employee of the Human Development Commission and a friend of the hospitalized psychologist.

Q. Dr Tanner, the document which our stenographer has just read into the records of these proceedings is an exceedingly strange one. Can you tell us what *really* happened to Dr Greer?

A. Well, it seems that for subjective reasons of his own Greg—I mean Dr Greer, of course—went to the Van-Ed classroom and set fire to as many of Emory Coleman's drawings as he could lay his hands on. He also burned the only surviving print of Dr Nettlinger's instructional film. Apparently he was found near the ruined projector with blistered hands and a look betraying his untenable mental state. A great deal of his narrative is therefore unreliable as a straightforward record of the case on which he was working. Only recently has he been able to acknowledge his illness.

Q. So he did set the fires himself?

A. No one has any reason to doubt it. Greer is a middle-aged bachelor, Mr Kahn, who's lived alone the entirety of his adult life. When Fiona Bitler requested a psychologist to help her maintain her balance against the disruptive influence of a little boy whose innate genius had recently manifested itself only in baroque, bitter drawings, the Human Development Commission sent Greg—Dr Greer—to help her.

Q. The boy is undoubtedly a genius?

A. That's what everyone, including Greg, has told me. It seems that Emory Coleman has the mental capacity to do just about whatever he wants to. For a long time, however, his potential's been obscured by his attempts to come to grips with his father's crime.

Q. Dr Greer wasn't able to help him?

A. Two aspects of the situation worked to undo Greg's objectivity and render his involvement in the case hopelessly counterproductive—a fact that Greg disguised, sublimated, or simply denied.

Q. What aspects?

A. First, he fell in love with Fiona Bitler. Second, he developed an almost obsessive dislike of Emory Coleman. Maybe this dislike stemmed from his perception that the boy stood between him and the object of his love. Maybe it came about because Emory's fondness for the color black and his penchant for showing the same dental-hygiene film over and over again drove Greg into spiritual catacombs he'd never explored before and didn't really want to get lost in. I'm speculating—but clearly it was Greg's mind that "eclipsed," not the paper flower in his narrative.

Q. And of course the Human Development Commission had no chance to send a replacement for Dr Greer because Fiona Bitler and her disturbed nine-year-old pupil disappeared from the City.

A. Yes, sir. The boy's mother believes that his teacher kidnapped him and smuggled him out by a transit-tunnel. Because Emory's real father assassinated Carlo Bitler, she fears that her son's life is at risk—even though the psychological profiles indicate that Fiona Bitler is incapable of physical violence, particularly against a child.

Q. Could it be that the Commission's failure to predict Dr Greer's little rampage has undermined Mz Coleman's faith in your assurances?

A. That may well be.

Q. Are you personally involved in casting these psychological profiles, Dr Tanner?

A. No, sir. Although we're both employed by the Human Development Commission, Greg's a psychologist and I'm a gerontologist and geriatrics researcher. My association with Greg—Dr Greer—has always been more of a personal than a professional one. We're drinking buddies.

Q. You're a bachelor, too?

A. I am.

Q. And your own work involves...?

A. Right now I'm trying to lay the foundations for a program that will revolutionize our treatment of the aged in this community. We hope to provide them with more fulfilling and dignified ways of confronting their remaining possibilities for life. It may take five, six, seven years but I'm—

Q. This is all very interesting, I'm sure—but it's irrelevant to our determination of Dr Greer's measure of responsibility in the disappearances of Fiona Bitler and young Emory Coleman.... When was the last time you spoke with Dr Greer?

A. I saw Greg yesterday, with the consent of his physicians. He's undergone a severe emotional trauma. It's difficult for me to see how he can be held responsible for something that happened *after* his breakdown. The disappearance, I mean.

Q. Do you think his ardor for Dr Bitler threw young Coleman back upon his teacher for guidance and support?

A. If it did, then Greg succeeded in spite of himself. That was what he was trying to do.

Q. Dr Tanner, you've been very helpful to this point—but now it seems we're talking at cross-purposes. You may step down.

A. Yes, sir.

Q. I'm afraid it may be some time before we get this matter straightened out to everyone's satisfaction....

The hearing continues with other witnesses.

CHAPTER TWO

Old Folks at Home

1 / *"Sold Down the River"*

At a stilly six o'clock in the morning Lannie sat looking at the face of her visicom console in their sleeper cove, Concourse B-11, Door 47, Level 3. Nausea was doing its stuff somewhere down in her plumbing: fizzes and bubbles and musical flip-flops. And Sanders—Sanders, her blue-jowled lummox—he lay sprawled snoring on their bed. If Levels 1 and 2 fell in on them, he'd still sleep, and he didn't have to get up for another hour. But Lannie intended to fight it, she wasn't going to the bath booth yet, no matter how tickly sick she began to feel.

That would wake Zoe, and she wasn't ready for Zoe yet—maybe not for the rest of the day.

Putting her arms across her stomach, Lannie leaned over the glowing console and tapped into the *Journal/Constitution* newstapes. Day 13 of Winter, 2040, New Calendar designation. Front page, editorials, sports; peoplenews, advertisements, funnies.

Then, in amongst the police calls and obituaries, a boxed notice:

WANTED: Persons over sixty to take part in the second phase of a five-year-old gerontological study funded by the **URNU HUMAN DEVELOPMENT COMMISSION**. Health and sex of applicants of no consequence. Our

selections will be based on a consideration of both need and
the individual interest of each case. Remuneration for the
families of those applicants who are selected. Contact DR
LELAND TANNER or his representative, UrNu Human
Development Tower.

Lannie, still clutching her robe to her middle, held this "page"
on the console. After two or three read-throughs she sat back
and gazed at the room's darkened ceiling. "Eureka," she
whispered at the acoustical punctures up there. "Eureka."

Sanders, turning his mouth to the pillow, replied with a
belugalike whistling.

She wasn't deceived, Zoe wasn't. She read the newstapes,
too, maybe even closer than they did, and if Melanie and
Sanders thought they could wooleye her with this casual trip to
the UrNu Human Development Tower, they needed to rethink
their clunky thinking. *I wasn't born yesterday,* Zoe thought—so
ludicrous a musing that right there in the quadrangle, on the
gravel path among the boxed begonias and day lilies, Sanders
craning his head around like a thief and Melanie drawing circles
in the gravel with the toe of her slipper, Zoe chuckled:
Clucka-clucka-cluck.

"Mother, hush!"

"'Scuse me, Lannie, 'scuse me for living." Which was also
reasonably funny. So she *clucka-clucked* again.

Sanders said, "What does he want to meet us out here for?
How come he can't conduct this in a businesslike fashion?"
Sanders was a freshman investment broker. He had had to take
the afternoon off.

"Not everyone runs their business like you do," Melanie
answered. She was a wardrobe model for Consolidated Rich's.

It was 2:10 in the afternoon, and the City's technicians had
dialed up a summery 23° C. in spite of its being the month
Winter. The grass in the quadrangle, as Zoe had already
discovered by stepping off the path, was Astroturf; and for sky
the young Nobles and Melanie's mother had the bright, distant
geometry of Atlanta's geodesic Dome. On every side, the white
towers of that sector of the Human Development complex
called the Geriatrics Hostel. Many of the rooms had balconies
fronting on the garden, and at various levels, on every side but
one (the intensive-care ward), curious faces atop attenuated or

bloated bodies stared down on them, two or three residents precariously standing but many more seated in wheelchairs or aluminum rockers. Except for these faces, the Nobles and the old woman had the carefully landscaped inner court to themselves.

"Home, sweet home," Zoe said, surveying her counterparts on the balconies. Then: "Sold down the river, sold down the river."

"Mother, for God's sake, stop it!"

"Call it what you want to, Lannie, I know what it is."

"Leland Tanner," a young man said, surprising them. It was as if he had been lying in wait for them behind a bend in the path, the concealing frond of a tub-rooted palm.

Leland Tanner smiled. More than two meters tall, he had a horsy face and wore a pair of blue-tinted glasses whose stems disappeared into shaggy gray hair—a pleasant-looking fellow. "You're Zoe Breedlove," he said to her. "And you're the Nobles.... I thought our discussion might be more comfortable out here in the courtyard." He led them to a gingko-shaded arbor on one of the pathways and motioned the family to a stone bench opposite the one he himself took up. Here, they were secure against the inquisitive eyes of the balcony-sitters.

"Zoe," the young man said, stretching out his long legs, "we're thinking of accepting you into our community."

"Dr Tanner, we're very—" Melanie began.

"Which means I'm being sold down the river."

"Damn it, Mother!"

The young man's eyes, which she could see like clear drops of sapphire behind the colored lenses, turned toward her. "I don't know what your daughter and your son-in-law's motives are, Zoe, but it may be that—on down the Chattahoochee, so to speak—you'll find a life a little better than it was on the old plantation. You may be freer here."

"She's as free as she wants to be with us," Sanders said, mounting his high horse. "And I don't think this plantation metaphor's a bit necessary." His foot always got caught in that wide, loose stirrup: his mouth.

Only the young doctor's eyes moved. "That may be true, Mr Noble. In the Urban Nucleus everyone's freedoms are proscribed equally."

"The reason they're doing it," Zoe said, putting her hands on her papery knees (she was wearing a disposable gown with clip-on circlets of lace at sleeves and collar), "is 'cause Lannie's gone and got pregnant and they want me out of the cubicle. They're not gonna get off Level 3 anytime soon, and four rooms we've got. So they did this to get me out."

"Mother, we didn't *do* it to get you out."

"I don't know why we did it," Sanders said, staring at the gravel.

Zoe appealed to the intent, gracefully lounging young doctor. "It could sleep in my room, too, that's the shame of it; it could sleep in my room." Then, chuckling again, "And they may be sorry they didn't think of that before hauling me up here like two Simon Legreedies."

"Dr Tanner," Melanie said, "we're doing this for her as much as for ourselves and the baby. The innuendoes about our motives are only—"

"Money," Zoe said, rubbing her fingers against her thumb like a usurer. "I read that box in the newstapes, you know. You're auditioning for old people, aren't you?"

"Sort of like that," Leland Tanner said, standing. "Anyway, Zoe, I've made up my mind about you." Under a canopy of gingko leaves he stared down at the group huddled before him, his eyes powerful surrogates for the myopic ones on the balconies.

"Don't take me," Zoe said. "It'll serve them right."

"From now on," the young man said, "we're going to be more interested in serving *you* right. And in permitting you to serve."

Sanders, her son-in-law, lifted his head and squinted through the rents in the foliage. "It's supposed to be Winter," he said. "I wish they'd make it rain." But an even monochromatic afternoon light poured down, and it was 23° C.

2 / To Marry with the Phoenix

She was alone with young Leland in a room opening onto the garden, and he had pulled the curtain back so that she could see out while they talked. A wingback chair for her, with muted floral-print upholstery. Her feet went down into a pepper-and-salt shag carpet. Tea things on a mahogany coffee table, all of the pieces a dainty robin's-egg blue except for the silver serving tray.

Melanie and Sanders had been gone thirty minutes, but she didn't miss them. It didn't disturb her that it might be a long while—a good long while—before she saw them again. The gingko trees in the garden turned their curious oriental leaves for her examination, and the young man was looking at her like a lover, albeit a cautious one.

"This is a pretty room," she said.

"Well, actually," he said, "it's a kind of decompression chamber, or air lock, no matter what the comfortable trappings suggest. Usually I'm not so candid in my explanation of its function; most prospective residents of the Geriatrics Hostel must be introduced into their new environment slowly, without even a hint that a change *is* occurring. But you, Zoe, not only realize from the outset what's going on, you've also got the wit to assimilate the change as if it were no more significant than putting on a new pair of socks."

"That's not so easy anymore, either."

He tilted his head. "Your response illustrates what I'm saying. I judge you to be a resilient woman; that, along with my interview with your family, induces me to select you as a candidate for the second stage of our study. I can use a term like air lock to describe this sitting room without flustering you. Because, Zoe, if you decide to stay with us, and to press your candidacy, you'll be very much like an astronaut going from the cramped interior of a capsule—via this room, your air lock—into the alien, but very liberated realm of outer space."

"First a sold-down-the-river darkie. Now a spaceman." Zoe shook her head and looked at the damp ring her tea cup had made on the knee of her gown. "Well, I'm old, Mr Leland, but I'm still around. More than you can say for slaves and astronauts, thank goodness in the one case, too bad in the other."

Young Mr Leland's violet eyes—he had taken those hideous glasses off—twinkled like St Nick's, but he didn't laugh, not with his voice. Instead he said, "How old are you, Zoe?"

"Sixty-seven. Didn't *they* tell you?"

"They told me. I wanted to see if you would."

"Well, that's correct. I was born in 1973, before the Domes ever was, and I came into Atlanta from Winder, Georgia, during the First Evacuation Lottery. Barely twenty-two, virgin and unmarried, though in those days you'd best not admit to the first condition any more than you had now. Met my husband, Rabon Breedlove, when the Dome wasn't a third finished. But a *third* of my life—my entire youth, really—I spent in the Open, not even realizing it was dangerous, the City politicians even said traitorous, to be out there." A few bitter black leaves adhered to the robin's-egg-blue china as she turned her empty cup.

"And how old is Melanie, then?"

"Twenty-eight or -nine. Let's see." She computed. "Born in 2011, a late child and an only one. Rabon and me had tried before, though. Four times I miscarried, and once I was delivered of a stillborn who went into the waste converters before we had a chance to put a name on it. Boy or girl, they didn't tell us. Then Melanie, a Winter baby, just when we thought we'd never have one. All the other times was forgotten, a pink and living tadpole we had then, Rabon and me."

"Your husband died when she was eight?"

"Embolism."

Young Mr Leland stood up and went to the window drapes. She saw how the shag lapped over his work-slippers, even though his feet were big: good and big. "The Geriatrics Hostel has two parts, Zoe, one a nursing home and hospital, the other an autonomous community run by the residents themselves. You don't need the first, but you can choose to be a candidate for the second."

"I got a choice, huh?"

"We coerce no one to stay here—but in the case of those committed to the Hostel's nursing sector it's often impossible for the residents to indicate choice. Their families make the decisions for them, and we then do the best we can to restore their capacity for reasoned, self-willed choice."

"What does it mean, I'm a 'candidate'?"

"If you so decide, you'll go into one of our self-contained communities. Whether you remain with that group, however, is finally up to you and the members of the group themselves."

"'Spose the old fuddy-duddies don't like me?"

"I view that as unlikely. If so, we'll find you another family or permit you to form one of your own. No losers here, Zoe."

Very quietly she said, "Hot damn." Young Mr Leland's eyebrows went up. "An expression of my daddy's."

And came down again into an expression amusingly earnest. "Your husband's been dead twenty years. How would you like to get married again?"

"You proposin'?"

Well, he *could* laugh. With his voice as well as his eyes. She was hearing him. "No, no," he said, "not for myself. For the first septigamic unit we want to introduce you to. Or for the six remaining members of it, that is. You'll have six mates instead of one, Zoe. Three husbands and three wives, if those terms mean anything at all in such a marriage convenant. The family name of the unit is Phoenix. And if you join them, your legal name will be Zoe Breedlove-Phoenix, at least within the confines of the Geriatrics Hostel itself. Elsewhere, too, if things work out as we wish."

"Sounds like a bridge group that's one short for two tables."

"You'll be doing more than playing bridge with these people, Zoe. No false modesty, no societally dictated inhibitions. And the odd number is a purposive stipulation, not merely a capricious way of messing up card games. It prevents pairing, which can sometimes occur on an extremely arbitrary basis. The old NASA programmers recognized this when they assigned *three* men to the Apollo missions. The same principle guides us here."

"Well, that's fine, Mr Leland—but even with those astronauts, you'll remember, only two of 'em went down honeymooning."

His horsy face went blank, then all his cheek- and jawbones and teeth worked together to split the horsiness with a naughty-boy grin. He scratched his unkempt hair: shag on top, shag around his shoes. "Maybe I ought to renege on the Phoenix offer and propose for myself, Mz Breedlove. All I can say to answer you is that honeymooning needn't be what tradition only decrees. For the most part, the septigamic covenant has worked pretty well these last five years at the Hostel. And your own wit and resilience make me believe that you can bring off your candidacy and marry with the Phoenix. Do you wish to become a candidate, Zoe?"

Zoe put her cup on the silver serving tray. "You know, Mr Leland, you should've been a comedy straight man." By which she didn't mean to imply that he was even half so humorless as Sanders Noble. No, sir. That Sanders could stay sour in a room full of laughing gas.

"Missed my calling. But do you want to?"

"Oh, I do," Zoe replied, taking what he'd served up. "I do."

3 / *Helen and the Others*

Dr Leland Tanner made a call on an intercom unit in the sitting room. Then, leaning over Zoe so that she could smell the sharp cologne on him, he kissed her on the forehead. "I'm going out now, Zoe. If you decide to stay, you'll see me only infrequently; your new family will occupy your time and your attention. There's no interdict, however, on associating with the culturally immature. If you like, you can see me or anyone else younger than yourself. Just let me know."

"Then I s'pose I shall, Mr Leland."

"'Bye," and he strode through the whipping shag, saluted at the sliding glass doors, and went out into the quadrangle. In only a moment he was lost to Zoe on one of the foliage-sheltered paths, and the calm, curious gingko trees held her amazed interest until an inner door opened and a thin woman with close-cropped gray hair came in to her.

"Zoe Breedlove?" A Manila envelope clasped in front of her, the newcomer looked *toward* the wingback but not exactly *at* it. A handsome frail woman with silvery opaque eyes and an off-center smile.

"That's me," Zoe said. The other's eyes focused on her then, and the smile firmed up. The woman navigated through waves of carpet to a chair opposite Zoe's and they faced each other across the tea service.

"I'm Helen," the woman said. "Helen Phoenix. Parthena and Toodles wanted another man, I think, but I'm happy Leland found somebody who won't have to compete with our memories of Yuichan. That would have been unfair to you."

"You-i-chan?" The word sounded foreign, particularly to a Dome-dwelling Georgia girl. Whereas Helen's accent marked her as no native to Atlanta. New York? Something cosmopolitan, that was for sure. Once.

"Yuichan Kurimoto-Phoenix. He was born in Kyoto, but he behaved like a raving Italian. Had execrable taste in everything; not a bit subtle. There's an unpainted plaster-of-paris squirrel on the bole of one of the trees in the garden—Yuichan's doing." Helen lowered her head. "A lovely man; just lovely."

"Well, I hope the others don't think I'm going to even try to take You-i-chan's place. I don't know anything about China."

The woman's smile died at the corners of her mouth, then slowly grew back. "Nevertheless," she said, "you may be more like Yuichan than you know. Which is all to the good: a bonus for us. And the question of your competing with Yuichan's memory won't enter into our appreciation of you at all, I'm sure of that. Toodles only favored another man, I'm sure, because she's a voluptuary and thinks Paul and Luther inadequate for our servicing."

Servicing. That probably meant exactly what she thought it did. Zoe leaned over the coffee table. "Would you like some of this tea Mr Leland left with me?"

"Please. And if you'll push the service to one side, Zoe—may I call you Zoe?—I'll introduce you to the others even before we go upstairs. That's an advantage you'll have over them, but probably the only one. We hardly begrudge it."

"Good. I could use an evener." And it was after pushing the tea service aside and while watching Helen take the photographs and printouts out of the Manila envelope that Zoe realized Helen was blind. The opaque eyes worked independently of her smile and her hands: the eyes were beautiful, somehow weightless ball bearings. Mechanical moving parts in a body that was all Siamese cat and animal silver. Without fumbling, Helen's small hands laid out the pictures and the data sheets. Reminiscently, Zoe touched one of the photographs.

"You can examine it all while I drink my tea, Zoe. I won't bother you."

The top sheet on the pile was neatly computer-typed. Zoe held it up and tilted it so that she could read it.

THE PHOENIX SEPTIGAMOKLAN

Covenant Ceremony:

Day 7 of Spring, 2035, New Calendar designation. Septigamoklanners:

M.L.K. Battle (Luther). Born July 11, 1968, Old Calendar designation. No surviving family. Last employer: McAlpine Construction and Demolition Company. Septigamoklan jack-o-trades and activity planner. Ortho-Urbanist, lapsed, age-exempted. Black.

*   *   *

Parthena Cawthorn. Born November 4, 1964, O.C.;
Madison, Georgia. A son Maynard, a daughter-in-law,
and three grandchildren: enfranchised UrNu citizens.
Last employer: Inner Earth Industries. Sgk artisan and
folklorist. Ortho-Urbanist, semiactive. Black.

Paul Erik Ferrand. Born October 23, 1959, O.C.;
Bakersfield, California. Family members (children,
grandchildren, great grandchildren) in the Urban Nuclei
of Los Angeles and San Francisco. Last employer: (?).
Unclassifiable Mystic, age-exempted. White.

Yuichi Kurimoto (Yuichan). Born May 27, 1968, O.C.;
Kyoto, Japan. Children, grandchildren, great-
grandchildren alive in Kyoto and Tokyo. Last employer:
Visicomputer Enterprises, Atlanta branch. Sgk legislator.
Neo-Buddhist, lapsed, nationality-exempted. Oriental.

Joyce Malins (Toodles). Born February 14, 1971, O.C.;
Savannah, Georgia. No surviving family. Last employer:
Malins Music, Voice & Dance. Sgk musician. Ortho-
Urbanist, lapsed, age-exempted. White.

Helen Mitchell. Born July 11, 1967, O.C.; Norfolk,
Virginia. A son in the Washington UrNu, a daughter in
the Philadelphia UrNu. Last employer: UrNu Civil
Service, Atlanta branch. Sgk mediator. Ortho-Urbanist,
semi-active. White.

Jeremy Zitelman (Jerry). Born December 9, 1970, O.C.
No surviving family. Last employer: University of
Georgia, Urban Extension, Astronomy Department. Sgk
historian. Recidivist Jew, age-exempted. White.

A mixed lot, Zoe decided: a party assortment. Over the
capsule-biography of Yuichi Kurimoto the word DECEASED
was stamped in large, double-lined red letters which did not
conceal the information under them. Zoe looked at the
photographs and tried to match them up with the résumés (they
weren't very good photographs); she got them all matched up,
but it was pretty apparent that some of the pictures had been

taken years ago. For instance, Paul Erik Ferrand, supposedly just over eighty, was a rakish, lupine man wearing a style of cravat that hadn't been fashionable in two decades. Before their names and faces meant anything, Zoe would have to meet these people. In the flesh.

"Is that what I'll be—a septigamoklanner, if y'all like me?"

"That's an institute word, Zoe, made up by someone who didn't know what to call a family like ours. Don't worry. None of us use it. You see, these information sheets contain only passed-upon, UrNu-validated 'facts'—impersonal and bureaucratic. Jerry or I, either one, could have put a little pizzazz into the sketches. Unfortunately, civil service sachems frown on pizzazz...." Her voice trailed off.

"Well, that's encouraging—'cause I think I'd have a hard time thinking of myself as a ...*septigamoklansperson*." A mouthful, that. "But in You-i-chan's biography here, it says he was the family legislator. Does that mean, since I'm coming in for him, I have to put on his shoes and be a legislator?"

"No, no. On these official data sheets everyone's given a position, as if we were baseball players or chess pieces. Really, though, we do whatever we do best, and by defining ourselves in that way we become ourselves to the others. Later, someone will probably put a label on what you are. It won't be a Phoenix who does it, though."

"Mr Leland?"

"Perhaps. A study is going on here, though we're mostly oblivious to it, and studies demand statistics and labels. A cosmic law, like gravitation and magnetism and whatnot."

"Well, if it was *age-exempted*, even an apple might not have to fall."

Helen's opaque eyes locked on her face. "An appropriate observation. But we do have a chance to do some naming of our own. Phoenix was our own choice, you know. Some of the other families in the Tower are Cherokee, Piedmont, Sweetheart and O'Possum."

"Oh, those are good ones, too." They were, too; had what Helen would probably call pizzazz.

"Yes," Helen said, obviously pleased. "Yes, they are."

4 / Climbing Jacob's Ladder

Zoe met them all at supper that evening. They ate in a room decorated with a quilted wall banner, and with several potted plants that Joyce Malins (Toodles) said she had bought from a slum-area florist in a place called the Kudzu Shop.

The Phoenix family had an entire suite of rooms, including a a kitchen, on the Geriatrics Hostel's fourth floor, and this evening Luther, Toodles, and Paul had shared the cooking: cornbread, frozen vegetables, and pasta with a sauce of meat substitutes. Better than Lannie managed after two hours of sloozying around in new clothes for the lechers at Consolidated Rich's; better than Zoe usually did for herself, come to that. The table was round, and wooden, and big enough for seven people, a metal pitcher of cold sweetened tea, and several china serving dishes. No attendants waited on them, Zoe noted, no nurses, no white-smocked young men with pursed lips. A biomonitor cabinet, to which they all were linked by means of pulse-cued silver bracelets, was the only alien presence in the dining room, and it kept quiet. (The people downstairs had a hookup to the monitor, though, Zoe was sure of that.) She self-consciously turned her own new bracelet, a handsome thing in spite of its being, also, a piece of medical equipment. Plugged in already she was, a rookie Phoenix.

Helen had introduced her. She was sitting between Helen and Jerry. Then, clockwise beyond Helen: Parthena, Paul, Luther, and Toodles. Jerry was sitting in a wheelchair, a lap robe over his knees. The others, like Helen, looked pretty mobile—even the eighty-year-old Paul, whose eyes resembled a Weimaraner dog's and whose mouth still knew how to leer.

"How old are you, Zoe?" he asked, after the opening small talk had faded off into mumbles and spoon-rattling.

Helen said, "Paul!" Like Lannie shushing her, Zoe—only nicer.

"Bet she ain't as old as me. Three-to-one odds. Place your bets." He smacked his lips.

"No one's so old as that," Jerry said. Jerry's hair was a dandelion puffball: just that round, that gray, that delicate. His face was red.

"I'm sixty-seven," Zoe admitted. Second time today. But saying so didn't age you, just worrying about it.

"Young blood," the wide-eyed, wide-faced black man said. That was Luther. His hair—Zoe was comparing now—was the kind of white you see on a photograph negative like the mallets on sledgehammers. "Hooooi! old folks, we're being transfused, we're gettin' new blood!"

"Toodles ain' the baby no mo'," Parthena said out of a tall, stern Zulu mask of a face. Plantation accent, Zoe noticed. Luther sounded more like Paul or Toodles than he did Parthena—except for the *Hooooi!* Except for that.

"How 'bout that, Toodles?" Paul said. "Puttin' your foot on the bottom rung of Jacob's ladder at last. I'm up the highest, but you've finally climbed on, too." Toodles, whose mouth was a red smear, a candy heart (even though no one wore lip ices or eye blacking anymore), lowered a forkful of squash to reply—but crazy old Paul turned to Zoe again: "I'm up the highest, but I'm never gonna die. I was born in California."

"Which is your typical Ferrand-Phoenix non sequitur," Jerry said.

"I've never made an issue of being the youngest one here," Toodles interjected. "And I'm not disturbed by losing that position, either." Her jowly face swung toward Zoe. "Zoe, I bought that fuchsia and the coleus for your arrival today. Parthena and I walked into that jungle off New Peachtree and haggled with the little Eurasian shopkeeper over prices. Then we carried our purchases back, pots and all—no help from these noble gentlemen."

"Course," Parthena put in, "that 'fo' she knew how old you was." Her Zulu mask smiled. Perfect dentures. And, taller than anyone else in the room, Parthena, even seated, loomed.

"Parthena, damn your black hide, you know that wouldn't've made any difference! It wouldn't've!" Toodles dropped her fork, her mouth silently working itself into a multiplex variety of lopsided O's.

"Joke," Parthena said. "Jes' funnin'."

"Well, what the hell's funny about my being younger than you old cadavers?" Her mascara, tear-moistened, was making crater holes out of her eyes. "What's so damn funny about that?"

"What's she takin' on like this for?" Luther asked the table.

"Humor her," Jerry said, winking at Zoe from under his puffball. "She thinks she's in her period."

Which brought guffaws from Paul and Luther and pulled the

roof down on everyone else. Rearing back as if beestung,
Toodles knocked her chair over and stood glaring at each
member of her family in turn. Not counting Zoe.

"Smart asses!" she managed. Then, more vehemently: "Limp
ole pricks!" Her mouth had begun to look like a pattern on an
oscilloscope. Zoe, in fact, saw that one of the miniature screens
on the biomonitor cabinet was sending delicate pale comets
back and forth across its surface: Toodles pulsing into the
hysterical.

In person, Toodles left off glaring and, without looking back,
moved painfully, heavily, out of the dining room. A minute or
two after her exit, the pale comets stopped whizzing. Not dead,
Toodles wasn't; just out of range. Another cabinet would pick
her up shortly.

"Silly biddy," Paul announced, chewing.

"Jerry's last remark was crude," Helen said. "A sort of
crudity, Zoe, that he usually doesn't permit himself."

"Please believe that," the crimson-faced man said, wheeling
himself back from the table. "Lately she's been upset. That she
was on the verge, though, I didn't think. I'm sorry, I'm honestly
sorry, you know." The chair powered him out the door.

"Hot damn," Zoe said. "Some debut."

"Ain' yo' fault," Parthena said. "She been eggcited. Las' two
week, she knew we was gonna fine a 'placement for Yuichan,
that's all."

"That's true," Helen said. "We argue like young married
couples do sometimes, Zoe, but usually not before company and
not very often. Ordinarily Toodles is a lovely woman. And the
only explanation I can give for her behavior is her excitement
and the menfolk's bad manners. Courting's always made her
nervous—always."

"As for the sort of crudity you heard from *her,*" Luther
added, "that's her style. She don't mean nothin' by it, though,
even when she's mad."

"Silly biddy," the time-blotched old Frenchman (or whatever
he was) reiterated. "Carry on like that, die before I will. . . . I ain't
gonna die." He was the only one who finished eating what was
on his plate. Once finished, long lips glistening, he let a red,
translucent eyelid drop lasciviously over an amber eye: a wink.
For Zoe.

5 / Rotational Reminiscence

Two hours later. The roof court of the UrNu Human
Development Tower, geriatrics wing. Temperature holding
steady at 21° C. Night had risen as the City's fluorescent suns
had been gradually dialed down.

The Phoenix had patched things up among themselves and
now sat in a semicircle at a tower railing overlooking the
Biomonitor Agency on West Peachtree and, ten floors down, a
floodlit pedestrian park. All the Phoenix but that oddie, Paul:
he still hadn't come up. Zoe put that old codger out of her mind,
though. The rooftop was open and serene, and she had never
seen such a pretty simulated twilight. Not much chance on Level
3, *under*. Now, winking on across the City's dying-into-the-
violet skyscape, a thousand faint points of light. The breath
sucked away just at the glory of it.

Jerry Zitelman-Phoenix maneuvered his wheelchair into
position beside her. (Ramps and lift-tubes made it possible for
him to go anywhere at all inside the complex.) "I want to
apologize, Zoe, for my uncalled-for remark in your presence."

"I always try to apologize to the person who needs it."

"Me, too. Look, you can see she's back." And she was,
Toodles—sitting with Luther, Parthena, and Helen and
animatedly narrating another episode of her afternoon's
shopping. "But you, too, need an apology for the disruption I
made," Jerry continued. "So to you also I say, 'Sorry.'"

Zoe accepted this apology, and Jerry began talking. He told
her that on Thursday nights—alternate ones, anyhow, and it
was Thursday night that night—the Phoenix clan had this
screened section of the rooftop for whatever purpose they
wished. He told her that tonight it was a game they called
"rotational reminiscence" and that they were waiting for Paul,
who never participated but who insisted on attending every
session. The rules, Jerry said, were simple and would become
clear once they started. Then, pointing to the darkened concave
hollow overhead, the honeycombed shell in which they all lived,
he told her that in his youth he had been an astronomer.

"Even now," he said, "I can look up there at night and

imagine the constellations rolling by. Oh, Zoe, it's just as plain as day. Which is one more of your typical Ferrand non sequiturs, Zitelman version thereof. But it's true, I can. There's Cassiopeia, there's Ursa Major, there's Camelopardalis. . . . Oh, all of them I can see. The Dome is no impediment to me, Zoe, but it's certainly no joyous boon, either. That it isn't."

He went on. He told her that the only advantage the Dome offered him was that he could just as easily imagine the constellations of the *Southern* Hemisphere passing in procession across its face. Sometimes he so imagined: Canis Minor, Hydra, Monoceros. There they all were, so dizzying in their splendor that he felt sure he would one day power his wheelchair right up into their diamoned-dusted nets and connect the dots among them with the burning tip of a raunchy green cigar. "Cigars I'm not allowed anymore," he said. "Not even the neutered ones with no tobacco, no tar, and no taste. And stars . . . ?" He pointed at the Dome.

"Well," Zoe said, "we got three stars at least. And they move."

Jerry's puffball rolled back, his vein-blossomed cheeks shone with wan reflected light. "Ah, yes. Girder-cars is what we've got there, Zoe. Torchlight repairs on the Dome. So they send out the magnetized girder-cars at night and let us pretend, with these insulting sops to our memory, that the sky hasn't been stolen. Pretty, though, I grant you." He was right. Artificial stars—only three—on a metal zodiac. How did the men inside those topsy-turvy trollies feel? What was that old song? She mentally hummed a bit of it:

> *Would you like to ride on a star,*
> *Carry moonbeams home from afar?*

"Damn that old zombie!" Toodles suddenly said to them. "Let's go on without Paul—he never contributes anyway."

"Yeah," Luther agreed. "Let's start."

Helen persuaded them to wait a few more minutes. OK with Zoe, A-OK. She listened as Jerry related how he had been involved in a bone crushing, paralyzing automobile accident in 1989, when most of the old "interstates" were falling into disuse: cracked pavements, weed-grown shoulders, brambly medians. He hadn't walked since. "When it happened, I'd never even had relations with a woman; impossible, after. At night, sometimes,

I'd cry. Just like that fellow in the Hemingway book—except his legs, they weren't crushed; it was something else. So I never got married until Dr Tanner accepted me for the study here. Then I got three wives at once. Now, in my old age, poor Yuichan dead, I'm helping my spouses court a fourth one. Who can say it isn't a strange and wizardly life, our pains and weaknesses notwithstanding?"

"Not me, Jerry," replied Zoe; "not me."

So Jerry went on and told her about how he had got his degree and then moved into the Dome and tried to teach astronomy by means of textbooks, slide programs, and old films. He'd done it for almost twenty years, at which point the City decided it was foolish to pay somebody to lecture about a subject with so limited an application to modern society. "Fffft!" Jerry said. "Fired. Me and others, too. A whole program, kaput!" He had to live on Teachers' Retirement and future-secure benefits in a Level 6 cubicle until—

"Howdy," Paul said. "Ain't you started yet?"

"Sit down," Luther told him. "What have you been up to?"

Paul, running his fingers through tatters of thin hair, lowered himself creakingly to the fore-edge of a chair between Parthena and Zoe. "Fetched up some night things for our fiancée. She didn't bring none with her." He looked at Zoe. And winked. "'Gainst my better judgment, too."

"You mighty sweet," Parthena said. "Now let's get on with it."

They did. The rules were these: (1) Silence while the person whose turn it was thought of a pre-Evacuation experience he wished to evoke for himself or, better, himself and the others. (2) An evocation of that experience in one word, the settled-upon word to be spoken, very clearly, only once. (3) An after-silence in which this word might resonate. (4) No repetitions from previous games. (5) An automatic halt after each Phoenix had had two turns. (6) And, in order to avoid a debilitating preoccupation with the past, no mention or replaying of any of the game's reminiscences before or after the sessions themselves.

Helen, a new Gardner-Crowell braille-writer in her hands, recorded the evening's twelve reminiscences and called down anyone who repeated any of the old shibboleths. As Zoe discovered, accusations of encroaching senility flew around the circle when this happened. No worries tonight, though. She had never played before, and there'd be no whistle-blowing no matter what words she spoke into the quiet ring of their anticipation.

"Three months," Toodles said. "It's been three months since we've done this. Back when Yuichan was ill."

"Go ahead, then," Helen urged. "You start, Toodles."

The group's silence grew. The girder-cars above them slid in slow motion down the steeps of the Dome. In three or four minutes Toodles dropped a word into the pooling dark, the well of their ancient breaths:

"Fudgecicles," she said.

Paul, Zoe noticed, had his head thrown all the way back over the top of his chair, his eyes all goggly and shiny. The old man's mouth was open, too. If he hadn't already moved his butt back into the chair, he would have fallen to the roof tiles.

It was Parthena's turn. Three or four minutes after Toodles' reminiscence, the tall black woman said,

"Scup'nins." Scuppernongs, that meant. A kind of grape.

When the word had echoed in their heads for a while, Luther said, "Paul isn't going to say nothin', Zoe. You go ahead now. It's your turn." No, Paul wasn't going to say anything: he was still mouthing Parthena's word.

As for Zoe, she was ready. She had thought of it while Jerry was explaining the rules to her. But it wouldn't do to blurt it out, it wouldn't do to show she'd been thinking ahead of the game. (Surely, they all did it, though.) So she waited. Then, leaning forward to look into the pedestrian park below, she gave the word to her new family:

"Fireflies..."

6 / Mount Fujiyama and the Orpianoogla

In their suite on the fourth floor the Phoenix slept in a circular common room, their beds positioned around a hub where the self-locomoting biomonitor cabinet (the first of three on the floor) had already taken up its brooding watch. Each bed had a nightstand, an effects-bureau, and an easy chair in its vicinity, as well as plasticloth dividers that, at a finger's touch, would roll automatically into place. Since no one seemed to use these, Zoe, grateful to Paul for having fetched her a nightgown, got ready for bed in front of the others.

Like having six Rabons in the room with you. Well, five—Jerry had powered himself off somewhere. "Like some time to himse'f 'fo' turnin' in," Parthena said. But even five Rabons was plenty, even if they were decent enough not to devour you with their eyes. (Rabon never had been.) Of the five, only Old Paul excepted. Again.

Anyhow, it didn't take this creaky crew long to start plying the waters of Nod. No, sir. Everyone off, it seemed, but Zoe herself. She even heard Jerry come whirring back into the snore-ridden room and hoist himself out of the wheelchair into his bed. In five or ten minutes he, too, was rowing himself under. Only Zoe had her head clear, her whole fatigued body treading against the desire to be drowned in sleep. My sweet lord, what a day. Every bit of it passed in front of her eyes.

Then Zoe heard the sobs. For a long time she listened to them. It was Toodles, two beds away, heart-troubled Toodles.

Feeling for slippers that weren't there, Zoe got out of bed. She walked barefooted to the easy chair beside Toodles, sat down, and smoothed back the woman's moist, frizzly bangs. "Can you tell me what it is?"

Uhnn-uh. Strangled, desperate noises.

"Is it about that suppertime business, Toodles? Hope not. Up against you I look like the . . . the Wicked Witch of the North." which was a Glinda-the-Good lie if she'd ever told one.

Subsiding strangles—"It isn't . . . isn't . . . that"—trailing off into hiccups. "Really . . . it . . . isn't . . . that." Apparently to prove this contention, Toodles pulled herself up to a sitting position. Across her rumpled lap she reeled in, inch by hand-wrung inch, a dressing gown that had been spread out over her bedclothes. A corner of it went to her throat, and was held there.

"What, then? Can you say?"

A modicum of control now. "Yuichan," Toodles said. "I was thinking of Yuichan. You see this robe, Zoe. . . . He gave me this robe." It was too dark to see well, but Toodles turned the robe toward her and displayed it anyway, an occasional hiccup unsteadying her hands. All Zoe got was a musty whiff of a familiar kidneylike odor.

"Here," Zoe said and punched on the reading light on Toodles' headboard. A circle of paleness undulated on the dressing gown. Execrable taste, Helen had said. And rightly. On one side of the robe, an embroidered snow-covered peak; on the other (once Toodles had lifted the limp lapel so that Zoe could see them), the words *Mount Fujiyama*. An ugly and smelly garment, no matter how you hemmed or whiffed it.

"Oh, I know it's not to everybody's taste," Toodles burbled. "But it reminds me of Yuichan. He mail-ordered it from San Francisco four years ago when he learned that there was a very sick Japanese woman in the nursing section of the Hostel. That was just like Yuichan. He gave the robe to that poor woman. A couple years later, when the old woman died and her son threw away almost all of her effects, Yuichan brought the gown back and gave it to me. Oh, it was tight on Toodles and smelled like piss all right, but I knew what spirit Yuichan gave it in and I had it washed and washed—till I was afraid it'd fall apart in the water." Toodles spread the dressing gown over her knees. "And tonight...tonight...it reminds me of him...of Yuichan...just ever so much." And propped her elbows on her shrouded knees and lowered her face into her hands.

The consolation Zoe gave Toodles was that of sitting beside her until the poor blowsy woman, mascara long since washed away, fell into a sleep as mortally shallow as the crater holes of her eyes.

But the next afternoon, in the room they called the recreation center, Toodles sat at the battery-powered orpianoogla and led them all in a songfest: thin, strained vocal cords reaching for notes those cords couldn't remember. In fact, only Toodles had an unimpaired range, a bravura contralto that could soar like an undercourse glissador or tiptoe stealthily through a pianissimo lullaby. With one arm she led their singing, with her free hand she rippled the keys, punched buttons, flipped toggles, and mixed in the percussion. Nor did her heavy legs keep her from foot-pedaling like an unbeliever on burning coals. The whole suite of rooms reverberated with Toodles' music, and Zoe, clapping and croaking with the rest, wondered dimly if she had dreamed, only dreamed, the midnight despair of this boisterous Phoenix.

"Very good," Toodles would shout at them between choruses. "Ain't you glad we're too old for them pricks who passed the Retrenchment Edicts to come in here and shut us up?"

Zoe was. Outlawed music they were souling on, outlawed lyrics and proscribed morals-corrupting rhythms. Old times. As they clapped and sang, Helen told Zoe that Toodles had once been a renaissance-swing headliner in a New Orleans hookah club. "Turn of the century and a few years after," Helen stage-whispered in her ear as they all clapped to the rumbling orpianoogla. "When she was forty she was doing a bushman pop-op-rah review in D.C. Forty! Quite professional, the old newsfax say." Since '35, when the ward reps and urban councilors panicked, those kind of performances had been totally *nyetted*, at least in Atlanta. Who knew, these days, what other Cities did?

"All right," Toodles shouted. "This one's *Ef Ya Gotta Zotta!* Way back to twendy-awht-tooo, evverbodddy!"

So they all sang, the orpianoogla singlehandedly—literally singlehandedly—sounding like the entire defunct, blown-away, vinyl-scrutchy Benny Goodman Orchestra of a century ago. Or Glenn Miller's, maybe. This was the chorus:

> *Ef ya gotta zotta,*
>   *Then zotta wa me.*
> *Durnchur lay ya hodwah*
>   *On that furji Marie.*
> *Ef ya gotta zotta,*
>   *Then ya gotta zotta wa me!*

My sweet lord. Zoe remembered the whole song, every kaporni word of all seven verses. She and Rabon had danced to that one; they'd done the buck-and-wing jitters in the remodeled Regency lobby ballroom. My sweet lord, she whispered: *Ef Ya Gotta Zotta!*

But after the last sing-through of the chorus, Toodles barreled out of the renaissance-swing retrospective and into a hard, hard computer-augmented tour of late Twenties/early-Thirties racked-and-riled terrorism. With the advent of this deliberate cacophony, Old Paul stopped stomping and let his mouth fall open, just as it had during the rotational reminiscence. The others, like Zoe, irresistibly fell to swaying in their chairs.

Toodles sang the ominous lyrics, and sang them so certainly that you could look at her full, jowly face and see that despite the sags, and wens, and ludicrous smeared lips, she was living every note, vivisecting every lurid word and dragging its guts out for the purpose of feeding her own and her listeners' irrational fears. (Which was fun: a musical horror movie.) Toodles sang and sang and sang. She sang *Walnut Shell Nightmare*, *Tomb of the Pharaohs*, *Crimson Clay Tidal Wave*, and *Outside Sky*. When the last note of the orpianoogla died away, a rain of bravos fell down on the (incredibly) beginning-to-blush Mz Joyce Malins-Phoenix. Even Paul joined in, though he stomped like a jackass rather than hallooed.

"Her first concert since Yuichan died," Helen whispered.

"Encore!" Jerry shouted. "That we wish more of!"

"Hoooi!" Luther cried. "I ain't heard her sing or play so well since Year-End Week in '38."

"I'm in as fine a voice as I was thirty years ago," Toodles said, turning on her stool. "It's hard to believe and it sounds like bragging, but by God! it's the gospel truth."

"Damn straight," Luther said.

"You ain' done, though," Parthena said. "Finish out now like we awways do, 'fo' we have to go eat."

Toodles, turning back to the keyboard, honored this request. Ignoring the buttons, switches, and resonator pins on the console, she played with both hands: an old melody, two hundred years almost. Everyone sang, everyone harmonized. Zoe found that, just as with *Ef Ya Gotta Zotta*, she remembered the words—every word, each one called to her lips from a time-before-time that had nothing to do with the Urban Nucleus, or with Sanders and Lannie, or with Mr Leland and the Geriatrics Hostel. And it wasn't timesickness or nostalgia that fed her recollection of the lyrics (some things you don't ever want to go back to), but instead a celebration of the solidity of the present: this present: the moment itself. They all sang:

> *'Way down upon the Swanee River*
> *   Far, far away,*
> *There's where my heart is turning ever,*
> *   There's where the old folks stay.*

They even sang the stanza about the old plantations and the plaintive line "Oh, darkies, how my heart grows weary," Luther and Parthena too, and none of what they sang distressed them. Stephen Foster somehow was and wasn't Stephen Foster when interpreted by an orpianoogla. Sticks and stones, Zoe thought, and names can never....

Why, only a week ago her own daughter had called her, during a moment of ill-concealed morning sickness, a mummified cunt. Zoe had chuckled. What else could you do? When you're two steps from the finish line, you laugh at the self-loathing insults of also-rans. You have to. Even in the melancholy performance of a nigh-on dead-and-gone work of a sure-enough dead-and-gone composer, Toodles' whole body laughed. Toodles was two steps from the finish line. They all were. And it certainly wasn't Death they were running at, not as Zoe saw it. No, sir. Something else altogether; something else.

7 / Parthena

That evening, after the orpianoogla-assisted songfest, Parthena, Helen, and Jerry saw to the cooking of supper. And after supper Zoe helped these three clean up in the galley beside the dining room (whereas, downstairs, three levels under, Lannie and Sanders had only a kitchen board in their cubicle and no dining room at all). A beautiful day it had been, a zippity-doo-dah day if she'd ever lived one. Not since Rabon...

"You quilt?" Parthena asked her as they put the last of the china away. But Zoe's attention was momentarily elsewhere. Jerry, in his wheelchair, was handing the plates to Helen, and the blind woman was stacking them cleanly in the hanging plastic cabinet over the sink. Before beginning, Helen had produced a pair of miniature black goggles, or binoculars, from a dress pocket and snapped these on over her eyes with seemingly only a thin metal bridge-piece to support them. With these in place she moved as if sighted. And yet this was the first time she had worn the goggles in Zoe's presence.

"Hey, Zoe," Parthena said again. "You quilt?"

"You mean stitch little squares together? Sew? Maybe. Things with my hands I could always bluff through. I'm a bluffer."

"Shoot, we ain' even asked you what you good at. Where you work 'fo' you got put on the Ole Folk Dole Roll?"

"Photography," Zoe said. "I took pitchurs. Still ones and moving ones. And I was good, too, you know. If you want to know the truth, some of my still pitchurs are pretty moving."

They all laughed. Zoe told them how she and Rabon had been a team for both the *Journal/Constitution* combine and one of the visual-media affiliates; neither wrote copy ("I didn't have the schooling and Rabon hadn't put his to use that way"), but they could both wield cameras, video portables, and the instant-printmaking varieties. She had been better than Rabon was, but from '01 to '09 she had been taken out of action four times by the onset of motherhood and he had got more commissions by virtue of his being insusceptible, as he put it, to pregnancy. But it had all been planned, and after Melanie was born the UrNu Sitter Mission Program had freed them both to pursue their careers. Sort of. They got docked an incredible number of earnies to have Lannie mission-sat for four hours a day, four days a week, she and Rabon splitting up the remaining hours and working less frequently as a team. But they'd done it, she and Rabon, and maybe it was only Lannie's having been their only child that caused her to grow up a gimme girl and a sometimes-sweet, more-usually-petulant young woman. What lovely portraits Zoe had made of her when she was little, ole sweet-treat Lannie. In a telecom to her that morning Zoe had asked her daughter to bring from her sleeper-cove only the few clothes she had there and the photographs on the walls, and Melanie had said she would bring them; maybe Mr Leland had them already.

"Well, if you can shoot pitchurs," Parthena said, "you can he'p us knock off that new wall banner what you seen on the quiltin' frame in the rec center. So you c'mon now, Zoe."

They were finished in the galley. Parthena led them out of there and down the corridor: seventy-six years old and as straight and skinny as a broom handle.

"Other work I got this evening," Jerry said. "If you all will excuse me." And he zoomed around them in his winged chair and disappeared into a room Zoe hadn't been in yet. A closetlike alcove between the rec center and the dining room.

Luther and Toodles were already at the quilting frame when they got there: a monstrous plastic contraption over which the layer of sewn squares, the synthetic cotton batting, and the underlining had all been tautly spread and whipped down. Zoe had seen the thing—"a Wright brothers plane made of sewing scraps"—during their afternoon songfest, but it had been behind them and partially hidden by a moving screen and no one had volunteered to explain its purpose or its function to her.

Now the screen had been shoved back against the wall, and Toodles and Luther were sitting at opposite ends of the frame pushing and pulling their needles through the three layers of material. Helen, still wearing her goggles, sat down between them, and Parthena and Zoe took up chairs on the other side of the frame, which was tilted like an aileron. It was 1903, and they were Orville and Wilbur, crazy-quilt pilots at a Kitty Hawk where the sands of time had transmogrified into linoleum tile.

"Helen," Zoe blurted, "with those goggles on you look like you're gonna fly us right out of here—right up to the Dome." Ooops. Was that the right thing to say to a blind person?

Helen raised her head and stared at Zoe. Straight on, the goggles—or glasses, or binoculars—gave her the look not of a biplane pilot but of an unfriendly outerspace critter. "Aren't they hideous?" Helen said. "I'd wear them all the time except for the way they look." And, expertly, she began plunging her own needle into the layers of cloth and forcing it back through.

Parthena showed Zoe how to do it, giving her a needle and thimble and making her watch her technique. "I taught us all how to quilt—but Paul he don' like it and use his weekend to think on keepin' himse'f a-live for awways. Jerry got real bidness to tend to. Otherwise, he 'most awways here. Now you keep yo' thumb in that thimble, gal, or that needle it gonna bite you. Look here—"

Well, Zoe had sewn before and she'd always been pretty handy anyway. Easy, take it easy, she told herself, and pretty soon she was dipping in and digging out as well as any of them, stitching those jaunty colored squares—yellow, green, and floral-print blue in a steppin'-'round-the-mountain pattern—to batting and lining alike. Much concentration to begin with, like a pilot taking off; then, the hang of it acquired, free relaxing flight. Nobody talked, not anyone.

When had she ever felt so serene and at peace? Serene and at peace, yes, but with a tingle of almost physical pleasure throwing off cool little sparks up and down her backbone. The quiet in the room was part of the pleasure.

Then Parthena began to talk, but not so that it violated the silence they were working in: "I use to do this up in Bondville, when my son Maynard jes' a little flea and the Dome ain' even half finished yet. Oh, the wind it blew then, it didn' have no Dome to stop it, and we use these quilts to sleep unner, not to hang them up on ole broke-up plasser walls. I still 'member how Maynard, when I was workin', would get himse'f up unner the frame—a wooden un my husban' made—and walk back and fo'th like a sojer so that all you could see was the bump of his head goin' from one end of that frame to the other, up and down, till it seem he warn' ever gonna wear out. Laugh? Lord, I use to laugh him into a resentful meanness 'cause he didn' unnerstan' how funny his ole head look."

She laughed in a way that made Zoe join her. "Now he got three babies of his own—Georgia, Mack and Moses—and a wife what can do thisere quiltin' good as me. Better maybe, she so spry."

They quilted for an hour. When they broke off, Parthena insisted that Zoe come back to the dormitory common room and see the "pitchurs of my gran'babies. Shoot, you like pitchurs and babies, don' you?" So Zoe went. She sat in the easy chair while Parthena, having lowered her bed to an accommodating height, sat like an ebony stork on its edge.

"This one my pert Georgie," Parthena said, handing her a picture of a handsome little black girl. "She twelve now and one sassy fas' chile. She gonna get out of Bondville all by herse'f, jes' on charm and speed." The two boys were older and a little meaner-looking; they probably had to be. None of them were babies. "I jes' want you to see I had me a fam'ly 'fo' the Phoenix. I ain' like Luther and po' Toodles what suffer till they was pas' sixxy without finin' a real home. Now, though, they got us an' we got them—but they come a long road, Zoe, a long road. Jerry, too. Sometime I jes' lif' up a prayer for how lucky I been."

"I never did pray much," Zoe said, "but I know what the urge is like." Yes. Like loving somebody in a way that didn't permit you to tell them; hell, yes, Zoe remembered.

They talked while some of the others got ready for bed. Parthena showed Zoe a set of dentures that had been made for her in 2026; she even made Zoe take them in her hand and examine them as if they were the teeth of an australopithecine. "They clean," she said. "I ain' wore 'em since twenny-nine. The reason I show 'em to you is 'cause they made by Dr Nettlinger."

"Who?"

"Gee-rard Nettlinger. He that fella what shot Carlo Bitler. Stood up in the middle of the Urban Council meetin' an' shot that tough, holy man. The day I heard that, I took out them dentures and never put 'em in again. They shoddy-made, anyhow. Only keep 'em so Maynard can sell 'em one day. People go all weedy-crazy over doodads what b'long to 'sassins. People crazy."

"Yes," Zoe agreed. "My daddy said it was the new idolatry."

"It idle, awright. Don' make a mussel-shell worth o' sense."

Then, somehow, their conversation got around to why the original family members had chosen Phoenix—rather than something light like Sweetheart or O'Possum—as the group's surname. Zoe said she had supposed it was because Atlanta was sometimes called the Phoenix City, having risen again from its own ashes after the Civil War (which Zoe's grandfather, even in the 1980's, had insisted on calling the War Between the States—as if that made some kind of significant difference). And when the Dome went up in that decade linking the old century with the new one, Atlanta had undergone still another incarnation. Were those part of the group's original reasons?

"They part of 'em awright," Parthena replied. "But jes' part. Another one is, we all come out of our own ashes when we 'greed to take the cov'nant. We all bo'n again, Zoe, like in Jesus."

"Well, I thought that, too, you know. That's what makes the name so good."

"Yeah. But Paul he like it 'cause the phoenix a 'Gyptian bird what was immortal, you see. It only *look like* it die, then it spurt back up jes' as feathery and fine as befo'. He a mean man on that p'int, Paul is."

"He ought to be happy with the Ortho-Urban Church, then. It says that the same sort of thing happens to *people* after they die."

"Ain' the same, though, Paul say. 'Cause people do die, no lookin'-like in it, and they don' get a body back at all. Paul he hung up on the body."

"You don't say? It's good to know he's not just a Dirty Old Man."

"Oh, he that, too, he sho' is." They chuckled together. "But it the other thing keep him thinkin' and rockin' and figgerin'. The Phoenix lucky. Mos' of us still got our mines. But Paul he eighty-some-odd and his been goin' ever since we marry. Mr Leland awmost didn' 'cept him in this program five year back, you see. Res' of us made him say yes. So Mr. Leland finally 'cepted him, hopin' we could haul him back on the road. We done it, too. Pretty much."

"Did Paul suggest the name?"

"No. Maybe. I don' 'member 'zackly. What I do 'member is that the name fit, it fit fo' all kinds o' reasons. One other, and maybe the bes' un, was a story my gran'daddy tole that his own daddy tole him. It was 'bout a slave chile, a little gal, what was made to watch the two-year-ole baby of the boss man, the 'marster' as gran'daddy say his daddy say.

"Well, that little baby fell down the steps while the slave gal was watchin' it—she took her eye away a minute and it bumped down them ole steps and took on a-hollerin'. Scared, you know, but not kilt. Well, when the white mistresses in the house heard this, they took on a-cryin' and carryin' on terrible, jes' like that baby been murdered. They kep' on till the marster himse'f come strollin' in and asked them what it was. When they tole him, he pick up a board and hit that little slave gal in the head. Kilt her. Then he gathered 'round him a bunch of niggers and ordered 'em to th'ow the gal in the river. The gal's mama begged and prayed and asked him to spare the gal fo' buryin', but he paid her no mine and made 'em th'ow the chile in.

"Now this is where the story get magical, Zoe. The little girl's name was Phoebe, and five slaves and the girl's mama went down to the river with her—the biggest nigger in front, carryin' little Phoebe with her bloody head hanging' down, mournful and cold. This big nigger he th'ew the gal in like the marster order him to, Phoebe's mama jes' moanin' and beatin' on herse'f, and then he walk right in affer the girl and hole himse'f unner water till he drown. The others they resolve to do the same. And they do it too, the mama goin' in las' and prayin' to God they all be taken up together.

"One night later, the white folks from the big house is walkin' by the river and all at once they see seven small ugly birds fly up outa the water and go sailin' straight at the Moon. The higher they get, the brighter and purtier and bigger they get, too—till at las' they stop in the sky like stars and stay still over the big house where them white folks live. A new constellation they become, which evvyone on the plantation call The Phoenix—'cep' this constellation don' move like it s'posed to but jes' sit with its wings spread, wide and haughty-like, over the marster's house.

"And that the story, Zoe. Jerry he say he never heard of no constellation call' The Phoenix. But with that Dome up there who gonna 'member 'zackly how the sky look? Nobody. Not nobody.

"An' I believe it still up there somewhere."

8 / Flashforward: At the End of Winter

Almost three old-style months after entering the Geriatrics
Hostel, not as patient or prisoner but as a genuine come-and-go-
as-you-please resident, Zoe sat on the roof one evening and
recalled the steps of her slow immersion in the Phoenix clan.
Supper was eaten: a calming warmth in her stomach and bowels.

Pretty soon the family would decide. When you're streaking
toward either seventy or eighty—as well as that something else
that isn't Death—long courtships are as foolish as whirlwind
ones. Three months is plenty to decide in, maybe too much.
Anyhow, they were formally going to pass on her, and it might
be that in giving her this hour of solitude, this retrospective
moment on the darkening rooftop, they were already engaged in
the process of their decision. Was it in doubt? And hadn't they
been so engaged all along, every day that Zoe had lived among
them sharing their lives?

One girder-car tonight, and a flight of pigeons wheeling
together in great loops in front of a huge neon Coca-Cola sign.

Look what had happened in these three old-style months:
For one thing, she had found out that the septigamoklans in the
Tower weren't living there as welfare recipients solely, as so
many helpless mendicants on the Old Folk Dole Roll. Most of
them had spent their lives paying into the medicaid and
future-secure programs of the City; since 2035, the year young
Mr Leland's study had begun, the quarterly benefits of all the
people in the Hostel had been pooled and invested. This was
done with permission from the residents, only a scant number of
whom denied the UrNu Human Development Commission the
legal administration of their estates. And against these holdouts,
no penalty at all. In any event, the dividends on these pooled
investments and the interest on several well-placed accounts
financed the feeding and the sheltering of the residents and
provided them with personal funds to draw on. They also helped
remunerate the surviving families of those who came into the
study.

Each family had a budgeter: Helen was the Phoenix
budgeter, and, wearing those little black vision-assisting
binoculars, she kept books like a born-and-bred C.P.A. (which

was C.U.A. now, Zoe remembered). Other times, she used her braille-writer. Anyhow, they weren't dole-riders, the people in the Tower—although Zoe had to admit that the Hostel's system was dependent upon the good offices and business acumen of those who administered their benefits. This drawback was partially offset by each septigamoklan's budgeter's having a seat on the Commission Board of Financial Planners, as well as by the judicious appeal to market-forecasting computers.

Down on Level 3 with Sanders and Melanie, Zoe's quarterly allotments—only a day or two after the future-secure printout chit arrived—got eaten up like nutmeg-sprinkled oatmeal. The Nobles garnisheed the entire value of the chit, without even so much as a countersignature, for granting Zoe the privilege of living with them. Only the coming of their child and the prospect of a lump-sum reward from the Commission had induced them to hand Zoe over. Just like a prisoner exchange, or the sale of a decrepit and recalcitrant slave. Yessir, Zoe thought: *Sold down the river.* But a river out of which it was possible to fly like a sleek bird, dripping light as if it were water. An old bird, Zoe was; a bird of fire being reborn in the Lethe of Sanders and Melanie's forgetfulness and neglect.

"A pox on self-pity," Zoe said aloud, surprising herself. Overhead, the torchlit girder-car had almost reached the acme of the Dome.

Well, what else, what else? Lots of things. She had met members of other septigamoklans, the O'Possums and the Cadillacs and the Graypanthers and oh! all the others, too. There'd been a party one Saturday night in the garden, with food and music and silly paper decorations. Hostel attendants had closed the patio windows and pulled the acoustical draperies in the intensive-care rooms, and everyone else had gone to town. Young Mr Leland, at their invitation, had been there, and nobody but Paul of all the Phoenix went to bed before four a.m. Sometime after midnight Toodles had led everybody in a joyful, cacophonous version of *Ef Ya Gotta Zotta.*

Then there were Sunday afternoons, alone with Paul or Luther, or maybe—just maybe—one of the girls. During the week, field trips to the Atlanta Museum of Arts ("Boring as shit," said Paul) and Consolidated Rich's and the pedestrian-park flea markets. Two different excursions to the new theater-in-the-round operahouse, where they had watched a couple of interesting Council-sanctioned hologramic movies. They were OK, sort of plotless and artsy, but OK. Back in their own fourth-floor suite, though, they could see old-fashioned two-dimensional movies; and just since Zoe had been there, the Phoenix had held a Rock Hudson festival and a mock seminar in the *Aesthetic of Late-Twentieth-Century X-Rated Cinema,* during which Jerry had turned off the soundtracks and lectured to quite humorous effect with the aid of a stop-action button and a pointer.

After one such lecture, when the rooftop was theirs, Luther and Zoe had laid out a croquet course; and, except for Jerry, in 23° C. weather (the internal meterologists had given them one or two cold days, though) they had all played without their clothes! Nude, as Helen said. And that had been one of those rare occasions *not* requiring meticulous attention to detail—quilting, putting away dishes, keeping books—that Helen wore her goggle-binoculars. And, not counting the pulse-cued bracelet, *only* the goggle-binoculars. The idea, lifted from an old book of short stories, had been Toodles', but Paul had given it a vigorous seconding. And so Zoe, like a girl going skinnydipping in the before-the-Dome countryside, shed her paper gown, her underthings, her inhibitions, and let the temperate air swaddle her sensitive flesh and her every self-conscious movement. Much merriment. And no repugnance for their blotched and lignifying bodies; instead, a strange tenderness bubbling under the surface merriment.

What, after all, did the bunions, and the varicosities, and the fleshy folds signify? Zoe could answer that: the onset of age and their emphatic peoplehood, male and female alike. Finally, that day, she forgot the sensuous stirring of the Dome winds, lost herself in the game, and became extremely angry when Parthena sent her ball careening off into an unplayable position. Yessir, that had been an all-fun day.

And what else? Well, the Phoenix had given her a still camera, and for the first time in ten or fifteen years she had begun taking pictures again. The camera was an old but still beautifully operable Double-Utility Polaroid, and the first project Zoe undertook was the capturing in stark black-and-white of the faces of her new family. Posed photographs, candid ones, miniatures, darkroom enlargements; group portraits, singles, double-exposure collages, meditative semi-abstracts. The best of these went up in the rec center. The Wall of the Phoenix, this gallery became, and it was framed on both sides by bright, quilted wall banners.

Paul and Toodles grew quite vain about certain of these

portraits and occasionally got caught staring at their favorites:
teenagers ogling themselves in a mirror. Vanity, vanity, saith
somebody or other, Zoe remembered. But Helen never donned
her little binoculars to look at her own photographed image,
even though she had more justification than either Paul or
Toodles. One day Zoe asked her why. "I haven't looked at my
own face since I was thirty," she said, "because I am quite
content with the self-deluding vision of my thirty-year-old one
that still resides up here." She tapped her head. Then she showed
Zoe an old photograph of herself, one that glinted in the
common room's fluorescents and revealed a woman of
disgusting, not-to-be-gainsaid beauty. "I can *feel* what I look
like now," Helen said. "I don't have to look." Even so, Zoe's
portraits of Helen did her no disservice; in fact, they launched a
thousand tiresome accolades from the men, Paul in particular—
when, that is, he wasn't all mesmerized by his own amber-eyed,
celluloidally distanced self. Well, why not? Zoe's pitchurs were
damn good, if she did say so herself, just by way of echoing the
others.

The month Spring was coming on. What else could she recall
about Winter in the Hostel? Visits by Melanie and Sanders. The
prospect of a grandchild. This last excited her, tickled her like air
on her naked body, and for it alone did she anticipate the
biweekly drop-ins of her daughter and son-in-law. No, that
wasn't true. Lannie she always had a hankering to see, whether a
baby was growing in her womb or not. Her daughter Lannie
was—her own flesh and that of dead Rabon, too. Their
daughter. Only fatuous Sanders did she have difficulty
tolerating, and he had never once called her anything as brutal as
a mummified cunt, not ever in his life. So what did you do?

Zoe, for her part, never visited them in their Level 3 cubicle,
and when they came to see her, thereby perfunctorily carrying
out their filial duty, she always greeted them in the quadrangle
where they had first put her on the block. That made Sanders
uncomfortable: he scuffed his street slippers in the gravel and
craned his neck around as if looking for the one mean old codger
in the Hostel who would use his balcony advantage to shoot
him, Sanders, with a blowgun or pellet rifle. Minor sport for
Zoe, watching her son-in-law sidelong as she asked Melanie how
she felt—if the morning sickness had gone away yet ("There are
pills for that, Mother!"), what sex the Jastov-Hunter test had
said the child would be, other things that Lannie was at last
willing to talk about.

But she never used her freedom to visit them on Level 3, and they never extended her such an invitation. No, sir. Not once.

Zoe tilted her head back and saw that the girder-car she had been following was nowhere in sight. My sweet lord, hadn't she been up on the Tower roof for a long time? And hadn't the time flown by? They were reaching a decision on her, the Phoenix were. That was it.

Was the outcome in doubt? Would Mr Leland send her into another incomplete septigamoklan (if one existed) because of a single person's snide blackballing veto? As Mr Leland had explained it, they could easily do that, blackball her. How would she feel if they did? As far as that went, did she herself want to marry with the Phoenix, to join with them in a new covenant?

Well, the answer to that was an easy one. The answer was yes. Yes, she wanted to marry with Luther, Parthena, Toodles, Paul, Helen, and Jerry. And her reason for wanting to was a simple one, too: she was in love.

9 / Spending the Afternoon with Luther

On her first Sunday among the Phoenix, Toodles told Zoe that although it was her, Toodles', turn to spend the afternoon with Luther, she would be happy to yield to Zoe. "I don't feel all that good," she explained, "and, besides, it's the only really hospitable way for me to behave, don't you think?" Propped up in bed, Yuichan's awful Fujiyama robe bundled about her shoulders, Toodles was eating a breakfast roll that a cartlike servo-mechanism had wheeled into the common room from the galley. A hairline smear of artificial peach jelly rode Toodles' upper lip like a candied mustache, and Zoe wanted to take a tissue and daub it away.

"If you don't feel well, should you be eating jelly rolls?"

"You know the old saying," Toodles replied, winking. "Jelly rolls is medicine. But I'm having mine this morning and don't need a dose this afternoon."

"Does 'spend the afternoon' mean what the young drakes and duckies call 'bodyburning'?" Why was she asking? She already knew the answer. Parthena and Helen were off to an Ortho-Urban service somewhere on West Peachtree, Paul was asleep across the room from them, and Jerry and Luther had both got up early and gone down the hall toward the rec center. Zoe had declined an invitation to attend services with Parthena and Helen. Now she wished she was with them.

"You ain't slow," Toodles said. "I'd've been blunter, but it embarrasses Errol."

"Errol?"

Flipping up the bed linen and extending a heavy leg, Toodles put one bunion-afflicted foot on the tray of the servo-cart. "Errol," she reiterated. The cart hummed and backed up, but Toodles got her leg off the tray in time to avoid a nasty spill. A doughnut did drop to the floor, though. "Temperamental, Errol is. . . . You're not thinking of saving yourself for after the covenant ceremony, are you?"

"Well, if I am, I been saving myself so long that my interest's now a whole lot greater than my principles." That was the punchline of a joke Rabon used to tell. It didn't suit Zoe's mood, which was cautious and a bit skeptical, but it perfectly suited Toodles'—she was delighted. I always play to my audience, Zoe thought; can't seem to help it. Aloud, attempting to recover, "I never was one to kiss on the first date, Toodles; just not the sort."

"Oh, I always said that, too. Anyhow, you've already slept in the same room with the Phoenix, you know. It's not like you'd be sacking out with some bulgy-britches thugboy." And at last she wiped the peach-jelly mustache off her upper lip. "Please say yes. Luther's liable to be hurt." And with her little gold remote-con box Toodles beckoned Errol (who, Zoe noted with some annoyance, was something of a whiner) closer to the bed so that she could take another pastry.

"OK," Zoe answered, almost as if it were someone else, not her.

So that afternoon she and Luther walked through the pedestrian courts outside the Geriatrics Hostel and stopped to eat lunch at a little restaurant that seemed to be made entirely of glass; it was nestled under the stone eaves of a much taller building, though, and had green reed-woven window shades to keep out of the glare of the Dome's day lamps. Atmosphere, Rabon would have said the shades gave the place.

They sat in a simulated-leather booth with potted ferns on both sides of them to cut off their view to the front door, and they drank Scotch-and-waters while waiting for the steward to bring them their meal. A Sunday drink. Well, that was something the Retrenchment Edicts hadn't outlawed. You could get one right after your favorite Ortho-Urban services, which was what half the people in this place, it looked like, were doing. The other half were sharing table hookahs and letting the thin smoke coil away from them through the decorative ferns.

"Good food," Luther said. "They do know how to throw together good food here." He was a little nervous, Zoe could see. He kept putting his malletlike hands on the table, dropping them to his lap, taking a sip of his drink, then sticking those heavy purplish hands back on the table. "You ain't disturbed that Toodles pushed you into this, are you now?" he asked, his brow comically corrugating.

"Luther, my daughter and son-in-law pushed me into this, *not* Toodles. And they don't even know when they're doing me a favor."

That loosened him, even more than the Scotch. He asked her questions about her family, he told her about himself. Their meal came—a vegetable dinner featuring hydroponically grown snapbeans, zucchini, tomatoes (stewed), and some sort of hybrid greens—and Luther, between bites, kept on talking. A warm rumble.

"I was born the same year Dr King was assassinated," he said at one point. "That's how I got my name. The shame of it is, I lived to see that sort of business over and over before the Cities went under cover—and then after the Doming, too. I wasn't quite six when I saw a young man shoot Mrs Martin Luther King, Sr, and several other people right in the old man's own church. My church, too. Then. More died after the Dome was up. That young Bitler was the last one, and it's been eleven years since we've had to walk our hungry-children miles to some good man's grave.

"You know, I was so sick I almost shot myself that year, I almost took a razor to my wrists. Back when you could breathe, when you could look up and see a sun or a moon, some men used to be born in the year a comet come through and wait their whole lives till it come back again so that they could die. That year, I was so down I knew it had been written that Luther Battle was supposed to come in and go out with another man's assassination.

"But I was with McAlpine Company in '29 in my thirty-second year with them, and we had a lot of work. Bitler had done made a lot of people angry, he had got a lot of ole dead

asses movin'. After he was shot, there was all kind of uproar to
tear down the surfaceside slums and stick up some kind of
halfway decent housing on top of the streets instead of under
'em. I was on McAlpine's demolition crews, not the construction
ones. Sixty years old and I was workin' off my anger and grief by
wreckin' ole tenements; it was the only way they let us make
anything of our own. I bossed the demolition of fifteen buildings
that year, workin' it all out so that walls come down clean and
the guts got hauled off neat. Cranes, cats, tractors, trucks, all of
'em doin' this and doin' that 'cause of how I told 'em to go. Only
thing that kep' me sane, Zoe—tearing down another century's
shithouses and doin' it with that century's equipment. Then the
uproar quieted off, the work contracts run out, and the Urban
Council didn't do nothin' to start 'em up again. We still got some
fuckin' ghettos in Atlanta, no matter what the ward reps say.
Bondville, one of the worst. Parthena's boy and her gran'chillun
still live there. . . . But that bad year was over, and I had survived
it, Zoe.

"Retired, then. Lived alone on 7, *under,* just like I had all the
years I was with McAlpine. The company had been my family
since all the way back to 1997. My mama and daddy was lucky:
they died before they had to see a Dome go up over their heads.
Me, I wasn't lucky: I had to sign on with McAlpine and help
build that damn thing up there."

"You helped build the Dome?" Zoe said. She'd never met
anyone who had, not anybody who'd admit to it, at least.

"I did. They was twelve different outfits, different companies,
workin' to do it, everybody goin' from blueprints they had run
off a computer somewhere up East or maybe in California. We
were a year behind New York and Los Angeles, McAlpine told
us, and we had to catch up. He was still sayin' this in '97, the year
I come on, three after the Dome Projec' started; and no one ever
asked why the hell we had to catch up with this foolishness that
New York and L.A. was pursuin'. Most of us hadn't had any
kinds of jobs at all before the Projec', so we shut up and did what
all of a sudden the City was givin' us money to do. Yessir, Zoe.
We started in a-buildin' a pyramid, a great ole tomb to seal
ourselves into and never come out again. Slaves in Egypt
might have to work twenty years to build a House of the Dead
for the Pharaoh, but they didn't have to lie down in it
themselves. We was more advanced. We done ours in ten and
managed it so that we could put the lid on ourselves from the

inside. No Moses anywhere to say, Hey! wait a minute, you don't want to live in this place forever! But we were pullin' down some decent cash, even if they was UrNu dollars, and didn't think there'd ever be a day you couldn't at least see a little square of sky somewhere, at least enough blue to make denim for a working man's britches. It was an adventure. Nobody thought he was just another one of Pharaoh's slavin' niggers. I didn't, anyhow. Even when I first come on with McAlpine, I felt like *I* was the chief mucketymuck myself."

"How come?"

"Well, we had to go up to the sections of the Dome's gridwork that we'd completed, and we always went up in girder-cars, just like the ones you see comb-crawlin' along after dark with their torches alight. You worked on platforms or from harnesses on the girder-car, and you was always right out there over the whole damn state, you could see everything—even when the wind was streamin' by you like it wanted to shake all your hard labor into rubble and scrap. Stone Mountain. All kinds of lakes. The mountains up by Gainesville.

"And kudzu, Zoe, kudzu like you never seen or can even remember. That ole madman vine ran itself over everything, telephone poles and broken-down barns and even some of them cheapjack townhouses and condo-minny-ums they hammered up all las' century. The whole world was green, dyin' maybe 'cause of that kudzu—but so green it made your eyes ache. And up there above the whole world Luther Battle felt like Kheops himself, or King Tut, or whichever one of them bastards built the bigges' tomb. And I never did say, Hooooi! Luther, why are we doin' this?"

After their meal, Zoe and Luther went back to the Hostel and rode the Tower lift-tube up to the fourth floor. Although she hadn't let him do it in the pedestrian courts on the walk home, in the lift-tube she gave him her hand to hold. Ten years after retiring from McAlpine Company he still had calluses on his palm, or the scars of old calluses. In the lift-tube he didn't talk—he was embarrassed again, as if his talking at lunch had been a spiritual bleeding which had left him weak and uncertain of his ground. Well, she was embarrassed too. Only Luther had an advantage: a blush on him wasn't so all-fired conspicuous as it was on her.

In the common room, which was unoccupied by group design and agreement, Luther took her to his bed and made the automatic room-dividers roll into place. Bodyburning, the young people called it now. That's what it was for her, too, though not in the way the term was supposed to suggest and not because Luther was a snorting dragon in the act. No, it had been a long time. Rabon was the last of course and this ready compliance to the rule of the Phoenix surprised her a little. For years she had been—what was Melanie's amusing vulgarity?— *mummifying*, and you couldn't expect to throw off the cerements, vaporize the balms and preservatives, and come back from your ages-long limbo in one afternoon.

So that afternoon Zoe experienced only the dull excitement of pain; that, and Luther's solicitude. But each Sunday—the next one with Paul, the one after that with Luther, and so on, depending on inclination and a very loose schedule—it got better. Since she had never really been dead, it didn't take so long as might the hypothetical attempted resurrection of a Pharoah. Not anywhere so long as that. For she was Zoe, Zoe Breedlove, and she no longer remembered her maiden name. . . .

10 / Jerry at His Tricks

What did Jerry do in that mysterious alcove between the rec center and the dining room? Zoe wondered because whenever Jerry had a moment of free time—after dinner, before bed, Sunday morning—his wheelchair, humming subsonically, circled about and went rolling off to that little room. And Jerry would be gone for fifteen minutes, or thirty, or maybe an hour, whatever he could spare. What provoked her curiosity was the midnight vision of his puffball hairdo and his sad hollow eyes floating out of the corridor's brightness and into the darkened common room after one of these recurrent disappearances.

On the Sunday night—more properly, the Monday morning—after her conversations, both social and carnal, with Luther, Zoe had this vision again and heard the crippled man unmindfully whistling to himself as he returned from that room: *Zippity-Doo-Dah*, it sounded like. And up to his unmade bed Jerry rolled.

Jerry rolls in at night, Zoe thought, and jelly rolls in the afternoon. A muddled, word-fuzzy head she had. It all had something to do with Toodles. And Helen, Parthena, and Luther. Only Paul left out, to date anyway. But these members of the Phoenix were all sleeping.

Sitting up and lowering her feet to the floor, she said, "Jerry?"

"Who is it?" She couldn't see his eyes now, but the macrocephalic helmet of his silhouette turned toward her, dubiously. "Is it Zoe?"

"Yep," she said. "It's me. Can't sleep." She pulled on her dressing gown (Sanders had brought most of her things to the Hostel on Saturday afternoon, but no one had come up to see her) and walked barefooted on the cold floor over to Jerry's territory.

The Phoenix could certainly saw wood. No danger of these buzzsaws waking up, it was enough to make you wish for impaired hearing. Except that each one of the sounds was different, and interesting: an orchestra of snorers. There, a tiny whistle. There, a snooglehorn. Over there, a tubaphone. That one, a pair of castanets. And...

Jerry grinned quizzically at her and scratched his nose with one finger. "Can't sleep, heh? Would you like to go down to the galley for a drink? Maybe some wine. Wine's pretty good for insomnia."

"Wine's pretty good for lots of things," Zoe said. "What I wanted to ask was, What are you up to when you get all antisocial on us and shut yourself up in the closet out there?" She nodded toward the door.

"You're a nice lady. You get a multiple-choice test. (A) I'm concocting an eternal-youth elixir. (B) I'm perfecting an antigravity device which will spin-dizzy all of Atlanta out into the stars. (C) I'm performing unspeakable crimes of passion on old telescope housings and the jellies in Petri dishes. Or (D) I'm...I'm.... My wit fails me, dear lady. Please choose."

"D," Zoe said.

"What?"

"I choose D. You said multiple-choice. That's what I choose."

As if struck with an illuminating insight (for instance, the key to developing an antigravity device), Jerry clapped his hands together and chuckled. "Ah, even at this late hour *your* wit doesn't fail *you*. I am bested."

"Not yet. You haven't given me a real answer yet, and I've

been talking to you for almost two minutes."

"Oh, ho! In that case, dear Zoe lady, come with me." Jerry Zitelman-Phoenix circled about in his subsonically humming chair and went rolling through the common room door. Zoe followed.

Down the corridor Jerry glided, Zoe now more conscious of the raw slapping of her feet than of his wheelchair's pleasant purr. Which stopped when he reached the mysterious room. "I would have preferred to wait for tomorrow, you know. But over the years I have learned to honor the moods of insomniac ladies. And, besides, what I have been working on is finished. It won't hurt for you to get a foreglimpse of the issue of my labors. It won't hurt *me,* anyway. *You,* on the other hand, may merely aggravate your sleepless condition."

At two in the morning, if it wasn't later than that, Jerry was a caution, a nonstop caution. Not much like Thursday night on the roof when he had talked about unseeable stars and his lifelong paralysis. Fiddle! Zoe knew better: he was just like Thursday night, if you were talking about the underneath part of him; the seeming change was only in his approach to the revelation of this self. Then, candor. Now, a camouflage that he stripteased momentarily aside, then quickly restored. Oh, it wasn't hard to undress this man's soul. You just had to warn yourself not to destroy him by letting him know that you could see him naked. Nope. Keep those pasties in place, wrap up the emotional overflow in an old G-string. And smile, smile, smile.

Because he was funny, Jerry was. In spite of his tricks.

They went into the little room, and he hit the light button. Zoe, standing just inside the door, saw a counter with some sort of duplicating machine on it, reams of paper, an IBM margin-justifying typer (they'd had those in the offices of the *Jour/Con* Combine), and a stack of bright, yellow-orange booklets. There were little inset docks in the counter, put there by Luther, so that Jerry could maneuver his wheelchair into comfortable positions.

Booklets. You didn't see booklets very often. One good reason: The Retrenchment Edicts of '35 had outlawed private duplicating machines. Everyone had a visicom console and better be glad he did. The Phoenix had two such consoles in the rec center, though Zoe couldn't recall seeing anyone using either of them. Why, since she'd been at the Hostel, she hadn't tapped into one at all. And now she was seeing booklets—*booklets!*

"I always wondered where Atlanta's pamphleteers holed up," Zoe said. "You preachin' the overthrow of our Urban Charter?"

Jerry put a hand to his breast. "Zoe lady, the name is Zitelman, not Marx. And I am first—no, not first; but last and always—a Phoenix." He took a copy of one of the booklets from the counter and handed it to Zoe, who had moved deeper into his crowded little den of sedition. "This issue, which has been in preparation for three or four weeks now, nay, longer, is for you. Not just this copy, mind you, but the whole issue."

Zoe looked at the booklet's cover, where on the yellow-orange ground a stylized pen-and-ink phoenix was rising from its own ashes. The title of the publication was set in tall, closely printed letters on the bottom left: *Jerry at His Tricks.* Beneath that: Volume VI, No. 1. "What is it?" she asked.

"It's our famzine," Jerry said. "All the septigamoklans have one. *Fam*ily maga*zine,* you see. Of which I am editor and publisher. It is the True History and Record of the Phoenix Septigamoklan, along with various creative endeavors and pertinent remarks of our several spouses. One day, dear Zoe, you will be represented herein."

Leafing through the *famzine,* Zoe said, "Don't count your chickens. . . ."

"Well, as an egghead who has already hatched his personal fondnesses, I am now seriously counting." He pointed a wicked crooked finger at her. "One," he said in a burlesque Transylvanian accent. "One chicken."

She laughed, patting him on top of his wiry puffball. But it was not until the next day, before breakfast, that she had a chance to read through the booklet—the advance copy—that Jerry had given her. In it she found artwork signed by Parthena, Helen, and Paul, and articles or poems by everyone in the family. Several of these were tributes, brief eulogies, to the dead Yuichan Kurimoto. The issue concluded with a free verse poem welcoming Zoe Breedlove as a candidate for marriage with the Phoenix. It was a flattering but fairly tastefully done poem. It was signed J. Z-Ph., and at the bottom of this last page was the one-word motto of the clan:

Dignity.

It was all too ridiculously corny. How did they have the nerve to put that word there? Zoe had to wipe her eyes dry before going into the dining room for breakfast.

11 / *In the Sun That Is Young Once Only*

Of all of them Paul was the hardest to get to know. Parthena had spoken rightly when she said that part of the difficulty was that his mind was going, had been going for a long time. He seemed to have a spiritual umbilical linking him to the previous century and the time before the Domes. He had been nine years old at the time of the Apollo 11 moon landing, thirteen at the time of the final Apollo mission, and he remembered them both.

"Watched 'em on TV," he said. "Every minute I could of the first one. Just enough of the last one to say I saw it."

And he talked considerably more lucidly about his boyhood in California than he did about everyday matters in the Hostel. His other favorite subject was the prospect of attaining, not in a dubious and certainly vitiated afterlife, but in the flesh, immortality. His only real grounding in the present, in fact, was the unalloyed joy he took in Sunday afternoons, at which time he performed creditably and behaved like a mature human being. The leers and the winks, it seemed, were almost involuntary carry-overs from a misspent youth."

"He gone sklotik up here"—Parthena tapped her head— "from the life he led as much as from jes' gettin' ole." *(Sklotik,* Zoe figured out, was *sclerotic.)* "Drugs, likker, womens, card playin'. Brag on how he never had a real job, jes' gamble for his keep-me-up. Now Mr Leland 'fraid to use on him them new medicines what might stop his brain cells a-dyin'. Easy to see, he done los' a bunch."

And with his washed-out, Weimaraner eyes and raw, long lips Paul sometimes seemed like his own ghost instead of a living man. But he could still move around pretty well, he drifted about as effortlessly as a ghost might. And one day, three weeks after Zoe's arrival, he drifted up to her after dinner in the rec center (she was making a photo-display board) and pulled a chair up next to hers. She turned her head to see his raw lips beginning to move.

"It's time for one of my services," he said. "You don't go to the Ortho-Urbanist ones with Helen and Parthena, so I expect you're a fit body for one of mine. This Sunday morning, right in here."

"What sort of services?"

"My sort." A wink, maybe involuntary. "The True Word. Once every quarter, once every new-style month, I preach it."

"The True Word on what? Everybody's got his own true word, you know."

"On how not to die, woman. The basis of every religion."

"No," Zoe said. "Not every one of them—just the ones that don't know exactly what to do with the here-and-now."

His long lips closed, his eyes dilated. She might as well have slapped him. In eighty years no one had told him that an ontological system didn't have to direct its every tenet toward the question of "how not to die." Or if someone had, Paul had forgotten. Even so, he fought his way back from stupefaction. "The basis," he said archly, "of every *decent* religion."

Jerry, who had overheard, powered himself up to the work table. "Rubbish, Paul. And besides, if tomorrow we were all granted everlasting life, no better than Struldbrugs would we be, anyhow."

Zoe raised her eyebrows: *Struldbrugs?* Paul kept silent.

"That's someone," Jerry explained, "who can't die but who nevertheless continues to get older and more infirm. Two hundred years from now we'd all be hopelessly senile immortals. Spare me such a blessing."

That ended the conversation. A ghost impersonating a man, Paul got up and drifted out of the room.

On Sunday morning, though, Luther went down to the rec center and took a box of aluminum parts, the largest being a drumlike cylinder, out of the closet where they kept the dart boards, the croquet equipment, and the playing cards, and assembled these pieces into . . . a rocking horse, one big enough for a man.

It was a shiny rocking horse, and its head, between its painted eyes, bore the representation of a scarab beetle pushing the sun before it like a cosmic dungball. Zoe, who was in the rec center with all the Phoenix but Paul, went up to the metal critter to examine it. The scarab emblem was so meticulously wrought that she had to lean over to see what this horse had crawling on its forehead. A blue bug. A red ball. Well, that was different: funny and mysterious at once. "What's this?" she asked Luther, who, mumbling to himself, was trying to wedge the cardboard box back into the closet.

"Pulpit," he said. He thought she meant the whole thing. No

sense in trying to clarify herself, he was still shoving at the box.
But *pulpit* was a damn funny synonym for *rocking horse*.

After wedging the parts box back into place, Luther dragged
a tall metal bottle from the closet and carried it over to the
biomonitor cabinet next to Toodles' orpianoogla. Then he set it
down and came back to the ring of chairs in front of the rocking
horse. A silly business, every bit of it. Zoe put a single finger on
the horse's forehead, right on the blue bug, and pushed. The
horse, so light that only its weighted rockers kept it from tipping,
began to dip and rise, gently nodding. No one was talking. Zoe
turned to the group and shrugged. It looked like you'd have to
threaten them all with premature autopsy to get anyone to
explain.

"Don't ask," Jerry said finally. "But since you're asking, it's
to humor him. He asked for the horse the second month after
our covenant ceremony in thirty-five, and Dr Tanner said OK,
give it to him. Now, four times a year, he plays octogenarian
cowboy and rides into the sunset of his own dreams right in front
of everybody. It's not so much for us to listen to him, you know."

Zoe looked at the five of them sitting there, afraid she
wouldn't understand: five uncertain old faces. She was put off.
They had been dreading this morning because they didn't know
how she would react to the living skeleton in their family closet:
the *de*-ranged range-rider Paul Erik Ferrand-Phoenix. Well, she
was put off. All somebody had to do was tell her, she was
steamingly put off. "O ye of little faith," she wanted to say, 'go
roast your shriveled hearts on Yuichan's hibachi. All of it
together wouldn't make a meal." But she didn't say anything, she
sat down with the group and waited. Maybe they didn't think
she had Yuichan's compassion, maybe they didn't think she was
worthy to replace their dear departed Jap. . . .

Just then Paul came drifting in: an entrance. Except that he
didn't seem to be at all aware of the impression he was making,
he was oblivious of his own etiolated magnificence. Dressed in
spotless white from head to foot (currently fashionable attire
among even the young—matched tunic and leggings), he
wandered over to the metal horse without looking at them.
Then, slowly, he climbed on and steadied the animal's rocking
with the toe tips of his white slippers.

He was facing them. Behind him, as backdrop, one of the
quilted wall banners: a navy-blue one with a crimson phoenix in
its center, wings outspread. Zoe couldn't help thinking that

every detail of Paul's entrance and positioning had been planned beforehand. Or maybe it was that this quarterly ritual had so powerfully suffused them all that the need for planning was long since past. Anyhow, knowing it all to be nonsense, Zoe had to acknowledge that little pulses of electricity were moving along her spine.

Slowly, mesmerizingly slowly, Paul began to rock. And softly he began to preach the True Word. "When we were young," he said, "there was fire, and sky, and grass, and air, and creatures that weren't men. The human brain was plugged into this, the human brain was run on the batteries of fire and sky and all of it out there."

"Amen!" Luther interjected, without interrupting Paul's rhythm, but all Zoe could think was, The City still has creatures that aren't men: pigeons. But the rocking horse began to move faster, and as it picked up speed its rider's voice also acquired momentum, a rhythmic impetus of its own. As Paul spoke on, preached on, an "Amen!" or a "Yessir, brother!" occasionally provided an audible asterisk to some especially strange or vehement assertion in his text. All of it part of the ritual. But then Zoe was caught up in it in a way that she could see herself being caught up. Very odd. She found herself seconding Paul's insane remarks with "Amen!" or "All praises!" or some other curiously heartfelt interjection that she *never* used. This increased as the rocking horse's careering grew more violent and as Paul's eyes, the horse going up and down, flashed like eerie strobes.

"Then before our lives was half over, they put us in our tombs. They said we was dead even though we could feel the juices flowin' through us and electricity jumpin' in our heads. Up went the tombs, though, up they went. It didn't matter what we felt, it didn't matter we was still plugged into the life outside our tombs, the air and fire and sky. Because with the tombs up, you really do start dyin', you really do start losin' the voltage you have flowin' back and forth between you and the outside. Just look at yourself, just look at all of us." (Could anything be more ridiculous than this reasoning?) "It's slippin' away, that current, that precious, precious juice. It's because our brains are plugged into the sun or the moon, one socket or the other, and now they've stuck us in a place where the current won't flow."

Even as she said, "Yessir!" Zoe was thinking that he, Paul, must have been plugged into the moon: loony.

But in another way, an upside-down way, it made a kind of loony sense, too. Even though everybody knew the world had been going to Hell in a handcar *before* the Domes went up, it still made a loony kind of sense. Maybe, at a certain time in your life—which was already past for her—you learned how to pass judgment on others, even unfavorable ones, without condemning. Zoe was doing that now. She beheld the madly rocking Paul from two utterly opposed perspectives and had no desire to reconcile them. In fact, the reconciliation happened, was happening, without her willing it to. As it always had for her, since Rabon's death. It was the old binocular phenomenon at work on a philosophical rather than a physical plane. Long ago it had occurred in Helen, too, the Phoenix "mediator," and just as Helen's little black goggles brought the physical world into focus for her, this double vision Zoe was now experiencing brought the two galloping Pauls—the demoniac one and the human one—into the compass of her understanding and merged them. Since this had happened before for her, why was she surprised?

"And the key to not-dying, and preserving the body too, is the brain. That's where we all are. We have to plug ourselves into the sun again, the sun and the moon. No one can do that unless he is resurrected from the tomb we were put in even before our lives were half over...."

The horse was rocking frenetically, and Paul's voice was swooping into each repetitive sentence with a lean, measured hysteria. The bracelet on Zoe's wrist seemed to be singing. She looked at the biomonitor cabinet beside the orpianoogla and saw the oscilloscope attuned to both Paul's brain waves and heartbeat sending a shower of pale comets back and forth, back and forth, across its screen. The other six windows were vividly pulsing, too, and she wondered if someone downstairs was taking note of this activity. Well, they were certainly all alive—very much alive.

Now Paul's eyes had rolled back in his head, and the rocking horse had carried him into a country of either uninterrupted childhood or eternally stalled ripeness. He was alone in there, with just his brain and the concupiscent wavelets washing back from his body. Still preaching, too. Still ranting. Until, finally, the last word came out.

Only then did Paul slump forward across the neck of his aluminum steed, spent. Or dead maybe.

Zoe stood up—sprang up, rather. Amazingly, the other

Phoenix—Toodles, Helen, Jerry, and Parthena—were applauding. Luther exempted himself from this demonstration in order to catch Paul before he slid off the still rocking horse and broke his head open.

"That the bes' one he manage in a long time," Parthena said.

Since the applause continued, Zoe, feeling foolish, joined in too. And while they all clapped (did sermons always end like this, the congregation joining in a spontaneous ovation?), Luther carried Paul over to the biomonitor cabinet, laid him out, and administered oxygen from the metal bottle he had earlier taken out of the closet. After which the wraithlike cowboy lifted his head a bit and acknowledged their applause with a wan grin. Then Luther put him to bed.

"You have to let him hear you," Toodles said. "Otherwise the old bastard thinks you didn't like it."

But he wasn't much good for three days after the sermon. He stayed in the common room, sleeping or staring at the ceiling. Zoe sat with him on the first night and let him sip soup through a flexible straw. In a few minutes he waved the bowl away, and Zoe, thinking he wanted to sleep, got up to leave. Paul reached out for her wrist, and missed. She saw it, though, and turned back to him. His hand patted the bed: *Sit down.* So she lowered herself into the easy chair there and took his liver-spotted hand in her own. For an hour she sat there and held it. Then the long, raw lips said, "I'm afraid, Zoe."

"Sometimes," she said carefully, "I am, too." Now and again she was, she had to admit it.

The mouth remained open, the Weimaraner eyes glazed. Then Paul ran his tongue around his long lips. "Well," he said, "you can get in bed with me if you want to."

And closed his eyes. And went to sleep.

12 / Somewhere Over the Broomstick

It had never been in doubt. Maybe a little, just a little, in jeopardy the first night when the menfolk insulted Toodles. Or maybe a bit uncertain with Paul, until after his rocking-horse oration and subsequent collapse. But never really perilously in doubt.

So when Luther came up to the rooftop on that evening at the end of Winter and said, "You're in, Zoe, you're in," her joy was contained, genuine but contained. You don't shout Hooray! until the wedding's over or the spacemen have got home safely. Zoe embraced Luther. Downstairs, she embraced the others.

On the morning after the group's decision, they had the covenant ceremony in the Hostel quadrangle. Leland Tanner presided. Day 1 of Spring, 2040, New Calendar designation.

"All right," Mr Leland said. "Each septigamoklan has its own covenant procedure, Zoe, since any way that it chooses to ratify its bond is legal in the eyes of the Human Development Commission. The Phoenix ceremony owes it origin to an idea of Parthena's." He looked at the group. They were all standing on a section of the lawn surrounded by tubbed gingko trees. A table with refreshments was visible in the nearest arbor. "That's right, isn't it?"

"That right," Parthena said.

And then, of all crazy things, Mr Leland brought a broom out from behind his back. He laid it on the wiry turf at his feet and backed up a few steps. "OK," he said. "What you all do now is join hands and step over the broomstick together." He reconsidered. "Maybe we better do it in two groups of three, Zoe, you making the fourth each time. Any objections?"

"No," Parthena said. "So long as she cross it in the same direction both times, so none of it get undone."

OK. That's the way they did it. Zoe went first with Helen, Toodles, and Luther, then a second go-round with Parthena, Paul, and Jerry. Jerry had to drive his wheelchair over one end of the broom handle.

"I pronounce you," Mr Leland declared, "all seven of you, married in the Phoenix. Six of you for a second time, one of you for the first." He took them all over to the arbor and passed out drinks. "Viva the Phoenix."

Zoe drank. They all drank. Toasts went around the group several times. It was all very fitting that when you were sold down the river, into freedom, you got married by jumping over a broomstick. How else should you do it? No other way at all. No other way at all.

Paul and Toodles, the oldest and second youngest in the family, died in 2042. A year later Luther died. In 2047, two days short of her eightieth birthday, Helen died. In this same year Dr Leland Tanner resigned his position at the Human Development Tower; he protested uninformed interference in a study that was then twelve years old. Upon his departure from the Geriatrics Hostel his programs were discontinued, the remaining members of the ten septigamoklans separated. In 2048 Jeremy Zitelman died in the Hostel's nursing ward. Parthena and Zoe, by the time of his death, had been returned to their "surviving families," Parthena to a surfaceside Bondville tenement, Zoe to the Level 3 cubicle of Sanders and Melanie Noble. Oddly enough, these two last members of the Phoenix died within twelve hours of each other on a Summer day in 2050, after brief illnesses. Until a month or two before their deaths, they met each other once a week in a small restaurant on West Peachtree, where they divided a single vegetable dinner between them and exchanged stories about their grandchildren. Parthena, in fact, was twice a *great*-grandmother....

After the broomstick-jumping ceremony in the garden court, Mr Leland took Zoe aside and said that someone wanted to talk to her in the room that he had once called an "air lock." His horsy face had a tic in one taut cheek, and his hands kept rubbing themselves against each other in front of his bright blue tunic. "I told him to wait until we were finished out here, Zoe. And he agreed."

Why this mystery? Her mind was other places. "Who is it?"

"Your son-in-law."

She went into the air lock, the decompression chamber, whatever you wanted to call it, and found Sanders ensconced in one corner of the sofa, playing with the lint on his socks. When he saw her he got up, clumsily, with a funeral expression on his face. He looked like somebody had been stuffing his mouth with the same sort of lint he'd been picking off his socks: bloated jowls, vaguely fuzzy lips. She just stared at him until he had worked his mouth around so that it could speak.

"Lannie lost the baby," he said.

So, after Lannie got out of the hospital, she spent a week in their Level 3 cubicle helping out until her daughter could do for herself. When that week was over, she returned to her new family in the Geriatrics Hostel. But before she left she pulled Sanders aside and said, "I've got some advice for you, something for you to tell Lannie too. Will you do it?"

Sanders looked at his feet. "OK, Zoe."

"Tell her," Zoe said, "to try again."

Interlude: The City Takes Care of Its Own

In 2035 the Urban Council and Conclave of Ward Representatives passed a comprehenseive series of statutes that came to be known as the Retrenchment Edicts. Deliberately designed to squelch dissent, encourage a blasé conformity, and provide penalties for antisocial behavior, these statutes were so numerous as to boggle mortal understanding. Moreover, to compound the difficulty, Altanta's legislators had given the term "antisocial" the widest possible construction.

You could be arrested for spitting on the street, singing in public places, distributing unauthorized mimeography, potting pigeons with a slingshot, preaching the doctrines of Bahai (or any other unsanctioned dissident religion), badmouthing the Council/Conclave, pushing your brother-in-law down a lift-shaft, pitching pre-Evacuation pennies, selling raffle tickets, or blowing up transit-terminals. After 2035, you watched your step or you invited the anonymous and often permanent oblivion of the bookerslam. There were those, in fact, who got jobbed righty out of downtown pedestrian courts and stoked unceremoniously into the wast-converters on Level 9. No one talked very much about this last unsettling means of enforcing the Edicts, but no one really needed to, either.

Such stringency, said the City's legislators, derived from an ever-ascending spiral of disorder, coercive demands, and cruel opportunism on the part of the disenfranchised and their well-meaning but deluded supporters. Carlo Bitler's brief reign as a spokesman for the disenfranchised had ended, predictably enough, with his assassination. In the years between his death and the passage of the Retrenchment Edicts (the Council/Conclave took some delight in pointing out), the streets, the p-courts, and the hive of the underCity had often been dangerous places to visit alone. After 2035, however, the situation had improved to the extent that a joove or a senescente could venture out without the least fear of an unprovoked assault.

This lull lasted a mere six years. In 2041, a series of small disturbances broke out in Bondville, most of which were efficiently quelled by uniformed and gauntleted riot trolls. One such "disturbance," however, induced the City's First Councilor—whose office had only recently come into being—to declare a curfew and a week-long period of martial law. In the hive, concourse trolls almost daily stumbled upon the mutilated corpses of derelicts who had run afoul of marauding human jackals.

Another period of stark repression followed, and after a time even the darkest and the deepest recesses of the City again seemed safe to walk alone. Tickleheeling pranksters ran through the hive—but they no longer carried weapons, and they goosed rather than murdered their unsuspecting prey. By 2043, in fact, the administrative tactic of full-scale repression had vindicated itself in many people's eyes. That pinpointing and solving the social ills conducive to discontent and violence might have been an equally effective measure, no one cared to concede. After all, the City took care of its own.

If you died, for instance, someone—somewhere—knew almost immediately that you had yielded up your soul. Each cubicle was a complex and virtually infallible monitoring system, and in the instant when you believed yourself most alone, straitjacketed in the fusty embrace of death, you could count on the impersonal, comforting fact that *someone knew*. . . .

CHAPTER THREE

The Windows in Dante's Hell

1 / The Combcrawlers

We received notification of the woman's death on the Biomonitor Console in the subsidiary control room on West Peachtree. A small cherry-red light went on; it glowed in the blue halflight that hangs about the console like the vague memory of fog. "Someone's dead," Yates' son said. "That light just came on." Yates' son is fourteen years old. His broad face was purplish in the fog of the control room, the sheen of flesh over forehead reflecting back a small crescent of the red that had just come on. Only a moment before, the boy had entered the building, stopped at my elbow, and waited for an opportunity to talk. Yates is my boss, the head of the City's Biomonitor Agency. Because our interests were similar, his son frequently came around to talk to me: I girderclimbed on the weekends, and the boy was just learning. But he had never come into the console area before, and when the red light began faintly pulsing on the monstrous board, his lank body had stooped toward it.

"Yes," I said. "Someone's dead. The board don't lie. 'Deed it don't." To sentimentalize the death of a cubicle-dweller is a soul-destroying business. I try to keep it light.

"I've never seen a dead person. Papa says that people get sick, that the board reports that all the time—but people don't die very often."

"People die all the time."

88

"I've never seen a dead person," Yates' son said. "Never at all."

"You're lucky you haven't seen a girderclimbing accident, Newlyn. You'd see death and terror and plummeting human beings all in one fell swoop." I am nine years older than Newlyn, and those nine years have taught me one or two things that I'm not always capable of communicating to those younger than myself. But I try—for their benefit, not mine. "When I was your age, I saw a party of six combcrawlers, hooked together with a glinting golden cord, lose either the magnetic induction in their girderboots or else all sense of the teamwork involved in dome-traversing."

Newlyn looked away from the board. His heavy forehead turned toward me; his African lips framed a faint exhalation: "What happened?"

"The climbers," I told him, "had reached a section of honeycombing about three hundred yards from the very apex of the Dome. Their backs were down, and inside the spun-iron gloves their hands were probably clinging like crazy to the track of the navigational girder they had chosen. They had worked out a complicated, a truly beautiful assault, on the apex. They were high above the City, bright specks on the artificial sky, and suddenly the fourth man in the contingent fell away from the group and bobbed on the elastic gold cord that held them together—bobbed just like a spider weighting the center of its web.

"From the top of the new Russell Complex, my father and I watched them—even though we hadn't gone up there for that purpose.

"The combcrawler couldn't recover, Newlyn. The fifth and sixth men broke away, flailing their arms around. It was amazing how slowly—how really distinctly—their fates overtook them. The first three men in the chain were sucked down toward us, and the whole broad sky under the Dome seemed to hold them up for a while. Then they fell, twirling around and around each other like the strands of one of those Argentine *bolas*, hypnotizing everybody in the streets. At last they fell through the canyon of buildings to our north and disappeared toward the concrete that I could *feel* impacting against them. It was terrifying, but it was beautiful. I resolved to become a combcrawler myself. All unbeknownst to my father, of course—he'd've suffered a multiple aneurysm if he'd known

about that resolution. You see, Newlyn, you're lucky. Your
father approves."

"But did you see them after they fell?" Newlyn asked,
unawed. "Did you see them lying in the street, dead?"

Annoyed, I said: "Hell no, I didn't see them! If my father was
the sort to frown on combcrawling, do you think he'd bundle me
off to ogle six crumpled, blood-spattered husks of humanity in
some crappy alley?"

Newlyn smiled. "Then you haven't seen a dead person,
either."

"Certainly I have."

"Where?"

"On the board," I said, smiling too. "There's one right there,
that pulsing red light."

"And who is it, then?" the boy said, continuing his
interrogation. "And where does he live?"

"Just a minute, lad." I leaned forward, recorded the
coordinates of the light, and at last gave it permission to go dead,
its dull cherry sheen fading out of the naked crystal and leaving
us, the boy and me, swimming in the blue dimness. (Wherever
possible, you see, the City conserves its resources.) I ran the
coordinates through the appropriate computer and found that
the dead person lay in a cubicle somewhere on Level 8. To be
exact: Concourse E-16, Door 502, Level 8. Another computer
gave me the corpse's name, age, and vital statistics—though
there weren't many of the latter.

"Well, who is it?" Newlyn asked.

"Almira Longhope. One hundred and seven years old.
Unmarried. No relatives. Caucasian. Came into the City at the
age of fifty-seven with the refugees of the first Evacuation
Lottery...."

"Let's go see her!"

"What?"

"Let's go see her. Somebody's got to go get her, don't they?"

"Somebody. Not us."

"Look, Mr Ardrey, that old woman died down on Level 8
because she was old and alone, probably. I've never seen a dead
person, you've never seen a dead person. Let's go and retrieve
her and keep them servo-units from eating her up like a wad of
dust. OK?"

"Newlyn, we're not going anywhere to gawk at an old woman
who couldn't get any higher than Level 8 in fifty years."

"It wouldn't be any gawking," Newlyn said. "It wouldn't."

And with that as a prologue and only a little more argument, I finally consented. The Biomonitor Agency does not ordinarily send human beings to dispose of the human beings who have died in their cubicles—nor does the Agency refrain from want of sufficient manpower or out of callousness. The problem is that human beings are invariably *too* compassionate; they represent feeling, and when that feeling confronts a corpse and all its attendant suggestions of loneliness, the living human beings suffer—and suffer profoundly. Therefore, the Agency usually dispatches servo-units to the cubicles of the kinless and the forgotten. It is best.

I appointed Arn Bartholomew to take my place at the console. I gathered from our files and resource rooms some of the things we would need. Then Newlyn and I went into the street.

Because it was Winter and because our meterologists maintain internal conditions that correspond with the external passing of the seasons, we wore coats. Newlyn, in his navy pea jacket, strode ahead of me like an adolescent tour guide, spindly, purposeful, curt. We walked across one marble square, circumnavigated a huge fountain whose waters were frozen in fantastic loops and falls, and jogged toward the monolithic lift-terminal that dispatches its passengers up and down the layered levels of the City in crystal lift-tubes. We jogged because it was cold. We jogged because it is difficult to talk while jogging, and we did not believe that we had, in actuality, committed ourselves to the viewing and the disposal of a . . . *dead person*. Jogging, we tried not to look at each other.

The Dome glowered above us; it seemed that it hung down with the weight of its own honeycombing, threatening to crush us. No one was up there. No one was crawling over the girders.

Then we reached the lift-terminal, found an open tube, and descended into the great hive of the City—descended in utter silence, descended through a nightmare halflight, a halflight freaky as the cold simulation of dawn. On Level 8, one stratum above the nethermost floor of the hive, we disembarked.

2 / *The Glissadors*

We found the concourse; we found the corridor. The people we passed in the corridor refused to look at us, passing us like wisps of smoke against the smudge-red illumination that contain us all.

Many of those who passed us were ghostly glissadors, hive inhabitants who spend so much of their time going up and down and about and through the various hallways that they have donned nearly soundless skates to conserve their energy and speed their labors. The skates are pieces of simulated cordovan footwear with a multitude of miniature ball bearings mounted in the soles. The City issues these glierboots to its sublevel employees. And Newlyn and I watched the graceful glissadors sweep past us through the gloom, their heads down.

Each time that one went past, Newlyn turned in a slow circle to watch. He said, "That looks like fun."

"It gets to be work," I said. "Everything gets to be work."

Still, I caught the next effortlessly volplaning figure by the elbow and spun him about before he could disappear into the dim distance. A small sound of protest escaped his lips, but he controlled his turn and wheeled about like a mute ballet performer. He was tall. Like Newlyn, he was the intense color of ripe wet grapes.

"Almira Longhope," I said. "Do you know her cubicle?"

The glissador stared at me: "What's her number, *surfacesider?*"

I told him.

"Then you keep following these here doors till you reach it." He threw up his arm and spun away. He looked at us briefly. Turning with sinuous skill, he strode out forcefully and skated off, off forth on swing.

"Why'd you stop him?" Newlyn asked. "We knew where we were."

I said nothing for a moment, trying to pick out the departing glissador's figure in the crimson light.

Newlyn said: "Well? Why'd you do that?"

"I wanted one of them to . . . to acknowledge us. I wanted to watch how one of them resumed his skating. Maybe it is fun," I said. And stopped. Newlyn was watching me. "Never mind. Let's follow the goddamn doors."

We did. We walked. Our feet *tap-tap-tapped* on the tiles, mundanely coming down one foot after another. In this fashion we eventually reached Door 502, a door which looked uncannily like the two doors on either side.

I extracted from my pocket the obscenely rubberoid sheath upon which were embossed the whorls of Mz Almira Longhope's right thumbprint, and slipped this sheath over my forefinger so as not to distort the print with my own outsized thumb. Then I held my forefinger to the electric eye for scanning, and the panel slid back, admitting us to the cubicle in which the dead woman must necessarily lie: unwept, unhonored, very nearly unborn. Newlyn preceded me into the odd closet just inside the cubicle's door.

At first we saw nothing. After our trip through the murky, glissador-haunted catacombs, the room's bright midday glare struck at us cruelly. We squinted. We blinked. And then there was the inevitable resolution of detail (in itself a haunting experience) as our eyes came back to us.

We found ourselves in an environment immensely strange. We were in a cramped artificial foyer. The walls on the inside of the cubicle had been altered so that they formed an octagonal area of space rather than a square one. Moreover, just inside the cubicle's doorway Newlyn and I stumbled upon a crude wooden step which we had to mount in order to see more than the tops of the wall sections opposite us. We climbed the step.

We stood then on a narrow dais, approximately one foot from the cubicle's real floor, that made an octagonal circuit about the entire room and provided an odd catwalk for the unexpecting, and certainly unexpected, intruder into Miss Longhope's spendidly insane sanctuary. It was a sanctuary unlike any that one would expect to find on the lower levels of the hive—or anywhere else, for that matter.

Banks of computerlike gadgetry, from which there emanated the faint and fitful winking of orange and red lights, stood against two facets of the octagonal wall. Against two more sections—the two flanking us—we saw tall glass cylinders that were polarized so that we could not see into them; these cylinders could have been anything, from models of the City's lift-tubes, to gigantic chemical beakers, to containers for space travelers in suspended animation. The mystery intrigued us, but something else drew our attention away. In the remaining four facets of the octagonal wall, directly across the room, we looked upon four distinct and different windows: view screens that permitted us to see panoramas that no living inhabitant of the Dome had ever gazed upon, unless we were possessed of a vivid clairvoyance.

Newlyn and I drank in these panoramas quickly.

From left to right these "windows" demonstrated a progression based on an expanding consciousness of the universe. The screen on the far left depicted a view of our own domed City, but from the *outside,* as if from a distant hilltop in the wilderness that we had so long ago fled; and darkness swirled over the Dome's imposing hump like a disturbed gas, uneasily hovering.

The second window showed us the dead face of the Moon from about ten thousand miles away. No man had set foot there for more than sixty or seventy years.

The third window gave us the etheral aloofness of Saturn and its incandescent rings.

And the fourth window, the one on the far right, made us look into the cruel depths of outer space—where the glassy indifference of a thousand sharp stars somehow stung us back into the here-and-now, sucking away our breaths. And since the biomonitor units in the cubicle had begun to refrigerate the air to compensate for the onset of the old woman's physical decay, our breaths were chill.

Newlyn reacted noisily: "What kind of place does this old woman live in, Mr Ardrey? What's it supposed to be?" As in the hallway, his body revolved out of the impulse of sheer wonder. "What the heck is all this stuff for?"

"I don't think it's exactly *for* anything."

"Everything's for something, Mr Ardrey. What's this stuff supposed to be? What's it do?"

I tried to make sense of my suspicions. We had stumbled into what was evidently an elaborate mockup, and the octagonal room could have been a wide variety of things: the hall of planets in a second-rate surfaceside museum, some sort of wildly improbable computer chamber, or—

"—The command pit of a spaceship," I said. "It's supposed to be the command pit of—"

Newlyn cut me off with a cry that might have come out of the mouth of someone a great deal younger: "Look, there she is!" He pointed down into the pit which I had been trying to identify; he pointed at the back of the huge swivel chair that dominated this intriguing area. Visible above the back of this chair, the back of a woman's head, matted over with frowzy iron-gray pleats, caught my eye and sent a cold wrinkle unwinding up my spine. Newlyn jumped from the dais, jumped into the command pit before I could say anything. As I had spun the glissador about in the hallway, he spun the arm of the chair and turned the ruined face of Almira Longhope, glassy eyes open, lower lip twisted, toward me—toward *me!*

I stared at the dead woman, feeling her accusation.

"She's really dead," Newlyn told me excitedly, running a finger over the silver lamé sleeve of her gown. "She's really dead."

"I know. I can see that."

Newlyn turned impulsively around, forgetting the old woman. He did not spin the chair in the direction of his turn. Instead, he simply walked around the chair and paused momentarily at the semicircular panel of "instruments" over which the dead woman had been gazing before he had disturbed her. He looked toward the four viewing screens. Dome, moon, planet, stars. The last three could have meant almost nothing to Newlyn, even though he had undoubtedly seen the night sky in visicomb presentations and read about the "promise of space" in pre-Evacuation literature. Besides, the four windows had no reality. The stars on the far right were sharp and cold, yes, but they existed only as glossy points on a piece of lusterless mounted silk. Each window, in fact, was just such a piece of lusterless mounted silk. Despite this, Newlyn stared at the viewing screen on the far right for a long while. "Look at that," he said before turning away. "Look at all that distance, all that space." At last he did turn away. He brought his attention back to the semicircular console in front of the old woman's command chair.

Reaching over it, he pushed buttons. One or two of them seemed to operate lights in the walls. He fiddled with levers. One of the levers controlled two mobiles that hung from the ceiling, seemingly as navigational devices, since each one represented a miniature spaceship moving gyroscopically inside a glass sphere divided into sections by thin blue lines. "Look at all this stuff," Newlyn said over and over again. He made low whistling noises, articulations of pleased astonishment.

Meanwhile, the corpse of Almira Longhope continued to stare at me. I was certain now that the bitch's stare was singlemindedly accusatory, even though her sunken features contained less malice than disappointment.

But for Newlyn's oblivious cluckings, the room was deathly still. And cold. The orange and red lights on the phony computers made no noise; none of the instruments on the semicircular panel hummed, or clicked, or whirred. I grew uneasy.

"Newlyn!"

He did not even look up. "What?"

"Get away from there. We've got things to do."

"Just a second, Mr Ardrey. This thing's got a purpose, I can tell." He was manipulating a dial on the command console. Soundlessly the scenes depicted in the four windows opposite us slipped into another continuum; to take their places there came the image of (1) an alien planetscape, (2) the craggy moon of a world not belonging to Sol, (3) an eerie double binary, and (4) a minute spiral galaxy as seen from the loneliness of open space. How far outward the old woman had permitted herself to venture! These new images—or perhaps simply the changes he had worked—exhilarated Newlyn. "Climbersguts!" he said, a bit of irritating slang.

"Goddammit, Newlyn, will you get away from there!"

He looked up hurriedly and faced me, his chin tilted a little. I had never spoken to him like that before. His eyes betrayed his hurt and bewilderment.

"You were the one," I reminded him, "who said we weren't going to come down here to gawk. Do you remember that? You were the one who wanted to make sure the servo-units didn't vacuum her up like a piece of dirt."

The boy dropped his head, chastened.

I was still angry. My fists were clenching and unclenching of their own accord. It was difficult not to look into the corpse's vein-woven eyes, lose all resolution, and return surfaceside to the control room on West Peachtree. Especially since we had stumbled on the mausoleum of an aged lunatic with an adolescent pituitary where her brains should have been. No wonder Almira Longhope, at the age of one hundred and seven, still resided in a three-room cubicle on Level 8: she had exhausted her monetary and spiritual resources constructing a tomb with faster-than-light-speed capabilities, patching together an epitaph out of old screenplays and pulp magazine stories, paying homage to the very worst of the products of the pre-Evacuation mass media. No wonder that she stared at me with accusation and disappointment; the dream, too, had finally died, and we had walked in on its naked remains.

Still chastened, Newlyn said: "All right, Mr Ardrey, what do we have to do now?" Finally he looked up. "I'm sorry. I'm sorry I—"

This time I cut *him* off. "Don't be sorry. It was a natural response, Newlyn, a very natural response." Then I told him that the first thing I wanted him to do was face the old woman toward her windows once again, and he did this for me. "The computer said that she had no relatives," I went on, "so we don't have to try to contact anyone. All we have to do is go through her belongings and determine if she's left a will or any papers. Then we must see that her body goes into the waste converter on Level 9 and file a report so that her cubicle can be sprayed. All this junk will have to be destroyed."

"It doesn't look like junk, Mr Ardrey."

"It's junk."

He didn't protest a second time, but his eyes, though superficially still penitent, cut away from me at an angle of vague reprimand. I ignored this silent cavil. He was young.

It took us a little while to find the entrance into her sleeping quarters because the artificial hull of her "spaceship" had been erected in front of the cubicle's internal doorways. (The entrance from the outer corridor, through which Newlyn and I had originally come, was disguised as the facing of an airlock, for the artifices of Mz Longhope were nothing if not thoroughgoing.) We walked around the catwalk that circled the vessel's command pit. We tested the firmness of the walls with our hands and knees. We scrutinized the phony computer banks and puzzled over the two glass cylinders. And, at last, we did find the doorway to the old woman's bedchamber.

Newlyn made the discovery. Running his hands over the surface of one of the cylinders, he was surprised to find a vertical seam. He pressed this seam, and the cylinder split apart and opened out. "Mr Ardrey!" he called. I went to him. Together we found that the other half of the cylinder also opened out, but in the direction of the concealed sleeping chamber.

We went through this unorthodox portal, down a single step,

and into the old woman's private alcove. Newlyn dialed up the lights.

The alcove contained a low bed, a study area, and the standard visicom console on which one can display reading material or run his choice of entertainment visuals. However, the visicom's screen was silver-gray. And dead. The fanaticism manifested so tangibly in the main living area did not appear so virulent here. I looked at Newlyn. The disappointment on his face mirrored the look on the old woman's corpse. In truth, however, he had nothing to be disappointed *about*. Almira Longhope's ruling passion had merely secreted itself away into drawers, boxes, diaries, packets of photographs, and a heavy blue ledger. One or two testimonies of this passion remained shamelessly in the open, although Newlyn had not noticed them.

"Cheer up," I said. "Look there."

Beside the old woman's bed, resting on her night table, there was a spherical lamp mounted on a tripod base. The lamp had hundreds of tiny holes in its surface, for in reality it was not a lamp at all but a simple version of the star-projectors that one of the old networks had marketed in such profiteering quantities before the Last Days of our great-grandfathers. Newlyn asked what the thing was: I told him. Then he wanted to see how the thing worked. Therefore, after he had dimmed the lights, I turned the projector on. At once stars appeared on the walls and ceiling—the constellations all misshapen and askew, however, because Mz Longhope had apparently not been able to devise a curved surface on which to project them. To Yates' son, the resulting distortion made no difference. Even after I had made him dial the lights up again, he stood over the star-projector with all the solicitude of a nursing mother for her newborn whelps. His face was silly with concern.

"How did she think up all these things?" he asked.

"She didn't. She just copied them."

"From what?"

"From a style of entertainment that existed before the Domes went up—similar to our visual entertainment tapes. Most of this stuff has its origin in one of their *shows*... back when they believed in interstellar travel and galactic civilizations. Or at least when some of them did. She's just copied everything from that one particular series of tapes—and from magazines and movies."

"When was it? When was all this stuff thought up?"

"Seventy years ago. Eighty years ago. I don't know, Newlyn."

He stared at the star-projector. He looked back toward the half-open cylinder beyond which lay the spaceship's command pit. His lips scarcely moved. "It's neat," he said pontifically. "It's some of the neatest stuff I've ever seen."

"That old woman wasted her life," I said. "She wasted it."

Turning my back on Yates' son, I sat down at the study center and began pulling drawers open. What I found confirmed my judgment. Newlyn, sullen and belligerent now, looked over my shoulder as I arranged the contents of the drawers and of several crumpled Manila envelopes on the surface of the desk. The stench of another time flew out of these envelopes like the moths that still flutter from the surfaceside grasses in Spring. I coughed. Like moths, the photographs and slips of precious paper seemed to beat about my head with their dusty hard-edged wings. In Mz Longhope's blue ledger I flipped randomly to one of the pages of broad childish handwriting.

I read one of the paragraphs on the page.

> Log entry: Tonight I saw the episode entitled "Between the Star Mirrors" for the third time. Is there an alternate Almira somewhere in the universe? I wish that I could break through for a moment and visit my other self. The Rigelian first officer is an honorable man in both universes. What would I be? Sometimes I am afraid that I am empty of stars in both places, but this is not true. Even my other self, just as I do here, would have all her alternate universe to reach into and to wonder at. But she would probably need to have help to reach out—just as I do. I hate the image that the mirror I hold up to the world returns to me. The image in the mirror clouds over every day, like the dirty sky and the people's ugly wrinkled unhappy faces.

I read this passage aloud to Newlyn. "Neat, huh?"

He said nothing. He picked up one of the laminated photographs, bent and yellowed in spite of the lamination, and ran his finger over the heavy intense face of one of the actors who had been in the series. In the photograph, the actor had a smooth triple-lobed cranium and no discernible eyebrows; he had signed his name across the bottom of the picture. Newlyn touched the signature, too—or tried to touch it; the dull plastic prevented him. Stymied, he studied the face.

"Look at this man's head, Mr Ardrey." He had forgotten his resentment of my skeptical attitude toward Mz Longhope's memorabilia. "Look at his head, Mr Ardrey. Where did this man come from?"

"A makeup room, Newlyn. It's just an actor pretending to be a member of a humanoid species that never existed. A nonexistent friendly alien."

He continued to look at the actor's picture. "Can I have this?"

"No," I said. "It isn't mine to give you. What do you want with it, anyway?" I took it out of his hands, gently.

He shrugged and looked at the other items on the desk. He feigned an interest in the ledger containing the old woman's "log entries," but I could tell that the writing there bored him.

I sorted the papers and photographs and put them back into the dingy Manila envelopes. There was nothing in the old woman's possessions of any conceivable value to the City. We had innumerable collections of such maudlin remnants of the pre-Evacuation days, should anyone actually wish to see such things. Museums. Chronos galleries. Pedestrian corridors lined with glass cases and curio-boards. No one was denied information about the past. And if Almira Longhope had anything at all worth saving, I supposed it to be the blue ledger. However miserable and cramped, at least it was a document of human suffering and therefore of some value to the urban archives.

But as I had mentally predicted he would, Newlyn had grown weary of this document. He had left the sleeping cubicle and gone back to the command pit of the *Sojourner II*. I finished putting away the old woman's possessions, the inconsequential leftovers of a lifetime misspent and horrifyingly sad.

Everything but the ledger.

That I carried with me, out to where Newlyn prowled among the winking lights and the ghostly crewmen who rode their drifting derelict through the ruinous voids of that lifetime.

Newlyn said: "What do we have to do now?"

"Find a telecom unit. The old bitch must have tried to make it an integral part of the equipment on this 'vessel.' Why don't you see if you can find it?"

This request pleased Yates' son; it gave him an excuse to finger the dials and levers, to examine the intricacy of the total construct. Meanwhile, the old woman surveyed us regally from the command chair. I realized that she was attired after the fashion of some anonymous producer's concept of a Rigelian priestess; a sort of scepter, or abbreviated staff, lay across her thin thighs. How magnificently, how pettily, she had met her death. In the cubicle's cold air her face seemed to be carved of ice. I had just looked away from her twisted lower lip when Newlyn called, "Here it is, Mr Ardrey. In this box over here. Where it says 'Communications.'"

"Where it says 'Communications,'" I echoed. "Very apt."

I mounted the catwalk, sat down, and made three brief calls. One to the main control room. One to the office of the administrative head of the glissadors on Level 8. One to the City agency of Flame-Decontamination and Refurbishing.

Newlyn said: "You're going to have them burn out the old woman's cubicle? You're going to let them set fire to all this stuff she's made?"

"She's done with these things, Newlyn. Somebody else should have access to what she can't use anymore. Even though this is Level 8, there are people waiting to live here. People from the level beneath us."

"Maybe they'd like it the way she has it now."

"Grow up," I said.

He wouldn't talk to me through the waiting that followed. He wouldn't talk to me when the glissadors came with their silent cart to carry Mz Almira Longhope's corpse through the murky corridors to the pneumatic scaffolding that would drop her to the waste converters on Level 9. He remained silent through the waiting that followed the glissadors' departure.

And when the men from F-D&R came into the cubicle with their canisters of the bactericidal combustgens, and their flame-suits, and their unbelieving goggled-over eyes, Newlyn cut his own eyes in reprimand and stalked out. He went into the corridor—went with blatant contempt for my colloquy with these men—and waited outside in the smoky halflight that drifted there. I explained the situation to the men from F-D&R. I gave directions. They nodded their insectlike heads. My explanation done, I went into the silent corridor and, with considerable difficulty, found Newlyn leaning in a crimson shadow against the opposite wall. I said something, but he wouldn't talk to me.

"All right," I said. "I'm going up. You can do what you like."

The *tap-tap-tap* of my footfalls was overwhelmed, just then, by the carnivorous *whooshing* of the F-D&R hand-torches. The corridor filled with this noise, and the tightly closed panel of cubicle 502 gave me the momentary illusion that the panel itself was glowing with unnatural heat, unnatural light. I hesitated briefly. Then I resumed walking. Seconds later, it became apparent that another series of footfalls was echoing my own, albeit in a reluctant and irregular way: *taptap tap taptaptap.*

3 / *The Hoisterjacks*

In the domed Cities (not simply in Atlanta, but in all the Urban Nuclei) there exist among the affluent surfacesiders, particularly among the adolescent boys of the wealthy and/or enfranchised, a significant few who have more leisure and more adrenalin than they can intelligently deal with. These few release their energy and defile their time in inutile pursuits that frequently terrorize the innocent, the unprepared, the preoccupied. They do not pick pockets. They do not engage in vandalism. They do not kill.

Instead, they practice the grotesque art of instilling a wholly meaningless terror in all those whom they assault with mad gestures and mad nylon-distorted faces. These boys—and, sadly, these few perverse adult males—go by the name of *hoisterjacks,* primarily because of their inclination to leap out of the darkness of the catacombs, to cling reasonlessly to the crystalline face of a lift-tube, arms full out, fingers gripping the maintenance handles on either side of the lift-tube door, and to scream like ravening hyenas as they press their already misaligned features against the glass.

One can in no way make adequate psychological preparation for the coming of a hoisterjack—even if one sees him beforehand.

I had entered the central concourse on Level 8, the concourse leading to the lift-station from which we had earlier disembarked, when I became aware of an echo on the tiles. An echo in addition to Newlyn's tentative *taptaptaptapping.* The echo was coming to me from the direction in which I moved, not from behind me. I looked down the ill-lit corridor, through the haze of red light. I saw the deeper glimmering of the lift-station and the translucent outline of the waiting lift-tube itself. I thought the cylinder's presence a fine piece of luck; we would not have to wait for transportation—and I would not have to make inane conversation to cover the depressing childishness of Newlyn's funk.

Then I saw, or believed I saw, two wraithlike figures cross the glimmering backdrop of the lift-station and disappear into an auxiliary hallway. I could not be sure. I paid little heed.

When I reached the lift-tube, I entered and held my thumb on the thin silver operating panel so that the door would not close. From out of the fog of halflight Newlyn came. He entered the cylinder and stood to one side, away from me. I did not remove my thumb from the operating panel.

"Let go of it," Newlyn said. "Send us up."

"What do you mean, 'Let go of it?' Who are you talking to?" Newlyn didn't answer. I repeated my self-defeating straightline: *"Who are you talking to, Newlyn?"*

"A bigshot *fire*man. A burnheaded topsider."

He spoke with such incredible malice, enunciating each consonant and each vowel as if they would carve flaming signs in the air, that I could say nothing. My thumb was on the panel; the door remained open. At last, gathering a little strength against my embarrassment, I said: "You knew what we had to do. And what we found in Almira Longhope's cubicle didn't make any difference. In fact, it deserved the combustgens and the spray even more than the ordinary furnishings of one of these places. What a waste, Newlyn! That sort of thing, that sort of crap, has to be burned out, cut away, buried. Everyone goes through that, Newlyn."

Yates' son sprang toward me and knocked my hand away from the control panel. The glass door slid into place. I dropped the old woman's blue ledger.

Then a number of things happened simultaneously.

A huge shadow leaped at us from the corridor and affixed itself to the surface of the lift-tube. Another shadow, less quick, fell away behind the first and disappeared as the lift-tube began, seemingly of its own accord, to ascend. An hysterical, mocking scream pierced the thin wall of glass that contained the boy and me.

And then (beneath the terrifying scream) another sound: Newlyn was trying to quench the sobs that rose in his throat. Unsuccessfully.

"It doesn't have to be—" he said. "It doesn't have to be . . . to be . . . unless you make it—"

I'm afraid that I pushed him. He was leaning into my chest,

and all my attention had shifted from him to the droop-lipped, acromegalic hoisterjack who clung to our lift-tube, leering, insupportably leering.

I shoved Newlyn aside and began pounding on the glass between me and the hoisterjack's hooded face. I wanted him to lose his grip. I wanted him to fall down the terminal shaft to the concrete of Level 9, there to split and pulp open like an overripe radish. I wanted to murder his iconoclasm and turn his impudence to bile.

Then I felt a fist against the side of my head and heard Newlyn shouting and sobbing at once: "Leave him alone, you bastard! Leave him alone!"

We grappled. The boy struck me again. I pushed him down. He came back and pummeled my chest. Now I realized exactly what I was doing, and the pain that it gave me could not have been more real, more cruel, more excruciating. I knew that we would not go combcrawling with each other this weekend, nor any weekend to come. I struck Newlyn solidly under the chin, and it was like striking myself.

He crumpled and sat on the crystalline floor, making low noises.

The lift-tube continued to ascend. I picked up Almira Longhope's ledger. I raised my eyes. The hoisterjack clinging to our little prison was grinning at me, grinning at me in cryptic triumph.

2045

Interlude: Volplaning Heroes

By the time of the Bondville riots in the early Forties, the glissador corps—established in 2008 as a kind of subterranean Pony Express—had become to a great many discontented urban youth a symbol of nose-thumbing independence and sassy *savoir-faire*. It was one of the few such symbols remaining to these young people. Even the fact that the establishment sanctioned and supported the corps failed to tarnish the image of these graceful quicksilver messengers. In their jumpsuits and glierboots, speeding self-propelled through the catacombs of the hive, the glissadors embodied—even apotheosized—the seemingly expatriated virtues of freedom and self-sufficiency. It was impossible not to admire them.

Even the Council/Conclave came to recognize the double-edged nature of the glissador corps' mystique. On the one hand, selfless service to the hive dwellers. On the other, the championing of unspoken resentments in a language of pure physical exaltation that flouted all authority. Although the City could technically take credit for the services rendered by the glissador corps, it could scarcely brook the maddening because impalpable insolence of its members. Worse, most of the glissadors were black. They communicated among themselves in an impenetrable patois of body signs, glances, and slang. Who could say what they were up to? The Retrenchment Edicts, then, contained several statutes devoted to monitoring their leisure activities and introducing a more representative cross-section of the population into their ranks.

The mystique of the glissador corps did not, however, diminish. Five years before midcentury only a handful of whites were members, and all had attained their tryouts through legislative manipulation. Then they had had to prove themselves in strenuous tests of concourse-running, swing-pivoting, and other forms of practical glierbatics. In this way the corps successfully resisted any and all attempts to dilute their ranks with mediocrities, of whatever color or political persuasion. Too, the First Councilor and his advisors understood that they dare not tamper too much with the glissadors, for they had long been the pantherine darlings of the hive. They were sleek, volplaning heroes.

But even if you were a glissador, even if you partook of that group's indisputable charisma, you were still a vulnerable human being with few more emotional resources than the next person and just as many acute and terrifying needs. You sought shelter, contact, even love, and you were freshly amazed by the complex strategies with which a fellow seeker could reduce the possibilities of life to a sad and threadbare concept of honor. . . .

CHAPTER FOUR

The Samurai and the Willows

1 / Basenji and Queequeg

She called him Basenji because the word was Bantu but had a Japanese ring, at least to her. It was appropriate for other reasons, too: he was small, and doglike, and very seldom spoke. No bark to him at all; not too much bite, either. And he, for his part, called her Queequeg (when he called her anything) because at first he could tell that the strangeness of it disconcerted her, at least a little. Later her reaction to this name changed subtly, but the significance of the change escaped him and he kept calling her by it. After a time, Basenji and Queequeg were the only names they ever used with each other.

"Basenji," she would say, harping on her new subject, "when you gonna bring one of them little bushes down here for our cyoob'cle?"

"They're not bushes," he would answer (if he answered). "They're bonsai: B.O.N.S.A.I. Bonsai."

More than likely, she would be standing over him when she asked, her athletic legs spread like those of a Nilotic colossus and her carven black face hanging somewhere above him in the stratosphere. Small and fastidious, he would be sitting on a reed mat in his sleeper-cove, where she intruded with blithe innocence, or in the wingback chair in the central living area. He would be reading on the reed mat (a pun here that she would never appreciate) or pretending, in the wingback, to compose a poem, since ordinarily she respected the sanctity of these pastimes. In any case, he would not look up—even though Queequeg's shadow was ominous, even though the smell coming off her legs and stocking-clad body was annoyingly carnal. By the Forty-Seven Ronin, she was big. Did she have to stand in front of him like that, her shadow and her smell falling on him like the twin knives of death and sex? Did she?

"Well," she would say, not moving, "they cute, those bushes. Those bonsai." And then she would grin (though he wouldn't look up to see it), her big white teeth like a row of bleached pinecone wings.

They shared a cubicle on Level 9 in the domed City, the Urban Nucleus of Atlanta. Basenji was Simon Fowler. Queequeg was Georgia Cawthorn. They were not related, they were not married, they were not bound by religious ties or economic necessity. Most of the time they didn't particularly like each other.

How they had come to be cubiclemates was this: Simon Fowler was thirty-eight or -nine, a man on the way down, a nisei whose only skills were miniature landscaping and horticulture. Georgia Cawthorn was eighteen and, as she saw it, certainly only a temporary resident of the Big Bad Basement, the donjon keep of the Urban Nucleus. Fowler, it seemed, was trying to bury himself, to put eight levels of concrete (as well as the honeycombing of the Dome) between himself and the sky. She, on the other hand, was abandoning the beloved bosom of parents and brothers, who lived in one of those pre-Evacuation "urban renewal" slums still crumbling into brick dust surface-side. And thus it was that both Simon Fowler and Georgia Cawthorn had applied for living quarters *under,* he perversely specifying Level 9 (having already worked down from the Towers and four understrata), she ingenuously asking for whatever she could get. A two-person cubicle fell vacant on Level 9. The computer-printed names of Georgia Cawthorn and Simon Fowler headed the UrNu Housing relocation list, and the need for a decision showered down on them like an unannounced rain (the sort so favored by the City's spontaneity-mad internal meterologists). Georgia didn't hesitate; she said yes at once. Simon Fowler wanted an umbrella, a way out of the deluge; but since the only out available involved intolerable delay and a psychic house arrest on the concourses of 7, he too had said yes. They met each other on the day they moved in.

They had now lived together for four months. And most of the time they didn't like each other very much, although Queequeg had tried. She tried harder than he did. She had taken an interest in Basenji's work, hadn't she? She had asked about those little trees he nurtured, wired, shaped, and worried over in his broken-down greenhouse surfaceside. And they were pretty, those bonsai: Basenji really knew how to wire up a bush. Queequeg had first seen them about two months ago, when she had gone into the shop to discover her cubiclemate in his "natch'l environment." Which was more than Basenji had ever done. He didn't give gyzym, he didn't, that she was a glissador, one of those lithe human beings who cruised the corridors of the hive on silent ball bearings inset in the soles of their glierboots. No, sir. He didn't give gyzym.

"How come, Basenji, you don' come see me, where I work?"

This time he answered, almost with some bite: "Dammit, Queequeg, you're in this corridor, then in that. How would I find you?"

"You could come to H.Q. To glizador-dizpatch."

A foreign language she spoke. And he said, "Not me. Your rollerskating friends close in on me."

"Which ones? Ty?"

"All of them. You're rink-refugees, Queequeg, fugitives from a recess that's never ended." And then he wouldn't answer anymore, that would be all she could pull from him.

It was probably lucky that the shift-changes kept them apart so much. They weren't really compatible, they weren't the same sort of people at all. Being cubiclemates was an insanity that they usually overcame by minor insolences like calling each other Basenji and Queequeg. That was their communication.

In fact, though the name had at first hurt and bewildered her (she had had to ask Ty Kosturko, a white boy apprenticing with her, what it meant), Georgia Cawthorn now knew that it was the only thing that kept her from falling on Simon Fowler's diminutive person and pounding his head against the floor a time or two. But for Queequeg, but for that insulting, mythopoeic nickname, she would have long ago harpooned her sullen little florist.

2 / *The Kudzu Shop*

Georgia/Queequeg, two days after the argument (if you could call it an argument) during which she had protested his never looking in on *her,* tried again. After the glissadors' shift-changing, after a sprayshower in their otherwise empty cubicle, she rode a lift-tube surfaceside and angled her way through the pedestrian courts leading to Basenji's shop.

Why I makin' myse'f a fool? she wondered. She didn't have any answers, she just let her long body stride past the ornamental fountains and the silver-blue reflecting windows of the New Peachtree. Distractedly swinging the end of her chain-loop belt, she examined herself in the windows: a woman, Zuluesque maybe, but no less a female for her size.

Simon Fowler's hothouse lay beyond New Peachtree in an uncleared tenement section much like the one she had grown up in (Bondville, across town). It was a shabby structure wedged between collapsing ruins, some of the useless glass panels in the roof broken out or crazed with liquescent scars. No wonder that her doggy little man kept moving down. Who'd walk into a place like Basenji's to buy a hydroponic rose for their most favorite bodyburner, much less something expensive like a ceiling basket or a gardenia bouquet? She didn't even know why *she* was punishing herself by seeking out the little snoot. Hadn't she already done this once? Wasn't that enough?

Maybe it was the willow he'd shown her. She wanted to see it again as much as she wanted to see him. Shoot, she didn't want to see him at all. *Tang,* the bell went: *ting tang.*

Moist flowers hung from the walls; ferns stuck out their green tongues from every corner; potted plants made a terra cotta fortress in the middle of the floor. And the last time she had come in, Basenji's vaguely oriental face had hung amidst all this greenery like an unfired clay plate, just that brittle and brown. He had been at the counter fiddling with the bonsai willow. But today Queequeg found no one in the outer shop, only growing things and their heavy fragrances.

"Basenji!" she called. "Hey, you, Basenji!"

He came, slowly, out of the long greenhouse behind the

shop's business area. He was brushing dirt from his hands, dirt and little sprigs of moss.

"You again," he said. "What do you want?"

"You sweet, Basenji. You damn sweet."

"What do you want?" He didn't call her Queequeg. That wasn't a good sign; no, sir. Not a good sign at all.

She thought a minute, hand on hip, her green wraparound clinging to the curve of her stance. She was a head taller than he. "I wanna see that little bush you had out here last time."

"You saw it last time, you know. I'm busy."

"You busy. You also ain' no easy man to do bidness with, Basenji. I thinkin' 'bout buyin' that bush. What do you think of that?"

"That you probably won't be able to afford it."

"I a saver, Basenji. Since I come on bidness, you boun' to show me what I come to see. You has to."

"That willow's worth—"

"Uh-uh," she said. "No, sir. I gonna see it before you sen' me packin' with yo' prices."

What could he do? A black Amazon with grits in her mouth and something a little, just a little, more substantial than that beneath her scalp cap of neo-nostalgiac cornrows: elegant, artificial braidwork recalling an Africa that probably no longer existed. (The same went for his mother's homeland, the very same.) Poor Basenji. These were the very words he thought as he stoically motioned Queequeg around the counter: Poor Basenji. He had even begun to call himself by the name she had given him.

3 / Pages from a Notebook

This docility, this acquiescence, he despised in himself. Earlier that morning he had taken out the notebook in which he sometimes recorded his responses to the stimuli of his own emotions; he had opened it to a pair of familiar pages. On the top shelf of the counter around which he had just led Queequeg, the notebook lay open to these pages. This is what, long before moving to Level 9, Simon Fowler had written there:

*   *   *

• *Bushido is the Way of the Warrior. But our own instinctive bushido has been bred out of us. Most of us have forgotten what horror exists outside the Dome to keep us inside. Whatever it is, we have not fought it.*

• *Seppuku is ritual suicide, reserved for warriors and those who have earned the right to die with dignity. Hara-kiri' (belly cutting) is a vulgarity; to commit it, and to think of it as belly cutting, one must be either a woman or a losel.*

• *My father died as a direct result of alcoholism. "Insult to the brain," said the final autopsy report. This is the same meaningless euphemism doctors listed as the cause of Dylan Thomas' death, over 90 years ago in the City that is now the Urban Nucleus of New York.*

• *The ancient Japanese caste of the samurai despised poetry as an effeminate activity. Sometimes I view it that way too, especially when I am writing it. A samurai would also despise the sort of introspection I practice in this notebook.*

• *Maybe not. The great shogun Iyeyasu (1542-1616) attempted a reformation of the habits of the samurai; he encouraged them to develop their appreciation of the arts. Iyeyasu died in the same year that William Shakespear died.*

• *Witness the example of that 20th century samurai and artist, Yukio Mishima. Can he not be said to be the latter-day embodiment of Iyeyasu's attempts at gentling his nation's warriors? Or was he instead the embodiment of the militarization of the poet?*

• *Bonsai is the art of shaping seedlings, that would grow to full size to an exquisite, miniature environment. Bonsai is also the name of any tree grown by this method. I am an expert at such shaping.*

• *Each citizen of the Urban Nucleus is an artifact of a bonsai process more exacting than the one I am master of.*

Our environment is a microcosm. We are little. We are symmetrical. But wherein are we beautiful?

• *Seymour Glass, who loved the haiku, who lived when a man could let a cat bite his left hand while gazing at the full moon, is the patron saint of suicides. He was not, however, a samurai.*

• *Although no courtesan, my mother was mistress of the geisha graces: poetry, dance, song, and all the delicate works of hand. Kazuko Hadaka, a Japanese. Kazuko gave me a gentleness not in my father. And my docility.*

• *I gave my mother to a monolithic institution, where she failed and died. Cause of death: "Insult to heart." Day 53 of the Month Winter, Year 2038, in the New Calendar designation.*

• *Yukio Mishima: "To samurai and homosexual the ugliest vice is femininity. Even though their reasons for it differ, the samurai and the homosexual do not see manliness as instinctive but rather as something gained only from moral effort."*

• *I have heard bonsai spoken of as "Slow sculpture." That it is. But so is the process by which the Dome shapes its inhabitants. Are we any more aware of the process than my bonsai are conscious of their protracted dwarfing? Or do my sculptures, as do I, think and feel?*

• *And what of those who are neither warriors nor gayboys? Does it not also require of them moral effort to establish the certainty of their manhood? If so, what regimen must these others undertake?*

• *Easier than discovering the answer, much easier, is to sink through the circles of our Gehenna. Can the willow ignore its wiring?*

• *Bushido, seppuku, samurai, bonsai, haiku, geisha. In this catalogue, somewhere amid the tension among its concepts: the answer. How to sort it out? how to sort it out?*

All of this was written in Simon Hadaka Fowler's tight, up-and-down cursive in black ink. A roll of florist's tape lay on the corner of the right-hand page of the open notebook. Thumbprints and smudges covered the two pages like official notations on a birth certificate. No one but Basenji, of course, would have supposed the notebook to be there.

4 / Layering a Willow

So Basenji, that doggy little man, and Queequeg, the lady harpoonist, went on through the greenhouse, whose various counters and table trays were all overhung by fluorescent lights, and out to the open patio between the collapsing buildings: Queequeg unaware of what was going on in her cubiclemate's hangdog head, Basenji uncertain as to what this persistent Zulu wanted of him. He led her to the rough wooden table where he had been working when she came in. He sat down. She looked around, noticing the shelves against the patio's shoulder-high walls and the little potted trees sitting on these shelves. In spite of the rusted fire escapes and hovering brick dust outside, everything in the patio compound was spick-and-span.

Then she saw the bonsai on the table. "That the one," she said, letting her shadow drop on him like a weight. "That the one I saw out front last time I come. Hey, what you doin' to it?"

"Layering it."

"You took it out o' that pot, that blue shiny one," she accused, leaning over his shoulder. Then: "What this layerin', Basenji?"

He explained that he was trying to establish two more of the sinuously stunted trees before the year was out and that you couldn't leave the mother tree in an expensive ornamental Chinese pot such as she had last seen it in; not, anyhow, if you were tying off tourniquets of copper wire below the nodes where you wanted the new roots to develop. Since Queequeg, for once, kept silent, he finished the last tourniquet and began wrapping the willow's layered branches in plastic.

"That the one," Queequeg said, "I wanna buy."

"Can't now, Missy Queequeg, even if you could afford it. This is going to take a while. But next year we'll have three trees instead of one, all of them fine enough for pots like the blue Chinese one."

"We?"

"The shop," he corrected. "The Kudzu Shop."

"I see." Her shadow, however she had managed to drape it over him, suddenly withdrew. She stopped by the shelves against the back wall, and he looked up to see her in front of them. "You got more of them bushes right here," she said. "Five of 'em."

"Only one of them's a willow, though." Skipping the willow, he named the trees across the top shelf. "The others are a maple, a Sargent juniper, a cherry tree, and another juniper." He had potted each one in a vessel appropriate to the shape and variety of the tree it contained. Or, rather, had repotted them into these new vessels after taking the bonsai over from his mother's care.

"Well, you sell me this other one, then. This willow like the first one."

"What you want with that *bush?*" he said, mocking her. "What you want with a runty ole willow, Queequeg? You gonna rollerskate with a bush in yo' arms?"—He could bite if he wanted.

It wasn't a bite to her; she ignored it. "Man, I gonna bring that tree into our cyoob'cle where you won' let me bring it. When it mine, I do with it what I want."

"These are bonsai," he told her then, as if she were a customer instead of his annoying cubiclemate. "They're real trees, not toys. Don't be deceived by their size. Just like any real tree, they belong outside. You can't keep them in any of the understrata and expect them to survive, much less the ninth one. That's why they're usually outside on the patio here, instead of in the shop or greenhouse."

"Look up," she said contemptuously.

He stared at her without comprehension.

"I say look up, Basenji, look up."

He did what she asked and saw a faintly golden honeycombing of plexiglass and steel; no sky, just the underside of the Dome. All the tumble-down buildings seemed to funnel his gaze to this astonishing revelation.

"What you call *outside?* When you *ever* been outside?"

"Nobody's been outside," he said. "Nobody who was born

here, anyway. Not outside the tunnels between Cities. The requisite, Missy Queequeg, is *weather,* and that we've got. Underneath there's only air conditioning or dry heat. In three days you'd kill any bonsai you took down there, maybe that willow especially."

"Well, I don' have to keep it down there all the time, you know. So I ready now. How much you askin'?"

"Two hundred dollars."

"What kind o' dollars?"

"UrNu dollars. Two hundred UrNu dollars."

"You crazy. You think this bush a money tree, Basenji?" Incredulous,she canted her hip, leaned forward, and looked at the willow as if to determine if its bark were gold plate.

"I've had that tree thirteen years. My mother started it, and she had it as least twenty before that. The others—the junipers, the cherry, the maple—are that old, or older. One or two of them may have been started even before there was a Dome. Handed down to my mother from—"

"If hand-me-downs precious, I a millionaire, Basenji." She moved to the greenhouse entrance. "You mighty right," she said from the doorway. "Without I auction off all my brothers' ole socks and nightshirts, I can't afford that bonsai."

She left him on the patio sitting over the unpotted and clumsily trussed willow. When he heard the *ting-tang* of the bell in the outer shop, he began to whistle.

5 / *The Interpretation of Dreams*

Simon/Basenji sometimes had a bad dream, not frequently but often enough. Before he had moved down to Level 9, the dream had been persistent about rubbing down his nervous limbs with night sweat: every three or four days the images would get a screening. But in the last four months, having reached bottom, he had apparently developed a degree of immunity to the dream. Once a week, no more.

Anyhow, here is the dream:

Always he finds himself on the floor of his greenhouse, under one of the table trays filled with fuchsia or rose geraniums. Like

Tom Thumb, he has no more height than a grown man's opposed digit. When he looks up, the bottom of the wooden table seems as far away as the honeycombing of the Dome when he is awake. Always he realizes that he has been hiding under the table waiting for night. And as the City's artificial night slides into place, he creeps out of the hothouse and onto the patio where we have just seen him layering a willow and talking with Queequeg.

A small orange moon hangs under the Dome, and the "sky" behind and around it is like a piece of velvet funeral bunting. No glow at all from the ordinarily fluorescent buildings beyond both his own patio and the collapsed tenements surrounding it.

Basenji wears silken robes, a kind of kimono. He resembles a musician or a poet. The robes are cumbersome, and he would like to discard them but discovers that the material is seamless.

He stands on a piece of brick tile and stares at the wooden shelves ranged above him against the back wall of the patio. So small is he, the shelves look to him like stone ledges on a mountain face. On the highest shelf sit the willow trees in their glazed pots; not only the willows, the other bonsai besides. The orange moon (how did it come to be there?) provides just enough light to make this monumental undertaking possible. The seamless kimono, cinched at his waist with a golden strip of silk, several times almost sends him tripping over its skirts to the patio stones. This fate is what combcrawlers and hoisterjacks refer to as the "glory of splatterdom." Incongruous as it is, this phase comes to Basenji's dreaming mind and offends by its slangy graphicness.

Not solely because it mocks death, though that has its part.

Shaking and damp on the topmost shelf of his patio, the arduous climb at last done, Basenji turns and surveys his holdings. How meager they are, even for a man the stature of his dream self. Now his robes seem even more ridiculous, sweat soaked as they are, and he tries again to tear them off. They won't come, they bind him in.

He succeeds, however, in tearing away from his garment the golden sash about his waist. This he wraps several times about his hands. The sash has tassels at regular intervals along its bottom edge: an overpretty belt. Basenji, perhaps summoning energy from his sleeping body, tries to rend it to pieces.

Thwarted, he ceases and begins walking back and forth along the shelf, looking at the miniature trees.

Finally he settles upon the older of the two willows, the one with the more artfully sculpted form, and expends his last reserves of strength and will getting into the Chinese pot and knotting the sash in a way he thinks appropriate to his purpose.

After which, using the sash, he hangs himself from the willow: a little man dangling unnoticed beneath foliage so delicate and veil-like that a picture of impact-upon-concrete rises before his backward-rolling eyeballs as if in reproach. What warrior has ever killed himself in so womanish a way? It is too painful, this thought. He is a Judas to himself.

But then the limb of the bonsai snaps: Basenji falls on his kimono-clad backside into the pot he sweated so hard to clamber over, just to get to a place where he could hang himself. Now this. Lying there bruised, the broken willow branch attached to him by a golden umbilical, he finds himself shamelessly weeping, whether out of frustration or out of remorse at having disfigured the bonsai, he cannot tell. He hopes that a robin or a cardinal (species officially sheltered inside the Dome) will come along to sever his bond to the willow and to devour him, piece by grateful piece.

High overhead, through cascading leaves, the little orange moon blanks out: an extinguished jack-o'-lantern.

After this, Basenji invariably woke up, sweating his inevitable sweat. It happened less often now that he had hit bottom, but it still happened. What he needed was a Joseph, or a Sigmund Freud, to unravel the symbolism. Not really. He could do it himself, he was fairly sure, if he genuinely wanted to. But he didn't. He genuinely didn't want to. It frightened him too much, the image-ridden virus of his nightmare.

Nevertheless, two or three pages in his battered notebook were devoted to an account very much like the one given here.

6 / Ty Kosturko

Outside the Kudzu Shop, she thought: Two hundred UrNus, that baa-ad news. And Basenji, he crazy.

Well, she wasn't going to go back down to their cubicle to wait until he came dragging in with the next shift-change (which he could observe or not observe as he liked, anyway). If she didn't have 200 earnies to squander on a potted fancy-pants bush, she at least had pay-credits to go shopping with, and she was sure enough going to prom a few of them for some kind of brightener; a compensatory purchase, something to make up for Basenji's nastiness. Then, afterwards, there was eurythmics for all the glissadors in the Level 9 Coenotorium. She just might go. It was pretty good sometimes, though about an hour of it was enough for her.

Georgia/Queequeg got back to New Peachtree as quickly as she could. Lizardly fellows, more evil-mean than the hoister-jacks in the hive, hung out in the City's crumble-down corners, and she didn't like the looks of some of the stoopsitters she was seeing sidelong. Basenji, in a rare moment, had told her once that he had been beaten up one evening leaving the Kudzu Shop; but since he never carried any money or kept any in his greenhouse building, the stoopjockeys and thugboys didn't bother him anymore. That anecdote, related offhandedly, had impressed Queequeg: no bite maybe, but ballsy enough to go in and out of a neighborhood worse than Bondville. In fact, she'd never been scared in Bondville, not the twitchy, uneasy way she was here.

Even so, she'd come to see Basenji twice, hadn't she? Right through the brick dust, and the potholes, and the unemployable street lizards (both black and white) "sunning" themselves on old porches. But no more. No, sir, not never again.

Back on New Peachtree, Queequeg slowed down. Her long stride turned into a kind of graceful baby-stepping as she turned this way and that in front of the store windows, looking at the merchandise on display behind the tinted glass, looking at her own tall body superimposed on the merchandise, a beautiful gaudy phantom about to strut sensually through the glass. Yoo-rythmics, she thought bitterly. Well, hell, she'd probably go anyhow. She was just getting used to it. Shopping first, though.

Queequeg went into the colossal, perfume-scented escalator lobby of the Consolidated Rich's building, the City's biggest department store and one of the few still in operation from pre-Evacuation times. The Urban Nucleus owned it now, though, and the building didn't look very much like the original one, a huge picture of which hung in a revolving metal frame over the shoppers crowded into the escalator lobby. Queequeg glanced at it perfunctorily, then picked her escalator and rode up to a mezzanine level high enough over the lobby to give her a good view of two of the adjacent pedestrian courts outside.

People preening and strutting like pigeons, which, once, the City had almost got rid of.

Standing at the mezzanine rail, Queequeg noted the tingling in her feet: high, high up. And she lived down, down, down, almost forty meters under the concrete. Not forever, though; one day she was going to ride an escalator right out of there. . . .

When she turned around, she saw a willowy white boy leaning back on a doodad counter and grinning at her like a jack-o'-lantern.

"Ty!"

"Hey, Queequeg," Ty Kosturko said. He had called her that, too, ever since explaining about Herman Melville and white whales. He was wearing a matching trousers and shirt, with cross-over-color arms and legs: pink and white: apple blossoms. Loose and gangly, he was as tall and as athletic as she, but less visibly muscular.

They had been glissadors for about the same period of time, seven or eight months, though he was one of the few whites in their ranks and had got his appointment by badgering his father, an influential ward representative, to exercise his influence. The boy had bragged of, or elaborated on, his threatening his old man with going hoisterjack if he, Ty, couldn't put on glierboots: it was all he wanted. And so the old man had capitulated; better his son a menial than a maniac.

"What you doin' here, Ty?"

"Same as you, I'd imagine."

"Yeah? What you think I up to, then?"

"Down-chuting your pay-credits, since you're so much like me. That's what I'm doing, getting out from under my money."

She showed her wide teeth. "Oh, I tryin', I tryin'. But I ain' got so much I can prom for anythin' I want." She told him of attempting to buy Basenji, her cubiclemate's, miniature willow. "No way I gonna down-chute 200 earnies, Ty. I savin' for to say goodbye to 9."

Ty was one of the only three or four glissadors to live surfaceside, an amenity owing to the fact that he rented from his parents. Therefore, the boy commiserated. "I know what you need, then. Come with me."

He took her hand and led her through the many counters on the mezzanine, moving so gracefully that she had to look at his feet to convince herself that he wasn't wearing glierboots even now. They climbed a stairway hidden behind the men's and women's lounges, and she tried to strangle her mirth as Ty Kosturko, leading her through the tie-dyed ceiling drapes and batik wall banners, affected the sleazy nonchalance of a dick on shoplifter lookout. Finally, Queequeg giggling, Ty nonchalantly rubbernecking, they got to a room with a rounded portal over which were these words: *Paintings & Prints.* Into this make-believe kingdom he led her, a gallery of white wallboards and simulated mahogany parquetry.

"If you can't get a tree for your cubicle," Ty said, "try a print. One of the Old Masters. Nothing better for flinging off a funk. Every two or three months I buy or trade one in."

And Georgia/Queequeg, who had never before been in the *Paintings & Prints* gallery of Consolidated Rich's, walked in awe among the wallboards. Here, since abstract expressionism had fallen into disrepute, were all the Old Masters of pre-Evacuation representational art: Whistler, Homer, Cassat, Albert Ryder, Remington, Thomas Hart Benton, Grant Wood, Edward Hopper, the three Wyeths, and others whom even Ty had no knowledge of. Even so, he dropped all the names he could and impressed Queequeg by telling her who had painted what, even when she covered with her hand the title plates on the frames. Only two or three times did he miss, and each miss he accompanied with gargoylesque grimaces.

"Damn," Queequeg said. "You good, Tyger."

Ty Kosturko bowed. Then he took her hand again and led her to another of the partitionlike wallboards. "Now this," he said, a sweep of the hand indicating the prints on display here, "is what you're looking for, Queequeg, this is what you can take downstairs to homey up your humble abiding place."

Queequeg, she didn't say him nay.

7 / *Appreciating Norman Rockwell*

About four hours after Queequeg visited him, Simon/Basenji left the Kudzu Shop, locked its doors, and made his way to the central lift-terminal on New Peachtree. It was the weekend, Friday evening, and he carried with him his battered notebook.

A false twilight was descending, by design, on the towers of the Urban Nucleus, towers looming over Basenji like shafts of frozen air. People were crowding toward the transport-terminal, and he added himself to the flow of pedestrians, virtually riding the current they made into the vault of the terminal.

In the hall fifteen crystal lift-tubes went up and down the levels of Atlanta. The air was smoky here, wine-colored. Every upturned face shone with nightmarish radiance. Pandemonium, Basenji thought. He half expected Beelzebub and a few of his cohorts to start pitchforking people into the lift-tubes, whose gliding capsules glowed with red emergency lights. Up and down the capsules went, packed with shadows instead of human beings.

Basenji found his way into a cordoned lane to a descent capsule and at last got aboard, with nearly a dozen others. "Sardine time," two teen-agers sang, "sardine time." Then Basenji felt the catacombs rise up around him like a hungry mouth. "Sardine time," the boy sang. They were all being swallowed. Like little fish...

Once down, it took Basenji, threading his way among disembarked passengers from other lift-tubes, almost ten minutes to reach his own cubicle. Standing outside it, he heard Queequeg laughing and an adolescent male voice saying, "That's right, you know. Absolutely on-target. I'm the foremost expert on pre-Evacuation magazine art in the whole cruisin' glissador corps, Atlanta or anywhere else."

Ty Kosturko. Friday night, and he had to share it with Ty Kosturko, the 21st Century's Kenneth Clark of popular culture. A boy who, when he wasn't wearing glierboots and uniform, dressed like a department store mannequin; who ooh'd and ah'd over his, Basenji's, Japanese figurines like a gourmet over well-simulated lobster Newburg. And his voice was so self-assuredly pontifical you could hear him right through the walls. Goodbye, Friday night.

Basenji put his thumb to the electric eye beside his entrance panel, which promptly slid back, admitting him. He stopped in the middle of the spartanly furnished central room. He placed his notebook on the back of the upholstered chair beside the door.

"Hey, Basenji," Queequeg said, turning from the opposite wall. She grinned at him.

"Hello, Mr Fowler," Ty Kosturko said. He called Georgia Queequeg but he didn't call Mr Fowler Basenji. Self-proclaimed expert or no, son of a ward rep or no, he at least had that much sense. But look at his clothes: pink and white: a lanky harlequin in drag.

"Look what I prommed for at Rich's today, Basenji. Ty, he holp me pick 'em out. Not too spensive, either." *Holp*. Plantation English, which was enjoying an unaccountable renascence among the City's blacks. "Come on now," Queequeg insisted. "Come look at 'em."

So Basenji crossed to the formerly naked wall and looked at the three prints they had affixed there, matted but unframed, with transparent wall tape. The prints were Norman Rockwells. They filled the cubicle with children, and loving parents, and the Apollo 11 Space team.

"Jes' ten earnies each," Queequeg said. "Which mean I don' have to auction off my brothers' ole socks. It all be paid for in two months, and you, you stingy Basenji, you gonna get to look at em too."

With Queequeg and Ty Kosturko on either side of him, Basenji felt like a matchbook between two tall, carven bookends. The lanky boy said, "The print on the left is called *New Kids in the Neighborhood*. It was commissioned by *Look* magazine in the late 1960s. The interesting thing about it is the way the composition's balanced, the moving van in the back kind of tying together the three white kids over here," pointing them out, "and the black boy and his little sister over here," sweeping his hand over to the black children. "Look at the way Rockwell's given the little girl a *white* cat, while the white kids have this *black* puppy sitting in front of them. That way, the confrontation's mirrored and at the same time turned around by the pets the children have."

"And what's the point of that?" Basenji asked.

"To show that the *color* on the two sides shouldn't make any difference. The painting has sociological significance for that period, you know. Rockwell was making a statement."

Basenji stared up at the print. "Cats and dogs," he said, "are completely different kinds of animals. Was the artist trying to suggest an innate...antipathy...between the children, as between cats and dogs?"

"Antipathy?" Queequeg said.

"No, Mr Fowler, you're trying to read too much into it now. The animals are just animals, a cat and a dog. An interpretation like yours would probably lead you to misconstrue Rockwell's intentions."

Basenji was silent. Then: "Well, go ahead. Tell me about the others."

"The one in the middle is the Four Freedoms series: *Freedom from Fear*. The one on the right shows you the first men to land on the Moon, with the NASA engineers and the American people behind them."

"But no cats or dogs," Basenji said. "Those men walked on it, and we can't even see it."

"Let's sit down so we can look at 'em easy," Queequeg said. "Forget 'bout the Moon." She and Ty Kosturko sat down on throwrugs while her cubiclemate lowered himself into the wingback. The notebook balanced on top slid down the chair's cushion. Basenji retrieved it and held it in his lap. Then the three of them stared, without speaking, at the prints.

Goodbye, Friday night. He hadn't been planning to do much with it, though. Go to his visicom console and read. Or try to make sense, in his notebook, of how he had come to a place where his privacy could be so effortlessly violated. Or maybe just sit and stare at a wall, a blank one.

Then Ty Kosturko said, "Come to the eurythmics with us, Mr Fowler. It's for glissadors, but you'll be our guest."

"Yeah," said Queequeg, touching his leg. "Otherwise, you jes' sit here all night thinkin' gloominess."

"No," Basenji said, earnestly shaking his head.

"Well, if you don't go," Ty Kosturko said, "we're not going to go either. We aren't going to let you sit here in solitary on Friday night. That's inhuman, Mr Fowler."

"No, it's all right."

"Inhyooman," Queequeg echoed her companion. "You ain' gonna sit here doin' nothin' on a Friday night. We won' let you."

So Simon/Basenji, not understanding why he had allowed himself to be so bullied, went with them to the Friday night eurythmics in the Level 9 Coenotorium.

8 / Eurythmics

In the Level 9 Coenotorium, which lay (it seemed) an infinity of concourses away from their cubicle, a hundred or so people moved about under shoddy Japanese lanterns: little orange moons, like decorations for a high-school dance. Most of the people were black, since most of the glissadors were black, and the lanterns filled the hall with a dismal orange smoke similar to the quality of light in the New Peachtree lift-terminal.

At the far end of the hall Simon/Basenji saw an elevated platform on which a man in white leotards demonstrated the proper eurythmic responses to the music of his accompanists, a flute player and a man sawing on a highly lacquered bull fiddle. The music had just enough melody to prevent its being censured as neo-avant-garde (a term even more ludicrous, Basenji thought, than the activities it was supposed to squelch). Ripples from the flute, reverberations from the bass...

Ty Kosturko led Queequeg and Basenji into the middle of the floor, where variously attired dancers surrounded them. Arms, legs, hips, bellies, and buttocks moved past Basenji in a stylized and regimented choreography. In fact, everything about these languidly swaying body parts was too damn deliberate. Planned. Everyone kept an eye cocked on the white ghost on the far platform, aping his well-tutored spasms.

"Is this eurythmics?" he asked Queequeg.

"Yeah. It ain' much, but it better than sittin' home. Some of 'em here even *likes* it. Come on now, you do it too." She began snaking her arms around her body, bending and then lengthening out her smooth naked legs. Ty, without touching or looking at her, did the same, his harlequin's body assuming and relinquishing so many odd postures that he, Basenji, was intimidated by its mechanicalness. "Come on," Queequeg insisted.

"I don't know—"

Ty Kosturko revolved toward him, very nearly brushing one of the ubiquitous paper lanterns. "Anybody can do this, Mr Fowler, it's all just mental, you know, and almost anyone can think." He did a premeditated butterflying movement with his arms and swam back to the little florist. "My father remembers the days of fission opera, renaissance swing, even terror-rock, when you could let the beast out and explode all over yourself without worrying about where the pieces'd land."

"Shoot, my brothers and me were *livin'* that a few months back. We'd jes' go out in the street and close it off and 'splode to somebody's ole records till the slum trolls and spoil-it squad come along and tell us to silent down." Without ceasing to gyrate, Queequeg chuckled. That was a human memory; you could almost feel homesick for old Bondville. Almost. "Us and the neighbors. Too many for the ole spoil-it squad to junk up in their jails."

"Yeah," Ty said. "Raggy music, abstract art, and free verse. Gone with the wind, my queen McQueequeg."

"I don' like that, that McQueequeg bidness, Ty. Anyhow, yo' own daddy, who say he 'member what it used to be, he one of them what voted it all out the door. He one good reason we got yoo-rythmics instead of music."

"I know that. And that's one good reason I'm a glissador instead of an accountant or an aspiring ad executive."

Basenji, forgotten in this exchange, walked over to a folding table in front of the hall's concessions booth and sat down. Bodies continued to hitch and snake and revolve past him, without any real expenditure of energy. No one threw back his head, no one pumped his knees, no one shimmied as if possessed. It was like watching a ballet performed by graceful wind-up toys, if that were possible. And Ty Kosturko looked like a sure choice to dance the part of Oberon, even though his competition was not inconsiderable.

Rock music, and atonal music as well. Abstract art. Free verse. And free-form video-feedback compositions. All gone with the wind.

Basenji didn't miss too many of these; his tastes ran in other directions. Nevertheless, he remembered when you couldn't walk down a surfaceside concourse without going by a row of imitation Mondrians and Pollocks. The Mondrians were there for their symmetry, the Pollocks for their vigor. Outside, in the parks and pedestrian courts, you could listen to people reciting Baraka, or Ishmael Reed, or maybe even their own unstructured verses; whereas today, if you dialed for the works of such people on your visicom console, the word PROSCRIBED rolled into place, and you could be sure that your key number had gone into the belly of a surfaceside computer. As for music, the Urban Nucleus itself had once sponsored, in the Omni, free retrospectives of artists like Schoenberg and the virtually deified Allman Brothers. Though never crushingly attended, these performances had always summoned genuine enthusiasts, and Basenji himself, on two different occasions, had gone to the atonal and dodecaphonic concerts. He remembered, too, a time when the Dome's citizens had access to the works of such early video experimenters as Campus and Emshwiller; programmed tapes to feed into your own visicom console. No more.

About eleven years ago—five years after the assassination of Carlo Bitler, a charismatic demagogue, and just one year after the disappearance of Bitler's wife—the Urban Council and the Conclave of Ward Representatives had together voted to remove the abstract paintings from public concourses, halt the outdoor poetry readings, and cease the funding of free concerts, except for those of designated classical works and contemporary popular music. There were simultaneous crackdowns on hand-operated duplicating machines, distributors of underground comix, wielders of portable video equipment, and unchartered, "fringe-riding" religious groups. Only the Hare-Krishna sect and the Orthodox Muslims, with histories of influence in the city going back to pre-Evacuation times, secured legal exemptions from this last stricture of the Council/Conclave's sweeping decree.

The year of these "Retrenchment Edicts" had been 2035, the same year that Simon Hadaka Fowler committed his mother to an UrNu geriatrics program. Three years later she had died. . . .

Since then, he had worked himself down from Tower housing, surfaceside to his cubicle on Level 9, *under:* it averaged out to a little better than a level a year. And now he was sitting at a folding table in the hive-people's Coenotorium watching the glissadors move about eurythmically under Japanese lanterns. Amazing, this turn in his life.

Although the bull fiddle continued to throb in a subsonic hinterland that he was dimly aware of, the flute abruptly stopped. Queequeg found him, and Ty (all fluttering apple blossoms) came trailing along behind her.

"You lef' us, Basenji," Queequeg said.

"I didn't know how to do that."

"Do you want to learn, Mr Fowler?"

"No," he said, looking up into the stratosphere where their heads always seemed to reside. "There are too many important things that I haven't learned yet." Implacably young, they stared down at him. "I'm more than twice as old as you two are," he added: a kind of apology.

Queequeg leaned down and pecked him on the cheek. "You right, Basenji," she said. "Anyhow, you done seen it. And I tired of it. Let's go on home. I fix us a drink."

Ty Kosturko tried to persuade them to remain, but, much to Basenji's quiet pleasure, Queequeg refused to be persuaded. "OK," Ty said. "Call me *mañana*, Mz Cawthorn."

Out in the murky corridors they walked side by side, she

striding smooth and silent, he newly self-conscious about his lack of stature, in a more acute way than he had been when all three of them had walked to the Coenotorium. Then the boy had balanced things a little.

But Queequeg, the lady harpoonist! Didn't the terrible fragrance of her, the smell of sweat-touched cologne and untrammeled woman, break over him like a *tsunami?* A tidal power set in motion not by the moon, but by the passions of vulcanism and earthquake! Anyhow, Queequeg's presence, her aura, diminished him to a cipher; he could not speak, even though their mutual silence, as much as her size and smell, was disarming. In the bleak corridors of Level 9, he was a samurai without a sword.

9 / Soulplaning

Georgia/Queequeg, she was damn glad to get away from that flute and fiddle, from the posturing zombie on the grandstand. It was OK for a while, but she didn't have Tyger-boy's knack of making what was "just mental" into a kinetic showplace for her instincts. She kept looking at what she was doing and wishing she could shake off her skin and emerge into an unclad rioting of the blood. To let the beast out, like even Ty said. Because he understood the other even if he could almost manage to bury his brain with the Friday night eurythmics. Shoot, they *all* understood the other, they were glissadors. And Ty, he could be sweet, he certainly could.

"You ain' sayin' much, Basenji," she said, after they had turned into a concourse perpendicular to the one to the Coenotorium.

"You aren't either, Queequeg."

"No, *I* was thinkin'. What you been up to, down there?" She grinned at him; he appeared to wince, just in the muscles of his face. So sensitive-crawly he couldn't take a bit of juicing, which was what he accused her of when she didn't whicker her nose off at one of his infrequent intellectual puns. Shoot, he only made them so she wouldn't get them, that was the point of his doing it. Whereas she wasn't trying to be nasty a bit. "I mean you been thinkin' too. What 'bout, Basenji?"

"About being a basenji, a little dog."

"No you ain'. I bet you wonderin' why I asked you to come to somepin I don' like myse'f."

"All right," he said agreeably.

"Well, I didn' ask you. Ty did. I jes' say Yeah to what he already asked. But I know why *he* done it."

"Why?" Now Basenji was just being polite, saying Why? because it was easier than jumping down on her with some rudeness. Well, she was going to tell him anyhow, he needed telling.

"Ty worried 'bout you, Basenji. He say you workin' nigger-hard to get as far down as you can, and you done got as far unner as this City gonna let you. Nex' step: the waste converters over on Concourse 13. But how and when you get there, that up to you, Ty say."

Basenji laughed; a sort of snort.

"So he asked you along. When we home, you make me 'splain why we keep goin' to them sickly yoo-rythmics. You hear?"

They walked the rest of the way to their cubicle without saying a word to each other, although Queequeg softly scatsang a bit and, once, wished out loud for her glierboots. Since a few of the apartments along the way had their panals slid back, she waved at the people she knew. Solidarity against hoisterjacks and down-from-up spoil-it squads.

Home, she fixed toddies (the air conditioning made it cool enough) and made Basenji sit down in his chair. A throwrug for her, her legs straight out before her like pillars of polished oak. Basenji was letting her determine his evening as he had never let her manipulate his time before. It was all guiltiness about the bonsai, she decided, that and maybe a little dose of the big head. After four months she had finally got him curious about something—even if, to be specific, it was only himself.

With the mug of hot liquor between his hands, he said, "You told me to make you explain why you and young Kosturko go to the eurythmics even though you're not enamored of it." He had a tic in one moist, narrow eye.

"You wanna hear that, Basenji?" If he did, maybe he wasn't so dragged out on himself after all.

And he said, "Please": a surprise.

"OK, then. Because we glizadors. They only twelve or fourteen of us on each level, you know that? Yeah. The City pick us 'cause we good—even Ty, whose daddy holp him get set up in the corps. They wouldn't've took him *only* because of who his daddy was. He can fly, Ty can. He belong on glierboots.

"Anyhow, we keep the unnerCity, the down-beneath part of it, together. We the Pony Express and the 707 airmail combined, we the fleet elite of New Toombsboro.

"In four months, jes' since I come down here, I been to the booondocks of this level and out again. I done run letters and packages 'tween ever' concourse. I been in on the dumpin' of twenny or so deaders down the waste converters, includin' one ole woman dressed like all in tinfoil and holdin' a baton so it wouldn' come loose. I skated through at least four gangs of them sockheaded hoisterjacks, and I gone up to substitute on other levels, too. We all do that, Basenji, and we fine at doin' it." Look at that Basenji, she thought; he listenin' to me, eye tic and all.

"Then one day the councilmen and ward reps, even the house niggers sittin' upstairs with 'em, say *No more tomtoms down there, no more axes and ivories,* and give us a yoo-rythmics program to chew on. Shoot, that don' kill us, we glizadors. We keep our heads on.

"Now, by *we* I really mean them what were glizadors in 2035 when the 'Trenchment E-dicts was passed. But that don' make no difference: a glizador's a glizador, even 'leven years later. So we—all of us, then and now—we went to what they gave us to go to. And some of us wooleye those council fellows by learnin' to like the bullshit they sen' down here for music."

Basenji said, "Are you sure they didn't 'wooleye' you, inducing you people to like the eurythmics? Wasn't that what the councilmen and ward reps wanted?"

"Nah. It may seem like it, but it ain'. They never wanted us to like it at all, they jes' wanted us to *do* it. But we knew what they was up to, we all the time knew—so we done beat their plan by likin' that stuff when we was s'posed to jes' do it."

"But you *don't* like it, Queequeg." Damn, he was listening almost closer than she wanted him to. A starved little slant-eye drinking his toddy and eating up her words: *smack, smack.*

"No. But it's tollable. I can stan' it 'cause I know I am a glizador. That make up for the music they done stole from us in '35."

"You were seven then," Basenji said. They were quiet. A moment later he leaned forward, and she could see the gray in his otherwise jet-black sideburns. "Don't you ever get tired?" he said. "Don't you ever get sick of going up and down the same ugly hallways? As if you were a rink-refugee forever?" He was asking about himself, really. About himself and her, too.

"No," she said. "No, I don'. You know what *volplane* mean?"

He shook his head.

"Use to, it mean what a airplane do when its motor quit. Down here, we *volplanin'* after a good run down a concourse, when the balls in our boots get rollin' like rounded-off dice. Yeah. That's real volplanin'. Jes' yo' whole body slippin' through air like a rocket or a arrow, goin' head up and flat out, gamblin' on the brains in yo' muscles to keep you from headin' over inna heap. Soulplanin', we call it when ever'thin's smooth and feathery, and it make livin' sweet, Basenji. It beat liquor and new peaches and a lovin' tongue, it beat mos' anything I can think of. Doin' it, you forget 'bout concrete and levels and how no one see the Moon no more. That's the truth. That's real soulplanin'. And Ty, he'd tell you the same thin', Basenji. That's why we glizadors."

Queequeg stopped talking and examined her cubiclemate's face. He was blushing a little, red seeping into his pale brown cheeks. Shoot, she'd embarrass him again, then. The air conditioning had leached away at her toddy's warmth, had put a chill on her legs. She drew them up under her, without a great deal of attention to the arrangement of her skirt. Another surprise: he didn't hurry to look away.

Good for him, he was usually prim as a prufrock, whatever that meant. Ty always used that expression, and somehow it was just right for Basenji. In a three-room cubicle, with the bath-booth between two sleepers, you couldn't practice or pretend any bodyshame, ritualistic or real, unless you were an expert. Which Basenji was. He was never anything but dressed, and if she dropped a towel in front of him or strolled nighty-clad out of her sleeper, *zup!* he was right out the door: prim as a prufrock.

But tonight, his cheeks looking like somebody brutish had pinched them over, he didn't let the drawing up of her Zulu's legs at all befuddle him. His eyes swept across her whole body, they flashed with a toddy-fed humor. He said, "And what will you do when you're too old to volplane?"

"I gonna las' till I forty at leas'. We got glizadors been lacin' on glierboots since ten years 'fo' I was bo'n."

"Then what? After forty? You could live sixty more years."

"I gonna do it, too. Die in the wunnerful year 2128, when they won' be no more Dome and the earth will have done took us back."

"But before that happens? And after you're through with the glissadors?"

"Babies. I have my babies to raise up. Then when I feeble, I got 'em to talk at and to baby me. If I need it. Which I won'."

"How do you know you won't, Queequeg?"

"I jes' like my mamma, and she don' need nobody but my daddy and not him all that much. She love us all, I mean, but she ain' gonna fall over if sompein happen to us. A quittin' streak don' run in her. Or me neither."

"Maybe." He said that cockylike and lifted his eyes from her. Whispering, he breathed out the word, "Babies," as if he didn't believe it.

Queequeg fixed Basenji another drink, which he accepted and slowly sipped off. But he wouldn't talk anymore, even though she plopped herself immodestly down in front of him. He went to sleep in the wingback. Thank you, thank you for a stimulating evening. Well, it had been: stimulating, that is. Moreso than any evening she had ever shared with him in the cubicle. He was sweet too, Basenji was....

Queequeg took the heavy mug out of his lap and removed his shoes. Then, mug in hand, she stood in front of her Rockwell prints. It hit her that she was almost like the parents in the *Freedom from Fear* painting, tucking in the children while thugboys beat up the citizens surfaceside and hoisterjacks terrorized pedestrians in the understrata. In their cubicle, though, it was cozy: air-conditioned cozy. A sad-making peacefulness suffused Queequeg and, shuddering with the ache of it, she put the mug on the kitchen board, dialed down the lights, shed her clothes, and lay in her sleeper cove gazing into the impenetrable darkness. Her hands rested on the planes of her lower abdomen, the tips of her fingers pressing into the wiry margin of her pubic hair. How still and big the world was. She felt connected to everyone in it, a deliverer of universal amity. And she was a long time going to sleep....

10 / *In the Descent Capsule*

Simon Hadaka Fowler, alias Basenji, woke up and lifted himself out of the chair where Queequeg had left him. He had slept dreamlessly: no visions of a tiny incarnation of himself climbing the shelves on his patio. Ordinarily, he did not go into the Kudzu Shop on Saturdays, at least not to open it; if he did go, it was to secure the plants for the Sabbath. Then he would retire back into the hive and his own private cell. This morning, though, he quietly changed his clothes and prepared to leave for surfaceside, two hours before the City's meterological technicians would dial up daylight.

Outside her sleeper he paused. "Queequeg," he said.

No movement, and the glowing clock on the kitchen board didn't give him enough light to see into her room. Very well.

Off Basenji went. Out of the cubicle, through the Level 9 concourses, up the lift-tube shaft (in a capsule by himself), across the pedestrian courts, and into that faintly inimical district where the Kudzu Shop tried to bind a collapsing empire together with flower chains.

On his door he put a sign reading OPEN. Then, by the fluorescents in the greenhouse, he worked until the artificial dawn gave him enough light to move out to the patio.

The morning went by. He even had a few customers. Queequeg stayed on his mind. Occasionally he shook his head and said, "Babies." Was that what she thought you relied on when your own strength ran out: your grown-up babies? Not altogether, apparently. She trusted her own resources too; she was just like her mamma. So she said.

At the noon shift-change Basenji looked at the newly layered willow in its covered stand; in two warm, sealed-over wombs of sphagnum moss it was beginning to generate new life. He hoped. A year it would take....

He watered the other plants on the patio shelves, then picked up the bonsai willow he had not altered and carried it straight out the shop door. The locking-up was made clumsy by his holding the miniature tree in its shallow oriental pot while he struggled with his key.

Then he walked all the way to the New Peachtree lift terminal with the willow swooning in his arms, half concealing his face. Aboard a descent capsule, seven or eight black men and women surrounding him, Basenji tried to pretend that he wasn't clutching a pot to his stomach, a willow to his chest. Not really. Grins on every side. The Big Bad Basement was swallowing them all, rising like irresistible water around them.

"What you got there, man?"

Basenji started to answer.

"A bush. He carryin' that bush home."

"That ain't no bush. That a tree, Julie-boy."

"Well, it don' got a proper growth, anybody tell you that."

A woman asked him, "What do you wanna take a pretty tree like that into the basement for? It doesn't belong down here, not that one."

Basenji started to answer.

"He takin' that bush to his dog," Julie-boy said. "He mos' likely got a dog hid out in his cyoob'cle."

"A dog?"

"Yah. A little one that don' make much noise. So he don' get junked by the concourse trolls."

"It's for decoration," the woman said, answering her own previous question.

"He takin' it to his dog."

Speculation went on around him, entertaining speculation. He couldn't get a word in. Then they were down: all the way down, without having stopped at any of the other floors: the Level 9 Express. Everyone disembarked.

"Take it on home to yo' dog," Julie-boy insisted. "See to it he don' has to hike his leg on the wall."

"Fuckin' fine tree," someone else said. "You got a fuckin' fine tree."

Laughter as they dispersed, although the inquisitive woman had already taken herself out of earshot of Basenji's jovial assailants. Huffy, huffy. As the others tapped off toward various corridor mouths, a wiry man with big luminous eyes turned back to him.

"You take care of it," he said. "It could die in a place like this. You tend it now." Then those eyes, too, revolved away from him.

Basenji, balancing the plant, at last turned from the lift-tube passageway, walked down a poorly lit auxiliary hall, entered a wide concourse, and reached his own cubicle. After he shifted the willow so that he could hold his right thumb to the electric eye, the panel slid back.

11 / Declaiming a Poem

Queequeg, when she woke up, was surprised and disappointed
to find that Basenji had gone off somewhere. Standing in her
penwah at the kitchen board, she ate a bowl of cereal
(fingernail-colored flakes that dissolved into a paste when she
moved her spoon around) and drank some instant orange juice.
She scatsang to herself and mashed a few imaginary muscadines
with her bare feet: muscadines and scuppernongs. Her daddy
always called the latter *scup'nins*. Sometimes you could find
both varieties of grapes in the City's supermarkets, especially in
the Dixie-Apple Comestibulary on the Level 4 mall. The
checkout boys and stockers didn't seem to know where they
came from: they were probably growing all over the Dome, right
over everybody's heads, out there where nobody poked his old
noggin anymore.

I bet Basenji could raise 'em up in the Kudzu Shop, Queequeg
thought, if he had enough room. Which he probably didn't.

She got dressed, a body stocking. What was she going to do?
Not shopping. She'd already prommed away enough pay-credits
for a while. The Rockwells. She sat down in Basenji's chair to
look at them. A sharp nub cut into the small of her back.
"Umpf." It was the corner of a beat-up old notebook, a
notebook wedged between the back of the chair and the seat
cushion. Queequeg pulled it out and began thumbing through it.

Lord, look at all the soot-smudged pages. Basenji wrote as
teeny-tiny as anyone she'd ever seen, as if this was all the paper
there was in the world and he wasn't going to waste none of it. As
she flipped along, the notebook opened out flat, of its own
accord, to two pages where his little handwriting was even
tighter than elsewhere. She read:

• Bushido is the way of the warrior. But our own
instinctive bushido has been bred out of us. Most of us
have forgotten what horror exists outside the Dome to
keep us inside. Whatever....

That was enough for her. Bushido. Boo-SHEE-doe.
Whatever that was. Some of the other words on the page looked

mighty funny, too. Back she flipped, leisurely thumbing. It was a journal, though not a very well-kept one. The entries went all the way back to 2039, seven years ago. A year or two in between didn't seem to be represented at all. She stopped thumbing when she saw this:

> *you gave me the willow*
> *with the loving remonstrance*
> *that the tree become*
> *something other than a decoration,*
> *the diffident point of an effeminate*
> *motif;*

Whew! Queequeg was reading this out loud. It wasn't any better than the other, but it looked pretty on the page. It had that to speak for it. And her. She spoke some more:

> *and though I still go*
> *through gardens looking askance*
> *at the total sum*
> *of your commands and my hesitation,*
> *the willow itself has become animate:*
> *a thief.*

> *what it has taken*
> *from the days I wear like leaves*

A line into the second stanza, Queequeg had levered herself out of the chair and begun pacing. She was declaiming nicely by the time she got to *leaves*. Then it stopped. She had to stop too, which was too bad because she'd almost reached the volplaning stage. Actually, there was more, but Basenji had very effectively crossed out the final two stanzas: violent red slashes. He had done it so well that she couldn't read any of the words in the obliterated lines, not a one.

So she started again from the beginning, gesturing with one arm and walking back and forth in front of the Rockwells. L-O-Q-shun. Maybe it wasn't so bad, after all. Bad enough, though. Anyhow, reading it again, she knew that it was about the bonsai she had tried to buy the day before. Or the other bonsai just like it.

At the bottom of the page Basenji had written the date, Winter 2041, and two more words: "Oedipal claptrap."

Queequeg put the notebook back in the chair, exactly as she had found it. For a few minutes she scatsang variations of the phrase *you gave me the willow,* still pacing. What had he gone off for? Maybe just to close up for Sunday. Anyhow, if he hadn't gone off, he'd probably be scrunched over his visicom console tapping into the *Journal/Constitution* newstapes. Last night was a fluke, one big fluke.

The clock on the kitchen board said 11:10. Queequeg went into her own sleeper cove and dialed Ty Kosturko surfaceside, up in the towers.

His mother answered: very, very politely. Finally Ty was on.

Queequeg said, "Meet you for lunch, Level 4 mall."

"Sleepy." He sounded it, too.

"How long you stay?"

"Till it was over. It got good then. Everybody talked."

"Well, I hungry, Tyger."

"Where on the mall?"

"The Dixie-Apple."

"OK. Thirty minutes."

"'Bye."

Quick, quick: a spray shower, which she should have taken last night. Then, a summer dress, orange and yellow.

Maybe they'd have scup'nins in the produce department, shipped in from the Orient or Madagascar (ha,ha) or the kudzu forests where no one supposedly ventured anymore. If they did, she'd buy her daddy some. Besides, it had been a couple of weeks since she'd been over to Bondville. She'd take Ty with her, turn him loose on her mamma....

Out of the cubicle she went, fifteen minutes ahead of the Saturday shift change. And up to Level 4 before the crowds came waterfalling down.

12 / Simon Hadaka Fowler

The cubicle was empty. But he found a cereal bowl and a juice glass on the kitchen board, both wearing the lacy residue of their contents. Staring through the branches of the willow, he saw that the clock behind the breakfast dishes said 12:40. Which had to be right: it was linked to a strata-encompassing system tying it into The Clock, a computerized timekeeper housed in a tower on

New Peachtree. So what? He was disappointed that Queequeg
wasn't in (an unusual response, he knew), but mildly gratified
that the time didn't make any difference to him. The
disappointment and the gratification canceled each other out:
quasi-serenity.

Put the bonsai down, Simon.

Holding it, he turned around. Where? In a place where it
would be displayed to advantage. Fine. But the central room of
their cubicle didn't offer that many possibilities. Beside his
chair? Under the Rockwells? Either side of the kitchen board?
Not good, any of them.

Well, it was evident to him why he had brought the willow
down to Level 9, it would be evident to Queequeg as well. Why
not let its placement say unequivocally what, just by exchanging
a glance, they would both know?

Very good. Therefore, Simon Hadaka Fowler carried the pot
into Queequeg's sleeper cove (the first time he had been through
that door) and set it at the foot of her bed. She had thrown her
nightgown, he noticed, over her pillow. Meanwhile, her
presence, her aura, hung in the room like a piquant incense, not
yet completely burned off. That was all right, too.

But an unmade bed didn't do much for the miniature tree,
and he wasn't going to touch her nightgown so that he could
remedy the bed's rumpledness. He moved the tree to the back
wall of the cove. Then he went into his own room and came back
with a rolled bamboo mat and a small scroll of rice paper, also
rolled. He put the bamboo mat under the glazed vessel
containing the tree and affixed the scroll to the wall with the
same sort of tape Ty and Queequeg had used for the Rockwells.
He went out and came back again. This time he stood a bronze
ornament on the mat next to the bonsai: an Oriental warrior,
sword upraised.

Scroll, tree, figurine: the display formed a triangle. Good.
That's what it was supposed to do. The scroll bore a poem that
he had written as a boy:

> *The moon and the mountain*
> *Mailed themselves letters:*
> *These were the flying clouds.*

His father had criticized him for messing up the syllable
count and for writing about inaccessible phenomena: Moon,
mountain, clouds. His mother had said it was OK, very nice. He

had never tried to straighten it out.

Simon Fowler went again to his own sleeper cove, shed his trousers and tunic, and performed his daily regimen of exercises, which he had forgotten to do that morning. Afterwards, he took a spray shower, conscious of the cool droplets clinging to the cabinet from its previous use. A smell of scrubbed flesh trembled in these droplets.

Fowler fixed himself lunch at the kitchen board. He decided, knowing Queequeg, that he would have the entire afternoon ahead of him. Maybe the evening, too. All right. His soul was at rest. Heaven would accept Simon Hadaka Fowler: moon, mountain, and clouds. For the first time in eleven years it seemed certain to him inevitable. Only the demands of conscience and honor remained. After lunch, he sat down at the visicom console and tapped into the *Jour/Con* newstapes.

13 / Wedding Bells

Ty Kosturko and Queequeg came in a little after eight, laughing and punchy-hysterical. They had been at each other in Georgia's old bedroom in the surfaceside Bondville tenement and hadn't really pulled either themselves or their clothes together even yet. The boy's long, neo-Edwardian shirt, embroidered flowers going up and down the sleeves, might have been on backwards: its design made it difficult to tell. And Queequeg's flaming scarf of a dress looked like an old facial tissue, everywhere crumpled.

Fowler, when he came out of his room to greet them, took all of this in at once, even the sexual compact between them. Especially the sexual compact. It had shone in their gestures and lineaments before, but then he had been either pre-emptively indifferent or unbelieving. Now he was neither: he smiled.

"Basenji," Queequeg said, putting an arm over his shoulder, "we gonna get married, Ty and me."

"That's right," the boy said, and dropped, grinning, into Fowler's wingback. He shifted uncomfortably, pulled a smudged notebook from behind him, and lowered it to the floor as if it were an incunabulum.

Fowler said, "Very good. Congratulations. Congratulations, both of you."

"After Quee—" Ty broke off and nodded deferentially to the

girl. "After *Mz Georgia Cawthorn* called me this morning, my mother gave me the mail. The UrNu Housing Authority says I can have a cubicle of my own. They said—"

"His daddy done holp him again, that what it was. How long *we* have to wait, Basenji, how long did it take *us* to fine a place?"

"Well, my daddy, Mz Cawthorn, wanted me out of the house. As far as that goes, I think my mother did too. But I digress. The Housing Authority said the cubicle was two-person only, Mr Fowler, up on Level 3, but that the double-occupancy requirement could be waived since the requisitioner's father was T. L. Kosturko. I didn't want that, but I didn't want to roost forever with mommy and daddy either.

"So when I met Queequeg at the Dixie-Apple—Mz Cawthorn, I mean—, I said, 'Move up with me.' She said, 'I got a cubiclemate.' I said, 'You haven't got a bonafide, signed-and-delivered bodyburner.' 'No,' she said, jes' a bodyburner.' So I said, 'Well, let's sign and bind, with options, durations, and special clauses to get worked out between now and the wedding.'"

"Which gonna be nex' Sattidy."

"She said OK. Which'll leave you without a cubiclemate, Mr Fowler, but the Housing Authority won't toss you out because of a wedding. You'll have a grace period and a chance to screen the first five people on the relocation list for the one you most want to move in with you. Which neither you or Queequeg got to do when you were thrown together from the top of the lists. So I hope you aren't upset with me for stealing your cubiclemate."

The boy had never seemed so earnest, not even while explaining the Rockwell prints or instructing him in the theory and practice of eurythmics. Maybe his shirt was on frontwards.

"No, that's fine," he told them. "But I want a clause permitting me visiting privileges."

"Yeah," Queequeg said. "You 'member that one, Ty."

The boy nodded and wrote a make-believe message to himself on the palm of his hand. "Anyway, Mr Fowler, we've already told Georgia's parents and you. But I've got to break the news to Ward Rep Kosturko and his lady, who'll be," rippling his wrist in demonstration, "determinedly delighted." He laughed, that incongruous falsetto. Then, looking at Queequeg, "Tomorrow's Sunday. I've met yours, you gotta meet mine. Come up in the afternoon, three or so. All right?"

"OK. You tell 'em who I am: a glizador, jes' like you." She

reached down and pulled Ty out of Fowler's chair. "Only better." They kissed, decorously, though he didn't believe the decorousness was for his benefit; they were simply expressing the calm their affection had come to.

"Good night, Mr Fowler," Ty Kosturko said. And he went out into the concourse, where he was at once absorbed by the red fog hanging there.

14 / *Georgia Cawthorn*

She was high, high, high. Like yesterday at the mezzanine rail in the Consolidated Rich's before meeting Ty. Like looking down on the pedestrian courts, out through the tinted glass. The world spread out like a map, the flat kind like they used in geography: Africa on one side, America on the other. So that you could fall off either end, right into the chalk tray. Well, she was volplaning back and forth across that whole landscape.

"Hey, Basenji," she said, walking toward her sleeper cove, "what you think? You 'prove?"

"I approve," he said, right behind her. In fact, he was following at her heels, which never happened: he didn't do that. But when she turned toward him from the darkened cove, he was right there. Like a little dog that's been left shut up all day, eyes begging, tail ticktocking. Except Basenji had his arms folded self-composedly and was standing straight and still at the edge of the shadow just inside her door.

Facing him, she dialed up her light. "Hey," she said again, smiling. Prim as a prufrock, he looked, but devilish too, a little bit of witchman in his Japanese eyes. Last night had not been a fluke; he was somehow turned around, wrinkles fallen out of his soul as if he'd hung it up overnight to drip dry. Neat on the outside, neat in: that was Basenji now.

He unfolded his arms and pointed at the wall behind her.

Georgia turned to look. She saw the willow, its blue ceramic pot glinting with highlights. Saying, "Oh, Basenji," she crossed the room and knelt beside the tree. "You givin' it to me?"

"No," he said.

Her head jerked up, her mouth turned down, before she could stop either of these involuntary responses. Damn.

"I can't. If it isn't outdoors most of the time, it will die. As I said yesterday, it needs weather. But we can keep it down here for the weekend. *You* can keep it."

"It won' die?"

"It shouldn't. Not because of two days downstairs." Straight and still he stood; a trifle stiff, too.

"Take you a seat, Basenji." She pointed him to the bed. He was going to protest, she could see it coming. "Go on now. Ty, he plonk down in yo' chair, you plonk down right there. An res'."

"Oh, I've had plenty of rest." But he did what she'd told him to. And he watched her as she picked up the bronze samurai. "The bonsai display is very formal," he said, "if you bother to do it right. There are always three points of focus, and the tree isn't necessarily the main one, although it always represents the corner of the triangle standing for Earth."

"Well, that seem natch'l enough. What this one?" She waved the sword-wielding warrior at him, then set it down in its place.

"A figurine representing Man." He pointed at the wall over her head. "The scroll stands for Heaven. Those are the three principal aspects of the universe: Heaven, Earth, Man. In the Shinto formulation, I think. I can't really remember anymore."

Georgia stood up to examine the rice-paper scroll. She read: *"The moon and the mountain/ Mailed themselves letters:/ These were the flying clouds."* That was OK. Nice. It beat the poem in his notebook all up and down. She looked at him sitting on the bed. His shirt was open at the collar, dark hair curled below his throat. (Ty's chest was as bald as a baby's.) Too, he smelled like soap.

"Each point of the triangle," Basenji said, "also represents a vital human attribute. Heaven is soul, Earth is conscience, Man is honor. You have to fulfill the requisities of all three." His eyes were merry, like the eyes of a preacher who didn't mind taking a nip now and again. A nip for a Nip. She grinned at him as he finished talking. "And that's not Shinto, or Muslim, or Ortho-Urbanism. That's my own formulation."

She sat down beside him. They looked at the display together. No nervousness in him at all, not even the teeniest blush under the almost translucent planes of his high cheeks. Serenity was riding him like a monkey. It was about damn time. For four months he'd been shooting up a jillion cc's of crotchetiness a day and staying together by making sure his clothes were straight. Then, last night. Now, today. Sitting in *her* sleeper cove, on *her* bed, with his collar open. OK.

Georgia Cawthorn took Basenji's left hand, which was calloused from his work in the Kudzu Shop, and bit it gently in the webbing between thumb and forefinger. Then she lowered the unresisting hand to her thigh and helped it push the hem of her crumpled yellow dress upward to her hip. His hand seemed to know what to do. Leaving it there, she began to unbutton his shirt.

"You ain' tired, are you?"

"No," he said. "Are you?" It was a sweet question, not sarcastic. She could tell by the way his eyebrows went up to a little *v* when he asked her.

"Well, I ain' gonna think about it right now." She moved a kiss across his mouth and let her hands come down to his waist. He, in turn, pressed her backward, slowly, like a gentleman, so that her cast-aside nightgown lay under her head.

Everything else happened just like it was supposed to, although she had to wait until the first round was over to get her dress all the way off. Then she got up, dialed down the light, and quickly came back to the hard muscular, curly-chested Basenji. They lay together in her bed, her head on that chest. She could certainly feel her tiredness now, weights in her arms and legs.

After a while she said, "You invited to the wedding, Basenji."

"Next Saturday?"

"If Ty and me get the papers set up."

"Well, I hope you do." He did, too. He was thinking of something else, though, just like she was thinking of going up to the Tower tomorrow and sitting down with Ty to figure out options and whatnots. Maybe they could finagle authorization to go glissadoring on the same level, so long as it didn't take Ty's daddy to finagle it.

After a while she said, "The way you dress, you been hidin' all them muscles you got." She touched one.

"I do push-ups," he said. Then, like a naughty boy: "And yoga."

She laughed. "Bet you could glizador. Bet you could even fine out how to soulplane, jes' you get started."

15 / The Geriatrics Hostel

Putting his arm over the girl's bare shoulder, Simon Fowler said, "I want to tell you a story, Queequeg, something that happened eleven years ago." All his life since then, he had been looking for someone to tell it to; the notebook had been the only listener he'd found. "It's a confession, I suppose."

"Well, if it happen 'leven years ago, it ain' gonna have to do with me."

He was silent. Did she want to hear it?

She recognized his hesitation. "No, that *good*. I don' *wan'* it to. You go ahead, Basenji."

And so he confessed, doing for his conscience what Queequeg and Ty Kosturko and the bonsai had somehow managed to do for his soul. "Eleven years ago I gave my mother to the UrNu Geriatrics Hostel. Do you know what that is?"

"I think so."

"Well, it's a place for old people, a hospital and nursing home. Some of the old people there aren't sick at all and live in a separate wing, almost a hotel. Most who go there, though, are waiting to die. Geriatrics Hostel. The name itself is a contradiction, meant to inspire hope when you know you shouldn't have any."

"I don' know what's hope-inspirin' 'bout a buildin' full of hostile ole people," the girl said. She waited for him to laugh. Which he didn't. "That's a joke, Basenji. One of yo' snooty *puns*. You ain' the only one smart enough to make 'em, whatever you think." She chuckled. "Good one, too."

"Touché." It had stopped him, he had to admit. To save face, he pinched her nipple. "May I finish?"

"Ouch. Yeah. Don' do that."

Georgia Cawthorn listened while he told her about taking his mother, Kazuko, who had been born in reconstructed Hiroshima in 1970, to the UrNu Geriatrics Hostel. His mother was only sixty-five, but he had been taking care of her as if she were a child for six or seven years, since Zachary Fowler's death in 2028 (the year she, Georgia, was born) of "insult to the brain."

Kazuko had taught him everything he knew about

horticulture, bonsai, and miniature landscaping; and he, after he was old enough to run it himself, had taken her with him every day to the Kudzu Shop, even though this had entailed pushing a wheelchair through the corridors of the Tower Complex, into and out of lift-tubes, and across spotless pedestrian courts and pitted, unrepaired asphalt. The medicaid physicians told him that they could find no measurable deterioration in her legs; perhaps her condition derived from an irresistible and ongoing loss of neurons, nerve cells, in the brain, a failure owing to oxygen deprivation. "Premature senescence," they said. Perhaps. In any case, they didn't know what to do about it since they had no long-range methodology for reversing vein constriction in the brain or for increasing her blood's oxygen payloads.

"One of them said *payloads,*" Simon Fowler said. "Aerospace jargon. The men in the descent craft *Eagle* were part of its payload."

"They talk like they has to, Basenji," She could see him nosediving into bitterness. But he pulled out.

"Finally, I went and talked to the people at the Geriatrics Hostel. They were soliciting tenants, patients for the hospital section, residents for their quasi-hotel. Part of a study, all of it. The director told me that my mother's apparent 'premature senescence' might in reality be a response to alterations in her life over which she had no control.

"'Look,' he said. 'Your mother was born in Hiroshima. She came to this country with your father before the turn of the century. She watched the Dome go up over Atlanta, actually saw the steel gridwork—over a ten-year period—blot out the sky. The United States turned into the world's only Urban Federation before she was even granted American citizenship. So instead she had to apply for enfranchisement under the new Urban Charter. You were born only after she and your father had obtained that enfranchisement. That made her what?— thirty-seven years old?—when you were born, Mr Fowler, no small adjustment in its own right. Twenty years devoted to raising you, then, while the Urban Nuclei cut themselves off from all contact with their own countrysides, not to speak of foreign nations, and your father degenerated into alcoholism. Then your father, the one person she knew who had seen her homeland, who could talk about it with her, was cruel enough to desert her. By dying. Mr Fowler, your mother's time sense has been upended, her cultural and her emotional attachments pulled out from under her. Her psychological metabolism has sped up to keep pace with the alterations she sees occuring in the external world. She is aging because she feels intuitively that she must, that it would be a chronometric impossibility for her *not* to be aging. Physiologically she is neither older nor younger than any reasonably healthy woman of sixty-five. We have other victims of the same malaise here, some barely into their fifties. The roots of this syndrome, in fact, are a century old. Older. Leave your mother with us, Mr Fowler, and we'll try to help her. That's all I can promise.'

"I said, 'All of her emotional attachments haven't been pulled out from under her. She has a son, you know.'

"'Yes,' the director said (his name was Leland Tanner, I believe), 'and from what you've told me, you've been castigating yourself for not being your father. Or an improved version of your father: all the strengths, none of the weaknesses. Your own sense of guilt runs very deep in this matter, Mr Fowler, as if you blame yourself for being both a late *and* an only child, neither of which conditions you had any control over. And you've done well to seek help here.'"

"You don' still feel that guilt, do you?" Georgia asked.

"I don't think so. If I ever felt it. But I'm not through confessing. The greater guilt is ahead.

"I gave—*sold*—my mother to the Geriatrics Hostel. They had been soliciting tenants, as I said, as subjects for a gerontological study, and they offered me a considerable sum to submit my mother to them. I did. They promised that she, along with the others, would be a recipient of intensive care and treatment, not simply a guinea pig for their researches. And in that, I think, the director told me the truth.

"During the first year I visited the Geriatrics Hostel every week, usually twice a week. Wednesday evenings and Sundays. They were working to alter my mother's time sense, to bring it in line with that of a normal woman in her sixties, maybe even to slow it down below the so-called normal threshold. The director did not believe in the biochemical approach, though, and that seemed good to me. No untested repressants or hallucinogens. Instead, they placed my mother in a controlled environment, a room in which everything took place at leisurely, but prescribed, intervals. They encouraged the reintroduction of Japanese motifs into her life, in the decorations of her room and in the material available for her to read. I brought a different bonsai with me each time I came; when it had been indoors for two or three days, an attendant carried it to the balcony outside my mother's window—which, on the director's orders, they kept curtained. But she still had scenery. A false window in the room opposite the curtained balcony ran hologramic movies of the Japanese gardens in San Francisco; my mother could watch the people come and go, come and go. Or she could wheel herself over to the wall and let a curtain drop into place here, too. More, they permitted her company from among the Hostel's other 'guests,' and they didn't shut her off from news of the City and the other Urban Nuclei; they just monitored and restricted its content.

"The first month, no progress. Not much the second one, either—though by the third month she had begun trying to walk, supporting herself on a movable aluminum frame they had kept in her room since the beginning. This didn't last. The director went by tunnel to a conference on aging research in the Washington Nucleus. While he was gone, someone proposed a room adjustment; patients were shuffled around. That did it. We *think* that's what did it; the results of this bungling didn't begin to show for a while. In fact, the new room my mother was given was exactly like the other, down to the false window and the hologramic movies of the San Francisco botanical gardens, except that the floor plan was a mirror-image of the other. Even the adjustment's having been made in its entirety during my mother's sleep couldn't compensate for this; the director later said it may have even complicated matters, since if my mother had witnessed the shuffling, her sense of disorientation would not have been so great."

"Thoughtlessness, Basenji. The program don' soun' bad, the director don' soun' bad."

"No, they weren't. But that's not the point. This is a confession, not an indictment. May I finish?"

"Go on. But let's pull up that sheet." The air conditioning, the interminable, almost imperceptible droning of the air conditioner. They adjusted themselves against each other under the rumpled drifts of linen.

"From that point on, my mother failed. When I came to visit her, we sat opposite each other and, more often than not, stared. She had sores on her legs and arms from lying so long in bed. She scratched the sores and the skin came away. The attendants left the sores undressed so that they'd be open to the air and the prospect of healing. I found myself fixing obsessively on these raw wounds; it was as if I expected on one visit to see her shin bone or elbow joint peeping through the worn flesh. And her eyes, the skin around them was sagging and red, falling into pouches. Queequeg, I expected—I was afraid—that one Sunday afternoon her eyes would roll out of her sockets into the little bags on her cheeks."

"Hey now!" She drew away from him, a reprimand.

"Come back," he said, and she did. "I wouldn't admit to myself the horror I felt, I still don't completely admit it. Later when I went to visit her I had to introduce myself; I had to tell Kuzuko Hadaka Fowler, my mother, who I was. It was just her eyesight, the director told me, not her memory. But then she would ask questions about my father, who she seemed to think was still living in the Tower Complex with me. Or she would speak in Japanese, which I had never learned. In English she would reminisce about what it had been like to survive the A-bomb blast of August 6, 1945, although not even her own parents had been alive when that first bomb was dropped. Even so, after the reversal in her progress, it was the key to almost everything she talked about. She once described for me the photographic images of human shadows burned into the sides of Hiroshima's buildings by the blast. Maybe she saw a few of them when she was a little girl, three or four years old, I don't know. One or two such images may still have existed then.

"At the end of the first year in the Hostel she wasn't even talking about that, just sitting in her wheelchair and nodding, or asking me every ten minutes or so what time it was. Which I wasn't supposed to tell her. I had been seeing a woman quite frequently during this time, but I finally stopped. The visits to my mother had started to tell on me: a depression I couldn't exorcise.

"I went three weeks without going to see her, my very first break in a year-long routine. Then, on a Wednesday evening, I rode a lift-tube from street level to the floor of her ward in the Geriatrics Hostel. When I came out into the hall, I heard an old woman's voice saying over and over, 'Please, please help me.' I saw her, my mother, in her wheelchair at the end of the corridor: nothing terrible seemed amiss. She looked all right. But she kept begging for someone to come to her aid.

"They were mopping out the rooms along the corridor, and several other 'guests' shared the hallway with her, all of them deaf, maybe even literally, to her pleas. I threaded my way through the wheelchairs, and when she heard me coming, knowing that I was neither a patient nor one of those who ordinarily tended to her, she stopped begging. She held her head up, and started nodding and smiling.

"'How do you do,' she said. 'How do you do.'

"I said, Mother, it's Simon, it's your son.'

"'How do you do,' she said. 'How do you do.' In the past my introducing myself had gained me at least a slow-coming acceptance. This time, only her grin and those terrible nods of the head. I waited. That was all I got. 'How do you do, how do you do.'

"Then I saw that the skirts of her robe—a hideous robe I had never seen before, kimonolike, with Mount Fujiyama embroidered over her left breast and the name of the mountain stitched across the right—well, the drape of this hideous robe was drenched. A pool of urine lay under my mother's wheelchair, droplets hung from the frame on which her feet rested. 'How do you do,' she said. She wasn't going to let a stranger, even if he had just introduced himself as her son, help her with something as personal as a bladder she could no longer control.

"Courtesy, dignity, self-reliance."

"'I'm your son,' I said. 'Mother, let me—'

"'How do you do.'

"'Someone help this woman!' I shouted. 'Someone help her!' Four or five time-savaged faces revolved toward me. An attendant came out of one of the rooms.

"I backed away from my mother, I turned and walked up the hall. Waiting for the lift-tube, I heard my mother saying again, 'Please, please help me.' The attendant took care of her, I think: I didn't look back to see. Then I left the Geriatrics Hostel and never went back again until almost two years later when they notified me that my mother had died."

Beneath drifts of linen Simon Fowler and Georgia Cawthorn lay against each other. He was thinking, Heaven is soul, Earth is conscience. These I have salved....

16 / *The Samurai and the Willows*

It was the Saturday of the wedding. The clock on the kitchen
board said 1:20. She kissed him. "You come on up now, the
Ortho-Urban chapel. You hear? We both gonna be late, Ty
gonna kill me."

"Go on, then."

"You comin', Basenji? You better come." He was smiling, the
way a quiet little dog smiles. And you never find out what it's
thinking.

"In time," he said.

"*On* time," she said, "you be *on* time." Enough. She went out
the door into the concourse, her shoulder capes, intense
burgundy, twirling with the power of her stride. No need for
glierboots, he thought.

Simon Hadaka Fowler went to his sleeper. He took his
notebook out of the drawer in the cabinet compartment of the
visicom console. He tore out two blank pages toward the back.
Then, pulling a metal waste can toward his chair, he dropped the
notebook in and set it afire with a pipe lighter from the console.
He pushed the waste can away from him with his foot.

This done, he began to write on the first of the two pages he
had saved back from the miniature holocaust in the waste can:

"Ty, Queequeg: I am leaving the Kudzu Shop to you. Here is
the name of a man who may offer you a good price for it, should
you not wish to keep it." He wrote the name and level station of
the man. "The bonsai on the patio I hope you will keep,
especially the willows. Under the counter in the main shop I have
left instructions for completing the layering and transplanting
processes of the willow now putting forth new roots. It should
not be too difficult if you follow them to the letter. They are
good instructions."

He leaned back in his chair and thought. Then he wrote:

"My mother once told me a story of two young Japanese men
who recklessly stormed the home of a great lord who they
believed had impugned the good name of their father. Perhaps
the lord had been responsible for their father's death. (My

memory fails me here.) In any case, the two young men—neither of them yet twenty—were captured.

"The lord whom they had tried to kill, however, was impressed by the young men's courage and refused to condemn them to death. Instead, he commuted their sentence to the mercy of committing seppuku, ritual suicide.

"To a Japanese, my mother tried to explain, the distinction between execution and seppuku is by no means a fine one. On the one hand, disgrace. On the other, the satisfaction of one's honor. An Occidental mind struggles with this distinction, attempts to refute it with reasoning altogether outside the context of its origin. It is only in the last two or three weeks that I have recognized this myself.

"To return to my story, which I am almost done with: The gracious lord whose home the young men had attacked even went so far as to include in this commuted sentence the six-year-old brother of the attackers, even though the boy had been left at home during their mission. Nevertheless, on the appointed day he sat between the two brothers and watched carefully as each one of them performed the exacting ceremony. Then, with no hesitation at all, he took up his knife and did likewise."

Fowler set this page aside.

On the second sheet he wrote: "Queequeg, I go in joy. This is no execution. You have commuted my sentence."

The equation in his mind he did not write down. Heaven, Earth, Man: soul, conscience, honor. Shortly, he thought, I will have salved all three.

Much later, when Georgia Kosturko-Cawthorn could weigh with some degree of objectivity what had happened, she told Ty: "He changed a lot. The blessed part is, he started askin' himse'f questions 'bout who he was. He got a long way. But he jes' never asked the last question, Ty, he jes' never asked it." In the spring of the year that followed, working from Basenji's directions, Georgia and Ty began two new trees from the layered bonsai willow. Both trees took.

2046

Interlude: First Councilor Lesser

The catacomb years between 2047 and 2072 belonged to a woman named Saganella Ruth Lesser, who attained the First Councilorship early in the first-named year and unwillingly relinquished it early in the latter. Her career therefore spanned a quarter of a century. During this period she strengthened her hold on the City by an unpredictable despotism that kept even her closest advisors doing defensive pirouettes.

First Councilor Lesser's sole abiding constant, unpredictableness aside, was her commitment to Ortho-Urbanism, the City's official faith. With two conspicuous exceptions (the Federated Urban Society for Krishna Consciousness and the Orthodox Muslims), nearly all other religious and pseudo-religious sects were outlawed and their devotees impartially but relentlessly persecuted. Jews, perhaps because they could so convincingly invoke the patriarchs of the Old Testament, were in favor one day and out the next. No one seemed to know exactly what to do with them. In or out of favor, however, the people of Abraham endured.

UrNu House—Atlanta's seat of government—and the First Ortho-Urban Worship Center off Hunter Street stood within hailing distance of each other. Many ward reps and city councilors discreetly acknowledged that the High Bishop Andrew Ogrodnik had as much to do with policymaking as they did. Ortho-Urbanism itself combined the ritual, the contemporary scholasticism, and some of the hierarchical designations of the Roman Church with a good many of the holy-roller appurtenances of pre-Evacuation primitivism. In the midst of elaborate holiday masses, for instance, you would hear members of the congregation, when irresistibly moved by the Holy Spirit, talking in tongues or crying "Amen!" or "Tell it, Preacher!" Moreover, post-ceremony "witnessing" was as popular, and as obligatory, as the orpianoogla-accompanied *Te Deum* during the celebration of communion. No one found these supposedly contradictory approaches to worship incompatible or jarring, and, a regular churchgoer, Saganella Lesser delighted in every one of them.

Outside the Worship Center, the First Councilor condemned, praised, commanded, or temporized just as she pleased. On religious and moral grounds, she took exception to the septigamoklans of Dr Leland Tanner. Well within the first year of her reign she managed to shut down several of the Human Development Commission's most humane and innovative programs for the elderly, eventually forcing Dr Tanner's resignation and then reluctantly approving his exile to the Washington Nucleus. In his absence, and in the face of the First Councilor's implacable hostility, gerontological and geriatrics research in Atlanta ground to a virtual halt. Meanwhile, on political and purely personal grounds, Saganella Lesser took exception to the mobility, exuberance, and unqualified prestige of the glissador corps.

Battle was joined.

Through the whole of the Fifties the First Councilor worked systematically to deprive the glissadors of their influence in the hive and so to undermine the foundations of their fragile but previously unadmitted power base. When glissadors quit or retired, she declined to approve the training of replacements. She ordered the concourse trolls, an arm of the urban police force, to take over many of the message-carrying duties and small private services once in the exclusive domain of the glissadors. And she embedded the manufacture and requisitioning of new uniforms and glierboots in so much bureaucratic excelsior that not even a man with a power shovel could get to the bottom of it.

Then, briefly, the First Councilor waged a subtle propaganda campaign against the glissadors. If a popular song or a holodation drama dealt with them, she approved it for release only if it presented the glissadors in a ridiculous or a distastefully self-seeking light. The results of this first campaign were negligible. Later, toward the end of the decade, the First Councilor refused to permit in the arts or the news media any reference whatsoever to the glissadors. They were *personae non gratae,* glierbooted embarrassments who didn't go away no matter how you opposed them. At the beginning of the Sixties, in fact, Saganella Lesser found them a more deeply entrenched irritant than such underground religious sects as the Mythodists, the American Hoodoo Criers, and the Piscapalians of Dagon Magus, none of which had the effrontery to be legitimate scions of the Urban Charter. Worse, neither ridicule nor neglect seemed to dim the luster of the glissadors among their subterranean constituency. Embattled, they shone like heroes.

Their undoing was the "Glissador Revolt" of 2063.

As no one of any discernment failed to understand, this so-called revolt was a heinous fabrication. Returning to the attack, First Councilor Lesser compelled the *Jour/Con* newstapes to run a series of stories indicting the glissadors for moral laxity, petty thefts, unsolved slayings, minor acts of urban terrorism, and, finally, a concerted and on-going attempt to bring about the downfall of her government. With each successive news release their villainy and their ambition grew more and more overweening. To keep pace with this virulent new propaganda assault and to insure their own credibility, the concourse trolls began making arrests. One and two at a time, bemused glissadors found themselves riding to street level between gauntleted trolls in severe, concealing riot casks. Once booked, they disappeared. Soon, as the authorities themselves had foreseen, the glissadors saw no alternative but to resist any further arrests and to call on the hive dwellers for support. At this stage, Saganella Lesser's cold war of propaganda and random attrition became an intense physical struggle whose outcome was never in doubt.

Within two weeks the trolls had halved the glissadors' numbers—by the draconian expedients of shooting uniformed glissadors on sight and imprisoning without trial or later recourse those who cracked under the unremitting pressure and surrendered themselves. The end came so swiftly that no one could counsel moderation or intercede on the glissadors' behalf. In the Level 9 Coenotorium where they often gathered socially after their work shifts, the remaining glissadors met to declare their innocence of any disloyalty to First Councilor Lesser and to petition her for a truce in which to resolve the recent devastating conflict. By a dread necessity they were ready to talk, to make concessions, to conciliate.

Despite having received the First Councilor's authorization to meet, along with an official safe-conduct to the Coenotorium, they had no chance to do any of these things. Once gathered in the meeting hall, they found that no representatives of the government or the news media were on hand and that the hall's only door had been bolted behind them. Every conceivable crack, seam, or air hole in the Coenotorium had been calked with a plastic foam, and the cold, insidious hiss they were hearing seemed to be emanating from the heating and ventilation systems. Cyanogen. They died with the gas in their eyes and throats. Then the room burst into flames, an inferno that raged only briefly—for there was no longer any air to support it.

(Among those who died were Tyler Kosturko and Georgia Cawthorn-Kosturko. In a Bondville tenement, in the care of his maternal grandmother, they left a thirteen-year-old son. Later, he would take his grandmother's last name and embark on a strange affiliation with several visitors to Atlanta who would irrevocably alter the City's future history.)

The outraged reaction that Saganella Lesser and her advisors anticipated was not long in coming—but it proved so feeble and localized that the concourse trolls carried it before them like a domestic argument in an auxiliary corridor. The lid was on. To keep it on, the First Councilor immediately instituted a rare smorgasbord of diversions: sales in Consolidated Rich's, mime performances and art displays on the Level 4 Mall, Dome-diving exhibitions, free concerts of government-sanctioned music in the Omni, bread and circuses, anything and everything to mask the stalking specter of repression. When the Council/Conclave announced a generous bounty on religious dissenters, it did so as if declaring a holiday.

Overlaid with this frenetic gaiety and this artificial fellow-feeling, any idea that the First Councilor may have committed an unforgivable atrocity sank from view and passed out of existence. Those who remembered kept their mouths shut.

In the meantime, Saganella Lesser had begun sending

"resource-reclamation teams" into the Open to find and bring back people who might be of use to the City. This enterprise she and her cohorts referred to as the "Fifth Evacuation Lottery." In order to conceal the fact that you could breathe the air outside the Dome, walk safely in the sunlight, and find primitive human encampments amid the rampant kudzu, the work of the resource-reclamation teams remained a secret from the populace at large. But if you were one of those who went out, you knew that you had been lied to for years. And the conditions of your life were ever afterward at the mercy of those who knew you knew....

CHAPTER FIVE

Allegiances

1 / Cleopatra Amid the Kudzu

Do you know what Kudzu is? *Kudzu.* Most people who live in a doomed city, even the Urban Nucleus of Atlanta, aren't likely to know. How many of you have been outside our huge, geodesic walnut? I know about kudzu for two reasons: When I was very little my grandmother used to tell me about it and, more impressively maybe, I am one of those who have been into the Open:

> *Japan invades. Far Eastern vines*
> *Run from the clay banks they are*
>
> *Supposed to keep from eroding,*
> *Up telephone poles,*
> *Which rear, half out of leafage,*
> *As though they would shriek....*

James Dickey's description of kudzu in the opening lines of a poem entitled "Kudzu." It's a good description, too, especially the part about the telephone poles shrieking. Not too many standing telephone poles out there anymore, but pine trees, old barns, collapsing fire towers—all of these do seem to be shrieking as the merciless kudzu clambers over them.

Kudzu. *Pueraria lobata,* native to Japan, imported during a

157

previous century to keep the red clay from washing away. Baroque, vegetable architecture.

My grandmother told me about it before I ever saw it. My last name is Noble, but Zoe, my grandmother, gave me my first one: Clio. I remember Zoe very well even though she lived with us only the last three years of her life and died when I was five. Also, I have a photograph of my grandmother that she took herself using a tripod and timer: a large black-and-white one. This photograph, which sits on top of my visicom console as I write this, gives me a handhold on Zoe's heart and on several generations of the past.

The past is important to me. Just as you have to hack your way out of furiously growing kudzu to attain a vantage point on the surrounding terrain, sometimes you have to rise above and survey the past in order to get the lay of your own soul. Zoe understood that, and I think that's why my parents, after once renouncing her and packing her off to the Geriatrics Hostel, let her, in her seventy-second year, stick me with a monicker like Clio. But, having bridged a generation and walked over that bridge into my grandmother's life, I find that I now like my name well enough.

In Greek mythology, you know, Clio was the Muse of History. (Trumpet flourishes, if you please.)

The piece of history that I'm now telling occurred just last year, but really it takes in many more human seasons than the month of Summer, 2066. It's the story of how three of us on a resources-reclamation team, in the employ of the Human Development Commission (the very same authority that, nineteen years ago, disbanded Zoe's experimental septiga-moklan in the Geriatrics Hostel), went out into the Open to fetch back several people to our Urban Nucleus.

Although I was only twenty-one last summer, I'd been out on three missions before the one this story is about: all routine, all predictable. We'd "reclaimed" a number of people with desirable technical skills or influential relatives in the City by going out, finding their kudzu-camouflaged encampments, and asking them to return with us. Upon the promise of enfranchisement and respectable jobs, they all had: every one of them. They were flattered that an rr team had been sent out for them.

Our efforts were part of what the bureaucrats in the Commission called the "Fifth Evacuation Lottery"—although it wasn't an evacuation at all in the way the first four had been, when the Domes were going up sixty and seventy years ago (1994-2004, in case you're counting: a neat decade). The Fifth Evacuation Lottery is another thing altogether, not an evacuation but a series of carefully planned manhunts.

The three of us who went out last summer were Newlyn Yates, the team leader; Alexander Guest, a man of swarthy complexion although, unlike Yates, not a black; and me, Clio Noble. Three was the optimum number for such teams; it had something to do with an old NASA policy.

Twice before I'd been on teams with Newlyn Yates, and I was a bit dithery about him: he did things to my sense of equilibrium, sabotaged it mostly. But Yates was all poker spine, set jaw, and unflappable decorum, and we'd never come close to bodyburning, despite the opportunities spending all that time in the Open naturally provides. Yates was awfully interior, he was ingrown. In the Open you couldn't get him to uncoil, he did everything as if by an invisible manual. Off duty, you never got a chance to see him.

Alexander Guest, a big mahogany-colored man with a craggy profile, was probably ten years older than Yates. He looked like he ought to be wearing moccasins and the traditional turban of the old Creek Indians—for good reason, it turned out. Before our assignment last summer, I'd never met him before, never even seen him in the Commission Authority Tower. He was just insane enough to *like* traipsing through kudzu; you could tell by the way the wilderness pooled up in his muddy eyes. He was insane in other ways, too.

But this I found out in the Open. On the day I met him in the rr section of the Human Development Tower, he just looked bummish and uncouth. We were sitting in plastic chairs in the carpeted anteroom of Yates' office, two zombies rising out of the deadness of sleep at six o'clock in the morning: even so, I had to admit that the craggy, brown man whose bulk seemed to overflow the fragile cup of his chair was more awake than I.

"'Lo," he said. An orotund rumble.

I nodded.

"Looks like we're gonna be team members. You know what this one's about?"

"No," I said. "Do you?"

"Think so." He said this matter-of-factly rather than smugly, but I still didn't feel like asking him the natural follow-up question. So, shifting in his wobbly chair (with him in it, it looked like it had been stolen from a Van-Ed elementary division classroom), he said, "What's your name, Mz?"

I told him.

"*Cleo,*" he said, missing it by a letter. "Short for Cleopatra. Married up with her brother and bodyburned with two Romans. Well, Cleo, you're the first red-haired 'Gyptian I've ever seen. Nice to meet you."

I didn't correct him about my name. I did manage the bogus courtesy of nodding again. That was all I could manage.

"History's a pastime of mine," he said after a while. "My name's Guest, Alexander Guest. That's how I'm listed in the UrNu census anyhow, and even here at the Tower. Really, though, it's an alias.

"The alias I'd rather go by," he said after musing for a while, "is Menewa. But it's hard to get people in an Urban Nucleus to call you that. All the forms say 'Last name, first name, middle initial.' You write down somepin like 'Menewa' they jes' stamp INCOMPLETE on the forms and send 'em back to you. You see, Cleo, I'm an Indian. The name Menewa. . . ."

Fortunately, he got cut off because Newlyn Yates, trim in a one-piece worksuit and street slippers, glided through the anteroom and into his office. Guest didn't have time to lapse into an incomprehensible Muskohogean dialect: the words "Come in" floated back to us as Yates disappeared, and the Indian Menewa and the Egyptian Cleopatra exchanged a glance, got up, and followed their black pharaoh-chieftain into the dark.

In the center of Yates' metal desk—once Yates had coasted the false wood surface aside—you could see an illuminated projection well; in fact, that was all we could see when we came into his office. Yates was standing behind the desk and he beckoned to us to take up positions opposite him. Then he pushed a button so that a map of the transit tunnels leading out of Atlanta to the other Urban Nuclei appeared in the projection well.

"We'll take a transit-car to this station," Yates said, pointing at the map. "The juncture of the Miami and Savannah tunnels, southeast of here. Then we'll have to go to the end of the Savannah tributary, dismantle the filter system on one of the ventilation units, climb through, and strike out on foot. The biomonitor-relay people have one of our targets placed at about forty-five kilometers due east of the tunnel juncture." Yates' father had once been the director of the City's Biomonitor Agency, but in the last fifteen years the Agency had extended its operations to include surveillance of :he natives of the countryside; this was in addition to the medical monitoring of all Dome-dwellers. A *target,* both then and now, was a human being who was being monitored.

"Hot damn," I said. An old expression of my grandmother's. "How did they manage that?"

"An implant tab at the nape of our subject's neck, they told me," Yates said. "A month ago—two months ago—he came into the City."

"Why?"

"The Agency told me he brought a truckload of peanuts up here, using what's left of the old highway system. While here, he was drugged, implanted, and afterwards pumped by a hypnotist-physician at Grady Memorial. He's not aware of the implant tab or the fact that he was questioned."

"Why didn't we just keep him here when he came to the City? It doesn't make sense to go out and fetch him now." I was doing all the asking: Alexander Guest, the gingerbread Indian, was standing hunch-shouldered and open-mouthed beside me.

"The man's name is Jonah Trap," Yates said, irritated with me, the projection well giving his face the demonic geometry of a mask. "A black. But we're not going after *him,* Mz Noble. We're after two people whose intelligence and ability the City needs and who're now apparently living with Trap near the old town of Toombsboro. You were selected for this assignment because one of the people is a woman: the Commission Authority believes you may be able, far better than Mr Guest or I, to persuade her to return with us."

"Why was I chosen?" Indian Alex said, surprising both Yates and me.

"I thought they explained that to you. You met Trap while he was here, they told me; they said youd even been into that area of the Open before. Is that true?"

"Yep."

"Then those are your reasons. You ought to be helpful." Then Yates said, "And in case the question seems to logically present itself now, *I'm* going because I'm good at taking teams out and bringing them back entire. The fact I'm black probably won't hurt much either, not in this instance."

"Well," I said, "who are the people? The man and the woman?"

"That Mz Noble, I can't tell you till we're on our way to Toombsboro."

"Why not?"

"If I could tell you that," Yates said, "I could tell you the other. Couldn't I?"

"Not necessarily. Maybe the Commission Authority just wants to be sure we don't spread our targets' names around before we leave. You could easily tell us that without telling us the names of the targets."

"Well, Mz Noble, if you have it all figured out, why ask?" Yates was an icicle with an iron bar inside it, and I had just put my lily-white foot so far into my mouth that I was gnawing on ankle bone. *Hot damn,* I said to myself.

Aloud I said, "I don't have it all figured out. I didn't even know we had a tunnel to Old Savannah: Savannah's not one of the Urban Nuclei. Never was, was it?"

"It's about one-tenth of a tunnel," Yates said, letting his finger trace the route in the projection well. "A dead-ender. Anyway the geology of the coastal region wouldn't permit the construction of a viable tunnel, even if there were people there to get to. Same with Miami. Most of the Trans-Seminole 'tunnel,' you know, is above-ground and hooded." He tapped the illuminated map. "Once we exit the main tunnel near the Ocmulgee Mound here," tapping again, "we'll head down the dead-ender and then surface well to the east of Macon. Then, a kudzu-fouled walk in the Open. We may be able to use the old State highway—57, I think—for a good part of the way. That should ease it a little for us."

Guest said, "That highway's torn up and overgrown, 57 is—at least over here where we're gonna come out." He shook his head. "Crazy."

"It doesn't matter," Yates said. "We'll get there, Mr. Guest." In five more minutes the briefing was over, and Yates turned us out of the office, out of the Tower, for the rest of the day. An open day.

"You like to get some coffee, Cleo?" Guest asked me.

"No thanks," I said. "See you at six o'clock tomorrow morning."

I went back to my cubicle on Level 3, *under.* That's where, a quarter of a century ago, my parents started from: Level 3.

2 / The General Toombs Cornstalk Brigade

The transit-tunnels are dark; they smell of the dampness of concrete. Even before construction on the Domes of the Urban Nuclei had begun, the entire Federation-wide network of tunnels was blasted into existence by an arsenal of immaculately sanitary H-bombs: *grrr-choom, grrr-choom, grrrrr-whumpf!* Strangely, we don't use the tunnels that much.

On the morning after our conference in the Human Development Tower, an open transit-car carried us in eerie silence to the Miami-Savannah juncture, where, before we turned into the Savannah tributary, I knew we were passing pretty darn close to the old Ocmulgee Mounds. At these mounds and the territory called the Ocmulgee Old Fields, the Creek Indians had long ago formed the Creek Indian Confederacy. Several prehistoric cultures had thrived here, too.

I started wondering. Maybe the Domes of the Urban Nuclei had been raised from the same impulse that had motivated Kheops in Egypt and the Mound Builders in Georgia. Oh, in these two cases I know the immediate motives diverge: Pharaoh wanted a splendid tomb whereas the Indians wished their flat-topped pyramids to serve as the thrones of the gods. But if Pharaoh believed himself a deity, a god incarnate, then his tomb was also a throne, and the common denominator in the two instances is humankind's need to exalt something larger than itself. A religious motive, finally.

Anyhow, that's my belief, and I'm not talking about the Ortho-Urban Church, either. I tried to voice it once or twice, but these ideas, spilling from the lips of a twenty-two-year-old woman with red hair, elicit only peeved looks ("The girl thinks she's Bertrand Russel, Tom") or curt dismissals ("Sophomoric bullshit, Clio"). So I now reserve these ruminations for accounts like this one. Except I probably won't be writing any more accounts like this one. Circumstances change.

But for the beam of a single headlamp, our resources-reclamation team rode in absolute darkness. The winds of our blast-borne passage smelled of concrete: concrete and iron. Yates slowed at the Miami-Savannah juncture and negotiated the turn into the southeastward tributary of the subterranean network; Guest had to get out and switch the transit-rails. Then off we went again, the Ocmulgee Old Fields behind us, well to the west. We'd been traveling for three hours.

I shouted into the resurging wind of our movement: "*Now* can you tell us whom we're going after?"

Turning his head, Yates permitted his thin profile to carve itself in the air: "Wait till we're out! You've waited this long!"

In fifteen minutes the wind began to die, the walls to lose their dizzying speed, and we glided into what I could only think of as Dead-End Station: yellow fluorescents casting a somehow greenish light over the platform here. You half-expected, when you were close enough to see more clearly, to find stalactites on the ceiling. Didn't, though; too mercilessly hot.

We got out and began unloading equipment and carrying it up to the platform. Yates wore a myriad of tools on his low-slung belt, as well as a holster of artificial leather: it contained a laser pistol. (One such weapon to each reclamation team, and the team leader carried it.) Then Yates pointed at the ventilation unit at the top of the tunnel's final wall.

"OK," he said. "Let's dismantle that grate."

Guest climbed up the maintenance rungs to the unit and began working to take the filter apart. The filter systems had been installed when the Federation had been worried about the tunnel's Internal Environmental Control (IEC, if you like initials), fearing that the Open's tainted atmosphere would spill into the network and strangle us with the wastes we had fled from. If that's what we'd fled from. The Open had never been so foully tainted as that. Never. The first reclamation team had carried oxygen canisters and over-the-head masks (which made them look like startled rhesus monkeys when they put them on: perforated speakers, plastiglass eyes, and all), but its members hadn't had to use this equipment. And ninety percent of Atlanta's people still believe you can't go outside. Most of them, if they knew differently, still wouldn't rush to recolonize the wilderness.

"This thing's rusted," Guest said, swaying up there on the maintenance ladder. "Won't budge."

So Yates had to go up and cut both the filter system and the grate out of their moorings with the laser pistol. After the area around the ventilation unit had cooled, we all climbed through, weighted with paraphernalia, into the Open: Guest first, then me, then Newlyn Yates.

And the first thing we saw was the deformed, rearing landscape: green temples, arabesques of kudzu, pagodas to the gods of rampant fertility. The Orient had invaded Georgia, invisible samurai crouched in the vines. The wilderness shouted at us, and the sky—this always amazed me—was a brilliant sky-blue.

The job they gave Clio Noble was tying flaming-red markers on trees and rotted fence posts, anything up-jutting. "Hell," Alexander Guest said. "She don't need to do that. You got a wrist-compass and I could smell our way back to the station." He lifted his big head and whuffled two or three times at the air, a comic and lordly bear in the chapel of the forest.

"Suppose something happens to you, Guest," Yates said. "Or to me. Maybe Clio . . . Mz Noble," he emended, "will have to get back here on her own." I grinned at him, and the martinet in Yates revived. "Mz Noble will set the rags, and that's it."

So off we went, angling northeast in order to intercept the ruins of State Highway 57, Clio Noble tying markers the color of her hair at intervals of roughly a hundred meters—unless the eclipsing vegetation or a turn in our progress demanded them more often. Languorously swinging his machete, Indian Alex marched point. Newlyn Yates, good team leader that he was, brought up the rear.

Two brown thrashers (once upon a time, the state bird) and a logy cardinal. Which was funny enough—in context, mind you—to make me chuckle out loud; in that knee-high kudzu "brown thrashers" was especially good.

"Don't get to laughing so hard," Yates said from behind me, "you forget to keep an eye open for snakes. They love this stuff."

Guest stopped and turned around. "My little brothers," he said.

I glared. He'd almost lopped off my head with his machete.

"'Scuse me," he said, wiping his brow with one mesh sleeve. "It's snakes, though. Since I'm an Indian they're supposed to be my little brothers: snakes, lizards, alligators, all like that. But I saw a green mamba at the Grant Park Zoo two years ago and got so crawly I had to get out of there." His shoulders shuddered. "Went right home."

"If you've been out here before," Yates accused, "you've seen snakes plenty of times."

"Yeah, but I didn't come 'specially to look at 'em." Then he said something both clumsily poetic and, right then, incomprehensible: "This Hothlepoya ain't no herpetologist: no, sir." And started hacking again.

We did see some snakes, too—as we always did in the Open. One was a coral snake, up from Florida no doubt, that we gave a wide berth. Guest waved Yates and me around it and whispered to me as I went by, "Hope we don't run across any asps, Cleo." I thought he was being a smart Alex until I deduced from his head movements and inflection that he really did hope that. Literally, he meant it. An asp in Georgia, a creature as alien as that!

At one o'clock we found some shade, a knoll in the forest of pine and kudzu. Some moss actually grew at the base of the slash pine we decided to camp under. For lunch. We drank from our canteens and nibbled at our dried rations.

"Well," I said. "How 'bout now?"

Yates looked at me. "How 'bout now what?" Imperial annoyance.

"Telling us who we've come after this time. I think it's a pretty safe wager we won't leak the word to someone disreputable."

"OK," Yates said. I noticed that Guest, his heavy jaw working on a dehydrated vitamin bar, was gazing off into the distant portals of kudzu, apparently indifferent to Yates' impending revelation. Well, he'd told me he thought he knew what this mission was all about; maybe he did.

Yates said, "Do you know the name Carlo Bitler?"

"I know we're not looking for him," I said. "He was a half-caste demagogue who was assassinated in the UrNu Capitol Building almost forty years ago."

"Thirty-seven. And he wasn't a demogogue, Mz Noble." Archly he said this: very archly.

"OK," I said. "Beg your pardon. Why do you mention him?"

"We're looking for his wife," Yates announced, "and for the son of the man who assassinated Bitler, Emory Coleman. We think the two of them are together. Fiona Bitler was Coleman's teacher in a Van-Ed program for precocious children before the two of them disappeared."

"Great Maynard's ghost!" I was really excited: that's an expletive for thugboys and sentimental politicians. "How long ago was that?"

"Thirty-two years."

"You've got it all memorized! How old does that make Fiona Bitler and the little boy she was teaching?"

"The 'little boy' is now forty-one, Mz Noble, and Fiona Bitler has to be in her mid-sixties. In thirty years people age." Which was about the stupidest thing I'd ever heard Yates say. He was melancholy, though. To cover his emotion he lifted the canteen and drank.

Indian Alex hadn't stopped munching. None of what we'd just been talking about impressed him, his eyes still veered away into pine copses and viny cathedrals. When he did look at us again, well into Yates' and my awkward silence, he said, "Toombsboro was named for Robert Toombs, I think." He wiped vitamin-bar crumbs from his hands. "Robert Toombs was an unusual man. Confederate general who escaped the Yankees in the last year of the war and ended up in London. Came back to Georgia later, but never would swear his loyalty to the Union."

"Yes, sir," Yates said, annoyance surfacing again. "Old Toombs was a real jewel."

"Bitler's your hero," I said by way of mediation (they hadn't asked for it, though); maybe Toombs is his. Everyone has his own heroes." I remembered a story about Toombs that a professor of mine had always relished telling: In an early year of the war the old secessionist had bragged to a friend that one Georgia brigade with cornstalks could defeat any bunch of Yankees sent against them. After the war the friend reproached Toombs for this bit of brag. Well, Toombs drawled (my professor drawled it, anyhow), we could of—but them Yankee bastuds wouldn't fight with cornstalks. (Ho ho.) But it wasn't a story that would amuse Yates, though; so, out there in the Open, I didn't tell it.

"Not a hero of mine," Guest said. "When that war broke out there wasn't an Indian left in Georgia, least not officially: only white men and Negro slaves. But Toombs was a man who knew where he stood, that's for sure."

"Let's go," Yates said. He was already standing up.

"Wait a minute," I said. "Heroes aside, what're Fiona Bitler and that old pupil of hers doing out here near Toombsboro? Strange place for them to be, isn't it?"

Without looking at me Yates began jockeying his implement-lined belt into place over his hips. Jonah Trap's farming out here, the reports say. He's Fiona Bitler's first cousin: son of her mother's brother. When she and the boy left the city in thirty-four, they naturally went to Trap."

"And they've been living out here thirty years?"

"Off and on. It isn't completely clear."

"So why do we, in this funky year of Our Lord, come out here to haul them back to a place they must've wanted out of?" Which was a question that needed asking. Most of the "indigenous salvageables" our resource-reclamation teams brought back to the City had never lived in it before, had never been enfranchised. Fetching runaways was business we didn't engage in. Let the trash go, one of our more intellectual ward reps liked to say.

"To persuade them to return. Emory Coleman's a genius, and Mz Bitler's husband's been vindicated over and over again for his so-called rabble-rousing. Streets have been named after him, schools, housing projects, churches. The woman ought to be able to come back to that. She always wanted natural change, that's why she was a teacher. She ought to be able to die in the City that finally recognized the rightness of her husband's goals."

"Fine recognition," I said. "Implementing the Retrenchment Edicts of '35 and crushing that so-called 'Glissador Revolt' three years back, when there wasn't any revolt at all; nothing physical anyhow." This was heresy, but Yates didn't respond to it. His loyalties were cruelly divided: the City employed him, but his pigmentation suffused him with an allegiance no mere emolument or law could undermine. Newlyn Yates wasn't that sort of human being; a soldier maybe, but no mercenary.

3 / Rasputin at the Battle of Horseshoe Bend

About five o'clock on that first day we stumbled out of the green mosques and jumbled pagodas into an open area of sorts. A universal ground-cover of kudzu still tripped us up, but now it rose no higher than our upper shins: we waded through it like kids in the shallow end of a recreation pool. Guest raked the blade of his machete through the vines and felt for the hidden surface.

The machete clanged. Guest scraped at the ground-cover. "Well, here she is, Mr. Yates: Highway 57."

And it was. The vines had simply grown across it. We followed the filigreed roadbed for a while, moving east, and had the easiest time of it the wilderness had so far granted us. Well before sundown, though, we stopped, moved off the roadbed into a copse of deciduous trees (wild pecans), and made our camp for the evening.

Twilight still twinkling in the tall pines and pecans, Yates told us to go to bed: he would roust us out early, he said, so we could steal a march on the heat. We prepared to sleep on the ground.

But tall thunderheads began rolling through the twilight from the northwest, and Yates ordered us to pitch our one-person tents in a kind of triangle, dig run-off trenches, and hurriedly finish supper. The woods began to boom, the branches of the trees to thrash about violently. Huge drops began to fall through the accumulating darkness and the stuttering leaves.

Well, no stars this night; no bloated moon and no vivid, glittering constellations. Too bad. Those are things that make being a team member worth all the agitation of soul. From my two previous trips with him I remembered that Yates had sometimes stayed up all night, transfixed, looking at the stars. (How did I know it was all night? Sometimes I stayed up, too, watching *him*.) Tonight, though, Yates crawled into his tent before the worst of the deluge hit and fell soundly asleep. A feat I couldn't emulate. It was too noisy. And my soul was agitated: we were going after Fiona Bitler and Emory Coleman!

It rained an hour, at least. When it stopped, I looked up and saw a shadowy bulk hunkering next to my tent: Alexander Guest, rocking on his heels in the slow, sloughing, red mud. "'Lo," he said.

"What're you doing?" I said. Not too civilly, maybe.

"First watch," he said. "Yates gave me first watch. You can't do it proper from a tent."

"Why do we need one at all?" I said. "Nothing out here but snakes, raccoons, and opossums." The answer was that Yates did everything by the manual, even down to assigning watches in the middle of thunderstorms.

"Can't sleep, huh?"

That question disturbed me a little. I was afraid (ashamed afterwards, though) that Guest was going to propose a mutual settling of the nerves, a little easy bodywarming as a prelude to sleep. I said, "No. But look at Yates. Don't you hate a man who can go off like that, and then stay off?"

"I don't hate anybody," he said obliquely. Then, staring into the dark: "'Cept maybe Andrew Jackson. I've never really forgiven Andrew Jackson."

"For what?"

"For the way he treated Indians, you know. When that man got elected President, the Civilized Tribes and ever' other Indian in Georgia was doomed. In ten years, violatin' first this treaty, then that, he had all of us cleared out of here: Yamacraw, Creek, Yuchi, Cherokee. That Jackson's one dead fellow I wish was alive, jes' so I could kill him again."

"I'd think his being dead so long revenge enough."

"No," Guest shook his head. "Death is a sweetness, it's the dying, you know, that's the devil-bitch, always hungry for new meat . . . I wish ole Jackson was new meat again so I could feed him to the devil-bitch."

Death as Goddess, Death as Avenging Female. Well, Indians had considered the white man's failure to isolate his woman during menstruation as the most heinous of obscenities. I could accept the devil-bitch metaphor from Guest even though it would have angered me from anybody else; I could accept it without approving it, just as I could understand but never approve the Indian's fear and awe of a woman in her cycle.

Thinking these things, I crawled out of my tent. It seemed rude to carry on a conversation from the comfort of my bedding while Guest squatted in the mud. Together we drew a log up to the rain-squelched ashes of our fire and sat down. Yates slept on. Should I assure Indian Alex that I was in a touchable condition?

Instead I said, "You told me yesterday your name was an alias."

"Sort of," he said. "it's the name on my birth certificate, but *Alexander* and *Guest* certainly ain't Indian names. I'd be closer to it using something like Alexander X, the way some of them old-time black Muslims did."

Guest told me that he was the descendant of Cherokee Indians who had escaped into North Carolina at the time of the Great Removal in 1838 and 1839. Somewhere along the line a great-grandfather had taken the name Guest. "The reason for that," the big man said, "is Guest is one of the most common forms of Gist, and George Gist was the Anglo name of Sequoyah."

"Sequoyah? The inventor of the Cherokee syllabary?"

"Yep. Which I can read. I got a nigh-on complete microfilm facsimile of the Cherokee Phoenix. The Indian newspaper run off at New Echota up in old Gordon County. Got it back in my cubicle."

The other reason that Guest was an appropriate name for

Alexander's family, he explained, was that they were "guests" in the City: none of them had ever been granted enfranchisement.

"What about *Alexander*?" I said.

"Well, that's from Alexander McGillivray. He was a famous Creek *micco* whose father'd been a Scotch trader. If you want to survive in the urban Nucleus, you know, you can't go around calling yourself Menewa. So I got me a compromise name: Alexander Guest."

"Why do you want to call yourself Menewa? Is that a Cherokee name?"

"No. That's the name of a Creek warrior who called himself Hothlepoya when he was young. That means Crazy War Hunter. He was an unusual man, Menewa was; more unusual than Robert Toombs, even."

And, talking slowly, the ground around us steaming so that ghosts seemed to be rising from the heavy, carnal earth, Alexander Guest told me the story of Menewa.

By 1812 the Creek Confederacy had fragmented into pro- and anti-American factions; most of the Upper or Alabama Creeks were hostile to the new American nation, while many of the Lower or Georgia Creeks, hoping for the best, determined to support and befriend it.

"A few of these Lower Creeks," Guest said, "was in the pay of the U.S. government. Which you can't blame 'em too much for—since they was givin' up land right and left and jes' tryin' to survive in a turned-upside-down world."

The principal culprit, as Guest saw it, was a half-Scot Lower Creek, a man named William MacIntosh, who led his people in a massacre of the anti-American party of a chief named Weatherford ("Them Scots jes' seemed to have a way with the Indian gals") after Weatherford had directed his own massacre of the soldiers and their families of Fort Mims in Alabama: a Civil War antedating the one that gave the world William Tecumseh Sherman.

"Got all that straight?" Guest asked.

"I don't know. What about Menewa?"

"Well, he was a chief of an anti-American faction called the Red Sticks, and he and MacIntosh probably saw themselves as the deadliest of enemies. At the battle of Horseshoe Bend in 1812, the Red Sticks was making a desperation stand against Jackson's Tennessee militia and some pro-American Indians, and things didn't go too good for Menewa. MacIntosh was there, and some Yuchi Indians, and maybe six-hundred or so Cherokee."

"Cherokee?"

"Well," Guest said defensively, "they'd been promised all sorts of things. Some of 'em even had friends among the white men. Also, they was pretty sure this country never was gonna be all Indian again. They was doin' what they thought they had to do, jes' like Menewa's Red Sticks was—unless they was gettin' paid to do it."

The battle lasted several hours. Jackson used cannons to bombard the Red Stick positions on the peninsula. Only seventy of the original nine-hundred Red Stick warriors survived, and three-hundred women and children were taken as captives. What about Menewa?

"He was shot seven times," Guest said. "Seven times! None of 'em kilt him, though. Then, when he woke up—he'd been left for dead in the brush, you know—he took a shot at one of Jackson's militiamen. That fellow shot back. He drilled Menewa right through the cheek, but that didn't kill him, either. Menewa woke up in the middle of the night. He crawled to the river, found him a canoe, and floated down the Tallapoosa to some of the women and children who'd hidden themselves there. Made it alive, too."

"Sounds as tough as Rasputin," I said.

"Sure. Far as survivin' goes, anyhow. But the real Rasputins at the battle of Horseshoe Bend was Jackson and MacIntosh. They took all the Red Sticks' land, all of Menewa's goods and property, too, and MacIntosh probably went off thinkin' he'd finished Menewa for good."

"He hadn't?"

"It took thirteen years, but Menewa got his revenge."

In 1825, against both Creek custom and law, MacIntosh ("who was gettin' paid regular from the state, mind you") ceded to Georgia all the Creek land that hadn't already been signed away in past treaties.

"So the Creeks, the big miccos who hadn't been talked to, got together and decided to kill ole Mac. On May Day a bunch of 'em attacked his house and killed the bastard. His son-in-law, too. A lot of Georgia history writes this up as some sort of tragedy, Cleo, but it was only what the ole traitor deserved. He knew it, too. You bet he did. The best part, though, is this: it was

Menewa who actually killed MacIntosh."

Despite this triumph over his rival, Menewa lived out a story whose conclusion wasn't so happy. In 1826 Menewa went to Washington himself to make a new treaty. He didn't give up any new land, but he promised the loyalty of himself and his people to the United States.

"The land got took over, anyhow," Guest said. "Governor Troup was a cousin of MacIntosh, and he didn't give a damn how many white men tramped all over the Creek and Cherokee territories. He jes' said to hell with this U. S government's treaty, and pretty soon some of the Creeks was beggin' for food or livin' in the woods and swamps and tryin' to get by there. Coweta Town, the capital of the Lower Creeks, was full of white land speculators, Cleo, and finally a micco named Eneah Emathla got some of the Creeks together to fight it. That's when Jackson, who was now your President, you know, told his secretary of war to send troops in and smash up this 'rebellion.' Know who helped the white soldiers do it, Cleo?"

Cicadas were whirring in the undergrowth; the night sky looked like a dyer's vat full of torn bed sheets. "Not Menewa?" I said.

"Yep. Him and about two-thousand of his followers."

"Why?"

"Because in '25, you know, he'd pledged his loyalty to the U.S. government. He'd even taken to wearin' a general's uniform, standard army style, and someone in Washington promised him and his followers they wouldn't have to trek off to Oklahoma like the rest of them."

"He sold out his people," I said.

"He kep' his word. And the government broke its. They marched Menewa, a battered old man, off with them all others, never to come back. And some who saw that old Red Stick say he wept to go."

"Look," I said. "He put his abstract honor above the material well-being of the Creeks. He gave his allegiance foolishly, then acted upon it foolishly."

"Damn straight," Guest said, "considerin' who he gave it to. They never once put their, uh, abstract honor above material well-being." Groaning like an arthritic septuagenarian, he stood up and kicked languidly at the muddy ashes of our fire.

Questioningly, I looked up at him.

"Your watch, Cleo," he said. "You can wake Yates in a coupla hours." Then he lumbered over to his rain-sopped tent, took off his boots, and went to bed.

4 / *Aldeberan Above, Alighieri Below*

That night I got about two hours' sleep. We broke camp at four in the morning and moved out: eastward on kudzu-carpeted Highway 57. In thirteen hours we probably traveled about thirteen old-style miles. (Twice we saw buckshot-riddled, rusted signs saying things like *Gordon 12, Irwinton 21.*) The going was so bad because in places the asphalt had crumbled like a stale graham cracker; briary thickets had reasserted their primacy.

A little after *Gordon 12, Irwinton 21,* upon which I had tied a red marker, I said, "There's got to be a better way."

"Like what?" Yates said.

"How about a helicraft?"

"There's two in the whole city now. Besides, some redneck out here would open fire if he saw one."

Having got a little beyond the junction of Highways 57 and 18 (the latter of which led to the old town of Gordon), we stopped in the evening and made camp again. Five o'clock or so. While gathering firewood with Guest, I asked him if he had known that our "targets" were Fiona Bitler and Emory Coleman. Through an opening in the trees I could see Yates shedding his gear and dragging rubbish out of the circle of our proposed encampment. To me, it seemed a good idea to know where he was.

Not, however, to Guest. "Sure," he rumbled. "I knew."

"How?" My voice was quieter than the Indian's: a shush by means of example, I hoped.

"I was the one that met Trap when he come into the City. I'm not employed by the Human Development Commission, you know. Usually I work at one of the Dome's receiving points. It's a job you can't do if you're enfranchised, you might get corrupted off the True Path."

"But Yates said you'd been out in this area before."

"Have. But not as a team member on a rr squad. Since I work

at the old Interstate 20 Receiving Point, I'm also an agent between the City and some of the farmers out there. There ain't a single self-sufficient Urban Nucleus in the whole Federation, 'spite what the councilmen and ward reps say. Amazes me that some people don't believe the truth of *that*. Anyhow, I've been into the Open beaucoups of times. And a few miles from here we ain't gonna have to wade through kudzu no more. Wouldn't've had to do *any* of this if the City wasn't so set on motherhennin' its chicks."

"Did you set Trap up for his drugging?"

"I did. But that business about puttin' an implant tab in his nape is jes' a lot of eyewash. Yates thinks it happened, but it didn't. Hell, *I* knew where the man lived, and the fellows at Grady Memorial got all the other information out of him with the hypnotizin', and the drugs too. Surprised 'em, what he had to say. You see, I got a friend at the hospital."

"Why'd you set Trap up? He must've trusted you."

"'Cause enfranchised or not, I had to sign an oath to carry out the City's biddin'—in all things, you know—before they'd even give me a job." Holding two fistfuls of dry kindling, my gingerbread Indian paused and looked intently at me. "And, Mz Noble, I put my name on the paper, I put my name on the paper—with no one sayin' he'd scalp me if I didn't." He started to turn.

I caught his elbow. "Do you know why the authorities want Mz Bitler and Coleman back in the City?"

"Probably not for a ticker-tape parade, Mz Noble."

"Then what?"

"Old Trap told the doctors his cousin and her pupil, who calls himself Nettlinger now instead of Coleman (Nettlinger was his real father's name, you know, and he was the fellow who shot Bitler)—anyhow, Trap said they'd spent several years in New Free Europe: The Scandinavian Polity, to be exact. That's dangerous. Now they're both back, the infection might spread—sort of like kudzu, I guess."

"So what will the City do?"

"Question 'em, lock 'em up someplace. Maybe worse. I don't know." Guest broke free of me this time, and of my questioning, and made his heavily delicate way back to the clearing, where Yates had begun, with the fuel he had gathered, to boil some drinking water. I just stood there. Oh, Grandma Zoe, what a picture of perplexity I would have made, what a study in bewilderment.

Hanging over the trees like lamps, stars abounded that night: they freckled the matte sky with gold, silver, silver-blue, red: a carnival of constellations. It was splendidly gaudy, like a gauche hat.

Yates, propped up on his elbows and forearms, his head thrown back, began without prompting to talk:

"Before I'd ever been into the Open, I used to dream about doing what we're doing now. Seeing the stars firsthand; not on film, or in picture-books, or done up by some crazy foreigner with rings and haloes around them, like they showed us in art-appreciation class. I wanted real stars, just like these.

"Even inside the Dome I felt connected to them, you know: they were like missing parts of my body the nerve ends wouldn't let me forget. Or maybe like pulled teeth that had little radio transmitters inside them, so that even when they'd been dropped down the disposer-converter in some dentist's office, they still kept sending me messages: an all-the-time toothache, no matter what I did. So I tried everything I could to get close to them, to the stars on the Other Side. They had something to tell me, you know, gaps to fill in.

"When I was fourteen a man who worked for my father in the Biomonitor Agency—his name was Ardrey, I won't forget that—started taking me combcrawling: you know, using girderboots and mesh gloves, expensive magnetized equipment, to climb over the inside of the Dome. Scary as it could be, even when you were just practicing easy assaults out on the perimeter of the City and doing a lot of vertical climbing instead of hanging upside-down over the whole skyscrape. I did that, too, though. Partly so Ardrey wouldn't think I was a baby, but mostly because combcrawling, when I did it, I felt like I was pressing myself that much closer to the real sky outside and the stars hiding behind the Dome. The Dome was just another skin to get through, and I tried to get through it combcrawling, scared as I was.

"Then Ardrey and I had an argument. It was about this old woman who died on Level 9, *under*. Since he worked for the Bio Agency, he had her cubicle burned out—even though she had the whole thing made up like the inside of a spaceship. Neatest and craziest thing I ever saw. We'd gone down there because I'd challenged Ardrey to go look at a deader in person. I think I thought dying was one way to get outside the Dome, scarier even than combcrawling but probably more effective, too. Anyway, Ardrey ordered this spaceship-cubicle she was living in, with these fake viewscreens of planets and stars, eaten up by flame-torches and refurbished for a new occupant. I hated him for doing it; I called him names. Stopped combcrawling, too: just never went with him again. My father had to sell back all the equipment he bought me.

"Three or four years later Ardrey was killed in a combcrawling accident. Now it's outlawed, nobody can do it. And I'm sorry I never made it up with that man, know-it-allish as he liked to act. Ardrey just did what my father would have ordered him to do if Ardrey hadn't gone ahead and done it himself. Simple as that.

"Now I don't have to combcrawl to get close to the stars; don't have to pretend some old woman's busted dreams are going to get me closer. Just look up, there they are—making my nerve ends tingle and my toothache throb even worse than when I couldn't see them. Can you tell me, why is that? Sitting here looking at them, I ache ten times as bad as when I was fourteen years old and girderclimbing in order to press myself right through the skin of the Dome to the torn-off pieces of myself: ten times as bad. Now why is that? Can you tell me, why is that?"

But he didn't really expect an answer, and Alexander Guest and I, sipping at our metal cups of insta-caffe, didn't break the silence. The Ferriswheel lights in the sky kept turning.

Yates rousted us out early the next morning, before sunrise, and we were on our way again. In two hours' time, just as the sun had begun to send sparkles through the foliage, the foliage itself fell away and we were staring at cleared fields. Too, the kudzu on 57 had been hacked aside and contained. We walked out of the vines and onto a recently compacted and graveled surface. On previous trips into the Open I had never seen anything like this, no manicured roadbeds and certainly no cultivated fields the size of these: garden plots and arbors I'd seen, but not farms, not grazing land. Well, Guest had hinted at such a possibility.

"Can I stop stringing up these silly rags?" I asked Yates. The road stretched out before us like an invitation, white-washed wooden fences paralleling it on both sides.

"Sure," Yates said amiably, coming up from the rear to lead us. "This is a 'civilized pocket.' My surprise to you, a gift for the two days' slogging we've done." He looked around happily. "They told me it'd be here."

Guest said, "Did they tell you it was more'n a pocket?"

Yates, sweat in the hollows of his eyes, stared at the big man.

"There's a strip of cultivated land through here," "Guest went on, "all the way to Savannah. And some of the towns have people in 'em, too. Not Toombsboro, it don't. But Irwinton and Wrightsville and Vidalia and beaucoups of others. Savannah's got thirty-thousand people, at least. Ships still run in and out of it, that's probably how Bitler and Nettlinger got to the Scandinavian Polity and back."

Blank of all expression, his eyes maybe a little caged-looking, Yates said, "Guest, you're crazy." But he had been hit with an Indian club and was standing dazed on doomed legs: just to hold him up, I wanted to embrace him.

"Wait till you see all the walkin' 'lucinations I can conjure, then," Guest said. "Far as surprisin' us with this gravel road goes, we're gonna run into U.S. 441 at Irwinton—and it run straight on up to old Interstate 20. We could've saved us two days and a heck of a lot of boot leather if the old Com Authority had let us come by way of 'em." He spit into 57's loose gravel.

"Guest," Yates began. "Guest...." Then, to both of us: "Come on."

We walked in the sunshine down the gravel road. Eventually we passed a house, and a man on a parboiled, rust-purpled tractor came down its enclosed drive pulling a flatbedded hay wagon. After expressing, by his movements more than anything else, his distrust and suspicion, the man said, "Yeah, old Jonah Trap lives on the other side of Irwinton. Get in. Take you that far at least."

Bald and leathery of neck, he did what he said he would—carrying us right into the Irwinton town square, where he let us off. Coming in, I noted that U.S. 441 bisected our own "highway" and ran off to the north, there to connect with Interstate 20 (as Indian Alex alleged) out of Atlanta. Anyhow, by some strange transmutation, we had all traveled into a rural community redolent of the life depicted on old John Deere and

International Harvester calendars. (It was popular early last year to decorate your cubicles with reproductions of "Americana." Now I was a piece of Americana myself: a living curiosity. And a curious one, too.) We watched our benefactor's tractor chug around a corner.

"Runs on methane," Guest said. "Distilled from pig's shit, or any other kind of droppin's you care to use."

Yates looked at the Indian with distaste.

"No worse than the City's waste converters," I said.

A few people staring at us from store windows and chairs under awnings, we went on through the little town, still on Highway 57, and followed the gravel road toward the site of old Toombsboro. The fields on either side of us waved with beans, or cotton, or corn.

As we got closer and closer to the dwelling place of our "targets," I began thinking about what sort of living accomodations a man like Trap would receive if he lived in the Urban Nucleus. Since most of the surfaceside ghettoes had been razed (they had torn down Bondville in the conciliatory aftermath of the "Glissador Revolt") he would most likely go under: most likely Level 7, or 8, or maybe even 9. The circles of Dante's Hell, our cynical professor types always called them. Except that in the UrNu scheme of things, the innocent get punished along with the guilty. A few of the absolutely shiftless sort have been consigned to the Big Bad Basement, but you can find plenty of those upstairs, too.

On Level 9, for instance, you have people whose greatest crime consists of being too young or too old or maybe of having only a "marginally utilizable skill," like grocery-stocking or message-running or waiting tables.

In addition, all the unenfranchised live on Level 9, which meant—as I had either forgotten or never really considered— that Alexander Guest had a cubicle in this final ring of our parochial inferno.

What were the sins of these damned, what enormities were they guilty of?

My father would say, "You're a bleeding, heart, Clio. Almost everybody's lived *under*, one time or another. Forty-five meters up or down just don't make that much difference."

And Mama Lannie, twirling her chiffon sleeves, would say,

"Oh, she's just young yet, Sanders, that's how she's supposed to feel."

As if sympathy were a glandular condition like acne. So that I would go off remembering how Dante had put the perpetrators of passionate crimes in less abysmal circles of Hell than those who had committed sins of malice and fraud. Which meant, to me anyhow, that whereas I ought to be sentenced only to Level 7 for killing my parents in an idealistic rage, Atlanta's councilmen and ward reps—for their manifold, premeditated treacheries—ought to find brimstone and pitchforks waiting for them on our two nethermost strata. Sayeth Dante, it is more heinous to abuse the intellect, which separates us from the beasts, than to abuse the emotions. Therefore, I was proud of my overactive and probably misfunctioning glands.

On Highway 57, without ever having met him, I was proud of Jonah Trap for shunning the whale's belly of the Urban Nucleus and forging a life for himself and his family in the Open. A black man—a poorly educated black man, mind you—in the renovated plantation house of a one-time "marster." No Level 9 for him, no Level 9 for his brood.

5 / *Sesame Street Down on Marster's Plantation*

When we reached Trap's house, we paused before it like astronauts on the rim of an unexpectedly quartz-shot lunar crater. In awe we stood there, or at least Yates and I did. From the graded roadbed we looked across a lake-sized lawn whose far edge, immediately before the antebellum mansion itself, was dominated by two gnarled, top-heavy oaks. *His* and *her* trees, they'd been called in New England: one for the Master and one for his Dame. Pools of shade undulated on the grass. The mansion had a portico supported by four Doric columns, and beyond the living complex—which included a neat, single-story structure off to the right—you could see the beginnings of terraced red fields.

A shieldlike wooden sign on the gate by the roadbed said *Phoenix Plantation*. A series of starlike points on the sign had been connected to make this figure:

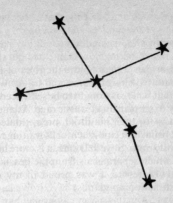

"What's that?" I said.

"The constellation Cygnus," Yates replied without a second's hesitation. "Sometimes called the Swan, or the Northern Cross. But it could be a phoenix, too, I guess: any sort of firebird that's born again every night."

A breeze rocked the sign. It was only nine o'clock or so in the morning, and I felt like I had been born again, right there on the edge of Jonah Trap's lawn: the Athena of Noble stepping from the sundered, feverish forehead of Newlyn Yates. Indian Alex, unperturbed by all this, was our staid midwife.

"Well, let's go see if anybody's home," I said. And I struck up the long circular drive that passed the oaks in front of the mansion. Scufflings behind me indicated that I was being followed.

A venerable-appearing black woman answered my knock at the wide, shaded door. I asked for Jonah Trap. She introduced herself as . . . Fiona Bitler, cousin of the man who owned the Phoenix Plantation; and without asking us who we were she invited us in, graciously.

Waxed parquetry in the anteroom. An enormous chandelier. An imposing carven china cabinet. Silence and coolness such as you might anticipate finding in an Ice Palace. And then, as we trailed the shorts-clad woman into an adjoining room (I hope I have legs that good when I'm sixty-five, and that they don't interfere with my looking venerable): the altogether incongruous sounds of children laughing.

"Come sit down with us," Mz Bitler said. "We've just started school for Jonah's grandchildren. As for Jonah, you'll have to wait till noon to see him."

School.

For the first time since coming into the Open together, Yates and Guest exchanged a sympathetic glance—but, along with me, they followed their hostess through the sliding wooden doors to the left of the long foyer and into an elegant, high-ceilinged "classroom." Mz Bitler motioned us to a row of rocking chairs behind the five black children—three boys and two girls—who did not turn their heads as we entered. Their gazes were fixed on the screen of a video-playback unit mounted on a high metal stand. Since I saw no electrical outlets or fixtures in the entire room, the complex must have drawn its power from batteries. The power source made no difference to the kids; they were successively intent, bemused, apprehensive, raucous, puzzled, and quietly delighted, all in accord with the images unwinding on the screen and the sounds sputtering out of the unit's speakers. A school of no little gaiety.

I leaned forward to watch: puppets, cartoons, animal films, adults singing and talking with children, letters and numbers flashing by, all of it spliced together with quick cuts and remarkable élan. Indian Alex, whose chair rested on the hardwood floor instead of the rug, had to keep himself from rocking in time to the activity: his movements made the floor squeak. Yates, holding himself erect (tricky in a rocking chair), just looked bewildered.

"Public Broadcasting Service program antedating the Domes," Mz Bitler told us. "When I worked with the Van-Ed people over thirty years ago, we had limited access to this series—for historical as well as educative purposes. You had to give cause for wanting the tapes, and sign for them—but you could get them. The year after I left, the tapes were proscribed; nobody got to use them, not for any reason."

On the screen two puppets, apparently outer-space creatures, were examining a telephone. They bobbed up and down, their googly eyestalks bouncing, and made high-pitched, repetitive noises: "*Yip yip . . . yip yip yip . . . yip yip.*" Trap's grandchildren, all of them under six, I'd say, were giggling. When the video-taped telephone rang and the unearthly creatures plunged out of sight in panic, the kids guffawed and bounced about and cuffed each other. Guest was laughing, too: a close-mouthed, resonating chuckle.

"Is that educational?" Yates said.

"In a way, I suppose," Mz Bitler said. "It's certainly *funny*." A new sequence was on now, though: an animated alphabet, each letter surrealistically metamorphosing into the one following it.

"How did Mr Trap get these tapes?" I asked.

"He bought them from a man whose father had taken them from an educational television station in the evacuated university town of Athens. The video equipment Johan had put together by an electronics hobbyist in Savannah. He has almost two years' worth of these tapes; he used them to start Gabriel's and Michael's education, not knowing what else he could do for them. Jonah can read, but only just."

We watched for fifteen or twenty minutes. Although Guest was engrossed in the program, Yates still had not loosened up. I touched the arm of Mz Bitler's chair and said, "We didn't come only to see Mr Trap. We came to see and talk to you also, Mz Bitler, and the man you took out of the City with you in '34. Gerard Coleman. Gerard Nettlinger. Whichever of those names he goes by now." Yates, whose reaction I had been unsure of, looked past Mz Bitler at me with an expression suggesting gratitude: I'd done something right!

"How did you know we were here?" she asked. "We haven't been, you see, for that terribly long: two or three months. In fact, Emory's been to Europe and back—again—since we arrived here in...what?...the middle of April?" That was old-style dating, not one of the Federation's "seasonal" months.

Yates glanced at Guest as if surprised by the big man's prescience: hadn't Guest, just that morning, mentioned the Scandinavian Polity?

"We learned Trap was your cousin," I said, "and just supposed you would be here."

Fortunately Mz Bitler did not ask how we had learned that Trap was her cousin or how we had known where he lived. "Well," she said instead, "you don't have to wait till noon to talk to me. This is almost over." We waited. When the program ended, she turned off the video-playback unit, then called to the children's mothers, who had been at the back of the house in the kitchen. Casta and Georgia, their names were. They nodded politely to us and herded their children into the wing of the house giving off the classroom. Mz Bitler led us through another high-ceilinged room to the cool gray kitchen they'd just evacuated.

"This is a good place to talk," she said, and we all sat down at a round oaken table.

Through the screened-in porch behind the kitchen I could see a grape arbor in the backyard, a portion of the cultivated field we had seen from the road, and an adjacent orchard beyond the arbor: these were peach trees, Mz Bitler said, and that's where the men were, out there picking the fruit. Trap and his family were people who still divided their labors into men tasks and women tasks. That was the only relic of unenlightened agrarian life predisposing me against them, and Fiona Bitler, a woman who had lived once in the shadow of her husband's passionate crusading, didn't seem at all perturbed by the dichotomy. A breeze lifted the kitchen curtains, and the planet seemed to stretch out around us like a new Eden (the man-and-maiden opposition still sadly intact). In comparison, though, most of the other "indigenous salvageables" we had gone out after had been living like ferreting beasts.

Yates said, "Where is Mr Coleman, Mz Bitler?"

"It's Nettlinger now. When he was old enough to decide for himself, he began using his real father's name again. Another of Guest's assertions corroborated. "At any rate, he's asleep. You're not likely to see him until this evening; he functions best at night, and, like an owl, that's when he comes out."

"He uses the name of the man who assassinated your husband?" Yates asked, his long, nervous hands poised on their fingertips over the table.

"It's his father's name, isn't it?" said Guest, who was leaning back in his chair, hands clasped at his middle. "Whose name you want him to use? Whose name *you* use?"

I could see Yates emotionally staggering, first from Mz Bitler's revelation, then from Guest's mildly delivered but unexpected assault: so vulnerable under the obsolete martial armor he affected in the field. "But his mother remarried," Yates countered, looking from the composed Indian to the composed black woman, "and his new father officially adopted him."

"Yes," Mz Bitler said.

"Well, do you approve of the change? From Coleman to the

name of your husband's assassin?" His hands looked as if they would momentarily flee from him.

"As a boy Emory had no say in the matter. The name was changed, *lipity lip,* just like that. Later he decided on the other. My approval—your approval—anyone else's approval—is beside the point." She looked at Yates. "Isn't it?"

"But how did it make you *feel*?"

"Emory isn't his father, Mr Yates, but his father lives in him. We don't renounce our pasts out of hand, even if we don't like them. We don't renounce our origins, our birthrights, our kindred. We acknowledge them at least. Then, if we don't like them, we move away from them into our selves." Fiona Bitler laughed. "Now, that's the sort of didactic pronouncement only a queen or a comfortable old whore can get away with, I give you leave to classify me as you like."

"A B C D," a thin voice said from the door. "E F G." It was one of the kids who'd been watching the video-playback unit: a boy wearing only a pair of cotton underpants. He didn't look much more than two.

Fiona Bitler motioned the child to her, and he climbed into her lap. "This is Carlo," she said. "Jonah's youngest grand-child." She introduced us all around.

"Hello, Carlo," I said.

The boy looked me directly in the eye. "A B C D," he said seriously. "E F G . . . H I J K." Pausing in the appropriate spots, he continued successfully to the end.

"Carlo has a twenty-six letter vocabulary," Fiona Bitler said. The namesake of her dead husband, the boy stayed in her lap for the rest of our conversation, occasionally reciting his letters in a voice that didn't disrupt Mz Bitler's narration but provided a contrapuntal undercurrent to it. And she took us back to 2034:

"I kidnapped Emory," she began. "Before that, I worked very hard to put myself in a position to teach the boy, not knowing exactly what I would do once I achieved this goal. I had followed Emory's development from only a month or two after Carlo's death down to the moment he was placed in my Van-Ed classroom, you see, and I felt an affinity with him for several reasons, not merely because he was the son of my husband's murderer.

"Maybe one reason was maternal: Carlo and I had never had any children. Planned them, yes, but never had them. The

strongest motivation, though, was the fact that Emory and I
shared a similar questionable blessing: precociousness. It had
brought me to the attention of the Education Authority of the
Human Development Commission at the age of four and lifted
my entire family out of the Bondville ghetto into Tower housing.
But that was just after the Dome was completed, before the
gradual return of a claustrophobically bred repressiveness. I
don't know what it accomplished for Emory, this precociousness, until he was accepted into one of the special-education
programs. I know that his mother and her new husband, John
Adam Coleman, lived in a Level 5 cubicle, *under*. So it didn't
accomplish for his family what it had once accomplished for
mine.

"He was eight when I met him for the first time, a thin,
spindly, almost palsied-looking little boy who could have passed
for an autistic child except for his occasional lapses into
sociability. He liked to draw, almost always in black purple
crayon, and sometimes he would come out of his corner to show
us these productions. Mockery, some of these drawings seemed.

"Toward the end of that year—the only one we had together
inside the Dome—he must have discovered who I was, and what
oblique relationship I had to him. After that, mockery emerged
in his actions as well as his drawings. He insisted on dragging
odd reminders of his father, Carlo's murderer, into the
classroom. The principal one was an old instructional film of his
father's: Nettlinger had been a dentist, and Emory, who was the
class projectionist when we showed films, would run this film
even when another one was scheduled. You couldn't stop him,
he wouldn't be reasoned with, and Fiona Bitler . . . well, Fiona
Bitler was losing control of things. So I asked for help.

"The Van-Ed people gave me a psychologist from the Human
Development Commission, a middle-aged man with a pleasant
disposition but something out of kilter in his eyes. Greer. Dr
Gregory Greer. The man tried. He tried his best. But what
happened was, he quickly alienated Emory and wrenched his
own objectivity apart by falling in love with me. I don't know
which happened first, maybe they occurred simultaneously—
but Greer couldn't admit either of them to himself: he was a
bachelor, his commitment was wholly to psychological
troubleshooting, and he didn't know how to handle a collapse
on two fronts, the personal as well as the professional. I don't
think I'm flattering myself about the personal aspect of the

situation; I may have even encouraged the man—in ways too subtle for me to pinpoint—to relinquish his objectivity. I don't know. I hope to God I never find out for certain.

"The result, oddly, was that Greer somehow threw Emory back into a strange sort of sympathy with me. Finally Greer suffered a nervous breakdown in the classroom where I taught: he came in the evening when nobody was there and set fire to Emory's drawings and the old film that the boy had been showing.

"Two days later Emory asked me to take him away from his parents. He said he wanted to live with me. During this same week, of course, Greer was hospitalized, and my life seemed as up in the air as it had been after Carlo's death. Sick I was: deeply, hollowly sick." Fiona Bitler stared into the peach orchard beyond the screened porch, a black Isis recalling her struggle to resurrect in her own life and work the image of her husband and the promise of their unborn children. Little Carlo was now blithely saying his numbers. "How I was tugged," Fiona Bitler said at last, "how I was cruelly tugged." Her arms were wrapped around Carlo.

"I cast about for help. Again. My mother, who was alive then, told me that a friend of hers who worked at an UrNu receiving point had heard from her brother: Jonah Trap had delivered some goods to the City. The friend might be able to get a message through to him, if mother had one she wanted carried. 'You've got one,' I told Mama, 'you've got a very special message you want carried.' And so one day after class in the Van-Ed complex I took Emory over to Mama's, and we all rode a transit-car to a lift-terminal as close to our friend's receiving point as we could. We didn't take anything with us, only ourselves, and that night we rode out of the City in the back of Jonah's pickup truck, under a tarp since we were afraid there might be patrollers out." She lapsed, suddenly, into plantation dialect and began to sing:

> *Run, nigger, run, the paddy-role will catch you,*
> *Run, nigger, run, the paddy-role will catch you.*
> *You better git away, you better git away....*
>
> *Run, nigger, run, the paddy-role will catch you.*
> *Run, nigger, run, the paddy-role will catch you.*
> *You better git away, you better git away....*

*   *   *

"A long, bumpy ride to the Phoenix Plantation, right here where we're all sitting now."

She let Carlo down. The boy made a circle around us, touching the backs of our chairs and sometimes putting his lips to the edge of the table. "A B C," he said gruffly; "A B C."

"Nicer here than in a subterranean cubicle," Mz Bitler said. "Isn't it? Even if you happen to be a kidnapper."

The morning passed much too quickly for me. The two young women, Georgia and Casta, cooked on a wood stove that quickly heated up the kitchen. Indian Alex and I helped Jonah Trap's daughter-in-law put the noon meal on the table, while Yates and Mz Bitler, two or three children tagging along, strolled through the scuppernong arbor and part of the peach orchard. When they returned for dinner, Yates took me aside and said that they had talked about her late husband and her own desire to see the City again. "It shouldn't be too hard for you to persuade her to come back with us," he said.

Trap and his two sons came in from the orchards to eat. More introductions. Gabriel and Michael, meet Mr Yates, Mr Guest, and Mz Noble. The kitchen was teeming with people, the linoleum floor sighed under us, additional wings on the table were folded into place and dishes dealt out like playing cards. Georgia took the kids into the backyard to eat on the lawn.

Fried chicken, sliced tomatoes, fried okra, fresh cucumbers, fried fruit pies, cornbread, slabs of home-churned butter, well water cooled in the earth. Amid this abundance, silverware rattled and platters of food went from hand to hand as if hovering on their own power.

Looking at Guest, Trap said, "You I done met, Mistah Guest. These people yo' frien's?" He pointed his fork at Yates and me.

"Yes, sir."

"Well, they plenny welcome, then. Will you ask the blessin', Casta?"

Casta asked the blessing: it wasn't an Ortho-Urban prayer, that's the main thing I remember about it. Between mouthfuls of food, then, Jonah Trap got our business straightened out: we wanted to invite his cousin and Gerard Nettlinger to return to the Urban Nucleus, at least for a kind of commemorative visit. (I think I was the bright one who used the word "commemorative.") Fiona Bitler said that Emory had been planning, for several years, to do just that; since returning from the

Scandinavian Polity two weeks ago, he had moved this contemplated visit to the top of his own personal timetable: he wanted a chance, in fact, to address a combined session of the Urban Council and the Conclave of Ward Representatives.

"Good luck to you there," Alexander Guest said.

"We're both enfranchised," Mz Bitler said. "Or were. Besides, I'd think our return would stir up enough interest to invite such a public address."

"A century ago," I said, "the Japanese permitted a rescued holdout in the South Pacific to speak to their parliament, almost thirty years after World War II." Not one of my better-received analogies. Jonah, Michael and Gabriel, Casta, Newlyn and Alex—they all stopped chewing to look at me: Scarlett O'Hara, Ph. D. in Comparative History.

"That's exactly right," Fiona Bitler said.

After dinner Trap and his sons returned to the orchards. The serving dishes on the table were covered with an embroidered cloth: no more cooking that day. Guest and I, working in wash/dry tandem, took care of the dirtied plates and silverware. But Emory Nettlinger was elsewhere, sleeping out the heat of the day, and the afternoon was much longer than the morning.

6 / Long King Is to Ogelthorpe
As Yates Is to Nettlinger

Fiona Bitler countered the length of the afternoon a little by giving us a bedroom upstairs and urging us to take naps: "If you want to talk to Emory this evening, you'd better get some sleep."

We had left our gear on the mansion's porch, in the portico. We hauled it up the stairs to our bedroom (the middle one of three in relation to the stairwell) and stacked it on the floor between the room's two brass beds. The beds had feather mattresses, though, and Alex refused to sleep on them, protesting a weak back. He made a pallet beside our gear and lay down on that. For the first time since we had been in the house Newlyn removed the belt supporting his holster and let his constricted facial muscles relax; he put the hand laser under his pillow. Even though all the heat in the mansion had seemed to concentrate itself in this one room, we all managed to sleep. The floors were so rickety that Newlyn didn't even feel compelled to set a "watch."

We met Emory Nettlinger himself that evening—after the supper Newlyn wouldn't let us go downstairs for. "One meal like that a day is enough," he said, shaking his head almost jovially. "Feather mattresses and fried food, it'll do you in."

Jovial or not, he wouldn't let us go down—until he was sure the Traps had finished the evening meal. Then we clumped in our boots single file down the stairs and, at Trap's direction, met Fiona Bitler and her former ward in caned lawn chairs under the "Master's Oak." It was almost twilight.

Nettlinger stood to shake hands with us. He was a short man with pallid skin, close-cropped blond hair making a point in the middle of his forehead, and eyes like bluish ice. The veins in his temples pulsed.

"You want to take us back to the Urban Nucleus," he said. "That's fine, Mr Yates. We're almost ready—almost—to go."

"Will you come with us tomorrow?" Newlyn asked.

"No. Tomorrow I'm not prepared to commit myself to. Nor would you and your people be ready for us to leave with you."

"Why not? That's what we came for."

"Sit down," he said, and Newlyn and I took up lawn chairs; Alex, true to form, sat down on the grass. "To answer your question," Nettlinger said, "you are ones who have been too long in City pent, and, like a great many other of the Urban Nucleus' citizens, you're going to require some…what shall I call it?…grooming? indoctrination? before you'll be truly ready to accept us."

"We've accepted you already," I said. "And Mz Bitler will find that the City's done a great deal to rectify the conditions her husband once complained of." This was Newlyn's line, I knew, but out here it seemed altogether true, not merely a part of the truth. Alex's fears were exaggerated. And I was supposed to be "persuasive."

"Maybe you've accepted *us*," Fiona Bitler said, looking at Nettlinger, "but we don't intend to come back to Atlanta alone."

"Trap's family will be welcome, too," Newlyn said. "It'll have to be arranged, but I think—"

"Jonah doesn't want to leave the Phoenix Plantation," she countered. "We're not speaking of them."

"Then who?" Alex said. "We s'posed to guess?"

Nettlinger said, "Do you know where we've spent most of our time in the Open? Not here, certainly. Not here."

"The Scandinavian Polity," Alex said.

"Eventually, eventually. I've just come from there, in fact. But when Fiona first took me out of the City, when I was a child, she arranged in Savannah to transport me to relatives of my father in Austria. That's when we discovered that Austria per se didn't exist anymore: the national units we supposed still intact had long since melded into the encompassing political entity of New Free Europe.

"At any rate, I insisted that Fiona accompany me, and we sailed to the continent on a steam vessel someone had christened the *Phoenix*. It was named for one that a man named John Stevens had built in 1808! A steam vessel, please note. Lately, we've traveled by air—since the Scandinavian Polity has aircraft which can compensate for the several inadequate coastal landing strips this 'country' still possesses—but we first left here on a *steam*ship!"

Nettlinger told us that he had acquired tutors through the intervention of a paternal uncle in Salzburg and that Fiona and these rotating tutors had taken him beyond the "kinetic relations" sessions and the "elementary" integral calculus of the Van-Ed program in Atlanta into physics and higher mathematics: wave theory, relativistic studies, subatomic physics.

"Oh, I gravitated to these studies naturally," Nettlinger said, smiling at Mz Bitler.

Moreover, he and Fiona had moved his schooling about: from Salzburg to Vienna, from Vienna to Munich, and, finally, when Nettlinger was sixteen, from Munich to Scandipol (formerly Kobenhaven), the designated administrative center of the Scandinavian Polity of New Free Europe. Here, his "schooling" ended, and he began work in a research-development institution, on aeronautical and space engineering projects that the Europeans, Eurasians, and Japanese had jointly commandeered, by default, from the abandoned NASA programs of the United States.

"Actually," he said, "'commandeered' is the wrong word, since what they had appropriated was neither hardware nor working plans but—this is very important—an attitude no longer countenanced in the Urban Nuclei because of the very nature of these Cities, these *Nuclei;* it's the eternal opposition of entropy and growth, perhaps even of autism and extroversion. 'Nucleus' says it all, Mr Yates: Atlanta sees itself, as do all the other Domed Cities, as the center of its own very narrow and circumscribed universe. And we're afraid that your own gracious . . . acceptance of Fiona and me will not be shared by Atlanta's authorities, primarily because of the argument we intend to bring with us."

"No," Alex said. "They're likelier to accept people than a argument. What is it?"

"To tear down the Domes and rejoin the community of men, which is also the community of life." Legs crossed, hands folded, the man looked remarkably priggish: prim as a prufrock. Even so, his voice was free of superciliousness.

Alex put a blade of grass between his teeth. "Doomed," he said. "You really are doomed."

Mz Bitler said, "That's why Emory's been telling you about the changes in Europe and about the course of his own education there. Since *you* find this hard to accept, you know the urban authorities are going to require some time to become comfortable with the changes in the outer world."

"But they aren't that startling," I said. "Here they are: Europe's become a single political unit, and Emory Nettlinger has studied advanced sciences in three or four different Cities."

The twilight had come together around us as if quilted out of sequined navy-blue cloth; fireflies were winking on and off under the trees. Fireflies, stars, and mosquitoes. I slapped at my exposed arms and squinted at the silhouettes of those around me: Mz Bitler was rubbing her bare legs as if similarly pestered.

"That's true," Nettlinger said, "but there's more." He suggested, though, that we go inside since the mosquitoes and the gathering dark made continuing on the lawn unpleasant.

Trap's sons, daughters-in-law, and grandchildren had all retired to bedrooms in the mansion's west wing. In the foyer we found Trap himself, preparing to go upstairs to bed.

"That owl there," Trap said, pointing to Nettlinger as we came in, "got him a place to stay in that ole overseer cottage. Can' stan' no early-mornin' scootin' about. Do all his thinkin' when the moon shine."

"A clear case of lunacy," Nettlinger said. "Good night, sir."

"Good night." Trap paused on the stairs. "Good night,

everybody." And went on up with the step of a considerably younger man.

In the parlor across the hall from the video-playback "classroom," Nettlinger resumed the process of our grooming. I felt even more removed from my own century than I had that morning in Irwinton. The parlor was illuminated by wall-mounted gas lamps, and the quality of the light—shifting, intangible, touched with the influence of lacquered floors and voluted window drapes—made the impetus of Nettlinger's words almost too choicely ironic for comfort. The setting was Victorian rather than antebellum, and Nettlinger was our intent, thin-faced tour guide leading us into a future that had already been part of the Old World's past. Legs crossed, hands folded, he sat in a chair that swallowed him.

"Did you know that during the construction of the Domes, shortly after the turn of this century, men walked on the Moon again? Did any of you know that?"

Newlyn's face was tattooed with blue and purplish highlights; he leaned forward on the edge of the striped sofa, hands hanging. "I don't believe that." But he wanted to, you could read the desire in his posture.

"No one in an Urban Nucleus has any reason to believe that," Nettlinger said. "So why should you? As a boy, I had no idea that such a thing could be. Fiona had never heard of a moon expedition beyond the American Apollo 17 mission. If *any* enfranchised citizen of the Domes knew that an Old World Coalition had put men on the Moon, he sat on the fact—smothered it beneath the wide twin buttocks of urban policy and patriotism. My own opinion is that no one knew, that no one in the City's hierarchy would have cared very much even if the fact had been conclusively demonstrated.

"The truth is, however, that continuously since 2023, two years before I was born, human beings have had a large and expanding base on the Moon: a base, a colony, a shipyard, an observatory...Enough. You must call it a City, I suppose: oddly enough, a *domed* one.... How do you feel when I tell you these things?" His eyes stopped on me.

Since Newlyn and Alex weren't going to answer, I said, "That it's too early for bedtime stories, is how I feel."

"OK," he said enthusiastically, his accent now more European than American Southern. "Expected. Anticipated.

How else should you feel? But it's the truth, and it's part of the reason Fiona and I aren't going trotting, *trit-trot, trit-trot,* into Atlanta tomorrow. The news is a shock, a jolt, it will undoubtedly throw a good many people and some of the UrNu authorities into confusion. And the note of dismay, or confusion, or even exhilaration, sounded by the broadcasting of this news—I must warn you—will only be the minor of that sounded by the rest of what I have to tell you. Do you understand me?"

"We've gone to the planets?" Newlyn said: *We've.* He was transferring the accomplishments of New Free Europe into the hands of humanity in general: *We came in peace for all mankind.*

"Beyond," Fiona Bitler said.

"To what?" Alex said. "To what?" He looked as if he wanted out of doors again, whereas I was proving susceptible to Newlyn's excitement: I found myself leaning forward, too.

"When I arrived in Scandipol," Nettlinger said, sidestepping, it seemed at first, Alex's question, "they had been working on relativistic and astrophysical concepts beyond those that had to do with the propulsion systems for Earth-Moon transport. Their compatriots on the Moon had, in fact, built a prototype of a vessel whose range would be interstellar rather than merely interplanetary.

"Gravitation wells and astrodynamics, metallurgy and stress mechanics; oh, it was a program drawing upon but otherwise divergent from the ones that had established us on the Moon.

"How to tell you? My mentor at the institute was Nils Caspersson, and my own contributions were minor. Everything had gone forward extremely well before my arrival, I could only hone—by virtue of my virgin perspective, if nothing else—the insights Caspersson and his fellows had developed over a period of three intensive decades. But I won't be self-servingly modest: I did contribute, I did lend my own quirky insights to these researches. Emory Nettlinger, seventeen years old.

"In 2043 our Moon-orbiting prototype was given probe-capability and mechanically test-advanced a range of four light years, nearly the distance of Alpha Centauri—although on this first unmanned flight our directioning was reluctantly, unavoidably random: a technological embarrassment, I must grant you. But we retrieved the vessel; we called it back to our solar system and confirmed by its onboard equipment, photographic and

chronometric as well as protoastrogational, the very real fact of
its advance. The surprise—the great, hoped-for surprise—was
the coincidence of shipboard, subjective time and Scandipol
Moon-base, subjective time: a round-trip of eight light-years in
ninety-three Earth-standard days. Not the negation of Einstei-
nian physics, oh no, but a kind of ballet kick over the glass stage
of interstellar space."

Nettlinger uncrossed his legs, pointed his toes, and
performed a funny, seated entrechat.

"Caspersson, Fiona, and I got drunk—oh, we got magnificently stewed, we did, in the dead of an old Kobenhaven winter,
snow sifting down outside like confetti from our friends on the
Moon. That's how it was, wasn't it, Fiona?"

"Like confetti," she said.

And I remembered Alex's saying, *Probably not for a
ticker-tape parade.* Right now he looked as unsettled, as
uncomfortable, as I had ever seen him: a bear on a lumpy
ottoman. But I was too happy for Newlyn to worry very much
about Alex's discomfort: Newlyn was a fourteen-year-old
gawking about in the spaceship-cubicle of that old woman on
Level 9, before Ardrey told him that it all had to be
"flame-decontaminated."

Nettlinger got carried away, maybe just from looking at
Newlyn, maybe from the simple joy he took in these
recollections. He went on to tell us about the concept he and
Caspersson called "light-probing" and about its controlled
implementation in a "fleet" of operable, manned vessels. "Six
light-probe ships," he said. "Why, that's a fleet. Who could want
more than that so soon? Who could afford a larger investment?"

Planned, constructed, equipped, and manned, and all by
Nettlinger's twenty-fifth birthday, too. Then broadcast, accord-
ing to itineraries computer-derived, to those stars within a
hundred-light-year range possessing the optimum likelihood of
habitable planets. Four of the vessels, it seemed, had returned
and gone out again with new crews!

"One way to our farthest target," Nettlinger explained, using
a word that had a numbing and familiar impersonality, "is only
7.2 years. The remaining two ships—if nothing hinders
them—ought to be back in our own system before Christmas,
perhaps slightly after the New Year at the very latest. If all goes
well."

"Oh, it's a New Year already," Newlyn said. "You got to

come back with us now, Mr Nettlinger," then turning to the woman, "Mz Bitler: both of you. Hot damn, who's gonna want a Dome over their heads when you can tell 'em things like that? Hey, nobody's gonna get apoplexy hearin' that, nobody! It's gonna wake up all them mummies sleepin' in the Basement, is all! That's what it'll do!" For the first time since I had been around him, Newlyn was falling into the speech rhythms suggestive of his blackness. But that *hot damn:* somewhere, some time, he had got that from me, Clio Noble.

"An' maybe not," Alex said from his footstool, his bulk almost shapeless in the pooled light next to the sofa. "I don't see it jes' that way, Mr Yates."

"How do you see it then, Guest?" They were using each other's names like weapons.

"The only way I can, where I sit from. When General Oglethorpe first landed in this state, to make a colony of it, you know, an Indian they called Long King came all the way from Coweta Town to see him. You know why?"

"Hell no," Newlyn said. "What's that got to do with anything, with anything at all?" He was shaking his head in exasperation.

"Wait a minute," I said. "Let him tell it, OK?"

"Please do," Nettlinger said. "Arguments against us we probably require more than blind enthusiasm. To forearm ourselves, you see."

"All right," Alex said. He looked up at the ceiling: the cracks and moisture stains fixed his attention. "Long King went to Oglethorpe to learn wisdom. He thought God had sent old Oglethorpe to *teach* the Indians since it was plain the English had more and knew more and must have been picked by Him to instruct 'em. So they gave up some land in payment for the instruction they was supposed to get. Later, the English got *all* the land and the only wisdom the Indians was left with was, You can't trust the English. But it was too late, they was on reservations in Oklahoma keepin' themselves warm with cholera." Alex looked down.

Everyone considered this, Newlyn annoyed that he couldn't give vent to his excitement—which was still effervescing in his head and hand movements. Finally Fiona Bitler said, "I don't think Emory's saying we're going to bring the population of the Urban Nucleus wisdom, or even advanced technological knowledge, necessarily. The offer is really the chance to rejoin a larger community."

"Oglethorpe," Alex said, "didn't say he was bringin' wisdom, either. The Indians jes' looked at the English and supposed it, is all."

"The citizens of Atlanta," Newlyn said, "aren't going to suppose they're inferior beings in need of instruction." His speech was crisp again.

"Who said 'inferior'?" Alex said. "Besides, you're one citizen that's supposin' jes' what Long King supposed when Oglethorpe got here. You're an Indian hopin' these people will take you back to England and show you off to the lords and ladies."

I chuckled, right out loud. And it was really me who had done it. Newlyn gave me his exasperated look, then said: "I think Guest's opinion is an eccentric one."

"A *minority* opinion," I said, and Newlyn didn't know whether I was supporting him or subtly ridiculing him: I didn't either.

"Well," Mz Bitler said, "eccentric or not, it's probably a view that will be held, with all sorts of variations, by enough people to make our hesitancy about going into the City the wisest course. You people may have to be our ambassadors, going ahead of us to pave our way. Because caution is called for, caution is required."

"Selah," Emory said, "Selah to that."

7 / The Citizens of the Urban Nucleus Considered as Indignant Desert Birds

At three in the morning we broke it off, Emory and Fiona telling us that the best procedure would be for us to go back to the Urban Nucleus and explain to the authorities what we had heard at Phoenix Plantation. Jonah would serve as a go-between for later preparations, if these were needed. Inconclusive; all of it, inconclusive.

Alex wouldn't sleep upstairs. He wouldn't say why, but it pretty clearly had to do with the conflict between him and Newlyn. "That lawn looks plenty good enough," he said when we were in our room. "Cooler than up here, too."

So I helped him carry his bed gear down the stairs (Fiona and Nettlinger were still in the parlor as we went by) and watched as he spread it out under the Master's Oak, cane chairs around it like a breastwork fortification. Resembling the hard, sinister bone under a face that has melted away, the Moon had come up: full. I couldn't see anything on it that might be the domed base of Nettlinger's narrative. Just the Moon, nothing more.

"Sweet Cleopatra," Alex said to me.

"What about the mosquitoes?" I didn't know why he'd said that, so I was heading him off.

"What about them back there in the kudzu? We made it, Cleo. I'm gonna make it out here tonight." He kissed me on the forehead, father to daughter. Our feet almost entangled in his sleeping bag, surrounded by cane chairs, we stood there. "Kiss me again, Cleo?" Asking, not ordering.

"Why?"

"Because Yates is gonna get more'n that, even."

It wasn't insulting somehow, it wasn't even self-pitying: only a statement of fact that I didn't at that moment believe in. I kissed Alex, putting my arms around the bulges above his waist, the ones my mother always called "love handles." Then it was over. Alex sat down in one of the chairs and looked at the Moon.

"You know what I want more than anythin' else in the world, Cleo?" He didn't give me a chance to answer. "Enfranchisement," he said. "That's all I want, that's why I do things like this one, come out here and all. One day—I keep thinkin'—they're gonna say to me, 'OK, Mr Guest, you can call yourself Menewa, and from now on you're fully protected by the Urban Charter. Jes' write Menewa on this form here and drop it in the mail.' That's what I dream about, even actin' as an agent between the City and all the Jonah Traps out here."

"Why?" I said. "What do you really owe the UrNu authorities? I don't know why you just haven't defected and stayed out here."

"I don't either, Cleo. 'Cept that I'm waitin' for my enfranchisement." He looked at me in bewilderment. "Ain't that the damndest?"

"Clio?" Newlyn said from one of the brass beds. I closed the door, and he said, "Is Nettlinger still up?"

"Talking with Mz Bitler," I said. I couldn't see Newlyn, he couldn't see me: the room bound us together in an indivisible blackness and a summer heat that the Moon still hadn't begun to siphon off.

"I think they're lovers," Newlyn said. "Bodyburners."

"She's twenty-five years older than he is," I said, finding the bed opposite his. Did he really think Fiona Bitler was a modern-day Isis, both mother and consort to her own Nettlinger/Osiris?

"How she look to you? Decrepit?" The blackness in the room had crept into his speech: City blackness, Bondville blackness, even though Newlyn had never lived a day in one of those razed tenements. *Under* maybe, but only Level 1 or 2.

"No. Hardly decrepit."

"Preserved," Newlyn said. "What you got to call 'preserved.'" But I was elsewhere, light-probing through my own gray matter. "What's wrong, Clio?"

"Guest. Alexander Guest."

"Look," he said, turning so that the bedsprings sighed and I could almost see his face resolving out of the darkness. "That man's a case. All this Indian history, all his foreknowledge of what's gonna happen if Nettlinger comes to Atlanta. And he claims to be... what? a Creek Indian?"

"Cherokee."

Newlyn was quiet a minute. "I know something about them, too, about the Cherokee. Indians and black men; coholders of honors in this world's dispossession stakes. But when the Cherokee got th'own out of Georgia, Mz Noble, some of 'em was rich enough to take their nigger slaves on the Trail of Tears. I always remembered that, whatever else of school I long since forgot. So if those black people was cousins in sufferin' to the Cherokee that dragged them along, they was cousins *twice*-removed. Did you know that, Mz Clio Noble?"

"No," I said. "Why are you so wrought up?" Our first quarrel, our first real quarrel. Start by using her first name but end up by spitting out the whole thing like a curse: almost flattering.

Newlyn lay back, the mattress sighed, the bedspring clinked. I took off my boots and socks and just sat there with my feet on the hardwood floor. After a while, Newlyn said, "Come over here, Clio. Please." It was seduction by ennui, not as I had imagined time and time again it would finally occur: loving violence and tender rapacity on both sides. I finished undressing, went over to Newlyn's bed, and slid myself onto his naked, clammy body.

Ain't this the damndest? I was thinking as it all unrolled like film footage consisting of nothing but blank frames. Then, head on his chest as he slept, I wondered if I had committed a sin of passion or of fraud. To which circle would Dante, that old anal-retentive, consign me?

After a half hour or so I got out of Newlyn's bed, put on all my clothes but my foot gear, and lay down on the floor. Went to sleep there, too; went to sleep there as if I had been lovingly embalmed by the hot night.

And woke up to the shrill, repeating shouts of someone downstairs, terrifyingly like war whoops from the ghosts of murdered red men: war whoops rising through Jonah Trap's house as if the prelude to a general massacre.

"Yip yip yip!" the shouts came. *"Yip yip!"*

"Jesus," Newlyn said, sitting up on his bed and swinging his legs to the floor. "What in Christ is that?"

But he was naked, and, answering him nothing, I went ahead of him to the door. I burst into the upstairs corridor to confront only darkness. No lamp anywhere, the hallway too tightly sealed for the spillings of moonlight. A commotion from the stairs, a creaking of the banister railing and successive hollow thumpings on the steps themselves. Continuing above these noises, the war whoops that had yanked us out of our sleep.

Holding my heart, my every pulsebeat, in the curl of my tongue, I edged down the hall and stopped on the very brink of the stairwell. A door was thrown open behind me, far enough away that I felt certain it was Jonah Trap, and not Newlyn, coming to provide moral reinforcement.

"Yip yip yip!" the shouts continued to come. Then, suddenly, they mutated into coherent language: "Yates! Clio! Get the hell out of there! Get the hell up!" It was Alex, and his voice was ascending through the foyer and the stairwell from the open door of the Phoenix mansion. Then he started the war whoops again, that strangled-sounding, banshee yipping. I couldn't see Alex because of the shadow of an eclipsing shape on the steps.

No: two shadows, two shapes.

They changed position and seemed to retreat as if in response to my presence. When they did, I could see Alex silhouetted in the doorway, moonlight pouring its waxy, bone-hard glow across the parquetry, the chandelier sparkling in a fitful run of tiny bursts. Then Jonah Trap was at my elbow, candle in hand.

The shapes that had formerly blocked my view of Alex were not at the bottom of the stairs; they were edging toward the entrance to the parlor. Not stealthily: diplomatically. One of them lifted its head and stared at me for a moment, as if trying to confirm a recognition. The other, its back to the first, looked guardedly toward the open doorway, where Alex had still not given up his hue-and-crying.

Behind Trap and me, Newlyn came clumping down the hall in his boots, and there was a movement in the third upstairs room, too.

"It awright," Trap said. "It awright, Mz Noble, you jes' go on back to bed. I take care of this now."

But I had already taken two or three steps down the stairwell, my weight on the lefthand banister. The creature in the foyer had not let go of my face, nor had I released its: a physiognomy carved out of maple or mahogany, but flexible in spite of its rigid appearance.

Lips that moved. Two parallel, vertical bridges separating the eyes and lips. Two brow-hooded eyes possessing large, hourglass-shaped pupils, one bulb of each horizontal pupil set to the front, the other bulb curving away to the side as if to provide simultaneous peripheral and frontal vision. The eye structures themselves looked like moist patches of canvas set into the wooden sockets of a primitive mask and glued there with a thin layer of mucilage. All of this, every bit of it, hypnotizing and unreal.

Guest, having seen people at the head of the stairwell, had finally shut up.

I took two more steps down the stairs. The other shape turned toward me. A face very similar to the first, perhaps taller from chin to crest. Each creature, behind its head, had a corona of bone or cartilage that extended its height and gave it an out-of-time, out-of-place regality. What were they? What were they doing in the foyer of Jonah Trap's house?

"Clio!" Newlyn said. "Clio, stop right the hell where you are!"

I looked back up the stairs. The number of lights there had proliferated, as had the number of people. Emory Nettlinger, wearing a dressing gown so hastily knotted at the waist that Trap's candle and his own lantern showed me Nettlinger's thin white legs, came jerking along the corridor and stopped above me on the landing. Fiona Bitler, carrying another lantern, came up behind the three men now standing there: her cousin, her lover, and Newlyn Yates, who was holding his hand laser trained on the shapes downstairs.

Alex shouted up to us, "They come out of that overseer's cottage! I saw 'em cross the lawn and come inside! When they started up the stairs, Yates, I started in to whoopin'!"

"Thank you for that," Nettlinger said, sotto voce.

"These are the 'visitors' he wants to bring into Atlanta!" Alex shouted. "This is what we're having to get *groomed* for!"

Somewhere in that huge house, a child had long since begun to cry. Without turning around, the two strange shapes below us retreated deliberately into the darkness of the parlor. Then little Carlo came out of the classroom opposite the parlor and stood in the middle of the foyer, dwarfed by shadowy adults and imcomprehensible events, naked and bawling. I started down to him, but Fiona, setting her lantern down and descending quickly, swept past me and caught the boy up in her arms. Trap's sons and daughters-in-law appeared in the entrance to the video-unit classroom, too, but Fiona, handing Carlo to Gabriel, turned them back.

An impasse. No one moved.

"We can't take 'em into the Urban Nucleus!" Alex shouted, still from the doorway. He was afraid to come in, afraid of the things he had followed up to the lawn to Trap's mansion. "If we do, Yates, I ain' comin' with you! I'll go on ahead and spoil ever'thin' for you, I'll tell 'em what Nettlinger's plannin', I swear I will!"

Newlyn ignored all this; he looked at Nettlinger. "Starmen?"

"Please, Mr Yates, put your weapon back in your room. Let me go down to them, they didn't know you were here anymore than you knew they were."

"It's not any wisdom I want to touch!" Alex was shouting. "It's not any wisdom worth goin' into bondage for!"

Several other children were crying now. Fiona slid the panel to, closing off the room that the families of Gabriel and Michael Trap had come through. This muffled the noises of their dismay and confusion.

"They ain' seen 'em befo' either," Jonah Trap said, his arm around my shoulders, and, although I had been steelily in control to this point, I realized I was crying. "They jes' like you and yo' gen'lemen, Mz Noble. It take some time is all; it jes' take some time."

We were midway down the steps, and I could see the two creatures in the parlor as if they were lepers hovering inside the mouth of a cave, cerements for garments, mummy-cloth unwinding from their arms—except that what I first saw as unwinding bandages were in reality the loose, ribbonlike extensions of their incredibly long forearms.

"Yates. Yates!" Alex was shouting, Mz Bitler beside him now. "You'd do best to shoot 'em, you'd really do best to take 'em out now!" But Newlyn had put the weapon away (though he hadn't retreated to our bedroom as Nettlinger had asked him to), and Fiona was trying to calm Alex, just as Jonah Trap was trying to comfort me. I don't know why I was crying, I didn't really feel in need of comforting: all I can suggest is that I was empathizing with Alex's panicky premonition of ruin.

"Can you believe this?" Newlyn said. He said it as if he believed it completely, as if he relished the spectacle of our astonishment, his own included.

Jonah Trap turned me so that I had to come back up the stairs with him, but I kept casting back over my shoulder. I saw Fiona lead Alex back out onto the lawn and close the front door behind her.

Nettlinger said, "Well, everybody's been given a good jolt, our visitors as well as ourselves. Please, Mr Yates, you and Clio go back to your room." He turned to Trap. "It's your house, Jonah. Tell them that it's an order, for their own sakes."

"No one get ordered here but chillun," Jonah said. "But I *sugges'* the same thin', Mz Noble, I strongly sugges' it."

Nettlinger went down the stairs, carrying his lantern. I wouldn't turn back to our room until I saw him go into the parlor and caught one more glimpse of the "starmen" who had thrown the Phoenix mansion into a four-o'clock-a.m. uproar. Then the little blond man pulled the glass-paneled doors to the parlor shut and returned the gleaming foyer to cool normality: silence and emptiness.

After Newlyn and I had gone back to our room, there were no more doors to be closed. Not physical ones, anyway.

Jonah Trap drove Alexander Guest and me back to Atlanta in a pickup truck built so long ago that its fenders and sideboards jounced about maddeningly. In the truckbed, a load of peaches—since he had to make the trip, he said, might as well do some business, too.

It was raining when we left, so we rode in the cab, not beneath a tarp in the back. West on Highway 57 to Irwinton we went, then right on U.S. 441 in order to make connection with Interstate 20.

As we drove, I kept thinking of all the red flags—flags of

warning, now—hanging on the green temples along our route out from the transit-tunnel. Through the wiper-cleared semicircles on the truck's windshield, we could see more vines rearing, jittering in the thin, steamy rain.

The rain finally stopped, and on the outskirts of Atlanta, late that evening, we saw the Northern Cross among the ragged, blown-away clouds.

Newlyn had refused to come back with us. Before we left, he gave the hand laser to Alex and told him it was his. Not to me, but to Alex. And not to slight me, either, but maybe to bridge the chasm between Alex and him. Riding back to the Urban Nucleus in Trap's pickup, the Indian pretty well knew he wouldn't have a chance to use the weapon. That didn't mean anything, though, that didn't matter. After seeing all the burning constellations, we were absorbed into the City through a receiving point, Alex's own, the one where he ordinarily worked. Trap unloaded his peaches.

So: one enfranchised team member had defected, the only unenfranchised team member had returned, and Clio Noble, full citizen, feeling an affinity for both these men and even for the vaguely sphinx-headed creatures who had ultimately decided their allegiances for them, came back into the City because—

They debriefed us, Alex and me. And we told them the truth, all of it. Then I quit my position with the Human Development Commission, my position as a resources-reclamation specialist. This was last year. Since then, for resigning with no acceptable reason they moved me out of my Level 3 cubicle to one on Level 9. My parents have asked me to move back in with them, but I'm an adult now and have kept myself in enough earnies to subsist on by waiting tables in the Gas Light Tower plaza. Mama, bless her, is trying to get me a job clerking at Consolidated Rich's.

"Or maybe even modeling," she says sometimes; "if it weren't for all those freckles. . . ."

I haven't seen Alex, even though he's supposed to live on Level 9 too, since our debriefing sessions at the end of last summer he has dissolved into the population as surely, as irrevocably, as a chameleon into kudzu. I just hope he's still alive somewhere, preferably not in this City, and that he's found some people who don't think he's crazy for wanting to be called Menewa.

Not long ago First Councilor Lesser announced that the

widow of Carlo Bitler and her former student, Emory Coleman, would be returning to the Urban Nucleus from a long sojourn in Europe. The spirit of the announcement makes me think that no reprisals are planned; the councilors and ward reps are touting it as some kind of coup. I just don't know. At the same time, I hope Newlyn comes back with Fiona and Nettlinger, though how safe his return would be is hard to assess. He did defect, you know; for at least a year he renounced the City—and *I'm* living on Level 9 for quitting my job, nothing more than that.

What's going to happen? Sometimes I think about Nettlinger's "starmen" and wonder if this great, mound-shaped tomb of ours is destined to be the cradle of a new community. I see their rough, masklike faces.

And even though we still don't understand each other, you me, or I you, I want you to answer me this: Are we now, all of us, living in Bethlehem? And, if so, in whose tax books must we enroll ourselves?

2066

Interlude: The Cradle Begins to Rock

Atlanta, in 2067, was not yet the cradle of a new community, but things had begun to change.

After an absence of nearly a third of a century, Fiona Bitler and Emory Nettlinger returned to the City, bringing with them two creatures from another solar system. First Councilor Lesser gave the repatriated exiles a penthouse suite in the Hyatt Regency; the aliens, meanwhile, were installed just down the corridor in an enclave of rooms artificially adapted to their specific physiological needs: darkness and cold.

Gathering the last names of their human benefactors into a single adjectival portmanteau word, the citizenry of the Urban Nucleus began referring to the aliens as the "Bitlinger starmen." Although Fiona and Emory had hoped to introduce the Cygnusians to the City's aroused and curious citizenry—primarily as a vivid way of demonstrating that outside the Dome lay not merely an unexplored world of possibilities, but an entire beckoning universe—their wards were at first reluctant to venture out, stirring from their ecologarium only on those few rare occasions when they met with First Councilor Lesser and other government officials in the Bitlingers' private suite. Why such shyness? It soon developed that the aliens were awaiting the arrival of others of their kind. Between 2067 and 2071, then, the First Councilor permitted five more Cygnusians to enter the

City from Scandipol, via the Amity Moon Base and 61 Cygni; and the aliens, shortly before the arrival of the seventh member of their strange connubial alliance, began to show a glimmering of willingness to meet the public.

In late Summer of 2071 the First Councilor's office announced that one of the alien visitors would make an appearance at the Dixie-Apple Comestibulary on the Level 4 Mall. This appearance was not scheduled until the Fall, however, several weeks away—with the result that curiosity about the Cygnusians began to build, sweeping like a contagion through every part of the upper City and all the levels of the hive. The winds of conjecture bearing this contagion began, inexorably, to rock the cradle of the Bitlingers' hopes.

One of those most severely infected was a young man named Julian Cawthorn, who lived on Level 9 and who incessantly mulled the small human ramifications of alien contact.

Long before Fiona Bitler and Emory Nettlinger brought their two starmen into the City, Julian had written stories about sentient creatures from outer space. The subject obsessed him; he felt that the Cygnusians, whose visages and forms he had seen only in newstape photographs, had spiritual access to varieties of knowledge outside of humanity's ken. He speculated endlessly about their lives, their minds, their purpose.

In Autumn of 2071, faced with eviction from his cubicle for failing to fulfill his "public-utility obligation," his mind revolving the gaudier possibilities of the imminent Dixie-Apple Savings Sale, Julian Cawthorn sat down and scratched out another story. When it was finished, he carried it to an editor at the *Jour/Con* newstapes whom he had been badgering for a job and a press pass to the second public event at which one of the Bitlinger starmen was supposed to make an appearance.

Here is Julian's story:

CHAPTER SIX

At the Dixie-Apple with the

Shoofly-Pie Kid

A Story by Julian Kosturko-Cawthorn

Going to the Dixie-Apple. Everybody was heading that way, down to the Level 4 Mall where this morning a visitor from the 61 Cygnus system was going to be on hand for the Dixie-Apple Autumn Savings Sale. Cullen knew it was a gimmick, the come-on of the year, but lately, holding his grief at arm's length, shucking about on the Dole Role with nothing else to do, he'd sniffed at every come-on tossed his way, just like a pigeon pecking along a trail of popcorn until the trap at the end's disclosed and there's no way to hop back out.

We're all of us pigeons, Cullen thought. And so he added himself to the crowd sashaying along the emporia-lined Mall toward the City's most popular comestibulary.

Everybody loved the Dixie-Apple Comestibulary, even folks not bigwig enough to belong to the Feasters Sodality, whose members had access to the Fresh Meat Retreat off the market's final aisle. Pigeon-pot pies were as close to poultry as people like Cullen ordinarily got, but he didn't much resent the feasters who had their way with both finer fowl and an occasional ill-butchered slab of beef or pork imported from the Open. No point in resentment. What did it get you? Because this question brought back the specter of Cullen's grief, he shoved it aside, refused to answer it. The Dixie-Apple was a happy place, after all. And it wasn't impossible to cope along fine on synthapro

208

comestibles and all the foil-wrapped baubles Management kept shelved and stacked about the market for the financially disadvantaged. Hey, nobody didn't like going to the Dixie-Apple!

Especially when their hither-ye-up of the week was a refugee from a sun that was rumored to be tottering toward nova. A Cygnusian, the newstapes liked to call it. Him, rather. Cullen wanted to see the Cygnusian. He'd been gimmicked as surely as everybody else.

Going to the Dixie-Apple. Got nowhere else to go.

Cullen waltzed past paraplegic scatsingers, vending-cart impresarios, Mall gals, fall guys, freaks, fops, and faerie folk until he found the caboose of the train of people snaking into the Dixie-Apple Comestibulary. No one in line but languid teeners and sleek middies, physically fit citizens all. These bored-seeming people did a disorderly lockstep toward the chromium doorways over which hung a cardboard-on-burlap banner proclaiming

DIXIE-APPLE AUTUMN

SAVINGS SALE

FEATURING, TODAY ONLY,

"CYGNOR THE CYGNUSIAN"

Today only, mused Cullen at the end of this line. Monday, Autumn the 16th. And "Cygnor" wasn't really the critter's name. That was what Management was calling him because his real name was an unpronounceable mystery, as vowelless as the Tetragrammaton. But when the L.P.A. still hadn't found you a job and your heart hurt something fierce, just going to see old Cygnor, whatever name he *ought* to be called by, was a way of shaking the Pluto-gloomy, smoky-Monday blues. 'Deed it was.

Nevertheless, it seemed that gloom was on most of these people. They looked blanched-out and logy. In front of Cullen were a pair of deep-purple squaws with papooses strapped to their backs, and even *they* looked a trifle faded. (One of the mamas did, anyhow. The other gave him a slow but zestful smile.) And under the merciless fluoros the gray ghosts in the D.-A. queue were so pale and sapped of pigment that Cullen felt sure his hand would penetrate their Caucasoid flesh like stainless steel through lemon jello. So right there at the end of

the line, in order to melt this gloom with jollity, Cullen let his
legs slide back and forth and sang aloud the lyrics of an old song
he'd just remembered:

> *Shoofly pie 'n' apple pandowdy,*
> *Makes yo' eyes light up*
> *'N' yo' stomach says, "HOWDY!"*

One of the squaws managed, by an aggressive use of her
elbows, to move up several places in the queue. The other
woman—she was no more than seventeen despite the kiddo in
her carrier—gave him another smile and patted her hands
together in time. The two women weren't together, apparently.
OK. Not everybody in this press-ganged, media-mounted crowd
was a washout. Nohsuh. This gal, baby on her back, had a
with-it rating right up there in the high positives. Cullen winked
at her. Cullen played to her. Cullen sang his song. *Tap tap,
stomp stomp, clap clap.* He concluded his performance with a
you-take-it! gesture. What eyes. As big as amber glass ashtrays.

"Nice," growled the big-eyed mama-child. "You goin' to see
it?"

"Him," Cullen corrected, not fussily.

"My daddy say it a it," said a little black boy squeezing up
from behind. He was shirtless, and his body, unlike most of the
others in line, had hue, solidity, suppleness. "My daddy say it a
'chine, he say it a disney'd 'traption. Nuts 'n' bolts 'n' all like
that."

"No more'n you or me," Cullen responded. He saw that
fifteen or twenty people were now riding the queue's caboose,
several of them peering about nervously, rubbing their chins,
shifting their weight from hip to hip....

The little boy's name was Sammy. He insisted that The Thing
inside was "a it, not a him." Insinuating himself between Cullen
and the big-eyed mama-child, Sammy said, "I got to buy some
Co' Cola. My daddy got to have his Co' Cola, that why *I* come."

"Amen," Cullen murmured. But in truth he was a believer, at
least in this. He knew that "Cygnor the Cygnusian" was really,
absolutely, a quasi-human sort of animal from eleven-odd light
years. He wouldn't've come if he'd thought otherwise—even
with pseulami and King Cotton peach in short supply in his
Level 9 cubicle, even with the smoky-Monday blues smoldering
in his bowels. Who'd fight this crowd for a peek at a mere
machine?

"Why'd *you* come?" he asked the mama-child, who was reaching over her shoulder to wipe her baby's nose. Canted to one side in its carrier, the baby stared bewilderedly at Cullen. Helpless. Hauled about at other's whims. What a cross, being a baby . . .

"Ever'body comin'," the girl said in a funny accent he hadn't noticed before. "So I come too, you know. My ver' first time."

Her name was Bayangumay, and as they moved toward the Dixie-Apple's doors she told Cullen her story. She was just up from the New Orleans Nucleus, where nobody'd even heard of any intersteller immigrants from the Swan. She was here because one dull-to-same, same-to-dull day in Summer her pledge-bound bodyburner—Jean-Paul, by name—had gone larki and shut her and little Etude out of the cubicle (Bayangumay said *cubbicle*) they all shared. For months their relationship had been sour, Jean-Paul just standoffish, funky mean, and even their baby had been a kind of experiment, an issue Bayangumay was only now beginning to see in its own "personhood." Before, Etude had been nothing but a political contract, a cease-fire agreement.

"Also," Bayangumay said, "Jean-Paul he want to see if . . . if he *work,* you know." She had a throaty voice, very deep.

"Worked?"

"Yes. If he workin' correkly, you see."

"My daddy don' work," Sammy offered, "'cause L.P.A. can't find him nuthin'."

Cullen ignored this. "What happened? When Jean-Paul shut you out?"

What happened was that Jean-Paul yogically stilled his heartbeat, collapsed into himself so far that his metabolic processes slowed to near motionlessness and his body temperature just dropped and dropped. The cubicle's auto-refrigerant system, a component of the biomonitoring equipment required by the UrNu Housing Authority, clicked on. The system had taken Jean-Paul for a sudden-deader and was humming hard and frosty to preserve his "corpse." That was just what Jean-Paul had wanted, that was precisely how he had chosen to go. He froze, Jean-Paul did, and that was the end of him, suicidally cool right up to the ultimate and ineradicable still point. Cold. A confounding iciness of the will and emotions, his mind, personality, and essence all clocked down to Absolute Zero . . .

"Wow," said Cullen under his breath.

Bayangumay only smiled. She had come to Atlanta through the transit-tunnels because Jean-Paul's older brother, Gustave, had used an esoteric personal contact to find her a job with Atlanta's Human Development Commission, as one of the all-night babysitters for the children of those UrNu employees working what was called the Cremation Shift. "You are an animal," Gustave had told her when he packed her off. "Jean-Paul was pure light, pure mind, and you sullied him, quenched the bright fever he lived by. Go." Just like in the holodation dramas they showed in L.P.A. waiting rooms. Out into the storm, young woman. Never darken my endeavor for *satori* again.

"Jesus," whispered Cullen, an incredulous hush in his voice.

Because the line lagged and because Bayangumay was new to the Mall, Cullen tried to tell her what it would be like inside the comestibulary. "You ever heard of Whoops-a-Deals?" he asked her. "You ever heard of So-Sorry Markups?"

"Beg pardon, Fly-Pie Mon."

"Ain't there a Dixie-Apple in the New Orleans Nucleus?"

"Oh, no. We get our groj-ree at computer terminal, you know, one big one each level. No elbows, no angers. Much better, I think."

And so Cullen warned Bayangumay that at the Dixie-Apple the stockers, butchers, and produce people were all given a weekly quota of goods to mismark and a specified range of prices within which the mismarking had to be conducted. The "accidentally" inflated prices were called So-Sorry Markups, the "accidentally" slashed ones Whoops-a-Deals. And because the shopping carts in the Dixie-Apple rolled at a steady, unnegotiable clip on invisible electric beams, you had to be quick to grab the infrequent Whoops-a-Deals, maybe quicker yet to avoid the more common So-Sorry Markups. Closed-circuit cameras were trained on the relentlessly herded shoppers so that you could be identified and docked an appropriate number of earnies if you were cheap enough to try sneaking a So-Sorry Markup back into the flow of goods at, so to speak, a point downstream.

Cullen throve on these contests with electronic surveillance. He was enviably good at snatching Whoops-a-Deals and bypassing So-Sorry Markups. If he did make a mistake he was also pretty adept at either lobbing the unwanted merchandise into someone else's basket while rounding a blind corner to deepsixing it in a frozen-food locker while pretending to rummage the ice-milk containers and pizza paks. Hey, shopping the D.-A. Way made the day dance, he told Bayangumay, where there wasn't nothing else to do . . . !

"System ver' curious," Bayangumay said. "Soun' fun, mebbe."

"Yeah," Cullen agreed, suddenly less enthusiastic. "Sometimes."

"I alway' come," Sammy interjected. "I alway' the one what do the shoppin' in my fam'ly. I know how, I do."

Cullen refrained from recounting the disadvantages of the D.-A. Way. The worst downer was that even if you'd only come for a bottle of catsup you had to hook up to an autocart—by means of a metal cuff with a nonknotting, flex-o-torque chain—and Injun-glide the whole gaudy gauntlet, up and back, up and back, all nine aisles, until you came cruising bruised and indignant into the checkout stands with your lone bottle of Reddrop Tomato Condiment riding like a gargantuan vitrified member in your autocart's kiddie seat. Sometimes the D.-A.'s herky-jerky system made you think dirty and talk to yourself, it surely did.

And it wasn't much comfort that the UrNu Food, Engineered Edibles, & Drug Authority argued that the D.-A. Way merely required you to budget, plan your needs beforehand, avoid small-purchase shopping, and develop both physical dexterity and highly desirable "reservoirs of patience."

Yessir, thought Cullen, P.A.T.I.E.N.C.E. As in, "Leggo that Whoops-a-Deal, you thugster, I had it first!" And there were enough pickpockets around that maybe "physical dexterity" wasn't so beneficial a gift to society as the people at F.E.E.D. seemed to think. Suddenly suspicious, Cullen flattened his hands on his slash pockets and looked about. A strange assortment of people on hand today, full of twitches and shuffles. Maybe it's just me. . . .

"What matter, Fly-Pie Mon?" Bayangumay asked Cullen. "You don't like shoppin' Dixie-Apple?"

"Sure," he said, surfacing from his reverie and his suspicions. "If you're a hive-dweller it's the only game in town."

No more time for talking. They were in the noisy, hoi-polloi-packed Dixie-Apple Comestibulary. A wall to their left blocked their view of the store's interior aisles. Each customer was a pinball awaiting the plunger that would send him shooting into a realm of targets, bumpers, traps, buzzers, and blatting lights. Yeah. The Dixie-Apple was a pinball machine, just like the antiquated ones in the Earnie Arcade across the Mall.

A steady stream of autocrats came careening through a pair of flapping doors in the lefthand wall. Then the carts cornered neatly and headed up the plunger-aisle that would finally feed them, one by one, into the guts of the machine.

Ping! Blat! Ping!

And somewhere inside this game, this engine, this electric maze was "Cygnor the Cygnusian," installed solely to maximize customer participation and boost corporate profits. So what? A glimpse of Cygnor, Cullen figured, was worth every extorted earnie he plonked down in homage to the grandiose crassness of the Dixie-Apple's campaign.

A man in a D.-A. uniform grabbed Bayangumay by the wrist, yanked her forward, and handcuffed her to one of the eerily cruising carts. She stumbled, caught herself, and then tripped off after her basket at the brisk, no-nonsense pace these carts demanded of everyone, regardless of age or infirmity. If you couldn't keep up, you were supposed to send someone hale and capable in your place. If you happened to fall while navigating the market's intricate ups and downs, your instructions were to drag the capsized autocart out of the flow of traffic and wait until an employee saw fit to undo your cuff, help you up, and escort you in hot dishonor to the checkout stands for identipix, x-rays, and a laminated reprimand.

Hey, though, little Sammy was taking off!

Cullen realized that, big-brotherlike, he had been gripping the boy's naked clavicles for the last fifteen minutes. He realized this when Sammy shot out from under his hands, skipped past the D.-A. manacle-man, and jumped into the autocart behind Bayangumay's.

"You!" shouted the attendant. "Not allowed! Not allowed!" He blew a whistle, but the Muzak oozing out of the wall and ceiling speakers, in combination with the human din inside the store, muffled the whistle's shrillness.

Spunky Sammy didn't even look around. Inside the wire basket he hunkered on his heels and rode toward the top of the plunger-aisle. Around that bend, a different world, miracles and marvels . . . !

"Me," said Cullen to the manacle-man. "Hook me up."

To keep from interrupting the flow of baskets, the manacle-man complied, and Cullen, too, trotted into the Dixie-Apple's maw.

How delicate and dainty this whole setup. Shopping baskets responding to electronic tractor beams rather than motorized wheel-ruts in the linoleum, which latter method would sure as Shiva provide more stability. But less excitement. There was excitement if you toppled. Irritation. Flusterment. What more could you ask for?

Blat! Ping! Blat!

Bayangumay and Etude went around the miracle bend. Then Sammy, a pygmy in a cage, the mesh of his basket outlining tiny, nappy squares on the back of his head. Then Cullen cornered, and the chill air of the market was quickened again and again by fluorescent flickerings and the cries of shoppers trying mightily either to flimflam Management or call down tsuris on those who would hinder them in their selections. Sometimes the same shoppers engaged in both kinds of crying.

"Three Whoops-a-Deals on peanut butter at the end of Aisle 1," a young man two carts ahead of Bayangumay shouted. "I missed 'em, I missed 'em" Peanut butter was protein, damn-near natural. Magnanimously he wanted to spare the others the torment of his failure.

A moment later he was crying, "You! You up there! Don't touch that Tetra Nabinol! That's what I came for, I have to have it!" He ended by weeping and calling out curses. Someone had gotten the last bottle. Two failures, amid this hubbub and babel, were more than he could be magnanimous about. Far away, the ringing of the automatic registers counterpointed his despair.

Cullen looked toward the still-hidden registers and finally saw "Cygnor the Cygnusian," Displaced Alien, one of the six refugees from the rumored Cygnus nova now living in the Regency penthouse downtown. There he was, clearly visible, seated on a revolving glass platform suspended over the comestibulary's central aisle—positioned so that you couldn't possibly miss him, no matter where in the Dixie-Apple you happened to be.

A heartstopping critter. A phizzog that would freeze lava. Nimbi played about his halo-crested noggin, and his mahogany countenance with its large, side-lying hourglass pupils turned this way and that with a spooky majesty. Emperor of Gog, Magog, and the Urban Nucleus too was Cygnor the Cygnusian.

Cool. Aloof. Impassive. You could *see* him all right, but you sure couldn't ask for his autograph or reach out to touch his arm just to see how that arm felt....

And on either side of Cygnor's throne Management had erected a pyramid of biodegradable toilet-tissue rolls, a nostalgia item for those whose bathbooths weren't equipped with Klens-o-Jet bidets (i.e., everyone in the five nethermost strata of the Basement). These pyramids revolved beside Cygnor as if in scaled-down synchrony with the Milky Way itself.

One cart ahead, little Sammy stood full up, put his right leg straight out behind him for balance, and swept a carton of soft drinks into his basket. Then, as the autocart cornered, he popped quick and pygmylike back into its cage and settled down for the rest of his ride.

They were heading into Aisle 3 now, and it was all Cullen could do to snatch the items he needed from shelves and frozen-food lockers as they sped toward the center of Ye Olde D.-A.

Displaced Alien, mumbled Cullen to himself. Debilitating Angina. Desdemona Applesmith...

Desdemona Applesmith, a girl he had loved, was two weeks dead of a cement-snapping, girder-gouging explosion that she herself had set off in front of a Level 1 branch office of the UrNu Housing Authority. This was Cullen's grief, this and the fact that for two full New Calendar seasons she had pretended to be ill of a rare variety of angina pectoris. Angina pectoris, a disease of the heart usually occurring only among middies and senescenti. Lord, he was a Dumb Ass for thinking of Desdemona while pinballing through this Grand Guignol machine. He had been a Dumb Ass for believing in her unlikely illness for so long....

A So-Sorry Markup came into Cullen's hand as if by its own volition, and he didn't even try to fob it off on the fox behind him.

Desdemona, why did you die?

Well, she had died for a cause: "The demolishment of the Urban Nucleus as both an architectural mode and an instrument of oppression." Her very own words, those. And Cullen hadn't been any dumber than Dezdi's physicians. Even while feigning illness she had burned with a passionate intensity, and two doctors, smitten with Dezdi although at loggerheads with each other, had eventually given her the medication she had so desperately fought and feigned for. Nitroglycerin. That was what you used, after all, to ease along the victims of angina pectoris, and, clutching her arms across her breasts, whimpering a little every time she spoke, Desdemona had wheedled and cajoled until the two star-struck medicos could no longer resist, City regulations be damned. Then, the illicit nitro in her possession, she had mounted a midnight commando assault on the UrNu Housing Authority, only to be hoisted with her own petard while trying to clamber out of range of the blast. The inside of the corridor, as one surviving witness later avowed, looked as if a miniature red sun had thrown molten streamers into every door panel and office front. In the larger picture, however, no harm done. Three days after a clean-up squad had eradicated every trace of her idealistic act, Desdemona died in Grady Memorial, holding Cullen's hand and murmuring over and over again, "My heart, my heart." Cullen now chose to believe that she'd been addressing not her pain, but him. . . .

At this point in his recollections a freezer bin of Popsicles and ices caught Cullen's eyes, and the rime glittering on their packaging seemed all at once so blinding and hurtful that he choked back a sob and scooped seven or eight of the Popsicles into his cart.

Beautiful, he thought. Such beautiful frozen delights. Touched and irritated at the same time, he barely kept from falling. Why did they have to handcuff you to these carts . . . ?

Now Cullen wanted only to take Bayangumay aside and tell her the story of Desdemona Applesmith. Outside the Dixie-Apple he'd listened to Bayangumay's story of Jean-Paul and the auto-refrigerant system with such intentness that he hadn't even thought of countering with a heart-breaking spiel of his own. He really hadn't. Only after seeing Cygnor surrounded by toilet tissue and zipping past a hundred of the comestibulary's in-house labels had dear, dead Dezdi popped into his mind. Only then. Maybe he was growing past his grief, maybe he was starting to shoofly-pie it in his soul as in his overzooty outward actions. . . .

Now they were heading into Aisle 4, barreling along.

Suddenly Cullen heard an explosion, a pop, and since nitroglycerin was on his mind he threw up an arm to ward off falling debris. No debris fell, at least not at once. Instead, the person in front of Bayangumay took a pair of wire cutters from his belt, snipped the flex-o-torque chain securing him to his autocart, and purposely turned the basket over, cluttering the

aisle with bottles, bags, and food packets. Then he ran.
Bayangumay's autocart sloughed through this mess and
toppled. Cullen saw a woman flash past him with a length of
chain dangling from her wrist and realized that she had just
duplicated the actions of the man. The cart behind Cullen was
spinning on its side, throwing out its contents like a centrifuge.
Up ahead, Sammy's basket plowed into Bayangumay and
knocked her down.

The woman with the chain dangling from her wrist didn't
even pause: she leaped over Sammy, sidled past Bayangumay's
basket, and disappeared into Aisle 5.

Most of the comestibulary's customers were screaming.
Overbalanced, Bayangumay was trying to struggle up from the
floor. Sammy was squatting on his haunches now, too
dumbfounded to move. Cullen yanked his cart off its invisible
tractor beam and watched as another hoisterjack dangling a
severed flex-o-torque strand slipped and slid through the mess
he and his confederates had wrought. Going by, the hoisterjack
made a triumphant gesture at Cullen and rolled his eyes.

For some reason all Cullen could hear was little Etude's
terrified screaming. He tugged his fallen cart toward the child.

Overhead, a pigeon was flying about under the fluoros, and
Cygnor the Cygnusian had begun swiveling his head to take in
the scope and degree of the debacle. The Muzak cut off, and an
alarm had begun to sound. Behind the checkout counters an
iron grating clanged down where ordinarily there was only a
blowing air-wall tinted blue by the lamps in its generators.

Cullen froze and stared at the Displaced Alien staring down.
The Dixie-Apple was all at once a closed system. This fact, the
visitor on the platform understood, was enough to ensure that
the pinballs banging about inside it would eventually come to
rest. . . .

Cygnor the Cygnusian had been the only one in the market in
a position to note the beginnings of this seeming riot. A moment
before, a young woman passing beneath his platform had
released a pigeon from a paper bag, blown up the bag, and then
popped it with the flat of her hand.

At this signal, at least two guerrillas in each of the
Dixie-Apple's aisles cut themselves loose from their carts and
kicked the baskets over. Then, more than likely knowing
themselves doomed, they ran for it. The hoisterjacks, Cygnor

felt certain were coreligionists of a proscribed understrata sect who feared that the Displaced Aliens now living in the Regency Hyatt House had it in mind to convert to Ortho-Urbanism, thereby giving an odious legitimacy to the City's oppressive "Official Faith." Who knew precisely what such people feared? Revolving above the clamor in the market's aisles, Cygnor both sympathized with the young guerrillas and recoiled from their terrible passion.

Meanwhile, an alarm wailed and the D.-A.'s P.A. system clicked on: "Please right your carts. Please remain calm. Management's working to restore order." The alarm very nearly drowned out the speaker's voice.

Cygnor watched. It wasn't really cold enough for him. A moment ago he had been thinking, on one track at least, of the darkened, air-conditioned suite on the top floor of the Regency which he shared with his five Cygnusian spouses. The temperature there always hovered around a delicious 0 on the Celsius scale, and Fiona Bitler, their sponsor, graciously saw to it that they didn't have to remain outside their suite longer than twelve hours at a time.

And he was thinking, not solely by chance perhaps, of the first human employee who had carried food and drink to Cygnor and the others. That man was gone now, but during the first few weeks of his employment he had made himself a coat of cat pelts as protection against the iciness of the Cygnusians' private enclave. Alley cats, poor man. But the coat had been primitively beautiful nevertheless, and when he tendered Mz Bitler his resignation he said he was going to go into business manufacturing these garments. Everyone, he said, should know the animal warmth he had discovered on the Regency's 21st floor, at the heart of his wards' surrogate homeland. A good man; a very good man. No one had heard of him since, and, more than once, through various locator services, Mz Bitler had attempted to find the mysteriously vanished Behram....

Pop!

Cygnor the Cygnusian saw a pigeon fly up, land briefly on one of the pyramids next to him, and then flap off into the fluoros again. Given impetus by the pigeon's departing toes, sixty rolls of toilet paper spilled from the platform and bounded into Aisle 5 like a rain of giant marshmallows. A cunning chaos was loosed in the Dixie-Apple. Cygnor understood it at once.

Guerrilla tactics. Insurrection. Anarchy.

Over there a young woman with a baby on her back, a victim of the hoisterjacks' misdirected zeal, was trying to regain her feet, and her baby, not surprisingly, was crying out its bewilderment and fear . . .

Cullen unfroze. Dragging his cart along behind him, he reached Bayangumay and lifted Etude out of the carrier the baby was riding in. Etude's panic was increased by being suddenly in the arms of a stranger, but Cullen bounced her lightly and sang "Shoofly Pie" under his breath while the Dixie-Apple threatened to fall into ruins about them, a pinball machine tipping toward *Tilt!*

"I kill 'em," Bayangumay said huskily.

A fourth hoisterjack, wobbly and overweight, came sprinting toward them from the foot of Aisle 4. His dangling chain was a giveaway. But he had to go on his tiptoes to negotiate the wreckage, and when he began picking his way through broken Co' Cola bottles, shirtless Sammy lunged from his crouch and tackled the man, who fell backward against a dairy locker, slumped down its glass facing, and lay there with his eyelids rolling and unrolling like tiny scrolls, a pinball tripped by a deadfall lever disguised as a little black boy.

"Lovely shit," said Sammy. He took the wire cutters from the hoisterjack's belt and returned to Bayangumay and Cullen. They freed themselves from their autocarts, and Bayangumay led the way around the corner into Aisle 5, midmost thoroughfare in the Dixie-Apple's innards.

"I kill 'em," she repeated.

Maybe that was what Gustave had meant, calling her an animal. Cullen could tell that this mama-child acted on instincts, passions, impulses. So long as she knew Etude was safe in Cullen's arms, Bayangumay was content to leave her baby there and pursue a fiery purpose of her own. Great Maynard's Ghost, didn't she spit along, though! Desdemona Applesmith was a *haunt* beside her, a phantom rattling fasces of icicles in her fists. The closest Dezdi'd ever got to the heat was the bomb with which she'd almost incinerated an office of the UrNu Housing Authority. Ye Olde Cremation Shift forever . . .

Stop it, Cullen told himself. Sure she's a haunt beside Bayangumay, 'course she's a phantom. She's *dead.*

Cygnor the Cygnusian was revolving toward them as they entered Aisle 5, and Cullen couldn't look away from the spaceman. The critter's head was reminiscent of an African tribal mask, his arms were like poles covered over with mummy cloth, and little Sammy's daddy, probably on the evidence of newstape photos, thought Cygnor "a it, a 'chine." That wasn't so. That just wasn't the case....

Bayangumay was kicking toilet-paper rolls down the aisle. Sammy was too. Cullen joined them.

Then they all stopped.

The hoisterjacks—stymied by the iron grate beyond the checkout stands, driven back through the market by a platoon of concourse trolls in riot gear—were swinging their cuff chains right and left and advancing up Aisle 5 toward them. Did they think the entrance at the end of the plunger-aisle was still open? It was closed off, but the hoisterjacks didn't seem to realize or care.

Retreat, Cullen advised himself. A flex-o-torque chain across Etude's face would scar her up good. Plastografting was mostly for surfacesiders; it was almost always denied immigrants from other Nuclei, especially financially disadvantaged ones. So Cullen started to fall back.

Bayangumay and Sammy, meanwhile, lowered their heads and went shit-kicking through the debris.

We're playing for earnies now, Cullen thought at them earnestly. Turn around, turn around. He clutched Etude to his chest and backed up against a wall of dry goods. This was going to be messy, no way to get around it.

Bayangumay closed with a female hoisterjack and jujitsu'd her to the floor with a hip shift and a quicker-than-the-eye levering of her hands. Sammy downed a male commando by butting him in the groin. The remaining thugsters backed up on each other and surveyed their fallen comrades with eyes flaring and guttering like points of phosphor. Did they think perhaps Bayangumay and Sammy were members of their own group? How else could these apparent strangers have freed themselves? Cullen saw, however, that none of the hoisterjacks recognized the belligerent mama-child or the gritty little black boy confronting them, and this fact was going to tell against his friends.

"Move now," warned a jittery fox. "We comin' through."

At which point, in surprising *deus-ex-machina* fashion, the cavalry arrived. Neither god nor machine, Cygnor the Cygnusian had just revolved toward the hoisterjacks crowded at the head Aisle 5. He dropped both feet over the edge of the platform and extended his legs until they reached the floor. Then, having levered himself off his throne, he collapsed upon the extensions and stood in the aisleway between the regrouping guerrillas and Bayangumay and Sammy.

Cullen judged Cygnor to be better than two meters tall even after the Cygnusian had telescoped his limbs. Unbudging and unbudgeable, he spread his arms between the stock shelves like a huge metal crucifix and so held the thugsters at bay. In less than a minute the concourse trolls arrived, took the offenders into custody, and began to escort them back to the checkout stands for pre-precinct processing.

When one of the trolls moved to handcuff Bayangumay and Sammy on the evidence of their dangling wrist chains, Cygnor shook his head and pointed to the hoisterjacks sprawled writhing on the floor. The officer, understanding at once, nodded to Cygnor and apologized to Cullen's two friends. The siege of the Dixie-Apple was over, and the store's alarm finally stopped wailing.

"OK," Bayangumay complimented Cygnor. "You do that ver' nice."

The Displaced Alien encircled the mama-child's shoulders with one long arm and walked her the final four aisles to the automatic registers, Sammy following two steps behind, and Cullen bringing up the rear with little Etude unconcernedly pressing his lips together with her pudgy hands. By the time they'd stepped over and around all the wounded patrons and scattered foodstuffs, the pastel air-wall was blowing again and Cygnor took them through it into an open section of the Level 4 Mall. He bowed, handed Bayangumay something, and, with the blessing of a security guard, returned through the air-wall into the shambles of the Dixie-Apple. Gone.

"See what he give me," said Bayangumay. She held up a roll of toilet paper. Outside of their lives, it was the only thing they'd managed to escape the store with. "Very sweet, I think."

Sammy studied it skeptically. Then he glanced back at the comestibulary, most of whose lights had suddenly gone out. "I still say it a 'chine. Y'all seen how it done its legs. Jes' one big-A mah-chine, me 'n' my daddy say." The boy hunched his bare shoulders and walked off down the curiously unpeopled Mall section.

"All my groceries," Cullen complained. He shifted Etude to

his right hip. "Now I ain't got a scrap for dinner. Nuthin'."

"You come my cubbicle for dinner, Fly-Pie Mon. Tomorrah we come shoppin' one more time. Much fun, I think. No?"

Cubbicle. Where was this mama-child from, really? The New Orleans Nucleus didn't seem far enough away. Not the way she talked, and moved, and thought. Cullen wondered if maybe Cygnor the Cygnusian wasn't a more comprehensible species of alien than Bayangumay. But so what, so what?

"Which way to your cubbicle?" asked the Fly-Pie Mon.

Bayangumay took Etude out of his arms and in exchange gave him the roll of toilet paper. Cullen tumbled it back and forth between his hands as they walked through the Mall together.

2071

Interlude: The Fall of Saganella Lesser

A turning point in the history of the Atlanta Urban Nucleus was the "conversion" to Ortho-Urbanism of the aliens residing in the Hyatt Regency. The first such conversion took place only five days after the Dixie-Apple Autumn Savings Sale which Julian Cawthorn's story "At the Dixie-Apple with the Shoofly-Pie Kid" anticipated and whimsically fictionalized. On the basis of this story, however, Julian managed to finagle from one of the newstape employees a press pass to the special weekend service at which a second Cygnusian was going to make his debut in urban society.

Press pass in hand, Julian met his future wife that Saturday evening, a woman named Margot Eastwin who was assisting the High Bishop Asbury Holman in the celebration of the evening's special mass; she was a deacon-candidate at the King Theological Complex, a fifth-year seminary student, and when the alien from the Regency penthouse unexpectedly answered Bishop Holman's traditional post-ceremony summons to accept Christ or to reaffirm a previous commitment to Him, Margot was sitting at the opposite end of Julian's back-row pew looking as dumbfounded as everyone else in the congregation. When Julian scooted across the pew to remind her that she was wanted at the altar, he set in motion the rattletrap machinery of their courtship.

But the alien conversion set in motion a great deal more. Events began occurring in such rapid and unpredictable sequence that no one appeared to have any control over them.

—A few hours after the special ceremony, when word of the conversion had gone echoing and reechoing through the hive, a Muslim named Abu-Bakr was slain and mutilated by a pair of thugsters who apparently felt that the alien's acceptance of Christ automatically sanctioned the murder of "infidels."

—Because Abu-Bakr had coincidentally been an employee of the Bitlingers, working in a menial capacity for the penthouse-bound Cygnusians, a unique and unusual job fell open. Julian Cawthorn, recommended to Fiona Bitler the editor at the newstapes who had given him his press pass, appeared for an interview and secured Abu-Bakr's job. He now found himself in frequent and intimate contact with the aliens who had for so long obsessed him.

—Julian eventually learned enough to write and publish, with Fiona Bitler's approval, an "ethnography" of the Cygnusians' weird penthouse society. Appearing in the *Jour/Con* newstapes, this document put forth the unpopular view that the aliens had "converted" to Ortho-Urban Christianity as a concession to the philosophical frailty of their hosts. It also accused First Councilor Lesser of using The Event in the First Ortho-Urban Worship Center as an excuse to ride roughshod over the City's minority sects.

—These charges brought about a major crisis. The First Councilor removed Haven Idhe from his senior editorial position at the *Jour/Con* newstapes, declared a period of martial law (recalling the Bondville riots of the early Forties), and announced that she was going to ask the High Bishop Asbury Holman to ordain all seven aliens as Ortho-Urban priests. This ceremony, to be held in conjunction with the graduation exercises of the King Theological Complex, was to take place at Grant Field on Christmas day, 2071.

—In the meantime, a nonperson by the name of Alexander Guest, alias Menewa, alias Menny, was organizing a small group of disenfranchised receiving-point employees into a cadre of urban terrorists. Guest was unable to reconcile the impending ordination of seven creatures from another sun with the fact that he himself had never been granted full citizenship in his own Urban Nucleus. Cryptically self-christened the Red Sticks, his tiny organization began stockpiling explosives and plotting to thwart the First Councilor's plans.

—On Christmas day, during the period of martial law, Julian Cawthorn attended the graduation ceremonies of Margot Eastwin's seminary class. (He had just resigned his position at the Regency and taken on a full-time job with the newstapes.) To witness the ordination of their seven alien wards, Fiona Bitler and Emory Nettlinger were also bemusedly on hand. But during the ceremony, with a laser pistol he had been keeping in reserve for more than five years, Alexander Guest stood up in the grandstands and fired upon one of the Cygnusians being ordained. As security police rushed to subdue Guest, a girder-car exploding high above Atlanta's streets blew a triangular hole in the Dome and showered Peachtree Canyon with debris. Fiona Bitler, witnessing these things, suffered a heart attack and died.

—Before the end of the year Emory Nettlinger returned to Scandipol, his hopes derailed and his career at the Light-Probe Institute perhaps not even recoverable. As supposed converts to Ortho-Urbanism, the seven Cygnusians whom he and his late wife had brought into Atlanta remained in the City as guests of First Councilor Lesser and the High Bishop Asbury Holman.

—One week after Fiona Bitler's death, on Year Day, 2071, Margot Eastwin and Julian Cawthorn were married. That evening, in their newly assigned cubicle on Level 3, they received an unexpected visitor and shared a strange, revelatory dream. Twenty-four hours later a bloodless *coup de polis* toppled the government of First Councilor Lesser and installed in her place the Council of Three, a triumvirate of religious moderates.

—Within days the new Council acted to expel the aliens from the City. Their presence was viewed, not without reason, as inflammatory and divisive. Nettlinger, in Scandipol, cooperated to the extent of hailing back to Europe five of the seven Cygnusians. Two could not return (their kinsmen managed to make known) because they were on the verge of death. To move them would be to profane the sanctity of their "final termination." Although much about the matter was unclear, the fact that two aliens must remain was not.

—A representative of the Council of Three approached Julian to see if he would act as an intermediary between the last two Cygnusians and the government of the Urban Nucleus. With the understanding that he could continue to work for the

Jour/Con combine, Julian agreed. He and Margot were given the same suite that Fiona Bitler and Emory Nettlinger had once shared. But when he took up his duties as intermediary, Julian found that he had very little to do.

—The Cygnusians (or Cygnostikoi, as he now preferred to think of them) had retreated deep into the rubble of their several rooms and created a kind of mausoleum for themselves. Here they holed up like animals in hibernation. They neither ate nor exercised, and each time Julian went into the dim, cold country of their dying he feared that he must emerge to announce their "final termination." On countless tours of their enclave he approached the aliens in the conviction that they were already dead. Only the shrinking of their double pupils under the glare of his helmet lamp—only that and an acid odor—proved the moment had not yet come, and he frequently returned to Margot shaken and confused.

—Two years into the reign of the new triumvirate Julian had begun to expect nothing of the aliens but an annoying mortuary stillness.

About this same time, an old man of Level 3—an exile who had only recently come home to the City of his birth—began impatiently seeking an occupation commensurate with his education and talents. Although no terrorist, no revolutionary, no Red Stick, he assumed a deliberate stealthiness and surrendered his hopes to a kind of guerrilla tactic. The darkness was his only ally . . .

CHAPTER SEVEN

Death Rehearsals

1 / *The Arrest of Tad Zimas*

At two o'clock in the morning the old man had to wait nearly twenty minutes at the Level 3 lift-platform for a tube to the surface. Then he rode to street level and disembarked into the wine-colored haze of the New Peachtree lift-terminal. Aware that he could get blackjacked or shivved, the old man hurried past the shadowy figures milling in the recesses of the terminal and shuffled quickly into the street. His destination lay a few short blocks away, through well-patrolled and -lighted pedestrian courts, and once safely in the p-courts he breathed more easily.

The old man was sweating under his greatcoat. He had expected wintry street temperatures, but the holiday benevolence of Weather Control—it was only four days until Christmas—made the coat a heavy if not absolutely dispensable nuisance. He unbuttoned it and walked with more freedom.

At a quarter to three he stood in the dim, tessellated canyon fronting the UrNu Geriatrics Hostel, to whose wide glass doors he presently began to climb on aching legs. Would he truly be able to spring those doors aside with a wave of his thumb? It had been twenty-six years since he had last gained entry by this method, but he had faith that he would succeed. Scanlocks were routinely reprogrammed to admit new employees, but to erase their responsiveness to every past employee required a keener vigilance than the bureaucracy was usually able to maintain. The old man believed his former prominence as an HDC administrator had worked to his benefit: the scanlocks would admit him because no one would have thought to deprogram them against the unlikely prospect of his return.

As the old man raised his thumb to the electric eye, he heard a continuous faint sluthering and saw the headlamp of a bike-mounted troll wobbling through the dark toward him. He passed his thumb three times through the plane of the glowing scanlock and wondered if it had indeed forgotten him—but, at last, the doors pulled sluggishly apart.

Even after twenty-six years he was among the Human Development Commission's computer-banked elite! By law, exterior doors opened only to section directors and chief administrators.

Inside, the old man watched the tall, self-stabilizing bicycle float off into the darkness. Strips of ghostly luminous tape adorned not only the bike's gigantic tires but also the helmeted troll's shirtsleeves and trousers. The troll was gone as a dream goes, evaporating irretrievably despite its momentary vividness. Thank God.

The old man saw that the Geriatrics Hostel was little different from what he remembered. Older maybe, as everything was older, but not much different—even if you took into account the renovations to which laborers were apparently subjecting the right-hand wing. In that wing were the suites and common rooms that had once belonged to the old man's long-disbanded septigamoklans, and he directed himself as if by an emotional sonar into the smoky radiance of its first-floor corridor. Building materials were strewn about, and so many vulcanized cables cluttered the gouged parquetry that the place resembled a viper pit.

No matter. In this building he could go anywhere he wanted to go. His passport was on the end of his thumb. Right now he wanted to go up. So he took an elevator to the floor on which the seven members of the Phoenix septigamolkan had lived during the dozen controversy-riven years of his grand experiment. If he remembered correctly, and if by some freakish dispensation of chance it had not been moved, there was a copying machine on the fourth floor. His memory of this specific copier, in fact, had suggested to him—after nearly sixteen weeks back in Atlanta—the possibility of gaining entry into the Geriatrics Hostel by the simple expedient of holding up his thumb. And the strategy had worked!

At least so far.

It struck the old man that if anyone intercepted him in the halls, he could pretend to be a patient from the hospital wing—an aimlessly wandering Struldbrug, a palsied deadhead, an all-but-a-goner. Who could act the part any better than he? No one. His entire professional career had pointed him toward the role.

On the fourth floor the old man found himself in the circular corridor surrounding the common room of the Phoenix clan. Not even a naked bedframe stood in the cavernous darkness of this room. In another empty room, with windows opening onto the building's interior courtyard, he looked down and saw that the laborers engaged in renovation had recently uprooted the botanical garden in the quadrangle in order to sink a swimming pool at its very heart. The excavation lay beneath him like a wound.

Numb and uncertain, the old man went back into the circular corridor and followed it until he had come to the locked room in which old Jerry Zitelman-Phoenix had once put together the quarterly famzine of his septigamoklan: a periodical devoted to the occasional artwork and poems of the family's seven elderly spouses. It was this room—if you could still trust *some* things to be where they were supposed to be—that contained the copying machine. When the old man raised his thumb to the room's electric eye, almost at once he heard the gratifying click of a bolt release.

The tiny room looked almost exactly as it had when Jerry Zitelman-Phoenix maneuvered his wheelchair from dock to dock in the work counter running the entire length of one wall. Copying machine. Margin-justifying typer. And paper supplies in boxlike cubbyholes beneath the counter.

"Hot damn," drawled the intruder.

From a pocket of his greatcoat he pulled the half-crumpled sheet of paper on which he had earlier composed the articles of his frustrated mental state. Then he plugged in the typer and programmed it to print out a clean copy of this curious manifesto. He did his best to arrange the material after the fashion of Ur-Nu-sanctioned advertising flyers. This accomplished, he removed the duplicator's blue-gray dustcover and began running off a ream of distribution copies. These issued from the guts of the copying machine like profligate, bright-yellow poker hands.

At which point the door opened.

The old man jumped. Confronting him was a small, pale, white-haired girl of twelve or fourteen. She was dressed like an adult. There were hints of carefully applied makeup at her lips, cheeks, and eyes. Her eyes, in fact, were large and luminous; they held and unabashedly appraised him.

"You're not supposed to be here," the pale child declared. "It's late and this room's off-limits to everyone but authorized personnel."

As soon as she had spoken, the old man understood that this was no child, but a woman in her mid or late forties with the delicate, birdlike physique of a girl just approaching puberty. The duplicator continued to deal out its gay, run-amok poker hands.

"You'd better shut that off," the woman said.

Turning bewilderedly to the machine, the old man pulled its plug and gathered together the stack of copies it had made. The tiny woman stood in the doorway watching him. She would be ridiculously easy to brush aside, but her bearing gave her an imperiousness that her birdlike size was unable to countermand. Besides, he hadn't come up here to hurt anyone.

"What's your name?" The tone of her voice suggested that she *had* mistaken him for a wandering patient.

"What's yours?" he responded, his courage coming back.

"Vivian Klemme." She scrutinized him more intently. "Why don't you let me escort you back to the hospital section?"

The old man, balked by her size and her conciliatory manner, briefly returned her stare. Then he said, "I've got to go, Mz Klemme," buttoned his coat, balanced his flyers against his chest, and squeezed past the woman into the foggy corridor.

She followed him. "You're not a patient, are you?"

"No."

"How did you get in?"

"I'd show you if my hands weren't full, but you can be assured I don't intend to try this again." As she accompanied him around the circular corridor, he deliberately refused to lock eyes with her again. When they reached the elevator he leaned against the button to summon it.

"Won't you tell me your name?"

"Tad Zimas," he said as the elevator cage arrived and the

door opened. "Please take one of my flyers."

Vivian Klemme—a childlike apparition in the halflight— removed a single leaflet from the stack in his arms. Then the door slid to and the cage began immediately to drop. All the way down to street level, all the way home to his Level 3 cubicle in the hive, the old man was haunted by the image of Vivian Klemme's youthful eyes in the kabuki whiteness of her adult face. And he regretted having lied to her.

Early the following afternoon the old man began passing out flyers to the people sitting shoulder to shoulder on the cold stone benches in the pedestrian court opposite Consolidated Rich's. The flat golden sheen of the Dome flowed down on Atlanta's encysted architecture like honey, and a pair of riot speakers somewhere in Peachtree Canyon was blaring a program of approved funkphalt Christmas ballads.

A red-haired man jumped up and waved one of the flyers in the old man's face. "This is seditious!" he screamed. "You can't go around handing out shit like this!"

A commotion erupted. Eventually a pair of trolls arrived on bicycles: a muscular deep-purple cop and a slender blond mosby, each outfitted with polymer casks and stunclubs. They immediately engaged in a colloquy with the red-haired man who had initiated the shouting, and he in turn began berating the grizzled, immovable derelict who had been passing out the flyers. Aware that he was going to be arrested, the old man gazed about unperturbedly.

Again and again his eyes returned to that section of the Dome which, he had learned, had been blasted open two years ago by a group of disenfranchised urban revolutionaries calling themselves the Red Sticks. The rent from that explosion had long since been welded tight, but you could still tell the repair work from the discolored geodesic honeycombing surrounding it. The old man derived a strange satisfaction from staring at its shiny scar.

"What's your name?" the deep-purple troll abruptly asked him.

Without hesitation he replied, "Tad Zimas."

The deep-purple spoke this name into his partner's computer backpack and waited for a digital readout. "Tha's a lie," he said matter-of-factly, looking around the mosby's shoulder. "They ain' nobody name' Zimas in the whole friggin' City."

"Where do you live?" the other troll demanded.

"Nowhere," the old man responded.

With that, the mosby relieved him of his remaining flyers, thanked the red-haired man for his testimony, and shook out a gleaming pair of hard plastic manacles. A moment later the old man was walking between the trolls' tall bicycles like a slave between a pair of mounted horse soldiers. Dozens of curious onlookers parted before the eerily cruising bikes and watched the old man go shuffle-footed but smiling into his captivity.

2 / The Flyer

CITIZENS OF THE NUCLEUS,
ECCE HOMO!

MY SOUL IS IMPRISONED!

• In Winter, at midday, during a fit of fair weather, the sky's fragile blue is backlit through ninety-three-million miles of night by a halo of feathery whiteness. An eyelash will scratch that blue. Each time you wink, the cold Winter light pours through.

• The faulted silts of the dusk are laid atop one another in layers of prismatic lava. An hour later, like so much collapsing plaster, they have all been shivered into blackness. The hour after sunset is the hour of the beautiful disaster.

• The evening sky is imprinted with the pattern of a black leopard's pelt, each cloud an ocelot link of chocolate or ebony. When lightning flashes through this pelt, the life behind its fur bristles and melts like pain. Afterwards, the rain.

• A rouge on the face of the night or a fever on that of the morning. Dawn's inflammation is ambiguous. The pallbearer and the midwife lie down in a common bed.

Their issue takes your heart away, scours your sky with its
rich placental blood.

• At bitter midnight, Summer drowsing even in the
interstellar ice, the sky is a shroud that grows. You watch
the darkness deepen, broaden, lengthen. No one escapes
the infinite sack it knits. And no one escapes its glitter.

*** ! THIS IS HOW FEEL! ***
MY SOUL IS IMPRISONED!

3 / *In the Hyatt Regency*

At five a.m. on Friday, two days before Christmas, in a
penthouse suite of the Hyatt Regency, the wake-up crystal on
Julian Cawthorn's left temple began sending pulse-cued
vibrations through his jaw and brain case. He pinched the
crystal between his fingers and eased out of bed so as not to
disturb Margot. This was going to be a busy weekend for her:
several full-scale masses in Bondville, three service-assists at the
First Ortho-Urban Worship Center, and a dawnrise ceremony
on the campus of the King Theological Complex. Christmas
busy.

Dressing in the dark, Julian tried to put together the
fragments of an interrupted dream. They wouldn't slot. The
entire surreal tomb-painting of his dream was melting and
sliding away from him. At last he shook his head and gave it up.

He was going down the hall to the cold, disrupted suites now
sheltering the last two aliens in the City—that was why he had
set the wake-up crystal for five. Pulling on his parka, he realized
that his subconscious anticipation of this visit had probably
triggered his dream. Although it didn't account for the specific
images of death and sex that had muddied his sleep, it at least
provided a general explanation. Satisfied as to the source if not
the precise content of his nightmare, Julian reached into the
closet for the helmet he'd worn while working full-time for the
late Fiona Bitler and Emory Nettlinger, her physicist husband,

the folks who had first brought into isolationist Atlanta a contingent of ungainly hominoid starmen.

The helmet slipped through Julian's hand and clattered about on the floor. "Damn," he managed bitterly.

Her head and upper torso emerging from the naked sheets with almost pantherine grace, Margot sat up and peered through the gloom toward him. At twenty-nine she slept so lightly that Julian could hardly ever get out of bed without waking her. (She sometimes playfully attributed his inability to wake up without mechanical assistance to his lingering "babyhood.") This morning he had nearly made it. That he hadn't, and that he had essentially thwarted himself, filled him with an unfocused rancor. Not only had he wanted to let her sleep, he had also hoped to keep his mission down the hall a small and innocent secret. Things were usually easier that way. Ignoring Margot, Julian picked up the helmet and checked its headlamp. When its beam shot through a deliquescent gel, immediately he turned it off and let the gloom again congeal the gloom again congeal around them.

"You were down there just last week," Margot said reasonably. "Isn't it a little too soon to be visiting them again?"

"They're supposed to be dying," he responded, gripping the helmet. "The Council of Three wants to know when one or both of them kick off, and so I go whenever it seems right to me."

"They've been lying in there for nearly two years, Julian. It's hard to believe they won't be lying there for a long time to come. Their metabolisms have apparently slowed down to fend off death, and there's just no point in continually going down there to genuflect before their big unresponsive carcasses. You're torturing yourself."

"Who genuflects?" Julian demanded heatedly. "I just want to see if they're still alive. All right?"

"I'm sorry," Margot said, apparently meaning it. "Go on, then."

Julian blew a kiss whose wet report could have embodied either affection or irritation, if not both together, and walked through the suite into the dim empty corridor of the hotel's topmost floor. At the far end, to his right, was the metal-plated door giving access to the chill, perpetually dark ecologarium where the aliens lay.

In spite of the nebulous forebodings of his dream, this

morning was no different from a hundred previous mornings during the past two years. When he finally stood beside the makeshift bier deep in the Cygnusians' suite, he let his headlamp play indifferently upon the aliens' huge, unmoving bodies and understood again that nothing had changed. Absolutely nothing.

Margot was sitting on a stool in the gallery. She was scrubbed and outfitted. Like a flag of truce, a snow-white clerical tucker draped the neck and shoulders of her tunic. When Julian skipped his helmet across the carpet and dumped his parka by the door, she merely crooked her finger at him. He took up the stool beside hers and poured out a tumbler of fruit-extract cocktail. The liquid was warm in his mouth, bittersweet.

"Nothing new?"

"Is that an 'I-told-you-so'?"

"No, it isn't!" Margot flared. "Sometimes I think you need to stick that wake-up chip inside your skull instead of merely on it. Listen, I know what a trial this business sometimes is for you."

"Do you know what I dreamed this morning?"

She controlled her anger. "You're waiting for another revelation of Ultimate Truth, aren't you? The last time one of those creatures communicated with us through the agency of a dream, you thought we'd been shown a mystery forever beyond the pale of human knowledge."

"And you dismissed the revelation as an irrelevancy."

"What difference could it have made to anyone on a day-to-day basis, Julian? We've been through this a hundred times. How could I go back on over two millennia of human experience because of a bizarre ten-minute session with the etheric intelligence of one of the Bitlinger starmen? What's ten minutes against two thousand years?"

"Nothing, apparently."

"Julian, what difference has the revelation made to *you?* Depressed and bewildered you because it wasn't objectively verifiable. And it seems to get worse for you with every passing day." She covered his brown hand with her own warm, translucent white one. "What exactly do you want from those pitiful sentient monsters down the hall?"

"To know," he said evenly.

"And what makes you think they truly know any more than we do?"

Withdrawing his hand from hers, Julian toasted Margot with his breakfast cocktail. "Great time of year for this discussion, isnt it? Christ's mass around the corner, the incense of orthodox salvation in the air."

As soon as he had spoken he knew his error. His wife regarded him with bright, unpitying eyes. She was a novice priest, secure in her faith, and he was a topless drum beating futilely in the infinite echo chamber of his skepticism. A marriage of faith and doubt. At moments of confrontation it required very little insight to perceive which quality was the stronger. He set his glass down and touched Margot's bottom lip with an apologetic finger.

"My turn," he said. "I'm sorry."

Margot accepted the apology wordlessly. Then she pulled a leaf of yellow paper from her carryall and handed it to him. "I meant to give this to you last night," she said.

An advertising flyer? Julian put it on the counter to read it. The first words to jump out at him were

MY SOUL IS IMPRISONED!

They seemed an uncanny gloss on the argument he had just had with Margot. His hands began to tremble.

"Where did you get this?"

"I taught my seminary class yesterday afternoon. One of my students brought it in and gave it to me. She said an old man had been handing them out in front of Rich's when a red-haired citizen took offense and called the trolls. He seemed to be one of the few people there who understood that the integrity of the Urban Nucleic Way was being impugned. The old man was arrested."

"These are descriptions of the sky," Julian said.

"Yes, I guess they are."

"Impressionistic descriptions of the sky." (But the words MY SOUL IS IMPRISONED! danced on the peripheries of his vision and made it hard for him to concentrate.)

"That's why the old man was arrested and hustled off. It spits in the collective eye of the Council of Three by implying that one of Atlanta's citizens is unhappy with his lot."

"He's hardly alone, is he?"

"I thought there might be a story in it for you."

Julian shook his head in exasperation. Although more

tolerant of religious dissent than its predecessor, the Council
continued to exercise subtle and unsubtle forms of censorship
over the news media. Because Eugene Chavers, the managing
editor of the combine, was in the Triumvirate's pocket, Julian
knew that every word he inscribed on the display screen of his
visicompositor signaled another perilous step on the tightrope
of accountability. You paid for the privilege of an elevated
vantage point on urban affairs by walking your tightrope in
deadly fear of an unrecoverable misstep.

Did Margot have no conception of these things? Far from it.
She understood the liabilities of accurate social reporting as well
as anyone. With lifted eyebrows Julian studied his wife as if she
had just uttered a heady blasphemy and forsworn the Church.

"It's a cry for help," she explained. "And the man was
arrested."

4 / *Eugene Chavers*

On the fifth floor of the newstapes building Julian flagged down
his boss with a bright yellow flyer. As Chavers approached him
from the stained-glass cage of the managing editor's office,
Julian had little idea of what he was going to say to the man, of
what sort of case he was going to present. The flyer gave a little
death rattle as he fluttered it aloft.

"Have you seen this, sir?"

A humorless man with the face of a granite lion, Eugene
Chavers was a holdover from the last days of Saganella Lesser's
administration; during the period of martial law brought on by
Julian's ethnography he was appointed to take Haven Idhe's
place. In a disconcerting if only partial way, then, Julian bore
the responsibility of Chavers' headlock on a position of
meaningful authority. A daunting, even a humiliating, footnote
to a squalid episode of urban history.

"I've seen one like it," Chavers replied, handing the flyer
back. He put a heavy, manicured paw on Julian's shoulder.
Why?"

"Do you know who wrote it?"

"The man who was arrested called himself Tad Zimas."

Julian permitted himself an expectant squint, nothing more.

"That's an alias," Chavers went on. "Tad Zimas is a simple backwards anagram of *samizdat,* which is Russian for 'self-publication.' In the twentieth-century Soviet state it also implied the underground circulation of typed or handwritten manuscripts among one's trusted friends. Our Tad Zimas, however, emerged from the underground to pass out his *samizdat* flyers in full Domelight. He gave the trolls not his name but a description of the illegal activity for which he was arrested."

"Do they know who he really is?"

"They determined his identity late yesterday afternoon."

Julian wanted to dislodge Chavers' hand from his shoulder, but he forbore and asked, "Well, who is he?" The uneasiness he had felt that morning had mutated gradually into a secret anticipation and excitement. The declaration MY SOUL IS IMPRISONED! flashed on and off in his consciousness as if a miniature scroll of neon were buried somewhere in his gray matter.

Eugene Chavers, moving on tasseled and embroidered street slippers, led Julian to a nearby visicompositor. He keyed the unit so that a name appeared letter by letter on the display screen:

L-E-L-A-N-D T-A-N-N-E-R.

"You're skying me," Julian heedlessly blurted. Tanner had once been the director of the gerontology and geriatrics programs for the Human Development Commission in Atlanta. That, however, had been more than a quarter of a century ago.

"Keep using expressions like that, you'll end up in detention too. In any case, that's the man's name." Chavers turned the visicompositor off and indicated by a gesture that Julian should follow him between a row of tall glass cabinets into his own stained-glass cage. A moment later both men entered the illuminated and ornately leaded chapel of his office.

Easing himself into a coaster chair, Chavers said, "You're not old enough to remember Tanner. How did you happen to recognize his name?"

"We have a bond."

Chavers narrowed his eyes. "What sort of bond?"

"My great-grandmother Parthena Cawthorn was a member of one of Tanner's first experimental septigamoklans. She lived in the UrNu Geriatrics Hostel with the other six spouses of her Phoenix marriage unit." Julian looked at the flyer in his hands with a sense of dread fulfillment. The links between Tanner and himself were many. . . .

"The septigamoklans were Tanner's downfall," Chavers remarked.

"Not until First Councilor Lesser took office. They lasted twelve years, weathered assaults from both ward reps and prelates."

"But they died, didn't they?" Chavers inserted his left hand in the glovelike, shiny orange ManiCureAll atop his desk and allowed the device to impart a look of blissful dippiness to the pendulous lower half of his face.

"Yes, sir," Julian admitted.

"First Councilor Lesser killed the septigamoklans, disbanded the families, and the Church never did recognize them as marriages of any social or moral validity. Tanner had to run for it when a politico of Saganella's savvy took over." Chavers was talking as if the woman still held her scepter. But he stopped abruptly and gazed over the top of Julian's head. "In any case, he's back, Tanner is—he's been back since the sixty-third of Summer."

"Let me do a story about him."

"I can't."

"Why not?"

"He's p.n.g. with the Triumvirate, just as he was with Saganella. Sanctioning his return from the Washington Nucleus and giving him cubicle-and-board are the only concessions it intends to grant him. They certainly don't want to publicize the fact that they permitted him to return, especially now that he's willfully violated a statute in the Retrenchment Edicts against *samizdat* activity." Chavers removed his hand from the ManiCureAll, blew on his burnished, bruise-colored nails, and turned the device upside down to accommodate his other hand. Julian noticed that the sideboard of Chavers' desk was lined with nail-polish cartridges—six or seven different colors, an arsenal of digital beautification.

"What's going to happen to Tanner, then?"

"Well, they could deport him to the Washington Nucleus or they could simply let him decline into gibbering senility in the bookerslam. He hasn't abided by the terms of his return-immigration visa, which he applied for as soon as he heard that Saganella had been deposed."

Chavers suddenly withdrew his right hand from the

ManiCureAll and plopped the device in his in-basket, where it resembled the severed extremity of a convicted urban traitor. Chavers then explained that after driving Tanner to resign late in 47, First Councilor Lesser had made it impossible for him to work anywhere else in the City—unless he wanted to flame-decontaminate the cubicles and concourse flops of poor dead derries. He hadn't submitted to this indignity. Eventually, however, some of Tanner's friends had prevailed upon a few minor government officials to intercede with Saganella on his behalf, and she had reluctantly permitted him to emigrate to Washington. There he went to work for that City's Anti-Aging Task Force and rose to its directorship in only four years. He had resigned that post during the Summer just past in order to return to Atlanta and the prospect of enforced idleness on an austere Dole Roll allotment.

"Why?" Julian asked. "Why did he do that?"

"Who knows? Saganella was out of the way, and he was a native Atlantan. Maybe he felt like Napoleon returning from Elba...before Waterloo."

Julian, without invitation, pulled up a chair and sat down. He placed his elbows on Chavers' desk and spoke through the steeple of his fingers: "This is a talented man. There's poetry in this flyer—"

"Disguised as prose. Violates the Retrenchment Edicts' requirement of unadorned utility in all documentary enterprises." He attacked one gleaming thumbnail with an emery board.

"All right. But I still don't understand why Tanner isn't permitted to work. Margot says this thing"—rattling the flyer—"is a cry for help. He probably wants to be able to *do* something."

"Like overthrowing the Council of Three."

"That's not really very likely, is it? Why can't he go to work for the Human Development Commission again?"

Chavers disposed of the emery board and walked to one of his office's stained-glass windows. "All right, Cawthorn, let's get this straight. The Council of Three permitted Tanner to return for humanitarian reasons—"

"But they won't let him work."

"Because"—Chavers didn't turn around—"the Church still remembers the septigamoklans: that's one reason. Second, the g-&-g programs at the Geriatrics Hostel have a new director already and too many Indian chiefs spoil the broth. Third, even if there weren't a new director none of the researchers over there wants anything to do with Tanner. And fourth, he's getting to be an old, old man."

"Wait a minute. Why are the people over there so dead set against his coming back?"

"They think he's a stone-age relic. He opposed chemotherapy, the use of synthetic drugs, the entire biochemical approach. Because of the uproar over the septigamolklans, Saganella's council/conclave cut back the funding for g-&-g research and discouraged scientific exchanges with Urban Nuclei of more liberal persuasion. Two strikes against Tanner right there: Holdovers from the Tanner period blame him for deserting them under fire, while the newcomers at the HDC hold him responsible for the funding cutbacks that followed Saganella's cracking of the septigamoklans. Now they've got a new director, a woman just up from Miami, and they *don't want Tanner back.*" With one elegant finger Chavers traced a leaded pattern in the stained glass and held the whole of Julian's attention.

"I'd still like to do a story about him."

"Cawthorn, that flyer contains five descriptions of the sky. In those descriptions is an implicit criticism of the Dome, and criticisms like that breed discontent among people who don't know any better. So ice your crusade, all right?"

"May I go *see* Tanner, then?"

Chavers turned around. "As a newstape employee or as a private citizen?"

"As a private citizen, I guess."

"Fine—but don't tell 'em *I* sent you and forget about putting anything about your visit in the newstapes."

Julian got up and turned toward the door. The rapping of Chavers' knuckles on a pane of colored glass halted him immediately.

"Did you know they're still using the Gregorian calendar in the Washington Nucleus?" Chavers inquired bleakly.

"No, sir, I didn't."

"Pathetic anachronism in this day and age."

As that seemed to be all he had to say, Julian left Chavers ruminating forlornly on Washington's atavistic measurement of time and strolled without a backward glance to the elevator. Five minutes later he was hurrying across the ceramic flooring of Peachtree Canyon with the Dome glowering down and five descriptions of the naked sky folded in his pocket like a bank note.

5 / Leland Tanner

A troll led Julian down the fluoro-lit corridor to a detention area consisting of several floor-to-ceiling thermoplastic cells. The prisoners inside them looked like department-store mannikins frozen in Lucite.

In the fifth plastic block on the right sat the old man. He perched on the unsupported bed-ledge coming out of the cell's rear wall, his mattress a safari-striped affair of some kind of wet-looking simulated leather. The wall above his perch was plastered with children's drawings, apparently from either the ecclesiastical nurseries or an urban-ed primary school. They lent an air of artificial cheerfulness to the cell, but the old man beneath them gazed raptly at his threadbare street slippers.

The troll—a mosby younger than Julian—admitted him through a virtually invisible door and then prowled up and down the corridor.

The cell was soundproof and comfortably heated—luxuries no doubt instantly revocable should a detainee ever arouse his guards' suspicions. A vent high in the rear wall reminded Julian that his parents had forfeited their lives to a poisonous gas fed into the Level 9 Coenotorium through a similar system....

"My soul is imprisoned," Julian said, shaking the old man's hand as Tanner rose to greet him.

"So is my body," replied the other. "I feel like a goldfish." The former gerontologist was very little stooped by age. He wore glasses with big violet lenses, and his face was mussed and expressively horsy.

Julian rushed to introduce himself, to point out that his great-grand-mother had once belonged to the Phoenix septiga-moklan, to insist that Tanner's return to Atlanta and his emergence from the anonymity of the hive undoubtedly had great significance for both of them. Margot's putting the flyer into his hands earlier that morning represented the pivot in a crucial concatenation of events whose outcome was as yet unforeseeable. Nevertheless—

But Leland interrupted him: "You're the emissary to the last two aliens, aren't you?"

Taking a breath, Julian admitted that he was. This fact had made him a minor celebrity in the Urban Nucleus, and although his relationship with the starmen had a bearing on his spiritual bond with the gerontologist, he hoped that Leland would wait to interrogate him about it until he had come to understand they were sibling pneumas engaged in an on-going quest for a common entelechy. Leland, in fact, might *already* understand the nature of Ultimate Reality—in which case it was he, Julian, who should be interrogating him, Leland, rather than the other way around. The catch-phrase MY SOUL IS IMPRISONED! seemed to suggest that Leland *did* understand.

"Wouldn't you like to get out of here?" Julian asked.

"Do you know how long it took me to get here?"

"As I understand it," Julian hazarded, "about twenty minutes."

"The last twenty minutes followed hard upon a period of twelve or thirteen weeks in which I made up my mind to do something, eight or nine hours devoted to the composition of my flyer, and one very chancy night over at the Geriatrics Hostel to run off copies." He shook a mottled finger at Julian. "I never associated the Cawthorn in the Hyatt Regency with the Cawthorn who was in my early septigamoklan. That's very interesting."

A half-naked prisoner in an adjacent cell pressed his face and hands against the intervening wall and leered at them. A middle-aged black man riddled with acupuncture scars, he was probably a devotee of an outlawed religious sect. The stainless-steel needles with which he had once declared the fierceness of his unorthodox piety were now evident only in the random tattoos of his wounds.

Julian tried to call both himself and Leland back to the matter at hand. "You wanted to be arrested?"

"I wanted somebody like you to come and get me out. I was tired of playing the role of a superannuated retiree in a cubicle still reeking of spray combustgens."

"So you took a potshot at the Dome by describing the sky beyond it?"

"Nothing of the kind. I'm an innovator, not a revolutionary. The articles on my flyer are not descriptions of the sky per se, but metaphorical declarations about five separate and distinctive psychological states—all of which I have experienced here in Atlanta since returning from Washington."

"Psychological states?"

"What else? Unlike Fiona Bitler and Emory Nettlinger, I'm not in a hurry to see the Dome dismantled. I just want an occupation."

"Have you told the trolls this?"

"I suppose I have—but it's all twaddle to them in whatever light I cast my intentions. All they choose to see is the sky."

"I think I can get you out of here," said Julian, casting an uneasy glance at the human pincushion who was now employing his tongue to draw a foggy bull's-eye on the transparent wall. "If I do, I'd like you to agree to being released into Margot's and my custody until we can manage to retrieve you from your untouchable status."

"Fine," Leland said. "Another death rehearsal."

"Sir?"

"Plato said, 'Practice dying.' But the best practice is undoubtedly living. If you can get me out of here and find me something to do, I'll go strenuously into death rehearsals again."

Julian nodded, then turned toward the corridor and hailed the blasé young mosby patrolling it.

6 / Intimations of Immortality

Dr Leland Tanner's "treason" was in the eye of the beholder rather than the heart of the captive—so Julian informed three different policemen, each of incrementally higher rank than the last, ensconced like buddhas in three separate niches of the New Peachtree precinct house. Although it took all afternoon, authorization finally came down to release Dr Tanner in Julian's custody.

Immediately Julian put through a telecom to the Bondville tenement chapel in which Margot was presiding over a series of Friday masses and told her what he had discovered about the old man who'd been arrested for passing out his illegally duplicated flyers. Leland would be let go, he explained, only if they agreed to vouch for his behavior and to keep tabs on his whereabouts. Orpianoogla music came faintly through the telecom line.

"Bring him home with you," Margot advised her husband. "Bring him home."

After redeeming the old man's ugly greatcoat, Julian and his aged foundling descended into the hive, disembarked on Level 3, and proceeded to Leland's single-occupant cubicle.

This apartment was drab and spray-scorched, and Leland began enthusiastically gathering up his personal effects as if in a hurry to be shut of the place. While he was filling a pair of briefcases with papers, microfiche files, and visicassettes, Julian went into the bath-booth to clean out the medicine cabinets, imagining that Leland would have an impressive store of organic (if not synthetic) anti-aging compounds: nucleic acids, antioxidants, natural hormones like thymosin. Chavers had said that Dr Tanner didn't believe in the biochemical approach—but what gerontologist turns his back on his field's most fruitful laboratory research, especially when many of its products are healthful natural derivatives? Even Margot took carefully measured units of some of these compounds, and she, despite a professional commitment to the doctrine of free will, was something of a fatalist about the moment of ultimate hammerfall.

But the only "drug" that Julian could find in Leland's bath-booth was a small store of Vitamin E—which the old man admitted taking only when he happened to think about it; in other words, "pretty damn seldom."

"My colleagues in the Washington Nucleus," Leland explained, coming to the door of the bath-booth, "convinced me that my antipathy to drugs was high-minded but archaic. They never really convinced me that it was wrong, though. Maybe that's because I would have had to admit that by withholding a number of available synthetic compounds from my patients here in Atlanta, I may have cheated them out of sizable stretches of life. In Washington, you see, I began to soften—a little—my opposition to the biochemical strategy, but the bumbling galens of geriatric medicine here in Atlanta don't know that. From what I understand, they don't know much of anything. Their City is an island, and the UrNu Geriatrics Hostel has become nothing but an antiseptic way station for the dying."

"The facility has a new director," Julian said.

Leland blinked at him in the mirror, a brief eclipse of his violet eyes behind the shadowy lenses. "Who?"

"A woman up from the Miami Nucleus, my boss tells me.

That's all I know about it. She's been here only a couple of weeks or so."

"Ah," Leland sighed. "I may have met her already." He wouldn't elaborate, but neither did he return to his own packing.

Julian, meticulously aligning the E-caps in the bottom of an overnighter, stared at the old man's reflection in the tiny mirror above the plastalloy sink. "How are Atlanta's researchers backward?" he finally asked. "What do you know that they don't?"

"A great many things, I'm afraid. That the gerontologists and geneticists in Japan and New Free Europe have joined hands in developing cell-modification techniques that not only prolong the body's self-repair capabilities, but also make it possible for amputees to grow new limbs as easily as a chameleon regenerates a severed tail. That these foreign researchers have discovered three distinct 'genetic clocks of aging'—one in the brain, one in the thyroid, and a diffuse one in the body's posmitotic cellular DNA. That they've probably devised either chemical or genetic means of stopping or setting back these clocks. That everyone overseas of any social or political stature may soon be a virtual immortal, subject only to flukish deaths of the 'broken-test-tube' sort or the absurd whimsy of deliberate suicide." Leland squinted into the mirror for Julian's reaction. "How's that for starters?"

Feeling vaguely trapped—he'd already cleaned out the cabinet and had nothing else to do in the bath-booth—Julian returned the old man's squint: "How do *you* happen to know these things?"

"Washington's better than Atlanta about permitting an occasional exchange of scientific and cultural information with foreign governments, a carryover from the days of union. But none of the Cities of the Urban Federation is a utopia of gerontological enlightenment. I've just recited a list of conjectures—hardly anyone over here truly knows what's happening outside our continental boundaries—but it seems pretty likely that our knowledge of the aging process and its biomedical deceleration is three or four decades behind that of the Europeans and the Japanese."

Immortality! thought Julian. But for the repressive stupidity of the Domes, we'd all stand on the brink of immortality! And the battle-cry MY SOUL IS IMPRISONED! sounded in his heart.

"And you don't want the Domes to fall?" he demanded.

"Whether they stand or fall isn't finally of much consequence," Leland replied. "I'd be happy if they simply let in the light."

7 / Suitemates

Two evenings before Christmas Dr Leland Tanner moved into the Eastwin-Cawthorn suite, just down the corridor from Cygnostik Land. Margot returned briefly from Bondville to welcome him into their home, then departed again for her remaining three masses, swirling away in a silken alb and trailing behind her the fragrance of incense. Julian, fretting inwardly over his prolonged absence from work that afternoon and Chavers' most likely response to it, fretted outwardly over the arrangements for their new suitemate's comfort and so ended up discomfiting him.

"I'm all right," Leland cried in mock distress. "Please sit down."

They faced each other in low-slung chairs through whose transparent tubular frames there migrated protean lumps of plastic, like antigens ballooning through an anemic bloodstream.

Surrounded by the glowing tubes of his chair, Leland seemed all elbows, knees, and eyes. "Very nice," he said, apparently without irony.

"They're like bumblebees," Julian ventured.

Leland, a gentleman, merely raised his eyebrows.

Miserable, Julian hurried to explain: "Looked at from an aerodynamic standpoint, the bumblebee ought not to be able to fly. These chairs resemble futuristic instruments of medieval torture—" *was he saying what he meant?*—"and yet they're really pretty comfortable."

"Interesting analogy."

Conversation lapsed. Julian treaded water in the reservoir of his stagnant social skills. What did he and this unemployed seventy-six-year-old gerontologist have in common?

Parthena.

But they'd already talked about her, that afternoon in the precinct house, and Julian didn't want to appear at a loss for new

topics of discussion. Globules of floating plastic passed under
his hands like disembodied pneumas in search of some
impossible apocalyptic reunion, dreamlike in their slowness.
Along with a mental image of the great-grandmother who had
died the year he was born, they induced in Julian a recollection
of the aliens at the end of the hall.

"Have you ever seen the Bitlinger starmen?" he asked.

"Only in photographs."

"Would you like to see them?" He half rose from the glowing
cradle of his chair.

"Not tonight, Julian. Eventually, I suppose. It's a little
frightening to think of confronting them face to face."

Sinking back into his chair, Julian began to wish that Margot
were there to help him. Although herself almost wretchedly shy,
since her seminary days she had learned to build delicate
empathic bridges between herself and others, passing over these
with a nimble confidence that Julian found impossible to imitate
or feign. (Afterward, though, she did yogic breathing exercises
to relieve her emotional fatigue.) Leland was a challenge. He
appeared aware of Julian's nervousness but almost wholly
indifferent to the fact that two creatures from another solar
system were hibernating only eight or nine decameters away.
Food? Sports? Literature? Immortality? What did you talk
about with such a man?"

"How long have you been waiting for them to die?" Leland
suddenly asked, taking Julian off the tenterhooks of his
perplexity.

"Ever since the Council of Three deposed Saganella," Julian
replied gratefully. "Almost two years."

"They're malingerers, then?"

"I don't know what they are, anymore. I've just about given
up on their ever doing anything but lying comatose until
Doomsday."

"If that's the case, they're virtually immortal, aren't they?"

Julian's heart beat a little faster. These words were an
approximate echo of what Leland had said in his Level 3 cubicle
about geriatrics research overseas: Japan and the NFE were
giving their people legitimate expectations of appreciably longer
life. In neither the European polities nor the territories of Japan
had science been made a theocratic shuttlecock. Julian, knowing
that the aliens were an umbilical to the outside, found himself
again worrying the notion of his fellow citizens' imprisonment

and what it cost them. He thought, *This is how I feel*. And, *My soul is imprisoned.*

In the meantime, Leland talked....

Margot got home almost two hours after Julian had seen the old man to bed. Limp with exhaustion, she came into her husband's arms on the hammocklike cushion of his chair. Amoeboid shapes twisted and pulled through the tubes of its lambent frame. The entire suite was adrift with shadows.

"You two get along all right?" Margot asked.

"Eventually, yes. We talked about the Cygnostikoi—after I'd offered to take him into their mausoleum for a visit."

Margot stiffened in Julian's arms. "Did he go?"

"No. He wasn't up to it tonight. Neither was I, really. My offer was a gesture of hospitality."

"Was that all you could think of?"

Julian shifted to get a better look at his wife's face. "Well, there was always Parthena—but we'd already hashed out the astonishing coincidence of her great-grandson's showing up to rescue the founder of her septigamoklan from the bookerslam."

Apprehensively, Margot asked: "You didn't discuss your— well, your 'revelation'?"

"I'm not an idiot, Margot. And I'm not a prophet of an alien faith, either. You have to have an easily communicable myth to dramatize the beginnings of a religious idea, and what happened to you and me on our wedding night doesn't seem to qualify. The Awakening of the Buddha, Prometheus on the Rock, Christ in His Passion—those are galvanizing mythopoeic images, Margot, they persuade by their accessibility and vividness. What we dreamed together was vivid but too private to qualify. So I didn't spill either my guts or my soul into Dr Tanner's gracious lap."

So conspicious was Margot's relief that Julian began to resent what her fled anxiety implied. She mistrusted his youth. She was afraid he would blunder—show himelf a fool—by the adolescent earnestness with which he undertook every public project and every private quest. That hurt, even if her concern was as much for him as for herself.

"You discussed the Cygnostikoi?" Margot carefully urged.

"He said just about the same thing you said this morning—that if they're dying they may be a long time about it. He was chatting, making conversation. He even warned me facetiously about holding my caretaker position here until death did us part—my death, not theirs. He threw out the idea that they may be *incapable* of dying, that maybe they'll just grow more and more decrepit without ever reaching an end. Like Tithonus, in the myth. Or like the Struldbrugs in *Gulliver's Travels,* who continued to age even though they couldn't die."

"Fit topics for a gerontologist," Margot said. "The ancients invented Tithonus, and Swift his Struldbrugs, as antidotes to the vanity of striving for physical immortality."

"Whatever," Julian responded. "The odd thing is that I'm not sure Dr Tanner is convinced of his own mortality."

"At his age?" Margot was smiling.

"Well, he speaks of life as a series of death rehearsals—but I don't think he believes in the inevitability of opening night. Not for himself, at least. He seems to consider himself a brother to Struldbrugs and close kin to our malingering Cygnostikoi."

"Do you still have his flyer?"

When Julian brought it out of the slash pocket on his hip, it looked as if it had been there for years.

Margot unfolded the flyer and snapped it out smooth. "Listen: *'You watch the darkness deepen, broaden, lengthen. No one escapes the infinite sack it knits. . . .'* Not the words of a man who's deluded himself that he's going to live forever. He just wants to live the time remaining to him to the fullest. A final Ulyssean fling, for as long as it happens to last."

"Maybe."

"He's come back to Atlanta when he could have remained in a position of authority in Washington," Margot insisted. "He set himself a challenge at a time in life when most people pretend that setting themselves a challenge is no longer an option."

Julian shifted positions again. "Well, Margot, he's set us a challenge, too."

Margot waited for an explanation.

"He wants us to use our influence to get him a job at the Geriatrics Hostel; he wants to go to work again."

"But we don't *have* any influence!" Margot protested.

"Which, of course, is the challenge. We'll have to braid together the filaments of the strings we pull."

8 / Braiding a String

In the festival week between Christmas and Year Day, Margot called on the new director of the Geriatrics Hostel. She laid out her case for Leland as if attempting to demonstrate a Thomistic proof for the existence of God. She outlined the nature of her mission, offered a glowing profile of the absent supplicant's professional career, and handed over all the pertinent references and recommendations.

"I've of course heard of Leland Tanner," said the woman who had recently assumed the directorship. "Why hasn't he come himself?" Vivian Klemme looked like an albino wren. Her white hair was cut short, and her hands were porcelain sculptures. Behind her desk was a false window featuring a hologramic view of deep, deep space—not the sort of decorative item you could find on the Level 4 Mall.

Because of the septigamoklans, Margot explained, the Church and the Council of Three still considered Leland Tanner a pariah. This past Summer, for instance, his every application for work—whether at the HDC, or private geriatrics hostels, or even Ortho-Urban day nurseries—had been turned back on him with unsubtle warnings to desist. Leland, Margot admitted, was perilously *persona non grata* with the religious and political establishment.

"Hiring him may involve a risk," she concluded lamely.

"Aren't you a representative of the Church?" Vivian Klemme inquired.

"Yes, I am." She added quickly: "But not today."

"Then you're at some small risk yourself, aren't you?" The woman gave Margot no time to respond. "Are you sure he'd accept a position subordinate to mine? I don't intend to go back to Miami for him—not unless the Council of Three tries to prevent me from appointing my own staff. They told me they wouldn't interfere."

Margot assured her that Leland would accept any position in the hostel that wasn't either demeaning or absolutely pointless.

"Good for him."

"Besides, he's met you before. And he's told both Julian and me that it would be a pleasure to work for you."

"He's met me?"

"Yes, ma'am—the night you interrupted him while he was running off his flyers on the fourth floor of the other wing."

"My goodness," said Vivian Klemme in surprise and consternation. She swiveled toward the view of deep space—a three-dimensional vista of stars and floating dust—and sat hidden by the back of her monstrous chair. "My goodness," she murmured again.

And Margot understood that Leland Tanner now had a patron at court.

9 / Leland Loves Vivian

In the nursing wards of the UrNu Geriatrics Hostel, answerable to no one but Dr Klemme, Leland went to work as a troubleshooter. He also supervised a research section for interning gerontologists, helped administer to select patients the battery of tests originally developed at Brookhaven to measure comparative rates of aging among the surviving victims of the Hiroshima and Nagasaki A-bomb blasts, and served as an advisor and social director to the ambulatory patients whose cruelest infirmities were not crippled limbs and fuzzied minds but boredom and loneliness. He was older than many of those he sought to comfort, and clearly looked it.

What kept Leland Tanner going was his deep, even overweening faith in his own usefulness. He lived simultaneously as if each day were his last and as if he were never going to die; these approaches to his work were amazingly complementary, as efficient at measuring the circumference of his days as the legs of a compass at inscribing a circle. Perfection. He was happy for the first time since immigrating from the Washington Nucleus.

Even the last two holdovers from his own controversial reign as director accepted him without hostility. He was older, they were older, it hardly seemed worth bothering about—all that shimmering water under the bridges of their divergent pasts.

Leland appreciated their renewed good will, people upon whom he'd once depended as family. He was careful not to allude to the major professional triumph and only political catastrophe of his career.

The septigamoklans.

In fact, he would have been able to forget the septigamoklans almost entirely if he hadn't eventually moved from the Hyatt Regency to a spacious apartment on the fourth floor of the wing under renovation. Margot and Julian, with whom he had lived for not quite two weeks, helped him make the transition, and he was as glad to be out of their hair as they were to see him go. Affection existed between him and them, genuine affection, but his presence in their suite had strained the young couple's relationship with each other in ways still opaque to his understanding. It seemed to have something to do with the young man's great-grandmother and the creatures to whom Julian and Margot scrupulously referred in his presence as the "Bitlinger starmen." For that very reason, despite his curiosity, Leland had declined all Julian's invitations to visit the aliens. Although he had never married, he understood how easily human relationships can be fractured or undone and he wanted no part in sundering this one—even if he didn't understand the nature of Julian's private expectations of him.

Now Leland was sleeping in the same room where Julian's great-grandmother had once set up the big wooden aileron of her quilting frame: the Phoenix clan's recreation center. Day laborers were completely restructuring this wing, turning its common rooms and refectories into offices, research laboratories, computer rooms, even surgeries. A major overhaul. In the meantime, however, he had a place to sleep amid the nighttime solitude of this upheaval; and after dark, haunted by the profiles of portable generators and vitrifoam-blowing machines, pursued by the odors of gypsum and heat-set epoxy, Leland would retire to the Phoenix clan's rec center to converse in dreams with their ghosts. In the mornings he was invariably as fresh as a sixteen-year-old joove.

A good thing. Leland soon discovered that Vivian Klemme's reserves of energy and self-discipline were staggering. She never sat down to a meal, not even one of encapsuled nutrients, but ate and drank on the run; as she saw to the hostel's daily business she would nibble furtively at a protein bar or take wrenlike sips of distilled water from a plastic dispenser. She lived in a first-floor apartment in the building's nursing wing, but from wake-up to turn-in she altogether avoided it, moving from task to task like a perpetual-motion dynamo. Leland had trouble keeping pace with her, so much so toward late afternoon that he could hardly fault the Triumvirate's choice of her as director.

And not merely because of her energy. Although she was close-mouthed about her intentions for the new facilities in the Hostel's old residence wing, Vivian did speak of reviving several kinds of research abandoned in Atlanta shortly after Leland's resignation of the directorship. Among these were *in vitro* studies of cellular aging; the construction, as a diagnostic device, of a fully equipped Schloss Chamber; any number of experiments using rats as test animals; and, finally, still unspecified biochemical and genetic inquiries. Leland privately deplored the lack of emphasis on confronting their patients' immediate *human* needs, but Vivian had at least appointed him to attend to some of these and he understood her reluctance to go public with peer-therapy programs, trial marriages, and rooftop sessions of nude croquet. All that was too reminiscent of the septigamoklans, and her reputation was already at hazard because she had insisted on making him, the notorious Leland Tanner, an important staff member. Besides, she could also single out the swimming pool in the quadrangle as a concession to her patients' physical as well as emotional needs.

For Vivian Klemme was far from a novice at handling people. She cared for the Tower's residents exactly as they required, matching each patient's need with so appropriate a response that Leland was frequently dumbfounded by her skill. On one occasion, only a week or so after joining her staff, he was himself an agent of Vivian's insightful resolution of a small crisis. They were together in her office when a steward in bibbed green linens interrupted their morning powwow and told them that an old man on the fifth floor had gone larki. Gilden was the patient's name, and he was eighty or more, a resident of Ward E.

Vivian and Leland went up together. Gilden, it seemed, had found an aerosol bomb of spray affixative in a maintenance closet. Shooting whiffs of acrid glue into the air as proof that he meant business, he had emptied the entire ward. That accomplished, and the nurses and stewards less than keen about trying to collar him, Gilden promptly removed his clothes and stationed himself in front of the ward's one full-length mirror. Now, with vehement self-loathing, he was cursing his own reflection and shaking the spray can at the mirror like a terrorist waving a hand bomb.

How many times in his career had Leland seen old men and old women cursing their mirrored selves? Too many times for the uninitiated to believe. He had watched them hawk saliva on their reflections, shred their hands in futile pounding, even smear their looking-glass doubles with excrement. Usually he had calmed such patients with talk, or waited for the inevitable subsidence of their rage, or (when less drastic approaches failed) ordered them either physically restrained or tranked with sedative pistols. In the aftermath of these episodes, however, Leland was often stricken with lingering bouts of depression and self-recrimination. Why hadn't he foreseen the trouble? Why hadn't he been able to handle it more effectively, more compassionately?

No one wanted to go near Gilden. The room stank of spray affixative. A young intern stood outside the door with red-rimmed eyes and a hideously marbled complexion, the victim of a face-on sphritz. Even though he protested that he had already rinsed his eyes and treated the affected skin, Vivian sent him away to be cared for. She also waved aside a nurse who approached the ward with a trank gun.

"I want you to go in there," she told Leland.

At first he was merely taken aback, then both appalled and fascinated.

"I'd do it," Vivian said, noticing his reaction, "but I'm a woman and that could complicate things immensely. You're nearly a contemporary of his. Disrobe and join him at the mirror. Tell him how much better he looks than you. Praise him for being able to act so decisively in clearing out the ward. Disparage your own appearance and achievements by way of contrast."

He must have hesitated.

"Mz Eastwin said you'd do anything for the Hostel that wasn't demeaning or pointless. Which do you consider this?"

Turning away from his wrenlike superior, Leland clumsily shed his clothes and began stacking them on the floor. In the ward Gilden's voice rose to a falsetto of chilling abusiveness. Vivian gestured impatiently: Stop folding your skivvies and get in there. No longer thinking, his skin as alien to him as a clammy rubber suit, he obeyed. The door swung shut at his back, and Gilden, aerosol bomb upraised, turned to face him.

Leland approached on bare, wrinkled feet, all the while belittling the shambling monster of his body and pointing out angrily how lenient time had been with Gilden's. He scarcely had to lie. Gilden had once been a powerful man, and the memory of his past self had evidently distorted out of all compass his perception of his present self. But as Leland, spouting comparisons and contrasts, padded toward him, he lowered the spray can and took on the look of one either drunk or hypnotized. The result was that he yielded the can to Leland, allowed a robe to be draped about him, and readmitted his numb and bewildered wardmates.

Vivian's unorthodox strategy had worked so well, in fact, that Gilden spent the entire afternoon delightedly recapitulating the episode for a counselor. Leland, meanwhile, escaped the straitjacket of his usual postcrisis funk....

It was a pleasure being second-in-command, a relief not to bear on his shoulders full responsibility for the Hostel's various programs. Leland had found a niche perfectly suited to his talents and his energy, a fact he well understood.

His gratitude to Margot and Julian took the form of invitations to holodation concerts at the Omni, of small, essentially whimsical gifts, and of shared meals aboard the expensive girder-car cafes that had begun traversing some of the Dome's most spectacularly lofty tracks. So long as Leland avoided serious conversations with Julian alone and refrained from visiting the couple in their Regency suite, his relationship with them seemed not only a viable but an enriching one. He began to regard Margot and Julian as he might a daughter and a new son-in-law. He saw them once or twice a week, usually in neutral but elegant surroundings.

Vivian Klemme, on the other hand, Leland saw every day. His gratitude to her, although initially tempered by skepticism about her qualifications, had mutated into a number of disparate feelings—respect, admiration, and, alarmingly, even physical attraction. Soon he realized that he was paying her court even as they discussed funding, set up laboratory experiments, and supervised the step-by-step construction of the Hostel's interaction chamber. The reports he wrote were love letters, and their daily rounds together in the hospital wards were codified mating dances of whose subliminal implications Vivian remained chastely, even resolutely, oblivious.

What was wrong with him? They made a comic pair. Even in his bare, wrinkled feet he stood just a little shy of two meters, whereas she had the stature of a joove still on the bloodless side of menarche. He had better than three quarters of a century behind him; she . . . well, she could hardly be more than fifty and looked a good deal less. The fact that they shared similar educational backgrounds and a common professional purpose was undoubtedly in his favor, but that, he had to admit, was about it. Nevertheless, for only the second or third time in his life (it was hard to remember after so long), Leland found himself falling in love. He could scarcely have been more surprised if awakened at midnight in Peachtree Canyon and informed by a bike troll that he'd been performing somnambular sodomy on streetlamps. His longing was indecorous, an affront to dignity. But it existed, and it was real, and he disguised it as best he could for as long as he could reasonably manage.

One evening, in a girder-car cafe called the *Genji*—its cuisine was eclectically Oriental—Leland told the Eastwin-Cawthorns what had happened to him. Although the City lay spread out below like a banquet of neon sherbets, he was in no hurry to get back down to it. With its gyroscopically self-adjusting tables and serving ramps, the *Genji* was a welcome haven from the turmoil of his earthbound passions.

"I'm astonished by this," Leland confessed. "Absolutely astonished."

"Tell her," Julian urged him gravely. "Why not?"

"It could jeopardize our professional relationship. I'm happy with things as they are."

"You *were* happy," Julian corrected him. "Tell her. Compose a flyer—five brief sonnets in prose—and scatter copies from the *Genji*."

Margot touched Leland's hand. "If you like, I'll invite you and Dr Klemme for one of Julian's gourmet ghetto dinners one evening next week. That way you needn't crawl out on the runningboard all by your lonesome."

"She may not come—she rarely goes anywhere."

"Well, let's see," Margot responded. "Let's just see."

Leland was again astonished; he'd been under the impression that Margot had found his presence in their suite more discomfiting than had Julian, and yet she was the one who had just extended a return invitation. Julian, too, looked surprised.

"Right," said Julian after a moment's pause. "Please come."

* * *

The next day, while watching Vivian instruct an interning lab assistant in the proper way to hook up a young rat to an older one in an experimental parabiotic marriage, Leland was hard put to keep from declaring his love on the spot. Maybe the surgical joining of the rats took on for him an incongruous erotic suggestiveness; maybe he was led nearly to the brink of disaster by the deftness of Vivian's hands and the endearing velvet childishness of her voice. In any event, his heart leaped, his lips began to move, and all he could do to save himself was cough violently into one gloved hand and beg the others to excuse him for a moment.

Who was Vivian? What was she?

Leland went downstairs. Walking in a dream, he invaded his superior's private office (the one near her living quarters) by lifting his thumb to the scanlock. Once inside, after noting the presence of a computer console and a data terminal, he rummaged all of Vivian's big metal drawers—which were either empty or obsessively neat, their contents by no stretch of the imagination remarkable. Staplers, paper clips, gummed labels, packages of graph paper. Disappointingly neat, disappointingly mundane. So Leland shut the drawers and turned to the data terminal atop her desk.

WHO, IS VIVIAN KLEMME? he asked it, keying in the question.

A message began unrolling on the dark green screen: THE NEW DIRECTOR OF THE URNU GERIATRICS HOSTEL.... APPOINTED BY COUNCIL OF THREE ON MONDAY, AUTUMN THE 65TH.... CONFIRMED IMMEDIATELY BY COUNCIL/ CONCLAVE.... ASSUMED DUTIES ON SATURDAY, AUTUMN THE 70TH.... HER DUTIES INCLUDE THE SUPERVISION OF

Leland overrode the message with another question: WHO WAS SHE BEFORE? WHAT IS HER BACKGROUND?

THIS INFORMATION IS NOT AVAILABLE TO UNAUTHORIZED PERSONNEL.

Leland, hoping that the mere fact he was using Vivian's private terminal would corroborate the declaration, lied: THIS IS VIVIAN KLEMME. The screen remained blank. THIS IS VIVIAN KLEMME, he insisted.

PLEASE SUPPLY YOUR ACCESS CODE.

Leland surrendered. Once again he was mystified by the fact that Vivian's name had never come to his attention during all the years he had worked in both the Atlanta and the Washington

Nuclei as the director of their distinct and very different anti-aging programs. Interurban communications had been severely restricted over the last three decades, but *something* ought to have filtered through about a woman of Vivian's prominence. How had she risen to a position of such eminence with so little fanfare and to-do?

The door opened. In an unexpected reprise of their very first meeting Vivian stood before him. Leland stepped back and waited for the woman he loved to evict him from her life.

"I wondered where you'd gone," she said. "What are you doing?"

"I used my thumb." Fascinated by the whorls, Leland held it up. Then he improvised irresponsibly: "I realized I needed some staples for a report. I was out. So Ciardi"—that was Vivian's secretary—"sent me down here to get them, knowing I could get in with . . . with my thumb."

By this halt-footed explanation Vivian was appeased—if she had ever required appeasement—and she led him back upstairs discoursing animatedly on the effectiveness of parabiosis as an experimental method and as a means of teaching elementary surgical procedures. She paid no attention to the fact that he had left her private office without the staples he had allegedly gone there looking for. The fragrance from her hair was a pheromone of maddening pungency. . . .

10 / Pilferage

During this period Julian was obsessed beyond the limits of discretion by Leland Tanner's presence in the City. He still had not shaken the conviction that Leland had come to Atlanta to help him lay to rest his nagging, even tiresome crisis of existential doubt. Often at night Julian would slip into a trance in which he feverishly muttered prayers to the alien soul of his great-grandmother, beseeching Parthena to act as an intermediary between Dr Tanner and himself, to bridge the dizzying chasms of his ignorance. Awake, he tested Margot's love and tolerance by making more and more frequent pilgrimages to the bier of the dying starmen, where he would stand in the frozen dark awaiting some sign that they knew who he was and recognized the urgency of his longings.

They never moved. They never even sent him dreams.

At work, Julian began to hound Chavers for a chance to do a story about Leland Tanner's return to Atlanta and the irony of his virtually anonymous employment at the Geriatrics Hostel.

"It's *supposed* to be anonymous," Chavers retorted irritably. "If Dr Klemme hadn't insisted on hiring Tanner, he wouldn't even be there. The Council of Three isn't happy with the arrangement, but they value Klemme so highly they're letting her have her way."

"Then let me do a story about Dr Klemme. She's been here nearly eight weeks and nobody's even interviewed her."

"Damn right," said Chavers. "So figure it out for yourself, Cawthorn." At which point a colleague summoned the managing editor out of his stained-glass cage and Julian was left in the middle of his luminous office feeling squelched and inconsequential.

He ambled to the desk and picked up Chavers' portable Mani-Cure-All. A cartridge of burnt-umber polish slipped out of the extension of its middle finger and rolled over the blotting pad, coming to rest beside a hard plastic object with a cryptic row of teeth on the end of its shaft. Julian recognized the object as a key to the master visicompositor—that quasi-omnipotent machine through whose maw every story in the daily newstapes was processed, to be blocked or extruded as its human key-bearer ultimately saw fit. With neither malice nor premeditation Julian picked up the key and pocketed it. Then he tore off the desk pad (which was covered with looping, burn-umber figure eights), righted and reloaded the ManiCu-reAll, and left Chavers' office like an inveterate sinner departing the confessional.

Ashamed and smug at once.

11 / Vivian Millar Escolona Tyndale Klemme, Alias Titmouse

On the evening on which he and Vivian were supposed to go to Margot and Julian's for dinner, Leland knocked at the diminutive woman's door in an agony of apprehension and suspense. Would she go? Would she send him on alone? That afternoon she had merely told him to call upon her for her decision—apparently believing (so parochial was her social sense) that Margot and Julian had no absolute need to know beforehand, either—and as he waited for the door to open, Leland stared at the toes of his plum-colored street slippers. Clutched two-handed at his navel was a huge and extravagantly decadent orchid, a hydroponic rarity.

Within the last two weeks a number of the interns, researchers, students, patients, secretaries, and gerontologists in the complex had begun to call Vivian "Titmouse." They did so openly, with Vivian's obvious approval, for Titmouse was a term of endearment rather than mockery, and Vivian had so few pretensions that she didn't care who addressed her familiarly and who didn't, so long as the work got done. Leland, aflame with a love alternately virginal and concupiscent, couldn't say Titmouse without stuttering. Whether he said it or didn't say it, he felt that he betrayed himself. And only the fact that he loved his work almost as much as he did Vivian Klemme made him fear the possible consequences of betraying himself.

Vivian never noticed. She never seemed to realize that Titmouse was the only word in the language he invariably flubbed and mangled. Even his embarrassment was unrequited.

The door opened and Vivian accepted his orchid. She was clad all in white—startlingly white ragsleeves and ivory jodhpurs that glistened like dental enamel. She had decided to go! And as Leland walked her out of the Geriatrics Hostel into the canyons of New Peachtree, he could not shake the conviction that he was smuggling a rare and fragile figurine out of its museum into the coarsening glare of everyday reality. People stared at them as they walked.

Visible only from the waist up, Julian stood in the gallery preparing an authentic ghetto dinner that, if smell was any indication, was going to consist of red rice, fried beans, collards, and barbecued pigeon. Vivian, Leland noticed, seemed vaguely unsettled by these several aromas. She had just enough social savvy to hide her discomfort behind livelier gestures and wittier small talk (she and Margot obviously appreciated each other, whereas Julian had at first fallen back from the tiny woman in a bewilderment akin to incipient dislike), but her sensitivity to the smells from the galley was sabotaging her poise.

At last Vivian excused herself and hurried off to the bathroom. She was gone nearly twenty minutes.

"I got the red-rice jones," Julian sang as she was gone. *"I gottom to the bottom of my huh-huh-huhngry bones...."*

His song and his good humor evaporated when Vivian, back from the bathroom, informed him that she wasn't going to eat. She explained she was on a diet severely restricting her intake of substances contributing to a buildup of lipofuscin in her body's postmitotic cells. Julian plainly didn't know what lipofuscin was and just as plainly didn't care. During dinner he ate with sullen relish, as if Vivian had declined his meal out of a motive as base and archaic as racial prejudice. Leland could think of no way to counter the young man's belligerence except to acknowledge it. (Not until much later did it occur to him that Julian's unseemly behavior may have derived in part from jealousy.)

"Lipofuscin," said Leland, "is a pigmented fatty substance that shows up in the cells of the muscles and nervous system as a person ages. In the brain and heart cells, too. All the cells, in fact, that have ceased dividing and can't repair or replace themselves. Vitamin E and a few other antioxidants help keep the lipofuscin buildup within reasonable bounds."

"If that's the case," blurted Julian, "why the hell can't she eat my gen-yoo-wine, down-home, City dinner?"

"Julian!" Margot cried.

Sitting cross-legged around a coffee table of smoky simulated obsidian, the four people stared at one another in mortification and chagrin. Leland wanted to turn Julian over his knee. He rued not having taught Vivian the etiquette of dining out. He hoped Margot would say something both intelligent and conciliatory.

Margot obliged: "Dr Klemme doesn't owe you any explanations, Julian."

Vivian's body had contracted so as to occupy as little space as possible. In awe and disbelief Leland watched her condensing. She was an innocent—she had never known sin—but she was intelligent, too. Her intelligence was in her eyes, which were now beginning to reassert a placid control of her body, halting its shrinkage and fixing upon Julian a gaze of unabashed steeliness.

"Have you ever heard of the McCay regimen?" she asked him.

Still sullen, still resolutely eating, he shook his head.

"Well, Clive McCay was a twentieth-century researcher at Cornell who prolonged the life expectancy of rats by underfeeding them. He limited caloric intake while seeing to it that his experimental animals received better than adequate supplies of essential nutrients. Metabolic rate remained surprisingly high in these rats, and their resistance to disease and tumor growth was *better* than that of the animals in the control group. In ways not then clearly understood—but which we've proved have to do with easing the body's chemical burden as it ages—the McCay regimen extends life. The life spans of some of the experimental animals, in fact, were doubled."

Julian, forgetting his anger, put down his fork. "Are you saying that you're on the McCay regimen?"

Vivian nodded.

Stung by a sudden realization, Leland objected, "But the McCay regimen is effective in mammals only if begun well before puberty. There's only one recorded instance of its being adopted for use by human beings, and that was . . . well, that was—" He stopped, his memory entirely trustworthy but his credulity strained to the snapping point.

"My father was Dr Augustus Millar," Vivian said. "Klemme was his mother's maiden name. I adopted it for use here in Atlanta. Several decades ago, when I wished to dissociate myself from the Millar Affair in order to get some work done, I took the name of one of my father's younger colleagues."

Julian and Margot exchanged blank, uncomprehending looks, but Leland could feel his heart beating like the feeble fist of a tiny old person trying to get out of the prison of his rib cage. Vivian recognized the young people's consternation and sought to remedy it, first extracting from them a promise to keep to themselves her secret. She also swore Leland to secrecy and reached across the table to take his hand.

"My father—Augustus Millar—was a gerontologist and an immortalist. He was—"

"What's an immortalist?" Julian asked.

"I suppose you could say it's someone who isn't immortal but who hopes to be through the application of biomedical technology."

"In the body?" Margot asked. "Does an immortalist strive for the immortality of the earthly body?"

"Definitely" replied Vivian. "He definitely does."

"But that's the ultimate presumption," Margot shot back. She looked at Leland with narrowed eyes. Although his concentration was shattered by the hostility of her expression, he could hear her telling Vivian something about Struldbrugs and the myth of Tithonus.

To which Vivian responded: "The immortalist believes he can extend human life *without* bringing along the debilities of age as baggage."

"Does he hope for literal immortality?" Margot pressed her. "Or is the term really just a metaphor for the ideal?"

"Some hope for literal immortality, others for whatever they can reasonably expect to get. The continuousness of consciousness, with or without the body. Most immortalists understand that outliving the universe is neither very likely nor especially desirable."

"Good for them," Margot said.

Julian ended a brief but uncomfortable silence by asking, "What about your father? Did he find a way to achieve what he sought?"

"I'm not sure. He died in the Twenties, but his body's been cryonically preserved in the Miami Nucleus by a company called TransDeath Enterprises. He expected—he expects, I suppose I should say—to be recalled to life by the end of this century." Saying this, Vivian looked as vulnerable as a twelve-year-old— but Leland, who knew the truth, searched her face for telltale evidence of her great age. Her youthful hand withdrew from his shiny, mottled one and dropped into her lap.

"Did your father put you on the McCay regimen?" Julian asked her.

Vivian spoke without meeting his eyes. "In the 1980s Augustus Millar called a press conference in New York City. At that time he was on the faculty of Columbia and a strong supporter of its Foundation of Thanatology. Without preamble he introduced me to a group of journalists whom he'd specifically invited and told them that I was soon going to go on the McCay regimen. Up until then I'd been on a supernutritional diet of my father's own devising. I was seven."

Leland watched Julian and Margot mentally computing Vivian's age. She was ninety-five or ninety-six and carried herself as if no more than half that. Her body, meanwhile, was a young girl's.

"My father declared that unless I were the victim of an 'act of God' I would be the first human being since Biblical times to live beyond two-hundred years of age. I was a potential female

Methuselah. Although everyone at the press conference would be dust by the time I proved my father's contention, other representatives of the media would be on hand to celebrate my two-hundredth birthday. My father hinted broadly that he might be there himself."

After glancing at Leland, Julian shook his head and asked Vivian: "But what about your mother? What did she think of all this?"

"My father was my sole guardian. He'd contracted marriage with a woman with the understanding that they'd divorce as soon as she bore him a child. By the terms of a nonrecourse clause in their contract the child would remain in my father's custody. I was the child. When the Millars' marriage of single intent was dissolved, my biological mother received a stock portfolio, a large sum of cash, and the assurance of a generous monthly stipend for as long as she kept her nose out of my father's affairs. We were never troubled by her again."

"Weren't you ever curious about her?" Margot wondered.

"No. I loved my father."

"Did he love you? Could he really expect that at seven you would understand what you were being committed to?"

"That's what the reporters at the press conference wanted to know. So my father allowed them to question me. I was mentally precocious even if I didn't look much older than most five-year-olds, and everything they asked me I answered—even when the questions were absolutely fatuous. 'Won't you miss ice cream?' one of the more stupid reporters asked me. 'I don't think so,' I told him. 'Well, why not?' 'Because,' I said, 'I've never had any and you can't miss what you've never had, can you?'

"Another reporter, perhaps a little more to the point, asked me if I thought my father had the right to impose the burden of his egotistical desire for longevity on *my* small shoulders, especially since I'd have to live with some pretty severe deprivations for the rest of life. I looked at my father. He was standing to one side, his hands behind his back, completely unperturbed. I told the press people that my father was giving me what he could never have himself. Was that wrong? Even if Dr Augustus Millar had hopes of being remembered for making a scientific point with somebody else's life—his daughter's—I knew that that wasn't his only motive. We loved each other, my father and I, and what other people thought didn't make a jot of difference to us. . . . So I've abided by the McCay regimen to this day. I've remained small because of it, though, and before I let my hair come back in white, I was often mistaken for a child."

No one said anything, and Leland knew that he would be unable to put another bite of food in his mouth, even at the risk of incurring Julian's sullenness. Vivian Klemme was in reality Vivian Millar, a name he had known from monographs and university texts since the beginnings of his own career, nearly sixty years ago. His superior—the woman he loved—was a casebook celebrity. But hadn't an "act of God" in the mid-Thirties put an end to the life of Dr Millar's daughter and so made of his almost Faustian experiment a tantalizing might-have-been? Were the three of them conversing with a ghost? Leland turned to Vivian with a head full of objections, contradictions, and inquiries.

Anticipating these, Vivian said, "I was supposed to have died the year that several of the Urban Nuclei adopted constitutional provisions similar to Atlanta's Retrenchment Edicts." She unpinned the orchid from her rag-sleeve jacket and smoothed one of its petals between her thumb and forefinger.

"I was living in the Miami Nucleus. With the complicity of several of my father's colleagues I staged my own death—a drowning in a research-center swimming pool closed to everyone but staff personnel. I lay on the bottom of the pool for nearly five minutes in a state of self-induced torpor I'd been rehearsing for weeks. The water was ice-cold, a precaution we'd seen to in order to ensure that my body would take full advantage of the automatic submergence response which shunts almost all of a drowning person's blood to his brain—the colder the water, the more efficient the response. It was early in the morning, you see, and I was supposed to have accidentally fallen into the pool while drunk or self-sedated. A co-conspirator in the company of a person ignorant of our plan 'happened' upon the scene of the accident and pulled me from the bottom with a very showy, panicked heroism. Another young colleague of my late father's was summoned to examine the victim and declare her dead. Then photographs were taken, and I was carried off to an interior room where I was able to revive myself without being discovered.

"A ten-year-old girl of Cuban descent who had died of severe immunological deficiencies in one of our urban orphanages was cremated in my place. I was later adopted by Gary Tyndale—the colleague who had pronounced me dead at poolside—and for several years I pretended to be the dead girl Remedios Escolona Tyndale. My small stature and my reclusiveness permitted me to maintain this role with pretty good success. It wasn't until coming to Atlanta that I began to use my Christian name Vivian again, and it's been hard to reaccustom myself to answering to it."

"Everyone's begun calling you Titmouse," Leland mournfully reminded her.

"I know. I told Ciardi to call me that and to spread the word among our younger staffers so that the name would finally work its way up to the high, the mighty, and the inhibited. Titmouse is what my father called me when I was a little girl."

"Why?" Julian suddenly cried. "Why did you go to so much trouble to rid yourself of your previous identity?"

"In my previous identity I was looked upon as a freak of nature, like a two-headed cobra or a primate with wings. My size had very little to do with this, although it made me instantly recognizable to people seeking me out. By the time I was in my early sixties I was more than ready to be shut of the notoriety. You'll never understand the freedom I experienced as Remedios Tyndale, even though I had to role-play in order to escape detection. For a long, long time it was unbelievably exhilarating. When it ceased to be exhilarating I revealed my identity to the urban authorities and extracted their permission to continue my gerontological research in New Free Europe. I haven't come here directly from the Miami Nucleus, I'm afraid, but from the Immortalist Institutes of the Polity of the Rhine."

This last revelation didn't seem to register immediately, for Margot asked: "Why do you take the risk of telling us the details of your deception, Vivian? Julian and I are little more than strangers to you."

"Hardly. I know both of you by reputation. I knew of you even before I returned from Europe to the Urban Federation."

Almost in unison Margot and Julian exclaimed, "How?"

"I knew you as the caretakers of Dr Emory Nettlinger's dying Cygnusians. I met Dr Nettlinger in Strasbourg last year, you see, and it was he who arranged with your City's government for me to accede to the directorship of the Geriatrics Hostel and its various research programs—most of which had lapsed. Dr Nettlinger and Fiona Bitler had always hoped that probeship flights and contact with an alien species would prove the most dramatic inducements for the Urban Nuclei to dismantle their

Domes and end their political isolation—but their well-intentioned experiment succeeded only in sowing the seeds of a new divisiveness. The Cygnusians became tools in the hands of your previous First Councilor."

As Vivian plucked one of the petals of her orchid and crimped it between her fingers, Leland suffered a pang of unutterable desolation. Somehow each word she spoke, each secret she revealed, carried her farther and farther from him, dismantling his hopes and klieg-lighting the frightful discrepancies between her goals and his own. Fifteen minutes ago he had feared that Vivian would regard a romantic alliance with him as impossible because of the prohibitive difference in their ages. He believed the same thing now, but the conditions of his fear had been turned upside down. Vivian would outlive him by perhaps as much as a century. How could he blame her if she refused to marry him? They were very nearly of different species, she a Galapagos tortoise of longevity, he an ephemerid—which wasn't all that damn funny if you happened to be the mayfly whose fugitive existence disqualified you as a suitor....

"It now appears," Vivian was saying, "that the most dramatic inducement for the Urban Nuclei to rejoin the larger human community isn't space flight and alien contact, but the prospect of immortality. Dr Nettlinger believes that by holding the prospect of immortality before the leaders of the Urban Nuclei we can blackmail them into coming out of their giant geodesic shells. My presence at the Geriatrics Hostel seems to indicate that there's some hope for this duplicitous approach." She laid the mutilated orchid on the table: delicate champagne-colored petals on a surface of ebony glass. "Because we desire the same thing," she continued, looking at Julian and Margot, "I've taken the risk of revealing myself. You won't betray me?"

"No," they responded together.

Leland watched Vivian's hand come across the reflective surface of the table to touch his own with admonitory gentleness. He was afraid of what she was going to say, he dreaded the fiery subtlety of her perceptions.

"What do you feel about this?" she asked him.

"I love you," he heard himself confess. The cloudy features beneath him in the obsidian were those of an old, old man.

A short while later Julian escorted Vivian Klemme and Leland Tanner to the elevator capsule that would take them to the Regency's lobby. As he was coming back to the suite he shared with Margot, he caught sight of himself in the metal door at the end of the corridor. He stared at his distorted image for a long time. His anger against Vivian Klemme had evaporated during the recitation of her incredible history. Although she had written off the aliens as instruments of Atlanta's social liberation, Julian still believed them the maddeningly unforthcoming keepers of his own spiritual enlightenment. If Tanner had been able to stay longer, he would have taken the old man into the cold and the darkness to see them.

Things had to change soon. Julian walked to the metal door and laid his cheek against it. Leland Tanner had his work and the satisfaction of a long and productive career, not to mention a bond with Julian's great-grandmother that Julian knew to have telling metaphysical significance. Margot had her faith. Vivian Klemme had long life, the scientific quest for immortality, and an immediate social goal. What did he, Julian, have? Only his doubt, a wife of preternatural tolerance and understanding, and two comatose critters from 61 Cygni who meant—he was sure—a great deal more than Vivian Klemme realized....

12 / The Rhenish Regimen

"Let me come in," Leland said when they stood outside Vivian's apartment in the Geriatrics Hostel. These were the first words he had spoken to her since leaving the Regency.

One liquid ragsleeve gesturing him inward, Vivian stepped aside to let Leland pass. Then they were alone amid the photographs, immortalist banners, and holograms of unfamiliar planets and alien starscapes that nearly concealed her light-yellow walls of perforated soundboarding. Never having been in her apartment before, Leland strolled about for a moment examining these prepossessingly unique decorations. One of them was a photograph of the press conference at which Dr Augustus Millar had announced a startling prolongevity program for a seven-year-old girl. In this photograph Vivian was no bigger than a rivet. Her face wore the distressed expression of a blacking-factory orphan—she looked like something out of Dickens. She belonged simultaneously to the past and to the future, territories for which Leland felt his passport was no longer valid.

"Not very flattering, is it?" Vivian said. "They never are."

He turned to her. "I love you, Vivian."

She put her hands in her pockets and ambled away toward her kitchenboard. "I saw it coming, but pretended I didn't because it complicates things."

"The age difference?"

"Because I'm celibate, Leland, and because I've never even considered living with or marrying another person. My work has always come first."

"We share the same work."

"Look at me, Leland. My body is that of a child. I've never menstruated, and although I have a strong empathic understanding of other people's physical needs, the thought of sexual contact between an adult male and myself appalls me."

Leland struck his fist into his open palm. "I'm not a libidinous joove, Vivian. Marriages—alliances, arrangements, ménages, whatever you want to call them—take place for reasons other than the bestowal of rutting rights. It won't be much of a hardship for me to forgo them. I want to live with you, Vivian."

"For reasons of possession?"

"I love you, God damn it!"

Vivian crossed the room and stood beneath an arrowlike felt banner on which a stylized human hand was shown closing about an infinity sign. "I can't allow myself to form any such...alliance."

"Why not?"

"Leland, even if I put you on a series of treatments with thymosine, DMAE, centrophenoxine—"

"All of which I would refuse. It's a little late to start thinking about living forever."

"All right. Even if you *were* to submit to such treatments, you'd be lost to me long before my own death. I've no desire to see a series of loving life partners cremated ahead of me, and once I've taken a partner I might later feel driven to take another. My self-sufficiency has survival value, Leland, and I've already seen more people die than seems quite healthy for the soul."

Leland removed his bifocals and gestured impatiently with them. "This evening you mentioned the prospect of immortality—that it may be the lever that overturns the Urban Federation. You've been in Europe. How close *are* they? How close are *we?*"

"The problem's multiplex, so many systems are involved, it's difficult to—" Vivian stopped. "The treatments you refuse, Leland, are highly effective in providing symptom relief from the aging process; some undoubtedly extend life by providing such relief. The Immortalist Institutes of the Polity of the Rhine, however, are on the verge of perfecting a biomedical program which will confer upon those adhering religiously to it the perpetual homeostatic condition of a man or woman of thirty. Another year or more and we'll have that program in amber, preserved and codified."

"With what catch?"

"One is expense. Another is that in order to benefit from the program you must begin it before your age-related autoimmune responses impair the body's ability to settle into it. The immune system itself is subtly changed, you see, and in persons of a certain age the body actively works to *reject* the immortality-conferring alteration. In these cases, it seems, death is actually hastened by the program."

"What 'certain age' is this, Vivian?"

"It varies from individual to individual—but the range appears to be between thirty-eight and forty-eight. The Institutes have hopes of pushing this back a little, but it won't be soon."

Leland shook his head. The infinity sign on the banner behind Vivian appeared to be swimming in and out of the segmented half-open hand that sought to nab it. When he put his glasses back on, the infinity sign rotated once about its longitudinal axis like a goldfish turning up its belly.

"How, then," he demanded, "can you say the Institutes are on the verge of 'perfecting' anything?"

"I'm speaking comparatively. A program that can be effectively begun before your thirty-fifth birthday is certainly better than one that has to be undertaken before puberty, don't you think?"

"In either case, I'm not very likely to qualify, am I? I'll never be a fit consort for an immortal."

"The Rhenish Regimen," Vivian began, approaching Leland with her hands open to receive his, "isn't likely to be of much benefit to me, either. My physiological age will probably put me beyond the range of absolute safety, although the fact that I'm still technically 'pre-pubescent' might be a point in my favor. Tests in Strasbourg were inconclusive. The only way for me to find out for certain would be to undertake the new program as soon as it's available."

"Will you do that?"

"Probably not. I've already had one unnatural death, and that was enough. Let the next one come as it may."

Towering over his childlike superior, Leland grew conscious of the absurdity of his courting technique. With his fingers hooked in Vivian's, he sidled blindly to a stool not much bigger than an egg cup, eased himself down, and drew Vivian toward him. His hands moved tenderly over the fragile boyish shell of her torso. When she resisted, his fingers—without his willing them to—tightened.

"I've always half believed," she said as he put his face near hers, "that the men who found me physically attractive were latent child molesters."

That stopped him. His hands fell away from Vivian's body. Through his neck and face there spread a crimson whose flame was most brilliant in the miniature lanterns of his ear lobes. Vivian escaped his embrace as he tried to comprehend the rationale of her attack.

"I'm sorry," she said, "but that's time-tested."

"I'd better go." From an ancient photograph Dr Augustus Millar peered at him skeptically. Multicolored banners hung down from every cornice like two-dimensional stalactites. And on one wall glistened a hologram of a world caught like a tennis ball between the gauzy racket faces of a double star: 61 Cygni, more than likely. A gift, Leland surmised, from Dr Emory Nettlinger of the Scandipol Light-Probe Institute.

"What exactly have you promised the Council of Three in return for dismantling the Dome?" he asked Vivian at her door.

"Since only one of the councilors is past forty, we've promised them they'll be among the first people on this continent to begin the Rhenish Regimen. I made a similar but more hypothetical promise to the authorities in Miami in order to gain their permission to go to Europe."

"But nothing we've done here has contributed to the development of this immortalist treatment, has it?"

"Parabiosis? The Schloss Chamber? None of these things is essential to the Rhenish Regimen, no. They're helpful to our interning gerontologists and our patients, but if you must know the truth, Leland, I've been temporizing, waiting for some sign of compliance from Atlanta's leadership and for progress reports from my colleagues overseas. The renovations in the old residence wing are an excuse to put things off until these developments occur. Like your friend Julian Cawthorn, I'm currently serving in something of a caretaker capacity here."

"You had me fooled, dear lady," said Leland as he slid the door back. "I never realized you were prostituting your science to a political end. I never realized you were dragging your feet even as you ran circles around me. I never realized...."

He eased the door to on its track and strode off gimpily toward the lobby and the elevators. The way seemed watery, inundated not only by darkness but by swells of mist and running wavelets of pain. The salt in his eyes stung like alcohol. I'm weeping, he informed himself. Great Mother of Fools, I'm weeping. I'm crying like a baby....

13 / Safari

That night he had uneasy dreams, plasmas of subconscious questing that bled toward one another without ever achieving union. Immiscible visions. He awoke several times and lay in a trancelike state of bemused despair. How funny to think that one day he would be dead. His emotion as he contemplated this disquieting fact had no substance, no reality. He felt like ... like nothing that any other human being would ever be able to understand, much less validate through the machinery of the senses. Like nothing. The whole reality of his existence lay elsewhere. The troubling part was that he couldn't reach into that elsewhere and touch the one true nerve of his being. He didn't even know where elsewhere was.

The next day Leland kept to the spacious rec center where he had his bed. No one sent for him. Pneumatic hammers sounded in the corridors, and laborers with tubes of synthetic oakum, portable ladders, gleaming coils of wire, and vitrifoam blowers trooped back and forth past his door like so many human drones. When they finally stopped, he realized it was evening and dutifully pulled on his clothes. Last of all, the unlovely greatcoat in which he had been arrested.

Approximately fifteen minutes later, as Julian, his expression a paradigm of beatific amazement, admitted him to his suite in the Regency, Leland was saying, "I'm resigning my position at the Geriatrics Hostel."

"Why?" The same look of blissful astonishment.

Margot wasn't home. Her absence considerably disappointed Leland because she had first gone to Vivian on his behalf and he owed her the courtesy of explaining what had happened. Or part of what had happened, anyway. Maybe she would be able to guess. Julian, in fact, looked as if he had already found in the rubble of Leland's scrambled motives a clue to what had taken place—but he closed his mouth on any further questions and tried to take the old man's coat.

"I'll need this, won't I?" Leland protested.

"Your coat?"

"I thought it was cold in there." He gestured toward the door and by implication toward the refrigerated sanctuary in which the aliens lay. "Is this a bad time to go? I'd like to see them."

"It's a great time to go," Julian declared, perhaps referring to Margot's absence, and he hurried off to gather together gloves, mufflers, hard-soled slippers, and his battered helmet with the lamp above its bill. "It's not quite zero degrees Celsius in there," he said when he got back. "Here. Put on these gloves. Wrap this around you." He helped Leland get ready. "Don't expect much more than a peek, though. They've been almost totally unreachable—if you're thinking about communicating with them—ever since Dr Nettlinger called their five compatriots back to Scandipol."

They left the suite and confronted their own images in the metal-plated door at the end of the hall. The future (Leland thought, taken aback by Julian's enthusiasm) is a mirror in which the past marches to meet itself. So had said somebody or other. . . .

"The converted suite's a hodgepodge of knocked-out walls and irregular crannies," Julian explained. "That's the way they wanted it. Just stay close." After the lock had scanned his thumb, Julian got the heavy door moving on its hinges.

A moment later the two men were standing in the arctic darkness. Julian pushed a button, calling to muted life a fluorescent tube above the door. By its flickering Leland was able to gaze a few meters into the gloom. The continuous throbbing of the unseen refrigeration unit gave this darkness a hallucinatory quality—it worked on the heart by keeping pace with it. Julian murmured, "Quite an icebox, isn't it?" and set off toward a destination still unknown to Leland. To deflect his own frightening disorientation, he reached out and put a hand on Julian's shoulder. Somewhere under the crush of his greatcoat his heart thudded wetly.

They passed a free-standing cubicle in which a swing of Julian's headlamp revealed a washstand and a commode.

Leland's voice betrayed his surprise: "Did they use that?"

"No. They reabsorb and put to use most of their 'waste products.' That was for the convenience of their human gophers."

Suddenly they came upon the leading edge of a wall that divided Leland's plane of vision into halves. On the right side of the wall, a familiar-looking variety of musical console. This apparition was lost to them when the headlamp pointed them into the farther darkness.

"Was that an orpianoogla?"

"The best the Bitlingers could buy."

"The aliens—they played it?"

"One of them did. For a time it was their principal means of direct communication with us."

The wall that had divided the dark left off abruptly, setting them adrift in a Plutonian immensity having no perceivable limits and only a corrosive coldness to suggest that it existed in physical space rather than merely in their dreams. We ought to be wearing pressure suits, Leland told himself.

"Through here," Julian said. "We're almost there."

The headlamp revealed a pair of leaning walls whose only function seemed to be to make a corridor through an open area not really requiring one. The two men entered the corridor, and Leland watched the beam of Julian's helmet lamp swing from wall to crazy wall as they moved inexorably through the dark. At last the tunnel debouched on a trapezoidal room whose rear wall was the longer of the two parallels.

Over Julian's shoulder, blinking into the riven gloom, Leland could see stiff gray draperies on the walls and an asymmetrical linen canopy sagging down from the ceiling. When Julian stepped aside, he had an unobstructed view of the sheet-covered bier at the very center of the little room. The bier looked to have been cobbled together out of three prosaic hotel doors, with some bent aluminum tubing for supports.

As if in mortuary tableau, the aliens lay atop the bier.

Leland glanced at Julian, who indicated by an arm movement that he should approach the starmen. Walking to one side, Julian tilted his head so that the beam from his lamp always fell directly ahead of Leland on the recumbent Cygnusians. In this way the two men made a complete circuit of the bier.

The Cygnusians lay back to back on the plane of the joined doors. They were huge, these creatures. Their faces were woody-looking masks with circlets of bone or cartilage standing up from the backs of their heads. Their eyes were patches of moist canvas, each "patch" containing a pair of pupils in the shape of a side-lying hourglass. Their bodies seemed to be nothing but cerement-shrouded arms and torsos grading into chitinous or metallic legs resembling those of otherworldly grasshoppers. No, the legs were humanoid in design—the fact that they were also big and brittle-seeming suggested the grasshopper image. The legs were bent outward in opposing V's that touched only at their feet and buttocks: a grasshopper angle. And they were dying.

"How do you know they're not already dead?" Leland asked.

"Look here." Julian shone his headlamp into the canvaslike patches of one of the alien's eyes. Instantly the hourglass-shaped pupils shrank to two tiny barbells of blackness.

"Couldn't that be an automatic response of the eye?"

"It could—but that's not the only proof I have." Julian wiped his finger along the alien's upper thigh and thrust his glove toward Leland. "Smell that."

"My smeller's not that good anymore, Julian."

"You'll smell this—it's an exudation that lubricates their bodies and protects them from what seems to us a prohibitive cold. It's the only 'waste product' they give off."

Leland bent toward Julian's glove. Ammonia? Vinegar? Whatever the smell suggested, it flamed into his nostrils and roared down his throat. He took a couple of self-defensive steps backwards.

"Are you ready to go?" Julian asked.

Was he? What else could he accomplish here? Communion with the aliens was impossible; he would have to content himself with simply having looked upon them.

And yet . . . and yet he had hoped that by coming here, that by looking upon these abandoned relics of Dr Nettlinger's first attempt to bring about the downfall of the Domes, he would find a means of discrediting or maybe even overstepping Nettlinger's more recent attempt involving Vivian Klemme Millar and her no doubt well-intentioned part in the barefaced bribery of Atlanta's current leadership. It mattered tellingly that immortality was the bribe. Who didn't want longer life? Life was a universal good. Living things had this knowledge *a priori,* with no other demonstration beyond their own splendid liveliness. Even these dying hominoids from eleven light-years away were fighting death; in their own exasperatingly incomprehensible and tenacious way they had been fighting it for over two years. Leland gazed upon them with a longing he couldn't voice and a sense of kinship he didn't know how to express.

The quest for immortality was a motive arising from profound, maybe even noble self-interest—but the quest for communion and adventure was a motive partaking of that inbred cooperativeness that had enabled humanity to evolve from a slouching primate to an angel of sublime contradictions. If you had to choose, if you were denied the option of synthesis, which motive was the more human and therefore ultimately the more noble?

I was rejected, Leland thought distractedly, because I'm going to die. For no other reason but that.

"All right," he agreed, aware that Julian was growing impatient with him. "Let's go."

But as Julian turned toward the bizarrely out-of-square tunnel behind them, Leland was struck by an anomaly in the aliens' posture. "Julian!" he barked hoarsely, halting the young man and then slowly passing a gloved hand above the Cygnusians' inert but awesome bodies.

"What is it?"

"Look at the way they're lying. There's no evidence at all of any separation between them."

"They're lying back to back—they're touching. That's the way it's always been with them." Julian's voice conveyed a hint of annoyance.

"They're not *simply* touching," Leland asserted, reaching out and pulling Julian toward the bier. "Their bodies have joined." He placed Julian's gloved hand on the shoulder of the nearer alien and guided it unresistingly into the crevice where the two unearthly bodies shared a seamless juncture.

Julian turned an expression of utter bewilderment toward the old man and then gazed back down at the aliens.

"Listen," Leland whispered, putting a hand to his pounding heart, "this may be a foolish notion—I can't really say—but I don't think both of them are dying. I think this is some sort of spontaneous parabiotic arrangement whereby the healthier of the two specimens sustains the life of the dying one. That's why it's gone on so long. That's why the joining has taken place. And that's why two Cygnusians had to remain here when Nettlinger had the others return to Scandipol.—Have you ever heard of parabiosis?"

Julian shook his head.

At that, Leland explained the basic elements of the surgical procedure that prolongs the life of an aged rat by connecting it shoulder to tail with a younger rat. He recalled Vivian's dismissing the technique as irrelevant to contemporary immortalist research, and he saw her students nevertheless diligently engaged in learning the procedure. His mind was awash in counterstreaming tides of method and theory—but he could conceive of no alternative to "spontaneous parabiosis" to explain the untoward back-to-back linkage of the Bitlinger starmen.

Julian murmured, "If that's the case, I may be an old man before either one of them dies. Hell, they may *survive* me."

"They may, Julian, but I won't. No need to worry."

"I'm not worried—I'm chagrined. One trip in here and you pick up on something I've never even noticed before."

"No need to worry about that, either. Let's go. I'm cold."

They backed into the passage behind them, did an about-face on the trapezoidal chamber, and made their way through the narrow tunnel, over an expanse of seemingly endless gloom, and past both the orpianoogla and the free-standing bath cubicle. End of expedition, thought Leland as they entered the corridor outside Cygnostik Land; end of safari.

Margot was waiting for them when they got back. As he came into the suite, Leland looked directly into her face and read there both bewilderment and suspicion. Her smile of greeting was acutely lopsided.

"We've got to get these stinkin' mittens into the laundry chute," Julian said, plucking off his own gloves finger by finger.

The vinegary stench of the alien exudation hung in the air like a veil: Margot stood on the other side of it. Leland removed his gloves and handed them to Julian, who disappeared into the galley toward the laundry chute, leaving his wife and the aged gerontologist to stare at each other—embarrassed, for different reasons, by a moment they had long anticipated even as they had refused to believe it would occur. The veil between them was not going to shift aside.

"I'm resigning the position you helped me obtain," Leland told Margot, examining his gloveless hands.

Margot, after starting to speak, bit down on her words and appeared to rethink the matter. Finally: "Where will you go?"

"To the cubicle on Level 3, I imagine."

"You'll move back in with us," Margot declared without an eye-blink's hesitation. "The other idea's absolute nonsense."

Leland looked into the galley and saw Julian returning through it. The young man approached his wife and slid his arm around her waist as if in gratitude for her understanding. The matter was settled. Leland shifted, studying their faces. Under his greatcoat the tracks of sweat running down his flanks seemed as searing and relentless as fuses. He bent his head in resigned acceptance of their offer.

14 / *Interior Dialogue*

Vivian Klemme is out of your life, Leland told himself that night as he lay in his bedroom in the Eastwin-Cawthorn suite. She is out of your life forever. Face that fact and exorcise her image.

What about your work, old man?

That, too—over and done with. From now on, if you still intend to "practice dying," you'll have to find new ways to do it. You're going to have to divert yourself. You're going to have to adjust.

Just as I adjusted on Level 3?

Let's hope you succeed a little better upstairs than you did down. Otherwise, old man, you'll prompt your own eviction.

That would be a tragedy?

I belong here.

In the home of a young married couple whose hospitality

derives in part from the young man's mistaken belief that you know something he doesn't and in part from the young woman's rigorous apprehension of her Christian duty? What's happened to your pride, old man? How can you impose and be imposed upon in these petty and undignified ways?

I belong here.

What in hidden heaven makes you think so?

God knows—

You don't?

Leave me alone. Let me sleep. Maybe I've simply convinced myself that I belong here because I *know* I don't belong on Level 3.

Maybe you have....

And so on, the ceiling going up and down as if in synchrony with the uneven rhythms of his heart. Even though the walls of the guest room were bare of ornament, Leland had the idiot notion that if he were simply to shift his eyes rapidly enough he would see about him the same banners, photographs, and holograms he had seen in Vivian's apartment. He purposely did not shift his eyes.

15 / Gnosis

For nearly three weeks Leland rattled about in Margot's and Julian's suite like a pinball lost in the maze of an earnie-arcade machine. His hosts worked during the day and left him to his own devices. The suite offered relatively few amusements, and what it did offer he found either empty of meaningful content or so repetitious as to fatigue his patience.

He tapped into the City's library of unproscribed visicom entertainments and lay in bed watching a three-day festival of twentieth-century television westerns. He could not get the films of Bergman, Fellini, Buñuel, Ray, or Kurosawa, and only the early, more antic comedies of Allen.

He played chess at a computer terminal. His chief pleasure during these games was vilifying the machine for its stupid moves.

He read Victorian novels. These had the soothing if passé virtues of literacy and length.

And sometimes, in the late afternoon before Margot and Julian had come home from work, he prepared elaborate gourmet meals, which the three of them would eventually eat in an atmosphere of tempered camaraderie.

By tacit agreement they refrained from discussing four topics: Vivian Klemme, immortalist research, Leland's long-term goals (if, indeed, he still had any), and the aliens at the end of the hall. In the first three instances Leland realized that *he* was the inhibiting factor. Margot and Julian, however, enforced the prohibition against speaking about the Cygnusians. These restraints on conversation made them all irritatingly considerate and deferential. A terrible formality descended on their interactions: the suite seemed to close in upon them like the walls of a room in a horror story by Poe.

By the fourth week of his residence in the suite Margot noticed that Leland had lost interest in sitting down at meals with them. When he ate anything, he ate alone in his bedroom. On those increasingly rare occasions when they engaged him in polite small talk, Margot began to detect strange lapses in his attention. By and large, he was as mentally keen as a freshman whiz at the seminary—but Margot sometimes wondered if Leland's disappointment at losing both Vivian Klemme and his position at the Geriatrics Hostel had not adversely affected his mind.

He invariably pulled himself out of his senescent nosedives with a sudden start, a shaking of the head, and a visible exercise of will—for who knew better than Leland Tanner what was happening to him?—but that he had to *work* to keep his spirit aloft and his brain perking seemed a heartbreakingly ominous portent of things to come.

Unpleasant things.

One evening the old man dropped a cut-glass tumbler on the table of simulated obsidian, shattering the vessel and sending tiny spears of glass into the concealing pile of carpet. "You worthless old fart," Leland cursed himself under his breath; "you utterly worthless old fart." He gritted his teeth and stared at his hands as if they had betrayed him.

More dismaying to Margot than the broken tumbler was Leland's verbal self-abuse. It seemed out of character—nor, on this occasion, did he shake his head and snap out of his senescent doldrums. He stared incredulously at his hands until she pulled an extensible vacuum hose from the galley baseboard and told him to get the glass out of the carpet before someone was injured. This activity restored him—belatedly—to himself, but the incident hung in Margot's mind like a portrait of someone who has only recently died: she couldn't take it down, but neither could she actively contemplate it.

Two nights later Leland began talking about the institution of the septigamoklans as if it still existed. Sitting in one of the living room's tubular chairs, the shadows of weird plasmas crawling across his pastel-green pyjamas, he spoke at length about Julian's great-grandmother Parthena, unaccountably using the present tense and praising Julian for having had the foresight to put himself in direct line of descent from such a splendid old woman.

"If there ever comes a vacancy," he said, "I'm going to court and then marry with the Phoenix. They ought to be *glad* to leap the broomstick with me. I was the one who married them all in the first place."

Later, in bed, Julian declared that Leland had been having them on, making them the butts of his increasingly ghoulish sense of humor. Julian was clearly agitated, though, and Margot understood that his agitation stemmed from Leland's manifold, unanswerable references to Parthena. She had placed Julian under a difficult restraint—the caution to keep their two-year-old "revelation" a connubial secret—when his every impulse was to spill the matter into Leland's lap and so discover what he believed to be the old man's hard-earned grasp of Ultimate Reality.

"His mind is going," Margot insisted, whispering the words. "He no longer has the clear-headedness or the savvy to have anyone on."

"All right," Julian replied petulantly. "Have it your way."

They lay in bed unable either to sleep or to settle their hostile feelings. They sighed, twisted away from each other, touched their own breasts or genitals in involuntary self-consolation and at last, hip by hip, lay staring into the darkness with sightless open eyes.

Then they heard Leland gasping, his breaths coming so hard upon one another that they sounded like the cries of one embarked either on orgasm or the very last stages of labor.

"He's dying," Julian told Margot. "I swear to God he's about to go."

They broke from bed, pulled on robes, and hurried across the corridor to Leland's room. Julian turned on a planetarium lamp, a recent purchase at Consolidated Rich's, and its multitudinous stars immediately speckled the walls and ceiling. Margot lifted the old man's head out of his pillow. His eyes opened in horror and surprise, taking in the faces of his rescuers and the unexpected backdrop of interstellar night against which they were so alarmingly outlined.

"Leland," Margot demanded, "are you all right?"

The old man's eyes, suddenly calm again, languidly intercepted hers. "I don't know. I suppose I am."

"What happened?" Julian asked. "What's the matter?"

"A kind of a dream. I dreamed I was being squeezed out of my present life and into another that didn't fit me."

The two young people exchanged glances—but Margot was struck by how lucid, how instantly alert, Leland again seemed. Like the flames of a pair of altar candles, a penetrating intelligence burned in his eyes. He was a different person from the old man who had been rambling on about Parthena as if she were still alive.

"Maybe," Margot said, "it's time we talked about how we're going to handle living together for the rest of our lives. If you feel up to it, Leland."

"The rest of *my* life, you mean, don't you?" The old man pointed at the robe lying across the bottom of his bed and eased his feet out from under the covers. "I'll go back to Level 3 tomorrow morning. The only thing that's important to me now is that I *not* be committed into the care of anyone at the Geriatrics Hostel."

"You're staying here with us," Julian announced angrily. Then, softening his tone, he said, "We're spiritual brothers, you and I. I know it, Margot knows it—you're the only one who resists acknowledging the fact."

"What makes you think so?" Leland pulled on and cinched his robe, his face cadaverous and his hands trembling. "Simply because Parthena once played a part in each of our lives?"

Julian laughed mirthlessly and took the old man's elbow. "My clue," he said, as the three of them left the guest bedroom and moved down the hall, "was a phrase on your flyer: 'My soul is imprisoned.' That made me think you had knowledge, that maybe you'd even had a revelation similar to my own—but we've never allowed ourselves to approach the matter before."

"*I've* been the obstacle," Margot interjected, dialing up the lights in the living room. "For what still seem to me pretty sound reasons. But it's time Julian and you open all the windows on this matter. Otherwise, none of us is going to get any sleep."

The two men found places near the coffee table of obsidian-reminiscent crystal, Leland on the sofa behind it and Julian on the floor. Her hands as cold as death, Margot sank to her knees beside Julian and looked back across the room at a triptych depicting in intricate mosaic three scenes from the ministry of Carlo Bitler, Fiona's first husband.

The enameled tiles in this mosaic were either white, wine-red, or shades of china blue, and they shone in the room's midnight dimness like the membranes of surgically revealed viscera. Once the tryptych had seemed attractive to Margot. No longer.

"I'm in the dark," Leland confessed, looking at Julian. "I don't know what sort of 'knowledge' you're talking about."

"Well," said Margot. "Let's tell him."

Julian put his elbows on the coffee table and clasped his hands. "It happened on Year Day, our wedding day, right after the coup that ended First Councilor Lesser's reign."

Margot sought Leland's curiously deep-set eyes. "That evening—the evening after our wedding—one of the aliens from the enclave down the hall came to the cubicle we'd been given on Level 3. Please try to imagine that, Leland: a starman moving afoot through the crowded concourses of the hive. They ventured out only rarely, and usually only with a security escort, and here was one of their number paying a private call on Julian, their retired step-'n'-fetchit man."

"But whatever for?" Leland asked.

Margot looked down at the table. "He had something to impart, something to tell us, and apparently he understood the sacrament of marriage well enough to believe that he should tell us on our wedding day."

"Tell you what?" Leland asked, lifting his fingers from his knees and then drumming them there impatiently.

"The ontological truth about the Cygnostikoi," Julian said.

Margot glanced quickly at Leland and read the confusion in the old man's face. "*Cygnostikoi* is what the Cygnusians prefer to be called collectively. It combines the Latin for 'swan,' *Cygnus,* and the Greek plural of 'gnostic,' which derives from *gnõsis,* 'knowledge.' In other words, our visitors consider themselves Gnostics from the Cygni binary."

"Gnosticism," Julian put in, "was an early Christian heresy."

Leland leaned back and crossed his legs. The white hairs on his exposed ankles glittered silver in the lamplight. "I still don't understand the connection." His eyes, deep in their hollows, moved from Margot's face to Julian's, and back again.

"The members of the Gnostic sects," Margot hurried to explain, "believed that the discovery of spiritual truth is more important than faith. They also believed that the world, or Creation, divides God from man, man from God; and that the salvation of humanity is also the deliverance of the deity. God saves Himself by reintegrating with that portion of his divine substance trapped in the lower world of his Creation. In other words, with every human being's spiritual attribute."

"Which is the soul, I suppose?"

"No," Margot countered, "the pneuma. The Gnostics believed that body and soul were products of a Demiurge, an archon or false god below the true God. The Demiurge believes himself to be the true God, however, and it's he whom humanity mistakenly worships. In the meantime, only the pneuma—an essence of divine substance buried deep in the psyche of every human being—actually comes from the God Beyond the World. This pneumatic essence in every one of us must reunite with God before the cosmos can be whole again."

Leland shook his head. "I *still* don't understand the connection. What does this heretical belief have to do with your aliens, or any of this with the visit you received on your wedding night."

Margot felt herself phrasing her response with bitter precision: "Gnosticism took many forms, most with very complicated cosmological systems involving spheres within spheres—often seven altogether—and a hierarchy of archons below the real God. The *chief* heresy, from which all the others flow, is the notion of a deity who is impaired by the act of Creation. In fact, the Gnostics believed that to have permitted Creation in the first place, God must have been tragically flawed. Hence, humanity's salvation is also God's."

"And is that what the Bitlinger starmen believe?"

Here Julian eagerly took up the explanation. "Only in part. Margot ought to have told you, too, that almost all of the early Gnostics were reincarnationists. They were called *gnostikoi* because they were supposedly possessed of a knowledge superior to that of the Christian multitude."

"The world," said Leland wearily, "continues to be overrunn

with people possessed of 'superior knowledge.'"

"The alien who visited us on our wedding night," Julian went on, undeterred by the old man's sardonicism, "told us that the physiological condition of being human is nothing but one of the lower way-stations on the pneuma's journey to reintegration with the true Godhead."

A silence held all three of them. Margot, glancing up at Leland, understood that her and her husband's words were at last beginning to have an unsettling effect on the gerontologist. He uncrossed his legs, leaned forward, and put his hands on the coffee table.

"One of the lower way-stations?"

"Look," said Julian, apparently aware that Leland had finally been touched in a promising way; "the Bitlingers—Fiona and Emory, I mean—brought the Cygnostikoi into our Urban Nucleus in the hope that their presence here would give us cause to reject our isolationism."

"But First Councilor Lesser tried to coopt the aliens for political and religious reasons of her own." Leland rose painfully and eased himself out into the middle of the room, blocking Margot's occasional glance at the triptych opposite them and forcing Julian to swing about on the carpet.

"Right," he acknowledged. "But what nobody—not even the Bitlingers—realized was this: that in going all the way out to 61 Cygni and encountering there a seemingly alien life form, in reality we had discovered ourselves!" Julian got up and joined Leland in the center of the room, reaching out to grip his right elbow and to clasp his opposite shoulder like a comrade. "To be specific, our future and our past selves. Fiona didn't live to know that she'd succeeded in this way and Emory probably still doesn't know—especially if he's begun to pin his hopes for the end of the Urban Federation on the biomedical pursuit of immortality."

Margot felt empty and excluded. She put her deathly cold hands beneath her arms and drew her shoulders in. "Tell him how your 'revelation' took place, Julian. Tell him of what it consisted."

Without stepping away from Leland Tanner or glancing back at his wife, Julian continued his explanation: "Our visitor—he was one of the five Cygnostikoi who returned to Scandipol after the Council of Three took over—our visitor told Margot and me that to achieve spiritual reunion with the

Absolute you have to climb toward it rung by rung. From the human rung to the Cygnostik rung, and so on toward our ultimate reintegration with God. There may be rungs before the human one and after that of the Cygnostikoi, but the alien who visited Margot and me was unaware of them. Only his return to Earth from his home world in the Cygni system jogged the memory of his preexistence here out of his subconscious."

Leland gently disengaged himself from Julian and shuffled toward the coffee table.

"I know you don't accept that, Margot. You couldn't continue to be what you are if you had swallowed such a story."

Julian whirled and clenched his fists. "Do you dismiss it as claptrap, then?" he asked defiantly.

The old man revolved a degree or so toward Julian, his hands hanging open at his sides as if to reveal his desire to soothe and placate. "It's just that it sounds like an intellectual construct, Julian, not a description of Ultimate Reality. How were you told these things? What makes you give them even a breath of credence?"

"Tell him," Margot urged, unsure now whether she was taking her husband's part or subtly sabotaging him. "Go ahead."

"The alien who visited us," Julian began, his eyebrows raised and his voice unsteady, "put Margot and me into a trancelike state in which—well, in which our consciousnesses merged. We became each other, the two of us shared one mind, and the message we received from our visitor was conveyed to us through a dream that we each dreamed simultaneously."

"A dream?" Leland asked reminiscently.

"Tell him the dream." Margot got up and walked past her husband into the darkness of the galley. Here she began fiddling with a small platinum crucifix, a gift from Julian on their first anniversary. "You won't be satisfied until you tell him."

"The Cygnostik who put us into this trancelike state," Julian hurried to say, "spoke to us from a shimmering plasma that bore the features and the voice of my maternal great-grandmother."

"Parthena?" Leland wondered aloud.

"Parthena," Julian belligerently attested. "She was once a member of your famous Phoenix septigamoklan. Earlier this evening you were carrying on as if she were still alive. Well, in a sense, she is. Her pneuma now resides in the psychic envelope of a creature from a planet eleven light-years from Earth."

Leland turned to Margot for corroboration. "Is that what

you experienced? You saw what Julian saw, heard what he heard?"

"Yes." She murmured the word without emphasis, almost without conviction, refusing to look at the agitated boy-man who shared her bed and whose solo dreams had never since their wedding night attained such a remarkable clairvoyance. Nor, for that matter, had her own.

Then she heard Leland Tanner laughing. The old man's chuckle was dry and unsympathetic, like a ratcheting New Year's noisemaker. Fearful of what Julian's reaction would be, she lifted her head in time to see him stalk down the hall and into their bedroom. The door slammed, interrupting Leland's pathetic chuckling just as effectively as if Julian had fired a pistol into the air.

Looking very old, Leland stared at her open-mouthed.

"That was unfeeling," Margot told him. "You're the first person from outside this suite to whom he's ever spoken of his 'revelation.'"

The mouth remained slack, the eyes shifted uncertainly.

"But I was unfeeling, too," Margot went on. "I made him tell his story when I knew you wouldn't be sympathetic. When I knew you had no idea what sort of spiritual brotherhood he believed the two of you shared."

Leland narrowed his eyes and peered down the hall. Then he shook his head and shambled to the carpet line between the living room and the galley. "Julian's just informed me that we're all going to be resurrected as Cygnusians—Cygnostikoi, rather. He insists that his great-grandmother told him so. And in spite of having received the same revelation under the same circumstances, you don't credit these nightmare notions any more than I do."

"No, I don't."

"Then why . . . ?"

"Because I understand exactly why Julian credits them. Our awareness of Parthena's presence that evening—of her image superimposed on our visitor's—was vivid beyond description, Leland. If my faith weren't as firm as it is, I'd probably be a fanatical champion of 'Cygnosticism' myself." Margot exhaled audibly. "But it is, and I'm not."

"It wasn't Julian I was laughing at," Leland whispered. "It was—"

"I understand that. But wouldn't it be amusing if the final

Cosmic Joke were . . ." She let her voice trail off.

"Were what?" Leland prompted her.

"Well, that the forms of genuine reality—when revealed—strike us as so ludicrous that we deem it beneath our dignity to believe in them."

Leland performed an excruciatingly slow pivot and, hands in the pockets of his robe, stared across the room at Fiona Bitler's enameled Triptych: a memorial to a man nearly forty-five years dead. "You're a capable devil's advocate," he said, scrutinizing the mosaic's central panel—in which Carlo Bitler stood with his head thrown back and his arms messianically outstretched.

"I hope not," Margot responded. "I try to speak from the firm center of my faith."

The old man glanced back at her, his face mummified by pain or anxiety and the sharp silver stubble along his jaw almost luminous. "And what about Julian?"

"He's not as lucky as I am, Leland. And neither are you."

16 / Death Rehearsals

Over the next twelve days Leland Tanner's condition steadily deteriorated, as if his falling-out with Julian were too much to contend with after the disappointments of losing Vivian Klemme and forfeiting forever his briefly renewed career. He no longer tapped into the City's visicom library, played computer chess, read Trollope or Wilkie Collins, or prepared exotic cuisines for Julian and Margot. He refused medication, extracted from Margot a promise never to commit him to a hospital, whatever else they might decide to do with him, and ate only when she imperiously commanded him to.

He took to his bed.

The incongruous thing about his surrender was that even flat on his back, even refusing food and medicine, he displayed an openness and an apologetic good humor that disarmed his hosts, sometimes causing them to doubt the existence of any malaise at all. Julian was half inclined to think that Leland simply enjoyed being waited on—except that the old man seldom asked for anything and took care never to require their help with his most intimate needs. Shambling, smiling trips to the john were his principal exercises, and he made these pilgrimages like someone bowing to the dictates of convention rather than conviction. He had become an amiable live-in zombie.

One evening, or morning, or afternoon (it no longer made any difference to Leland), Julian sat down beside the old man's bed and leaned forward into his plane of vision. "You awake?" he asked.

Leland opened his eyes and blinked owlishly.

"I wanted to apologize for trying to tie you into my private revelation," Julian told him, "for turning my back on you when you refused to be bound by it." He hesitated. "I just wanted—wanted to apologize."

"You took your sweet time, didn't you?" Leland favored the young man with an ambiguous smile, his lips skinning back like a chimpanzee's.

Julian, after rocking aside, said nothing.

"I'm the one who's sponging his room and board," Leland managed, still through skinned-back lips. "And if I know anything about dominion in marriage—which I probably don't—it was Margot who engineered your apology."

Julian again rocked into view. "In part," he conceded. "It's not easy living with an irate Ortho-Urban deacon—they seethe, like baked forbidden fruit."

The old man's grimace may have been meant to convey amusement, sympathy, disgust, or pain. Julian was unable to distinguish among the possibilities.

"I also wanted to tell you," he went on, "that Dr Klemme has announced a breakthrough in her anti-aging research. The newstapes carried the story yesterday afternoon. It seems that the Immortalist Institutes of one of the European polities have perfected a treatment that's effective even in people well beyond middle age. No details, though, about how soon anyone in the Urban Federation is likely to benefit from the discovery."

Leland closed his eyes—the lids resembled translucent grapeskins. "The apology was enough," he murmured. "The other—dear Lord, what are we going to do with the other?" He turned his head aside on the pillow.

Confused, Julian backed out of the room.

A day or two later, while Julian and Margot were away at their jobs, Leland Tanner slipped into a weird mental rhythm whose waves seemed to buoy and sustain him:

I rise to my death like a whale stabbed in the lungs. The sun is up there, even if the whale can't see it. I'd like to see the sun, too. The real one.

Cold winter light. Prismatic lava. Leopard's pelt. Infinite sack. Streaks of cancerous lipstick on the face of my bride.

I'd simply like to see the natural brightness beneath which our forebears were calved. We go back a long way. *Habilis. Erectus. Sapiens.* And so on.

The whales stayed in the water. Maybe they knew what they were doing. Maybe they knew.

But they rise to the light—

And I? Right now I would swear that my soul, my pneuma, is climbing to light rather than plunging to darkness.

Homo sapiens immortalis.

Hot damn, as I remember somebody saying. Hot damn and hallelujah, even if black is the oldest color. It outlines and separates, yes—but it unites in its ultimate triumph. In that union there's a glitter that won't wink out. It's a glitter you can climb toward even when you're stabbed to the pit of your breath.

Break the watery skin that contains you and throw back a spray whose liquid stippling leaves no wake.

What comfort? What comfort?

The silver pinpoint at the pit of the sack—

And then Leland Tanner thought: I cease when I cease. Pathetic and glorious, Ramapithecus to Panmanterra, tree toad to Titmouse, I cease when I cease....

Margot was the one who found him dead. She shut his eyes, which had started open at the last instant of consciousness, and spoke a prayer above his body.

Within two hours a team from the underCity had removed Leland Tanner's corpse from the Eastwin-Cawthorn suite, transported it back into the hive, and committed it to the waste-converters on Level 9.

Ashes to ashes.

17 / Reprise and Refrain

Julian awoke in a nightsweat. Margot seemed to be sleeping. He eased himself out of bed and rummaged about in the closet for the paraphernalia he required in Cygnostik Land. It was three nights since Leland's death, and he was putting on his parka when Margot sat up and said, "You're not going to try to go in there at this hour, are you?"

He gestured vaguely. Margot was a gray shadow in the gloom, and he felt as if he were trying to communicate with her ghost.

"Does it have something to do with Leland? I haven't really slept since. . . . I thought you were doing all right, though."

"I had a dream. Nothing like the one we shared on Level 3, Margot—but it came to me from down the hall."

"What kind of dream?"

"A stirring. That's the only way to describe it—a stirring. I'm being summoned."

A moment later lights began flickering on throughout the suite. When Julian declared that he was going to need their hibachi, Margot knew that he intended to be gone a long time. "I can stand the smoke better than the cold," he said, and she insisted on filling the hibachi's brazier with carbon-light briquettes and starting them with a disposable coil. Then, as if she were passing a censer to a fellow cleric, she slipped the hibachi's handle into Julian's glove.

By the time he entered the alien enclave his dream was rapidly receding from the foreground of his consciousness, and he began to wonder about his motive. Was he doing this in atonement for allowing Leland to die in their suite alone? He really didn't know.

He took himself deeper and deeper into Cygnostik Land, past all the familiar out-of-kilter landmarks and into the corridor whose amok-leaning walls eventually squeezed him into the aliens' trapezoidal mausoleum. He set his hibachi down and made a circuit of the bier, cursing the Cygnostikoi for summoning him from his sleep, and demanding to know what they wanted of him. They looked exactly as they had when

Leland accompanied him into their death chamber and convinced him that one of the aliens was sustaining the life of the other. Parabiosis. Literally, life by life. The Siamese twins from 61 Cygni. Awe-inspiring even in their motionlessness, they were not at all the half-mechanical monsters Julian had imagined them before being thrust into his positions as gopher and emissary.

Still, it was irritating to find them unchanged, as unaffected by Leland's death as they had been by Leland's first and only visit. They were as they always were, and God! what a provocation that was.

Julian gathered the strings of his parka's hood together and pulled them tight. Then he sat down at the foot of the Cygnostikois' makeshift bier. He clutched his shoulders, chafed them with his gloves, and rocked back and forth above the seething vermilion coals in the hibachi. Their liquid glow was hypnotizing. In it he saw constellations—volcanic eruptions—oozing blood—cellular holocausts—the protoplasmic flow of genesis. Eventually, despite the cold, he nodded off to sleep.

The light-show in the brazier sifted away into ashes.

When Julian awoke again, it was because he was being called. His head snapped back, and he saw that the Cygnostikoi on the bier were swaying in a way that suggested joint endeavor. Although their legs still bent outward, their feet had separated and he was staring right up into their shared perineal area, watching in almost voyeuristic fascination as the naked seam at the juncture of their buttocks split vertically. The lips of this seam began protruding—folding moistly back upon themselves—and a heavy acid fragrance filled the chamber. Julian got to his feet.

The Cygnostikoi were in labor. In their crazy parabiotic oneness, the birthing of their young was apparently a shared activity comparable in some ways to the human sex act. Julian was half panicked. The peristaltic rippling of the aliens' lower abdomens threatened to expel new life—strange life—directly into his hands. Pushing outward through the common birth canal, forcing even farther apart the lips of the perineal seam, the edge of a small Cygnostik crest was making itself visible. A misshapen head soon followed, and the eyes of the creature blazed at Julian through a clinging, mucoid film.

Here I am. Here I am....

Julian stepped to the table. If he didn't do something, the

infant would be dropped on the end of the bier. He cupped his gloved hands beneath the emerging creature, then closed them gently around its shoulders in order to assist the delivery. He felt an inharmonious mixture of fear, pride, and indignation. What if it had been a breech presentation? What if he hadn't been in his suite when the adults summoned him? What if what if what if what if what . . . ?

Muttering imprecations at the adult Cygnostikoi, his breath flowing out in streams, Julian took the weird infant in his arms. As big as a human baby of two or three months, its whole body was sheathed in a ruby-tinted gel. What now? Did he pull down a piece of wall bunting and swaddle the creature against the cold? Did he dry it off? turn it upside down and swat its small, curiously proportioned butt? The eyes blazed at him searchingly through their film, and he wondered quite seriously if the infant was imprinting his features in its neural pathways and labeling that imprint "mother." God forbid.

At last, prompted by intuition, Julian moved. He carried the Cygnostik child to the parent facing the door to the chamber and stared down at this prepossessing alien. One of its startlingly long arms lifted toward him, and a hand touched the sleeve of his parka. Julian repaid this questing tropism by easing the baby into the other's grasp. Immediately the child was tucked down into the fleshy cerements of the adult's torso and taken out of Julian's sight as well as his hands. The other parent remained as rigid as ever, light-years distant, spent or traumatized.

Suddenly Julian's body was wracked by tremors. The beating of his heart was like a troop of drummers goosestepping down Peachtree Canyon, insidious but remote. He had to get out—he had to get back to Margot—and he hurried from the scene of this fearful alien nativity like a man striding naked into the irresistible gales of Change.

18 / Sky

Late the following evening, long after he ought to have been home, Julian returned from work to find Margot sitting abstractedly over their bedroom's glowing visicom unit. She turned to him in confusion, even alarm.

"Look," she said, gesturing at the visicom screen. "In today's newstapes, a verbatim reproduction of Leland's flyer."

"I keyed it in this afternoon."

Disbelievingly, Margot asked, "With Chavers' approval?"

"Without. Several weeks ago I filched a key to the master visicompositor from Chavers' desk. This afternoon I took advantage of a senior staff meeting to go into the composition room and use the key."

"But why, Julian?"

"In atonement, I guess. Or an attempt at it."

"Is that why you're late? Were you fired?"

"Disciplined, let's say." Julian approached the console and took his wife's hand. "Haven't you been outside?"

"Not since I came home from the seminary—two hours ago."

"Didn't you see what they're doing?"

"Julian, I don't know what you're talking about."

"I was too late to commit treason," he said.

Then he led her out of their suite and up to the roof. Almost directly overhead a crew of maintenance cars ringed a new-made window in the honeycombing of the Dome. Through this gap were visible a number of pulsing, acid-sharp stars—for the Dome, after more than three quarters of a century, was coming down. Holding hands, Julian and Margot stared up into the unfathomable artifice of the reborn night.

2073-2074

Science Fiction Bestsellers From Berkley

Frank Herbert

____	CHILDREN OF DUNE	04075-5—$2.25
____	DESTINATION: VOID (revised ed.)	03922-6—$1.95
____	THE DOSADI EXPERIMENT	03834-3—$2.25
____	DUNE	04376-2—$2.50
____	DUNE MESSIAH	04346-0—$2.25
____	EYES OF HEISENBERG	04237-5—$1.75
____	THE GODMAKERS	03919-6—$1.95
____	THE SANTAROGA BARRIER	03824-6—$1.75
____	SOUL CATCHER	04250-2—$1.95
____	WHIPPING STAR	04116-6—$1.95
____	THE WORLDS OF FRANK HERBERT	03502-6—$1.75

Philip José Farmer

____	DARE	03953-6—$1.95
____	THE DARK DESIGN	03831-9—$2.25
____	THE FABULOUS RIVERBOAT	04315-0—$1.95
____	INSIDE • OUTSIDE	04041-0—$1.75
____	NIGHT OF LIGHT	03933-1—$1.75
____	RIVERWORLD AND OTHER STORIES	04208-1—$2.25
____	TO YOUR SCATTERED BODIES GO	04314-2—$1.95

Berkley's Finest Science Fiction!

ROBERT A. HEINLEIN

ROBERT SILVERBERG

26

Journey through space with these exciting science fiction bestsellers!

880-6906
5-28